TIM WAGGONER

CROSS COUNTY

WIZARDS OF THE COAST
DISCOVERIES™

CROSS COUNTY

©2008 Tim Waggoner
Cover Art and Design ©2008 Wizards of the Coast, Inc.

Published by Wizards of the Coast, Inc., WIZARDS OF THE COAST DISCOVERIES, and its logo are trademarks of Wizards of the Coast, Inc., in the U.S.A. and other countries.

Printed in the U.S.A.

Book designed by Matt Adelsperger
Cover Photography ©2008 David Madison/Veer

First Printing: September 2008

9 8 7 6 5 4 3 2 1

ISBN: 978-0-7869-5038-6
620-21935720-001-EN

Library of Congress Cataloging-in-Publication Data

Waggoner, Tim.
  Cross county / Tim Waggoner.
    p. cm.
  ISBN 978-0-7869-5038-6
  1. Sheriffs--Ohio--Fiction. 2. Psychics--Fiction. I. Title.
  PS3623.A354C76 2008
  813'.6--dc22

                                                      2008002710

U.S., CANADA,
ASIA, PACIFIC, & LATIN AMERICA
Wizards of the Coast, Inc.
P.O. Box 707
Renton, WA 98057-0707
+1-800-324-6496

EUROPEAN HEADQUARTERS
Hasbro UK Ltd
Caswell Way
Newport, Gwent NP9 0YH
GREAT BRITAIN
Save this address for your records.

Visit our web site at www.wizards.com

DEDICATION

To Mary and CeCe—thanks for listening

ACKNOWLEDGMENTS

Thanks to Phil Athans and Mark Sehestedt for their understanding and support during a difficult time in my life. If you ever decide to visit Cross County, you'll always be welcome to stay at Sanctity. The Crosses are keeping a special guest room ready for you: one located on the mansion's lowest level, at the end of a forgotten corridor, with an iron door that only locks from the outside. . . .

CHAPTER ONE

Night wind. The rustle-skitter of dead, dry leaves on pavement. Cold, white stars scattered across a clear night sky, pale-yellow quarter moon hanging in their midst—distant, remote, and uncaring. Birdsong, cricket chirp, and the Doppler-rush of traffic passing on the highway close by. Still early in the evening, so keep to the shadows. Stay unseen. The parking lot, poorly lit by the glow of a single fluorescent light set atop a wooden telephone pole, is empty, save for a single car—an old Ford with a dented front quarter panel. Good. The more shadows, the better.

Show time.

. . . . .

Debbie Coulter was getting ready to shut off the lights when she heard knocking at the door. She glanced at the clock behind the counter and saw it was 9:18, almost twenty minutes after closing. She'd locked the front door at nine and turned off the neon sign outside so that CAFFEINE CAFÉ no longer blazed into the darkness, but she'd left the lights on while she finished cleaning up, like she usually did. Rhine was one of the largest towns in Cross County, due primarily to its proximity to Route 75, and truckers often detoured off the highway to fill their thermoses with Debbie's rich dark roast coffee, which was pretty damned tasty, if she did say so herself. It might be one of her regular customers at the door, in desperate need of a caffeine jolt to keep him awake while he drove through the night. Of course, her regulars knew that she closed at nine every night. The café was mostly a one-woman operation since her husband Les had passed away a few years back, and while she employed several local teenagers to help her out, she couldn't get any of them to stay later than eight, especially on the weekends. But that was okay. She didn't mind closing by herself. Rather liked the peace and quiet. But just as her regulars knew the Caffeine Café closed at nine, they also knew that Debbie had been known to unlock the door and let them in if she was still around and hadn't poured the leftover coffee down the drain yet. Debbie hated to disappoint her regulars, and while she liked quiet, she didn't like it that much. And she did have some coffee left. . . .

The knocking came again, louder this time, insistent.

"All right! Just hold on a minute!"

She put down her spray cleaner and rag, came out from behind the counter and walked to the front door. She was breaking in a new pair of walking shoes, and their rubber soles squeaked on the cracked, yellowed tile floor as she walked. As she did at least a hundred times a day, she told herself that she was finally going to start fixing up the damned place—put in a new floor, get new chairs and tables, replace those godawful orange curtains. Maybe she'd start next spring. By summer, definitely. Sure, she'd been making the same vow for at least a decade, but this time she really meant it.

She stopped before the glass door and reached for the lock, but her hand froze halfway. Taped to the outside of the glass was a small poster, turned inward so she could see the photo and writing on it. Looking back at her was the grainy photocopied image of a smiling teenaged girl. A Homecoming picture, Debbie recalled, or part of one anyway. The girl's date had been cut away and her face had been enlarged, hence the picture's graininess. Debbie hadn't seen the girl's face for almost twenty years, but she knew it as well as her own. Better, in fact, for it had been burned into her memory—along with three others. She saw those faces whenever she closed her eyes, saw them in her dreams, and now she was seeing this one taped to the front door of her café, her own reflection in the glass superimposed over the image.

HAVE YOU SEEN THIS GIRL?

The girl smiling, eyes bright with joy and hope. Below the picture, these words:

MARIANNE HENDRICKSON, 17, LAST SEEN SATURDAY, MAY 11 OUTSIDE THE TASTEE FREEZE IN RHINE, OHIO. IF YOU HAVE ANY INFORMATION ABOUT HER DISAPPEARANCE, PLEASE CALL THE CROSS COUNTY SHERIFF'S DEPARTMENT. The sheriff's phone number came next. No e-mail address, though. The poster had been made eighteen years ago, before the world got wired, and well before Amber Alerts.

Emotions surged through Debbie—fear, anger, but strongest of all was shame. Her hand snatched out of its own accord and disengaged the lock with a single savage twist. She gripped the handle, shoved the door open, and leaned out into the night.

"You think this is funny, you sonofabitch? Do you?" She yelled so loud her throat felt instantly raw. "You come here and I'll show you something funny!" She paused, listened, heard only cars going by on the highway, a soft whisper-rush like the sound of waves breaking on some distant dark shore. "What's wrong? Don't have the stones to show yourself?"

Still nothing. Only the sound of her own breathing, ragged and rough. She was down to half a pack a day, but the way her lungs and heart were going now, she knew she should quit screwing around and stop smoking altogether, unless she wanted to drop dead from a massive coronary like Lester.

"Goddamn kids," she muttered. She reached around the door, took hold of the poster, and tore it off the glass with a single vicious swipe. The edges where the flier had been taped ripped and triangular pieces of paper remained stuck to the glass, but she didn't care. She'd remove them later. Right now all she wanted to do was get the hell out of there and go home. She stepped back inside, closed the door, and locked it. She started to crumple the poster, but something made her stop. She walked over to the counter, sat on a stool, spread the paper out before her, and stared at Marianne's now wrinkled paper face. The poor girl had never lived to get actual wrinkles, though, had she? She'd died young and pretty, body sleek, skin smooth ... where the knife hadn't touched, at any rate.

Every few years a new batch of kids turned into teenagers, and there were always some who decided to get their rocks off by tormenting the mother of Carl the Cutter. The trees in her yard had been TP'd so many times over the years that she'd finally had the goddamned things cut down. Enough eggs had been smashed on her windows to make breakfast for every starving Third World orphan for at least a year. Plastic skulls left in her mailbox, rubber knives dropped on her doorstep, and last Halloween some bastards had draped a shredded blow-up doll drenched in red paint over the CAFFEINE CAFÉ sign. But no one had ever done anything like this before.

Debbie ran her fingers over the wrinkled surface of Marianne's face.

This was worse than all those other times, for while they were essentially thoughtless cruelty, this ... this had taken planning. Finding a copy of the poster, waiting for her to be alone in the café, taping the poster to the door when she wasn't looking . . .

It was the amount of forethought put into this that made it cut so deep, that reopened wounds that Debbie knew would never fully heal, no matter how long she lived.

My baby paid for his sins, she thought. *He's been in the ground six years now. Why can't they let him rest in whatever peace he's found?*

Debbie stared at Marianne's grainy black-and-white face one last time before crumpling the poster up once more, this time squeezing it into a compact wad. She pushed off the stool and, holding the wadded-up poster in a fist so tight it shook, she walked back to the front door. Without bothering to look outside to see if anyone was watching, she flipped off the light switches on the wall, and the café plunged into darkness. Not completely, though. Fluorescent light filtered in from the parking lot, and the lights were still on in the kitchen. She headed there now, fist still tight and shaking, knuckles white, fingernails digging into the soft flesh of her palm.

The kitchen was mostly done for the night. It'd been slow this evening, and she'd managed to get the bulk of the cleaning finished around eight. There was only a little bit still to do, but she didn't feel like working any more tonight. Screw it. She'd come in an hour earlier than usual tomorrow and take care of it then.

She gave the poster-wad one final squeeze and raised her arm, prepared to toss it into the large plastic trash container sitting in the corner next to the fridge. But she stopped herself. The container was empty. She'd taken the trash out to the Dumpster already, and if she threw the poster in there, it would be waiting for her when she returned in the morning. She knew it was dumb, but she couldn't stand the thought of Marianne's wadded-up face lying there. She'd obsess over it all night, and she knew she'd have a hard enough time getting any sleep as it was. The last thing she wanted to do was lie awake and stare up at the ceiling while she thought about this goddamned poster as the hours slowly ticked away toward dawn. But she sure as hell wasn't about to take the damned thing with her, either.

She walked over the sink and held the crumpled wad of paper between her thumb and forefinger. With her other hand she reached into the front pocket of her jeans and brought out her lighter. She smiled grimly, glad that she hadn't gotten round to quitting smoking yet. She pinched the paper ball by a loose corner and held it out over the sink. She flicked the lighter to call forth a flame and stared for a moment at its flickering orange glow. The tiny fire seemed warm and comforting, almost cheerful somehow. Then slowly she moved the lighter until it was less than an inch beneath the wadded-up flier, and she watched as the paper on the bottom began to turn brown, then black, its edges curling, turning to ash, pieces breaking away and drifting gently down into the sink. She raised the lighter a fraction of an inch higher, and the remainder of the crumpled flier caught flame.

At that precise instant, the sound of glass shattering cut the silence. Startled, Debbie turned to glance over her shoulder, forgetting that she was holding a piece of flaming paper. She yelped in pain as heat seared her fingers, and she dropped the blazing wad into the empty sink. The crumpled flier hit the bottom of the metal basin with a soft ringing thud, rolled to a stop, and continued burning, flames reducing Marianne's photocopied face to black ash.

Normally, Debbie would've stuck her burnt fingers beneath the tap and turned on the cold water full blast. But she barely registered her burn. She was too busy holding her breath and listening. She couldn't see out into the front of the café from here at the sink, especially with the outer lights off, but she thought she heard a soft scrabble-scuff of movement. For an instant she stood like that—burnt hand lifted as if it were still holding the crumpled flier, head turned to look back over her shoulder—frozen with indecision. Should she call 911? Should she make a run for it? She tried to remember where her cell phone was. In her purse, she thought, but where the hell was *that*? Here in the kitchen? Out in front? She *always* knew where her purse was, *never* lost track of it. But for the life of her, she couldn't recall where it was.

For the life of her. Unfortunate choice of words.

She heard a soft metallic *click,* and cold fear twisted her stomach. She realized then what was happening. Someone—probably the joker who'd plastered the flier to the front door—had broken the glass, reached through, and was disengaging the lock. Whoever it was, and whatever he or she wanted, they were coming inside.

Debbie wanted nothing more at that moment than to get-the-hell-out-NOW!

Adrenaline coursed through her system, jolting her memory. Her purse was right here, tucked underneath the sink, where she always put it. Moving with a liquid grace born of desperation and fueled by terror, Debbie spun her head around, knelt, snatched up her purse, straightened, and started running for the back door. Her new running shoes came in handy now, their rubber soles slap-slap-slapping as she ran, nicotine-coated lungs heaving, heart pounding loud as a bass drum in her ears. With all the noise her body was making, Debbie feared she wouldn't be able to hear anyone approaching her from behind, and she tried not to think of all the knives she kept in the kitchen, and how very, very sharp they were.

It was only a dozen steps or so to the back door, but it felt like it took hours to reach. Her shoulder slammed into the door and she gripped the knob, twisted, but the door wouldn't budge.

Christ oh Christ, he's locked me in! she thought wildly, and hot tears burst from the corners of her eyes. Then she remembered. Of course the back door was locked. She always kept it that way. She fumbled with the lock—a deadbolt—clicked it back, and threw the door open. She practically fell out onto the asphalt of the narrow alley behind the café, but she surged forward, stumble-stepping into the night, lurching and wobbling until she got her balance back. A single fluorescent bulb over the back door lit the alley, and the pool of light it created was too weak to do much to push back the darkness. Anyone could be out here waiting for her at either end of the alley beyond the edge of the light. One or a hundred, she wouldn't see them until they started coming toward her, grinning as they anticipated the fun they were going to have with her.

Stop it! she told herself. *Just get to the car. Everything will be okay if you can just get to the car!*

Debbie ran to the end of the alley without encountering a single maniac, let alone a hundred, and continued around the side of the building. Her Ford was parked in front of the café, and she'd be safe once she reached it—*if* whoever had broken in was alone, and *if* they hadn't turned around and rushed out the front to prevent her escape. As she rounded the corner, she looked toward the café's entrance, saw no one running toward her, and let out a sob of relief. She reached into her purse for her keys, saw her car, and then stopped so fast her feet nearly skidded out from under her. Someone had spray-painted yellow symbols all over her car—a triangle bisected by a jagged line resembling a cartoonish bolt of lightning. Large, small, the symbols covered every inch of the vehicle, including the windows.

Debbie started shaking, and a small whimper escaped her throat. She dropped her keys and her purse, turned away from the car, and ran into the street, her whimper dying in the birth throes of an ear-piercing scream.

· · · · ·

Across the street from the Caffeine Café, sitting in the dark doorway of Holloway's Cards and Notions—so silent and still that he might have been merely one more shadow—Tyrone Gantz watched Debbie Coulter flee in terror. He made no move to help her: didn't call out to ask what was wrong, didn't rise to his feet and go to her aid. Indeed, the thought of doing anything more than sitting and watching didn't even occur to him. Tyrone's sole purpose in life was to bear witness, not interfere. It was his *raison d'être*, and he'd die before failing in his sacred duty. If necessary, he'd let Debbie die as well. Her loss would be a shame, but at least her death would be witnessed.

She was a heavy-set woman, well padded, though not obese, but she moved now with a litheness and speed that Tyrone wouldn't have thought her capable of. Sheer terror was a powerful motivator, he supposed. Debbie ran north down the middle of Wilkerson Street, tears streaming down her pudgy cheeks, her screams punctuated by hitching sobs. When she reached the corner of Wilkerson and Fairfax, she turned and Tyrone lost sight of her, though her screams were still clearly audible. He turned his attention to the café.

A moment passed, then two, and a shadowy figure pushed open the front door and stepped outside. As the door swung shut, a piece of glass dislodged from the broken pane, tumbled to the ground, and shattered. The sound should've been nothing compared to Debbie's shrill screams, but it seemed loud as a shotgun blast to Tyrone. The person who'd emerged from the café displayed no reaction: didn't startle, didn't so much as turn to look in the direction of the noise. A small thing, but it showed concentration, Tyrone thought. Or perhaps single-mindedness.

Tyrone had spent the better part of his adult life watching from the darkness, and his night vision had grown quite sharp over the decades. He squinted now, trying to make out the features of the person who'd terrorized Debbie Coulter so thoroughly. Perhaps it was due to the parking lot's poor illumination, or perhaps Tyrone's old eyes weren't as strong as they used to be, but he was unable to discern more than the most rudimentary details: medium height, medium build, hooded sweatshirt, pants, running shoes . . .

But nothing of the face. It was as if there *was* no face, only a pool of darkness where a face should be.

Before Tyrone could make out anything more, the shadowy figure sprinted off, running south on Wilkerson—opposite the direction Debbie had taken. The figure made no sound as it ran, no labored breathing, no shoes slapping on asphalt. It kept to the shadows, avoiding the blue-white glow of streetlights, and soon the apparition was gone, merged once more with the darkness that had birthed it.

Interesting, Tyrone thought.

He continued to sit in Holloway's doorway for the next thirty minutes, waiting for the sheriff to arrive. But after seeing no lights and hearing no sirens, he began to get bored. He stood up, stretched his stiff back, put his hands in the pockets of his treanchcoat to warm them against the autumn night's chill, and started off down the sidewalk in search of something else to witness. He knew he'd find something soon.

This *was* Cross County, after all.

CHAPTER TWO

Ray killed the engine and turned off the lights. Grinning, he turned to face the girl sitting next to him, ready to use one of the smooth-ass lines he'd been practicing in his head all evening. Either, *There's only one reason why anyone ever comes out to the old Deveraux Farm. You know it, I know it, so let's get to it*, or, *You may be a Cross and I may be just a townie, but tonight let's forget all that and just be a man and a woman.* But before he could speak, the girl sitting next to him said, "Let's roll down the windows."

It wasn't a request. Crosses never asked. They told.

The girl began lowering the passenger side window, but Ray didn't move. He didn't give a damn who she was. He wasn't about to take that attitude from any girl, no matter how sexy. The '78 Camaro was his pride and joy. Sure, it was old, needed a new paint job, and the engine knocked and rattled too much, but it was *his*. He was the captain of this ship, and he decided what to do and when to do it.

He wasn't going to, but then he felt a pressure inside his skull, like a headache was coming on. Without thinking, he reached out, took hold of the handle, and rolled his window down. Not because *she* wanted him to, but because it was a beautiful evening. Cool, crisp night air, crickets chirping softly, nightbirds singing in the trees . . .

Yeah, right. You're full of shit and you know it.

Maybe so, but at least his headache, or whatever it was, was gone now. Besides, she was hot as hell, and—though he hated himself for feeling this way—the fact she was a Cross made her even hotter. The Crosses were royalty here in the county that bore their name, and it was every man's ambition to lay one of their women, to "get crossed," as they called it. Ray was nineteen, and he attended trade school, learning to be a welder. There was nothing particularly special about him, and though he wanted to "get crossed" as much as any other horny-ass sonofabitch in the county, he'd never really thought he had a shot. Until tonight.

He still couldn't believe his luck. He'd stopped in at the Burrito Bungalow after classes for a Coke and a taco-burrito combo, and *she* was there. He knew she was a Cross girl right away. Not because of her clothes—while she looked smokin' hot in her blouse and shorts, they weren't anything fancy or expensive—but because of the way she carried herself, as if she owned the world and the world damn well better know it. She'd been in line ahead of him, and he'd been checking out her ass and thinking about how there was no way in hell a girl like her would even look at him, let alone talk to him, when she turned around and asked if he had a light for a cigarette. He didn't smoke, but she hadn't seemed to hold that against him.

Soon after that, they were sitting down at a table outside and eating together. Well, he'd eaten. She'd just had a Diet Sprite. They made small-talk about how the high school football team would do this year, about the Harvest Festival coming up in a few weeks, and Ray was working up the nerve to ask her out, when she suggested they meet again at the Burrito Bungalow later that night and "go for a drive or something."

So if she wanted the windows down, he'd put them down, grin

as he did it, and say, *Thank you, Ma'am, may I have another?* if he had to. Putting up with a little attitude was a small price to pay for a chance at some prime Cross pussy.

Of course, if he *didn't* get it . . .

She reached forward to turn the radio on, and Ray watched the fabric of her blouse stretch tight against her breasts as she moved. He could see the outline of her nipples, and he knew she was wearing a sheer bra. If she was wearing a bra at all.

Just being out here alone at night with a Cross girl had already gotten him half erect, and now his penis stiffened the rest of the way, straining painfully against the constraint of his too-tight jeans. But it was a *good* pain, oh yes it was.

She fiddled with the channel selector for a few seconds and stopped when a Black-Eyed Peas song came on. She glanced at his crotch then and smiled slyly.

Damn, girl! See something you like?

He wished he was bold enough to actually say stuff like that. Instead, he said, "So, you like hip-hop music, huh?"

Lame, lame, lame!

Her smile fell away, and she turned to look out the windshield. She shrugged. "It's okay."

Ray feared he'd said something wrong, but he couldn't think of anything else to talk about, so he continued in the same vein, figuring it was better to be talking about *something*—no matter how stupid—than saying nothing at all.

"I like country mostly, but I'll listen to just about anything. Long as it's got a good beat, you know?"

Despite the coolness of the evening, the girl had shorts on. Short-shorts. She'd been sitting with her shapely legs crossed, but now she straightened then out, spread them apart a little, and Ray caught a glimpse of inner thigh. He wasn't sure, but it looked like she wasn't wearing any panties. This was too good to be true! No one was ever going to believe that he'd hooked up with a hottie like this, but so what? *He* knew it was happening, and that was all that mattered.

"So why the Farm?" he asked. He'd almost said, *Come here often?* but he'd corrected himself at the last moment. Wouldn't be cool to imply she was a slut, even if it were true. *Especially* if. But he was genuinely curious. Parking here had been her idea, and while he'd have gladly driven to the lowest circle of Hell with her if it meant getting Crossed, the Devereux Farm did seem an odd choice of make-out spot for a high-class piece like her.

The girl looked out into the night. The Deveraux property was overgrown with weeds and tall grass, and a strand of trees partially blocked the view of the abandoned house and lopsided barn. Even if it wasn't dark out, they wouldn't have been able to see much of anything from here. Still, the girl stared wide-eyed through the windshield, as if the darkness was no impediment to her vision.

"I don't know," she said. "Guess because I've never been here before." The words were casual, but her tone wasn't. She sounded half-scared, half-thrilled.

Excellent! This was the reason lovers came here, after all: to get all good and shivery, to flirt with death a little and then flip the grim reaper the bird by performing the ultimate life-affirming act. And Ray—considering that his penis was throbbing in his pants like a bomb on the verge of exploding—was more than ready to perform. Time to make his move.

Like it was the most natural thing in the world, he reached over and put his arm around the girl's shoulders. She stiffened at his touch, but quickly relaxed and scooted closer to him. She lay her head on his shoulder, and Ray, feeling like the biggest stud of all time for getting this far with a Cross girl, debated whether he should wait a few moments or make a grab for a tit now. He had just decided to go for the boob, when the girl said, "It's so weird."

Ray, with more than a little disappointment, decided it would be best to keep his hand to himself for the time being. "What is?"

"This place. It's so peaceful. You'd never imagine in a million years that something so awful could happen here."

"Yeah, I guess." He didn't really think about it much. He'd grown up hearing stories about Carl the Cutter, and while he knew they'd really happened, they were no more real to him than urban legends like Bloody Mary or the madman with the hook hand. Just another spooky legend to talk about around a Harvest Festival campfire.

The girl went on, her tone becoming increasingly dreamy as she spoke, almost as if she were becoming hypnotized by her own words. "He killed four people . . . that we know of. Kidnapped them, then killed them . . . way out here, where no one could hear their screams. They say when he was finished with his victims, he'd decorate them by carving a strange design on their bodies." She paused, blinked a couple times, and when she turned to look at him, her voice had returned to normal. "Do you think that's true, or just some bullshit somebody made up? About the designs, I mean."

Ray felt a sudden chill that had nothing to do with the night air, a chill that seemed to come from the inside rather than out. The chirping of the crickets took on a sinister edge, almost as if they were mocking him, and the rustle of the tall grass in the breeze sounded too much like someone moving out there in the darkness—someone trying hard not to make any noise. Ray took a quick glance around, but he didn't see anyone . . . or *anything*.

Of course, that didn't mean there wasn't something out there, just that he couldn't see it, whatever it might be.

Stop it, you asshole! Despite himself, Ray was starting to get majorly creeped out, but he was determined not to show it. He had the sense that the girl might be testing him, and he feared that if he displayed any signs of being a wuss, she wouldn't give it up to him tonight—or ever, for that matter.

So he responded as casually as he could. "My dad told me the same thing once, so it's probably true. Either way, those folks are still just as dead, right?" He couldn't believe he'd said that! That was some hardcore shit! She was bound to be impressed now.

"Tough guy, huh?" She sounded amused, and Ray wasn't sure how to take it. Maybe she was pleased, but maybe she was making fun of him, too. Maybe both. Women were complicated like that, and Cross women even more so.

He decided to go with it. "That's me. Tough as nails." Telling himself that it was now or never, he reached out, cupped her right breast in his hand and squeezed.

The girl yelped and practically leaped to the far side of the seat, as if her tit had been zapped with a taser gun. "What do you think you're doing?"

Exactly what we came here for, was what he wanted to say. But he couldn't maintain his bravado in the face of her shocked, angry glare. "I'm sorry! I-I thought that was what you—"

"Well, you thought wrong! I came out here with you tonight because you seemed like a cool guy, and I wanted to get to know you better. *Not* because I'm a whore who screws every guy she talks to for a few minutes at a fast-food joint!"

Ray was beginning to feel like a real shit-heel, but he was also starting to get angry. Why should he feel bad? This bitch had led him on, hadn't she? He hadn't imagined all those signals she was giving off. She was playing with him, that's all—getting her kicks slumming around with a town boy and being a cock-tease.

"Screw this." He started the car, and the Camaro's ancient engine rumbled and belched to some semblance of automotive life.

"Well, you're not going to screw *me*, that's for sure!" she said. "But you *are* going to let me drive back to town."

He looked at her as if she were insane. "After all this shit, you want me to let you drive my *car?*"

"I don't care about driving this piece of shit. But I've been in situations like this before, and halfway home the guy who's pissed as hell he didn't get what he wanted stops the car and orders you to get out and walk the rest of the way. I don't intend to be humiliated like that again."

Ray, who'd just been contemplating doing that very thing, said, "Despite what you may think, I'm not a complete asshole. I wouldn't do that to you."

"Prove it. Let me drive."

Ray hesitated. He'd worked three jobs over the summer to make enough money to pay for both the Camaro and his welding classes, and he'd never let anyone else drive his car since he'd gotten it. On the other hand, maybe he could salvage something from this mess by being a good guy and allowing her to drive back to town. Maybe by then she'd cool off a little, realize that she was at least partially to blame for what had happened, and he might be able to convince her to go out with him again. She was crazy, but she was also gorgeous, and he definitely still wanted to nail her if he could. He decided it was worth a shot.

"All right." He opened the car door and climbed out from behind the steering wheel. The girl scooted over to take his place, and she pulled the door shut with a heavy, metallic *chunk!*

As Ray started to walk around the rear of the car, brake lights flared red, gears ground, the engine roared, and the Camaro leaped backwards.

"Shit!" Ray jumped back to avoid getting run down by his own car. Through the driver's side window, the girl grinned at him and wiggled her fingers as she waved goodbye.

"You bitch!" Ray ran toward the car, but the girl put it in drive, hit the gas, and the Camaro surged across the grassy field, throwing up chunks of sod as it went. The girl flipped on the headlights, and Ray kept running after her and swearing, even though he knew it wouldn't do any good. Moments later, the Camaro exited the field, whipped onto the road, and took off with a squeal of tires. By the time Ray reached the road, his car was nothing more than a pair of crimson lights dwindling in the distance.

He stood there for a long moment, then at the top of his lungs he shouted, "Shit, shit, *shit!*"

Then, with nothing else left to do, he took a deep breath and started walking.

·····

Goddamned bitch!

Ray walked with his arms crossed, wishing he'd worn a jacket tonight. It might only have been September but it was *cold* out here! He'd only been walking for a few minutes, though. Maybe he'd start to warm up before long. He briefly considered running—more for the heat he'd build up through the exertion than because he'd reach town faster—but he decided to hell with it. As pissed off and depressed as he felt right now, walking and shivering suited his mood much better. Besides, he was only a couple miles outside Rhine. He could tough it out.

Out here, there was nothing but farm land, and Ray walked

past rows of dried corn stalks rustling in the wind and whispering fields of hay and alfalfa. The stars spread out above him like sharp-edged diamonds scattered on black satin, their cold illumination almost dazzling without the lights of town to dilute it. All in all, if you had to get ditched by a Cross girl and walk home, it wasn't a bad night for it.

He was starting to feel a little better and had just begun to whistle the hip-hop song that had been on the radio earlier, when he heard something moving through the field to his left. His mouth went dry and his whistle choked off. He stopped and listened.

The field was full of waist-high grass, separated from the road by a simple barbed-wire fence. Either the farmer who owned this land was letting the field go fallow or he couldn't afford to plant anything here this year. Economic times were rough in Cross County—unless your last name was Cross, of course—and they were even worse for the area's farmers. Ray's Uncle Jimmy grew soy beans, and he'd been talking about giving up and selling his land ever since Ray could remember. Fields like this were full of animals, especially at night. Deer, possum, raccoon, rabbit . . . just about anything could've made that sound, really. Even coyote. They'd been slowly but surely making their way into Ohio over the last ten years or so, and Ray had heard stories that bear were starting to come back as well. Intellectually, he knew that whatever animal it was, however big or small, it would be way more scared of him than he was of it. But he couldn't keep from imagining a giant black bear rising out of the grassy field, rearing up on its hind legs, mouth opened wide to reveal its sharp teeth, roaring like some sort of ancient prehistoric beast just before it came for him.

Ray kept listening, but he heard nothing more except for the sound of his pulse thrumming in his ears. Sweat beaded on his forehead, and he felt hot, almost feverish. Then he let out a small bark of a laugh as he realized he wasn't cold anymore. Fear was good for something, at least!

He felt someone tap him gently on the shoulder. Startled, he spun around and saw starlight glint off the metal of a blade as it swept toward his throat.

CHAPTER THREE

Joanne Talon stood at the edge of the ditch, shining a flash-light on the body so the coroner could see as he worked. An EMS vehicle was parked a dozen yards away, lights flashing, the two EMTs standing around, smoking cigarettes and talking in low tones. It was too late for them to be of any help to the victim, and they knew it. Tonight, their job would be to bag the corpse once Doctor Birch was finished and transport it to the hospital morgue. A meat delivery, they called it. An easy, if boring, run.

One of Joanne's deputies who worked night shift—a pot-bellied middle-aged man named Alec Bernstein—stood over by a blue SUV, interviewing the man who'd discovered the body and called 911 on his cell phone to report it. The man, dressed in blue turtleneck and jeans, had an irritated expression on his face, as if he had important places to go and resented being kept from them.

That'll teach him to do his civic duty, Joanne thought.

The coroner's car was parked behind her cruiser, the flashing lights painting the doc's Lexus alternating shades of red and blue.

On a sheriff's salary, she couldn't even afford to spell Lexus, let alone own one. *I am definitely in the wrong business*, she thought.

She saw a pair of headlights approaching from the west, and she knew who it was long before she could make out the Jeep's details. The driver pulled in behind her cruiser, cut the engine, and stepped out of his Jeep. Dale Ramsey was a tall, lean man in his early sixties, with thinning white hair and a neatly trimmed salt-and-pepper mustache and beard. He wore thin-framed glasses and, despite the lateness of the hour, a gray suit, maroon tie, and black Rockports. Dale always wore a suit when he was working, no exceptions. In fact, Joanne could count on the fingers of one hand how many times she'd seen him wear anything else. Sometimes she wondered if he slept in a suit.

Dale stopped when he reached Joanne's side, put his hands in his pockets, and gazed down into the ditch.

"We have to stop meeting like this," he said. His voice was husky, like a long-time smoker, though Joanne had never known him to touch a cigarette.

"Is that going to be the headline your story?"

Dale smiled. "Hardly. I don't think the good citizens of Cross County share your skewed sense of humor."

"Tell me something I don't know."

Dale was the editor and chief reporter for the area's weekly newspaper, *The Cross County Echo*, a position he'd held since before Joanne had been born. He never took notes or tape-recorded anything, but he never forgot a detail or misquoted a source. And while he had a computer in his office, he only used it for typing final drafts of stories. Dale was a throwback to an earlier age, a "newsprint Neanderthal," as he put it. He always managed to show up whenever something important happened in the county—sometimes even before she got there.

"Why don't *you* tell *me?* I *am* the reporter, you know."

Joanne smiled. "True. I did the initial walkthrough and took pictures while Alec marked off the scene. I spoke with the guy who discovered the body, and Alec's taking a statement from him now. Terry got here a few minutes ago, and he's giving the body a preliminary once-over. I'm no doctor, but I think it's safe to say the victim didn't die a natural death."

"You think?" Dale said.

The boy—he couldn't have been more than nineteen, twenty at the most—lay on his back in the shallow ditch, eyes open wide, staring sightlessly up at the night sky. The front of his t-shirt was soaked with what appeared to be blood, and his throat had suffered some manner of injury. Joanne was willing to bet it had been cut, but she'd wait for Terry's verdict. She'd been in law enforcement too long to jump to conclusions about anything.

Terry—more formally, Dr. Terrance Birch—crouched next to the body, probing it gently with rubber-gloved hands. Joanne wasn't worried about his disturbing any evidence. Though the office of coroner was an elected position in Cross County, Terry was a skilled doctor with a great deal of experience at crime scenes. In short, he was a pro. *And* he was Joanne's on-again, off-again lover. Unfortunately, more off than on these days.

"Was he killed in the ditch or dumped there?"

The coldly casual tone Dale always affected in the presence of death bothered her. There was such a thing as taking professional detachment too far.

"From what I've seen, I'd say neither." She nodded in the direction of a wide circle of small orange cones she'd set up on the road less than ten feet away to mark a pool of what appeared to be blood. "Looks like he was cut over there, staggered a few steps, fell into the ditch, and then rolled onto his back." She'd placed a series of plastic orange flags mounted on wires into the ground to mark the blood trail from the road to where the body lay.

"Any sign of a weapon?" Dale asked.

"Not yet, but we've only searched the immediate scene so far. We'll search a wider area once Terry finishes and the EMTs take the body away." She hated talking like that, referring to dead people as *bodies*. She also hated the fact that it bothered her a little less each time she did it.

"Anyone recognize him?" Dale asked.

"No, and there's no wallet on him."

"Any tire tracks?"

"Not that we've found so far. If there was a car here, it doesn't look like it pulled onto the shoulder or left behind any skid marks."

"So . . . what? The poor boy was just out for a late-night stroll in the country and someone walked up to him and slit his throat?"

"Too early to tell." But that's exactly what it looked like to Joanne. She hoped Terry might be able to shed more light once he finished his examination.

Dale nodded toward the man Alec was interviewing. "I take it that's the guy who discovered the body?"

Joanne nodded. "He was driving home from a poker game—or so he says. From the way he stinks of cheap perfume, my guess is he was out cheating on his wife and doesn't want to admit it. At any rate, he was driving down the road when his headlights washed over the ditch and he caught sight of the body. He stopped, walked over to the edge of the ditch, and called out to see if the boy was all right. It didn't take him long to realize the boy was hurt bad, and he ran back to his SUV, got in, locked the doors, and called 911. He was waiting for us here when we arrived."

"You think he did it?" Dale asked.

"No. He wouldn't have called it in if he had. Besides, if he cut that boy's throat, he'd have blood all over him. But he's clean."

"I'm surprised he stuck around after he called. You think he'd have been worried the killer might still be nearby."

"I wondered about that, too," Joanne admitted. "I figure either he was in shock and it didn't occur to him that he might be in danger or, more likely, he was already late getting home to his wife, and he realized that staying to cooperate with the investigation would give him an alibi."

Dale smiled. "So he's more afraid of his wife than a mad slasher, eh?"

"Looks that way."

Dale glanced up and down the road before turning back to Joanne. "Quiet tonight. You'd think the vultures would be out in force."

Vultures was Dale-speak for TV news reporters. Cross County didn't have its own local television station, but they were close enough to both Dayton and Cincinnati for their reporters to come out—especially for a grisly murder like this one. But none had.

"Maybe we've been lucky and they haven't gotten wind of the murder yet," Joanne said.

"Maybe," Dale allowed. "But you and I both know it's more likely that someone's pulled a few strings to make sure there's going to be no on-the-scene TV coverage. Someone whose last name is Cross."

Before Joanne could reply, Terry called out. "I'm ready."

As soon as she'd arrived on the scene, Joanne had slipped sterile hospital booties over her shoes, as had Alec and Terry. She was about to tell Dale to stay where he was, but he reached into one of his suit jacket's outer pockets and pulled out his own pair of blue booties. Joanne shook her head. She should've known.

She stepped carefully as she walked into the ditch to crouch next to Terry and the body. A moment later, Dale—booties on—joined them, but he remained standing. She didn't worry that Dale might disturb any evidence. He'd been present at more crime scenes during the course of his career than she had in hers.

"What have you got for me, Terry?" As soon as the words escaped her lips, Joanne regretted them. Terry could be something of a tease at times, especially when he was handed an impossible-to-resist double entendre like that.

His mouth twitched, as if it were attempting to form a smile, but he fought it down and maintained his professional composure.

"I doubt this will come as any great surprise to either of you, but the cause of death appears to have been exsanguination due to throat laceration. Looks like a knife wound of some sort—a single stroke. Whoever did the cutting knew what they were doing and was damn cold-blooded, too. A cut like this was made swiftly, without hesitation. No defensive wounds are apparent, so either the victim knew his assailant or was taken by surprise. The swiftness with which the cut was made would argue for the latter, but I'll be able to tell more once I've finished the autopsy."

Even when he was discussing such grisly details, Joanne thought Terry had a sexy voice. Low, soft, with a bit of a sardonic tone. She'd always thought that if he hadn't chosen to go to medical school, he would've made a great late-night radio DJ. He was dressed in a blue windbreaker, jeans, and running shoes, and possessed the lean build of a marathon runner, though he didn't compete. He was in his late thirties, ten years older than Joanne, and had chestnut-brown hair and matching eyes. His neatly trimmed mustache held more black than brown. When she'd first met him Joanne had thought the contrast in colors odd, but over the years she'd come to accept and even like it.

"Is that all you've got to show us?" Dale said.

"Show the *sheriff*, you mean."

While Terry tolerated Dale's presence at crime scenes, he wouldn't tolerate even a hint of dispespect toward Joanne's authority. She was the youngest sheriff ever elected in Cross County—for all she knew, the youngest ever elected in Ohio. Most people in the county accepted her in the job, but there were some who thought her too young, especially for a woman.

But there was no need for Terry to defend her. Not only was she perfectly capable of taking care of herself, Dale was the last person who'd deny her authority. After all, he'd been the one who'd convinced her to stand for election in the first place.

Terry reached out, took hold of the bottom of the victim's t-shirt, and pulled it up.

"Now there's something I didn't think I'd see again," Dale said, his voice nearly a whisper.

Outside of old crime scene photographs, Joanne had never seen it before. Carved into the flesh of the victim's stomach was a triangle, bisected with a jagged line that resembled a bolt of lightning.

Joanne's mouth went dry, and there was a roaring in her ears, like the sound of the ocean inside a seashell, but a hundred times louder. Nausea surged through her gut, and the bones in her legs felt like they'd turned to jelly. She felt a nerve-jangling tingle at the base of her skull, and she began trembling as if caught in the throes of a winter wind.

She'd experienced these sensations too many times before, and she knew what they meant.

"This is bad," Joanne gasped. "Very bad."

CHAPTER FOUR

She sits naked on a cold stone floor, her body shivering to generate warmth. She's so tired, and she wants to lie down, but she knows she can't. The more of her skin that touches the stone, the faster her body heat will be leeched away. If she wasn't so weak, she'd stand or crouch so that only the bottoms of her feet were pressed against the stone, but it's taking what little strength she has left simply to stay awake. She may only be nine, but she understands one thing very clearly. If she falls asleep and slumps over onto her side, she will die.

Darkness surrounds her, but she's been in this place long enough—though she doesn't know exactly *how* long—that she's no longer frightened of it. At first she feared there was someone or something with her here in the blackness, moving slowly toward her inch by silent inch, reaching out with long cold fingers. But after hours of hearing nothing but her own breath and heartbeat, she knew she was alone. Then she began seeing ebon shapes in the darkness swirling and dancing before her eyes. Strange, amorphous forms resembling one-celled organisms viewed through the lens of a microscope. Illusions, she eventually decided. With nothing to see, her mind had created its own images, like a bored artist doodling on a blank piece of paper. At least for a time the inky swirls had provided some measure of entertainment, but after a while they'd vanished. Just like the emperor's new clothes: once an illusion was revealed to be an illusion, you could no longer believe in it, even if you wanted to. *Especially* if you wanted to.

So she sits and shivers and stares at the darkness. She has no idea if her eyes are open or closed, but it doesn't matter. The view's the same either way.

Slender warm fingers curl over her right shoulder from behind, and warm air puffs against her ear as a voice whispers her name. A raspy scream tears loose from her throat and slices through the dark like a razor.

. . . . .

Joanne opened her eyes and saw softly glowing blue shapes hovering in the air before her. It took several seconds before she understood the shapes were numbers, and several more before she could make any sense of them.

4:54.

She continued staring at the numbers until she realized she was looking at the time display on a microwave. She was in a kitchen . . . her kitchen. She realized then that her fingers ached, and she looked down to see that she was gripping the counter so hard that her knuckles were bone white. With an effort, she relaxed her hands and let go of the counter. Her fingers were stiff and she shook out her hands to work some life back into them. She wondered how long she'd been standing here gripping the counter like that. Minutes? Hours? There was no way to know.

Twenty years ago . . . but in some ways—too many—it was as if it had happened only yesterday, was *still* happening right now, this very second, and was never, ever going to stop.

The light over the sink was on, but Joanne nevertheless walked over to the switch plate by the doorway and turned on the ceiling light with fingers she couldn't keep from trembling. Right now, the brighter the better. She got a glass from the cupboard, went to the sink, and filled it with tap water, concentrating on keeping her hand as steady as possible. She liked the taste of bottled water much better, but she was too practical to waste money on little luxuries like that, especially on her salary. She gulped the water, not caring that some of it trickled down the sides of her face and dripped onto the front of her red silk pajama top. That and a pair of panties was all she wore when she slept, no matter the time of year or the temperature.

When she'd finished the water, her throat still felt dry and constricted, so she refilled the glass, gratified to see that her hand no longer shook, and then sat at the small wooden table in the breakfast nook. Every morning—when she didn't have to go in to work early, that is—she sat here with her coffee and a toasted onion bagel with butter and looked out the window as dawn came to Cross County.

She lived five miles outside of Rhine in a small farmhouse, though she only owned a couple acres of land. When the previous owner had decided to retire after his wife passed away, he'd sold most of his property to a neighboring farmer. That man had decided to use his new land to grow Christmas trees, and while he wasn't getting rich, he did better than many of the county's farmers.

Normally Joanne liked looking out her window at the regular rows of small evergreens, but she left the blinds closed for now. It was still night, and after the dream she'd had, she wanted nothing to do with darkness for a while.

As bad as the dream had been, she was more disturbed by the fact that she'd apparently been sleepwalking. It had been a long time since she'd done that. The last time she'd slept over at Terry's place, actually—which was *why* it had been the last time. She'd had a nightmare then, too, though she hadn't told Terry about it. She'd never told anyone about the nightmares: not her parents, and none of the few lovers she'd had in her life. She'd never even told the therapist her mom and dad had forced her to see when she was nine. For one thing, the details faded soon after she awakened, though she never forgot the darkness and the cold. But for some reason she felt that the nightmares were a private thing, something she didn't want to share . . . or perhaps wasn't supposed to.

Thinking of Terry made her long for his presence. Right now she wanted nothing more than to feel his strong arms wrapped around her, to press her ear to his chest and hear the reassuring sound of his heart beating, to feel his breath warm and tingly on her neck, feel his moist gentle lips slide against hers. For a moment she was tempted to give Terry a call and ask him to come over, but the moment passed. She didn't want to wake him, not after he'd been out to a crime scene so late. Let him sleep. Maybe they could get together tomorrow night.

Joanne took a sip of her water, wishing it were something a hell of a lot stronger. She had booze in the house—half a bottle of merlot in the fridge and a bottle of Royal Crown whiskey Dale had given her for her last birthday that she still hadn't opened. But she resisted the temptation. She'd gotten in around three, and though she'd only been asleep for a couple hours, she needed to get back to work as soon as possible. Homicide investigations weren't exactly the kind of thing you could put off until you were well rested. She knew from experience that she would have a hard time going back to sleep after a nightmare bad enough to cause her to sleepwalk, and the amount of booze it would take to put her down would make it damned hard to get back up when she'd need to. Better to stick with water for now, as unsatisfying as it might be.

She closed her eyes and once more saw the mutilated corpse

of the teenaged boy lying in the ditch. The image in and of itself didn't disturb her. Cross County didn't have the amount of crime that urban areas did, but the boy wasn't the first dead body she'd seen in her career, and she knew he wouldn't be the last. What bothered her was the feeling she'd experienced at the crime scene—the nauseating, overpowering sensation that Something Was Wrong. She was a pragmatic person, not given to putting stock in hunches and intuition, though she knew law officers who swore by them. She believed in gathering evidence and making rational inferences based solely on that evidence. That was how she'd been trained, and that was how she operated.

Usually. But there were times . . .

The electronic tone of her cell phone made her jump, causing her to spill water onto the table. She put the glass down and looked in the direction of the sound. Though she'd left her phone on the nightstand when she went to sleep, it now rested atop the counter next to the stove. Evidently she had brought her cell into the kitchen with her when sleepwalking. She couldn't stop being sheriff, it seemed, even when unconscious. She couldn't decide it that was comforting or not.

She got up, walked over to the counter, and answered the phone, half-hoping it was Terry.

"Sheriff Talon." She didn't say *hello*, just in case this wasn't a personal call.

"You should be asleep."

Joanne couldn't help smiling. "So should you, Dale."

"I don't need much sleep these days. I pulled out my notes on the Coulter murders."

Dale would never say *Carl the Cutter's murders*. He was never flippant when it came to death, not even indulging in gallows humor as many cops and reporters did in order to come to terms with the darkness that too often accompanied their jobs. Dale had too much respect for death to ever treat it lightly.

Joanne tore a paper towel off the roll attached to the bottom of a cupboard and walked back to the table to mop up the water she'd spilled.

Just hearing Dale's voice made her feel better. "If you're in a mood to work, why don't you come over here?" Joanne said. "My shower needs to be re-grouted."

"Sorry," Dale answered. "Typing's the only manual skill I possess, and even then I'd be hopeless if it wasn't for spellcheck. I don't have any of the crime-scene photos from Coulter's murders, but I do have some sketches of Coulter's calling card that Stan made for me. The design looks exactly the same as the symbol carved into the boy's belly."

Stanton Manchester had been Joanne's predecessor, serving as sheriff of Cross County for almost thirty years before retiring. Precisely one week after Joanne had stepped into the job, Manchester had taken a lamp cord, tied one end to the knob of a closed door, wrapped the other around his throat, got down on his knees, leaned forward, and strangled himself. He hadn't left a note, but Dale had told Joanne once that Manchester hadn't needed to.

Everyone knows why he did it. A man sees a lot in three decades on the job. Things that he can't forget, no matter how hard he tries. Stan saw too much, that's all.

Joanne wondered if that was truly the reason why Manchester had committed suicide. She also wondered if, when she retired, she'd end up doing the same thing.

"It's a copycat, Dale. And don't tell me that the sheriff's office and you are the only ones who know about Coulter's mark. It became public record during his trial. Besides, you know how people talk around here. Anyone who'd seen the corpses—cops, EMTs, the coroner at the time, morgue attendants—any of them could've described the symbol well enough for someone to copy it. It's not as if it's all that complicated an image to reproduce."

"True. But why copy it now, almost twenty years after the original murders and six after Carl's execution?"

Joanne wadded up the wet paper towel, walked over to the sink, and threw it away in the wastebasket underneath.

"You know I don't like making guesses without facts, Dale." She returned to the table, sat down, and took a sip of her remaining water. "You can come up with as many ideas as I can. Maybe whoever killed the boy decided to carve Carl's design into his belly to throw suspicion off him or herself. Maybe the killer's simply crazy."

"I know one thing. There's nothing *simple* about this murder. If there was, you wouldn't have had one of your patented Feelings."

Joanne could hear the capital F in the way Dale stressed the word. She grimaced. "I should've known you'd notice."

"I see all and tell little." Dale's tone was light, but Joanne wasn't certain he was joking. "So . . . how bad was it?"

She recalled the roaring in her ears, the stabbing pain behind her eyes, the nausea roiling in her stomach, the memory so intense she almost felt the sensations anew.

She swallowed to prevent her gorge from rising, and thrust the memory away. "Bad enough," she said, her voice raspy and strained.

Several seconds passed before Dale responded. "I'll keep digging then. I'll let you know if I find out anything. Try to get some sleep, Joanne." He paused. "Sounds like you're going to need it."

Dale disconnected before she could reply. She continued holding her phone to her ear for a moment, as if she thought he might call back to say goodbye. But Dale wasn't a hello-goodbye kind of person. He wasn't inconsiderate. He just thought social niceties were a waste of time. She put the phone back on the kitchen counter and returned to sit at the breakfast nook table.

When Dale said he'd "keep digging," Joanne knew he meant more than going through his old files. Decades ago, before coming to Cross County, he'd been a crime reporter in Chicago. She knew the reason he'd left the big city for life in rural Ohio had something to do with the deaths of his wife and daughter, but she didn't know the details. Whenever she asked, Dale would only say they'd died in an accident and then change the subject. Joanne understood that it remained a painful subject for him, even after all these years, and so she never pried any further.

But big city or Ohio countryside, Dale was a hands-on reporter, which meant that he would start his own investigation into tonight's murder. Joanne knew she should try to dissuade him. A civilian, no matter how well-meaning, shouldn't interfere with a police investigation, but in many ways Cross County was a world unto itself, with its own rules. This would hardly be the first time Dale had pitched in to help the Sheriff's office. Besides, Joanne doubted she could stop Dale even if she wanted to. And she didn't. Dale had his own sources of information, his own connections, some of which Joanne knew, most of which she didn't. If her Feeling had been right, and something truly awful was coming, then she was going to need all the help she could to deal with it.

When it came right down to it, despite Dale's less-than-forthcoming nature, Joanne trusted him more than anyone else she'd ever known. After all, if it hadn't been for him, she wouldn't be alive right now.

■ ■ ■ ■ ■

Dale sat on his couch, leaning forward, elbows on his knees, as he looked down at the newspaper clippings spread out on the surface of his coffee table. Dale's apartment was located in downtown Rhine on Fairfax Street, above the *Echo* office. It wasn't much—living room, kitchenette, bathroom, bedroom, a couple of closets—but it was big enough for him. He didn't spend a lot of time here anyway. Usually, he was downstairs working or out somewhere, investigating a story or just visiting folks, maintaining relationships with sources and sniffing around to see what was happening in the county and if it was worth writing about. His furniture, what little he had, consisted of Goodwill rejects, and every time he sat on the couch, he remembered just how uncomfortable the damned thing was, and he vowed to get a new one soon ... when he got around to it.

The blinds in the living room were up—Dale never lowered them. He didn't feel a need to here on the second floor—and glowing fluorescence from the streetlight spilled in from outside. It was the only illumination in the apartment, but it was enough for him to see by. Dale had spent a good part of his life in the darkness, and he'd long ago learned to be comfortable among the shadows.

He'd lied to Joanne. He was tired, but he didn't want to go to sleep, not yet. He had work to do. Besides, whenever he lay down and closed his eyes, he found himself thinking of Marianne and their daughter Alice. Alice would've been close to Joanne's age today if she ...

Well, he'd left a lot of things behind in Chi-town when he'd departed, and his love of sleep was least among them.

If Joanne had been here—not that she'd ever been to his apartment—she would've been surprised to see that he'd removed his suit jacket and tie. She'd have been even more surprised to discover the clippings Dale was looking at had nothing do with the Carl the Cutter.

LOCAL GIRL REPORTED MISSING.

NO CLUES IN CHILD'S DISAPPEARANCE.

POLICE CONTINUE SEARCH FOR MISSING CROSS COUNTY CHILD.

LOST GIRL FOUND!

Dale had written some of the articles, but not all. His paper, *The Cross County Echo*, only came out weekly, and the case had caught the attention of newspapers throughout Ohio: Cincinnati, Dayton, Columbus, even as far away as Cleveland. And the papers' fascination with the story had only grown after the girl was recovered.

MISSING GIRL, MISSING MEMORIES. LOST FOR SIX DAYS, GIRL ASKS, "WHERE WAS I?"

POLICE AT A LOSS TO EXPLAIN GIRL'S DISAPPEARANCE.

But among the blaring, sensationalistic headlines, one caught and held Dale's attention like no other—

GIRL FOUND WANDERING IN WOODS BY *ECHO* REPORTER.

It was one of his articles, and though he hadn't re-read it for years, he recalled it word for word. It was one of the finest pieces of fiction he'd ever written.

Oh, some of it was true. He *had* found Joanne and he *had* returned her to her parents, but the rest was nothing but lies. Necessary ones, perhaps. But lies nevertheless. Dale had been a reporter all of his adult life, and he regretted having to falsify this story. More, he regretted having to lie to Stan Manchester about what had really happened. Stan had been a good friend, and while the sheriff hadn't pressed the issue, Dale strongly suspected Stan knew he'd lied. While they'd remained friends, there had been a distance between them after that, one that had persisted until Stan killed himself. But in order to bring Joanne home, Dale had been forced to make a deal, and part of the bargain was his silence.

At the time, he'd believed he had no choice. Now he wasn't so sure. But despite his regrets, whenever he looked at Joanne, he knew he'd made the right decision. She'd grown into a fine woman, and she'd served the people of Cross County well as sheriff. As good as Stan Manchester had been at the job, Joanne was better. And though Dale knew he could take no credit for Joanne's accomplishments, he couldn't help feeling an almost fatherly pride in her.

But Joanne had paid a price for her freedom as well. She had no memory of what had occurred to her during the six days she was missing, though Dale suspected some of the details found their way into her dreams from time to time. For twenty years she'd lived with the gap in her memory and the uncertainly of what might have happened—or worse, been *done* to her during that missing time. But as difficult as living with that mystery might be for Joanne, Dale knew it was in reality a blessing, though of course he could never tell her that.

Joanne had paid a second price, as well—her Feelings. She'd never experienced them before her disappearance, and even now they came upon her rarely, only when some sort of danger threatened. The more intense the Feeling, the greater the danger. Like the time three years ago, when two blocks of Rhine's historical district were wiped out by an arsonist who turned out to be an autistic child. Or last summer, when an entire Cincinnati family who'd come to the area for a Memorial Day picnic on the shore of Lake Hush was drowned, fifty feet from water's edge, lungs filled with water, clothes bone-dry. From what Joanne had said, and *not* said, on the phone, the Feeling she'd experienced at the murder scene tonight had been a real doozy, stronger than either of those other times.

Whatever was coming, however bad it would get, Dale would help her. He always had. He just hoped that, whatever price they might have to pay this time, it wouldn't be too steep. He wasn't sure either of them could afford it.

· · · · ·

The less than imaginatively named Cross County Administration Building was located just a couple blocks over from Dale's place. The mayor's office was there, along with the sheriff and fire departments, and the township trustees had a meeting room there as well. But eight miles northeast of town, on the other side of Mare's Nest Woods, with a view of the western edge of Lake Hush, lay the true county seat. Sanctity.

Well over two hundred years old, the building resembled a castle constructed entirely of dark gray stone. Decade upon decade of ivy growth covered much of the structure, making it seem as if Sanctity, instead of being built one brick at a time, had instead emerged fully formed from the earth, ivy vines thrusting it upward from the hidden, dark depths where it had been born. And maybe they had.

The mansion grounds were silent and still. No birds sang, no raccoons or deer moved cautiously across the grass, and even the night breeze made no noise as it moved through the forest and across the ebon waters of the lake. All was quiet ... exactly the way Althea Cross desired it. And whatever Althea desired, Althea got—or else.

While Joanne sat drinking water in her kitchen and Dale sat on his couch looking at old news clippings, Marshall Cross—freshly showered, shaved, and wearing an obscenely expensive Italian suit—stood in the hallway outside Althea's room. Regardless of the hour, no one appeared before the matriarch of the Cross family in anything other than formal dress, not even her children and grandchildren. Marshall was trying to decide what his mother would desire most in this particular instance. Should he leave her alone to sleep, or should he wake her and inform her of the night's events?

Marshall himself had been awakened less than an hour ago, when he'd received a call from Stuart Ennist. The EMT possessed a modicum of Cross blood, hardly enough to note, but he enjoyed feeling that he was of service to "his" family, and Marshall deposited a little extra something in Stuart's bank account every month, just in case his sense of familial duty ever began to waver. Stuart had told Marshall about the homicide that had occurred earlier tonight, and while the murder of a local boy mattered little to Marshall—it wasn't as if the kid was a Cross, after all—one of the details Stuart had passed along *did* matter to him. Very much. But what he couldn't decide was whether or not it would matter to Mother. Marshall Cross was not normally an indecisive man, but there was much at stake here, and he had to make sure to play this smart, right from the beginning.

He was still trying to decide when he heard a door open farther down the hallway.

Althea insisted that all members of the immediate family reside at Sanctity, and that those closest to her—and she decided who deserved that honor based on a complex and ever-shifting set of criteria that she kept to herself—have their quarters on the same floor as hers. The nearer your room was to Althea's, the higher your status in the family. Marshall's suite of rooms was across the hall from his mother's. The door that opened now was on the same side of the hall as Althea's, two down on the left. Marshall hadn't turned on the hall lights when he'd stepped out of his suite, and no light spilled out of the open doorway to show him who was coming out. But he didn't need to see to know who it was. He'd long ago memorized every inch of Sanctity, from the common areas that everyone in the family knew about to the more . . . *restricted* areas. Thus he wasn't surprised when a moment later, the sound of bare feet padding on hard wood drew close, and he heard the too-adult voice of his daughter whisper, "Father? Is that you?"

Marshall didn't relax upon hearing Lenora speak. No Cross ever fully relaxed in the presence of another, regardless of how close they were. A healthy dose of suspicion was not only vital to advancing in status within the family, it was often the key to survival as well.

"What are you doing up?" Marshall asked, his whisper coming out more harshly than he intended.

The dim silhouette of the woman who had once been Marshall's little girl stopped three feet away from him. Not completely out of reach, but far enough away to grant her a good head start if she needed to turn and run. Marshall felt parental pride that he'd taught his little girl well, but he also felt a wave of sadness. Lenora was more distant around him than strictly necessary, even by Cross standards. Things between them had been strained at best since her mother had . . . left.

Lenora wore a silk robe over her nightgown, and if she thought it odd that her father was standing in the hall in the middle of the night, wearing a suit and smelling of freshly applied aftershave, she gave no sign. "Not that it matters, but I'm hungry. I'm going down to the kitchen. You—" She yawned, and when she resumed speaking, she sounded a bit more awake. "You want me to bring you back something?"

Twenty-three years old, and she's still getting up in the middle of the night for a snack, just like when she was a toddler. At least,

Marshall amended, that's what it looked like. He wondered if the real reason his daughter had awakened was because she'd sensed something bad had happened tonight. He wondered if she also sensed his own ambivalence about how to handle it.

"Thanks, but I'm all right. You go ahead."

He couldn't make out her facial expression in the dark, but he saw her cock her head to the side, and he heard the mocking smile in her voice. "You may not be hungry, Daddy, but if you were all right, you wouldn't be standing outside Grandma's door, wearing a suit this time of night."

He felt Lenora press him, testing his mental defenses to see if she could get a rise out of him. She was his daughter, and therefore strong, but she was no match for him. He pushed back, and she winced, letting out a tiny mew of pain.

Though it was too dark for him to make out her features, he felt Lenora's anger, tempered by fear. Marshall kept his own emotions in check as he waited for Lenora to make another move—if she was foolish enough.

Lenora turned away, breaking eye contact, and she moved past Marshall down the hall, continuing on her way downstairs to the kitchen in search of her snack. Though Marshall's impassive expression didn't change, inwardly he was proud of his daughter. She might have lost her battle of wills with him, but she wasn't going to slink back to her room and hide in shame. Even in defeat she was going to hold her head up high.

But after several steps Lenora stopped and looked back over her shoulder

"Go on in. You know she'd want you to. She *always* wants you to." Then Lenora faced forward once more and resumed walking.

Marshall didn't know what infuriated him more: that Lenora had seen him hesitating in front of her grandmother's door, or that she was right about what he should do. For an instant he was tempted to reach out with his mind and strike back at her, but he knew that was what she was hoping for. To make him lose control. So he drew in a deep breath and held it as he waited for his daughter to reach the end of the hallway and begin descending the spiral staircase. He then let the breath out slowly, allowing it to bear his anger away with it. He then gently rapped a knuckle on Althea's door. A few moments later, a commanding and quite wide-awake voice called out.

"Come in, Marshall."

He felt his mother's words as a command, an inward pull that he was powerless to resist. If Lenora were still here, he knew she'd be loving every second of this.

Fighting back a wave of resentment that bordered on fury, Marshall opened the door and stepped into his mother's room.

CHAPTER FIVE

By 6:45 Joanne had showered, dressed in a clean uniform, and was pouring a second cup of coffee into a travel mug when her cell phone rang. She hoped it was Terry, expected it to be Dale, but it turned out to be neither. It was Ronnie Doyle, her second in command.

"Hey, Ronnie. I was just about to head in."

"You might want to take a detour over to the Caffeine Café first, Sheriff." No matter how many times Joanne had told him to call her by her first name, Ronnie never did. He said he didn't think it was respectful. His voice sounded muffled, and she knew he was wearing his mask. No surprise there. He'd probably just gotten in and hadn't had time to finish the morning sterilization of his work station. He always wore a surgical mask when using cleaning chemicals.

Joanne sighed. "I don't suppose it's because you want me to pick up a sack of donuts." Like he'd ever touch any of Debbie's baked goods. Ronnie only ate food that he prepared himself.

"'Fraid not. Mrs. Coulter called a minute ago and said she had a visitor last night."

Even before Ronnie began providing details, Joanne felt a tingling at the base of her skull, a cold fluttering in the pit of her stomach, and she knew that what had already been shaping up to be a bad day had just gotten worse.

■ ■ ■ ■ ■

Joanne pulled into the parking lot of the Caffeine Café at 6:56 a.m., only to discover that someone had beaten her there. She recognized the Hummer parked next to Debbie Coulter's maroon Ford. Not that it took much effort to do so, considering the CROSS 2 vanity plates the Hummer sported. Debbie was already there, standing next to her car and speaking with Marshall Cross. Debbie looked up and waved as Joanne parked, but Marshall didn't. He was too busy examining the Ford, scowling as if he hoped to intimidate the vandalized vehicle into revealing its secrets to him.

Joanne tried to keep her expression professionally neutral as she got out of her car, but inwardly she was seething. She wasn't surprised to see Marshall here. The Crosses always knew what was going on in the county that bore their name. What pissed her off was that normally Marshall held back while the sheriff's office did its job.

"Morning, Debbie . . . Marshall."

Debbie turned to nod at Joanne as she approached, but Marshall continued staring at the Ford, arms crossed, brow furrowed in an unhappy scowl. Joanne didn't make much of that, though. Marshall normally wore what she thought of as the "Cross glower." She used to think he used the expression to intimidate people. But after her first couple years as sheriff, she realized he didn't need to do anything special to make people uncomfortable around him. His presence alone sufficed.

Marshall was a tall broad-shouldered man in his mid-fifties, though he looked ten years younger, at least. He was clean shaven—immaculately so. Joanne had never seen so much as a hint of a whisker on him, regardless of the time of day. His hair was coal-black and untouched by gray. Most of the women in town figured he colored his hair, but Joanne wasn't so sure. When people colored their hair, the new shade always looked a bit off to Joanne, and it never seemed to pick up the light the same way natural hair color did. Marshall's hair caught and reflected the light just fine, thank you. He was fit, without so much as an ounce of extra weight on him, and he possessed large, thick-fingered hands that seemed more suited for a manual laborer than a member of the local gentry. Dale had once referred to them as "strangler's hands," but though he'd meant it as a joke, Joanne hadn't laughed. She never would have admitted it to anyone, but she found Marshall handsome, in a cold, remote "I'd spit on you as soon as look at you" kind of way.

"Nice suit," she said. "Is it new?"

"Good morning, Joanne." Marshall rarely responded to her digs, and he never addressed her by her title. Crosses might show respect to those they thought had earned it, but they never showed deference. "Looks like we have a new artist in town."

Joanne examined the Ford more closely. Ronnie had filled her in over the phone on the details of Debbie's complaint, so she'd had a good idea what to expect. But she still felt a chill at seeing the same design that had been carved in the dead boy's belly spray-painted dozens of times on Debbie's car. She didn't need any special Feelings to know this couldn't be coincidence.

"Did either of you touch anything?" Joanne asked.

"When I got here this morning, I went inside to see if anything had been stolen," Debbie said. "I didn't touch too much, and I haven't gone any nearer to the car than this."

Joanne had investigated numerous complaints of vandalism from Debbie over the years, all related in one way or another to her infamous son. Debbie had invariably been seething with anger on those occasions, but now she was subdued, drained. Scared.

"*Was* anything stolen?" Joanne asked.

Debbie shook her head. Like Marshall, she kept her gaze fixed on the Ford, but she wasn't examining it. She looked as if she half-expected the engine to turn over, the transmission to slip into drive, and the vehicle to rush toward her in an attempt to run her down.

She's not just scared, Joanne realized. *She's terrified.*

Joanne turned to Marshall. "How about you? Did you touch anything?"

Marshall looked at her, his scowl deepening. "I'm not an idiot."

Joanne felt her anger rising, and she fought to keep it from getting the better of her. She'd grown up in Cross County, and she resented the Crosses as much as anyone. More so these days, because they had no compunctions about interfering in sheriff's business. But being diplomatic was part of the job, especially in these parts, so she kept her mouth shut, though it sure as hell wasn't easy.

Downtown Rhine was hardly a bustling metropolis at its busiest, but Joanne was still grateful that it was early. The shops—Holloway's Cards and Notions across the street, the Winter Mill Art Gallery and Second Time's the Charm, the pre-owned clothing and furniture consignment store, next door to the café on either side—hadn't opened yet. That meant no nosey neighbors, at least for a couple more hours. Traffic on Wilkerson was light so far, but the few vehicles that did pass slowed as they went by, drivers taking a good long look at whatever had brought both the sheriff *and* Marshall Cross out bright and early on a Monday morning. Joanne knew that more than a few of those drivers would pull out their cell phones and start spreading the news. By noon, the whole county would be gossiping about it and rumors would be flying—all of which would make her job harder than it already was. *Especially* when word of last night's murder got out.

She heard the sound of a car approaching, and she turned to see another cruiser pull into the lot and park next to her vehicle. Ronnie popped the trunk, got out, removed his camera and evidence collection kit, closed the trunk, and started toward them. The stereotype of the local yokel law officer was a good ole boy wider than he was tall, but Ronnie was the opposite. He was six five and rail thin, with slack features that made him resemble a half-starved hound dog. He was in his mid-fifties, his short hair a bright white, and he moved with the deliberate stride of someone who never hurried but always managed to get where he was going. He was completely unremarkable—except for the way he dressed. He wore a surgical mask and a pair of white rubber gloves. Not because he wished to take extra precautions while gathering evidence. He always dressed this way when he went out.

Joanne assumed Ronnie had severe allergies, obsessive-compulsive disorder, or both, but she'd never come out and asked him. He'd been an assistant sheriff before she'd taken over, and he'd been content to retain the position under her command. Despite his quirks, he was an excellent second in command, and she didn't wish to make him uncomfortable by prying into his . . . condition, whatever it might be. As far as she was concerned, as long as he did his job, what did it matter if he had a few eccentricities?

"Morning Mrs. Coulter, Mr. Cross." Ronnie gave each a friendly nod, but he didn't make eye contact with Marshall. He then turned to Joanne. "Where would you like me to get started, Sheriff? Inside or out?"

Normally Joanne might've collected the evidence herself, or at least helped Ronnie do it, but she had a homicide to investigate. Besides, Ronnie was meticulous in everything he did. He was just as good at evidence collection as she was, probably better. She was about to tell him to start on the car when Marshall spoke.

"Do the Ford first. As soon as you're finished, I'll have it towed away and repainted. It won't be long before news crews get wind of what happened last night and start crawling all over town, looking for sensational images to take video of. I don't intend to let them see *this*." He nodded toward the vehicle.

Joanne bristled. "Ronnie works for me, Marshall. Remember?"

Still, she saw his point. The media couldn't get pictures of the symbol etched in the dead boy's flesh, so they'd go nuts over the car. They'd insinuate all manner of sinister connections between the murder and last night's vandalism of the car belonging to the mother of Carl the Cutter. The TV stations would ransack their archives for footage of Carl, would dredge up every sordid detail of the killings, his trial and execution . . .

As sheriff, Joanne dreaded the chaos the media vultures would bring in their wake, for it would only make her job all the harder. But more than that, she felt sorry for Debbie. The poor woman had been at the center of media feeding frenzies too many times in her life. Joanne could only imagine the fresh hell a new one would put her through.

"Start with the car, Ronnie," she said, though she wasn't able to keep the irritation she felt at Marshall out of her voice.

Ronnie glanced sideways at Marshall before giving Joanne a nod. "Sure thing, Sheriff." He set the evidence kit on the ground then started taking photos of the Ford.

Debbie looked worried. "I haven't called my insurance company yet, Mar—Mr. Cross. I don't know if they'll pay to have the car repainted." She frowned at the vehicle. "To tell you the truth, I'm not sure I want to keep it anymore. Not after this."

Debbie's slip of the tongue wasn't lost on Joanne. She'd almost called Marshall by his first name. Joanne had been around both

Debbie and Marshall numerous times—Debbie especially, whether as a customer or as sheriff looking into her latest vandalism or harassment complaint. But this was the first time Joanne had seen Debbie and Marshall together. She wasn't surprised that Marshall was acquainted with her. If he didn't know everyone who lived in Cross County, he was at least aware of their existence. And though he didn't strike Joanne as a coffee-and-donut kind of guy, it was possible that he was an occasional patron of the Caffeine Café. Although Joanne had never seen him here before this morning.

But there was something more about the way Debbie was acting around Marshall. Not friendly, exactly, but familiar—and far too comfortable. Not only didn't Debbie act frightened of Marshall, but from the way she kept looking at him, it almost seemed as if she were trying to draw strength from him. Interesting.

If Marshall noticed or cared about Debbie's breach of etiquette, he showed no sign as he replied. "Don't worry about it. I'll take care of everything. If you don't want the car repainted, I'll have it destroyed and replaced with whatever make and model you'd like."

Marshall said this casually, as if he were doing no more than offering to pick up the check at a restaurant. For him, there was probably little difference, Joanne thought. The Crosses were wealthy, obscenely so, if County legend were true. But no one seemed to know just how the family had come by its money. Profits from the slave trade, some said, while others suggested bootlegging during Prohibition or profiteering during both World Wars. Others with a less sensational turn of mind claimed the family had grown rich by successfully investing in the stock market one generation after another. Still, the fact remained: no one knew for certain save the Crosses themselves.

"That's . . . very generous," Debbie said. "But I don't know—"

"Generosity has nothing to do with it," Marshall interrupted. "Whoever did this insulted you, and an insult to any citizen of Cross County is an insult to my family. It's our duty to take care of it."

Marshall spoke a bit too formally, a bit too stiffly, for Joanne to completely buy his words. She had no doubt he was serious about what he said, but she thought there was more to his offer than simple noblesse oblige. Her suspicion only deepened when she saw the way Debbie's eyes softened as she replied.

"Thanks."

Marshall's gaze, however, remained cold and unemotional, and he accepted Debbie's gratitude with a curt nod.

"Sorry, Debbie," Joanne said, "but I'm afraid you're going to have to take a rain check. Your car is now part of an ongoing investigation, and I won't be able to release it until we're finished with it." She turned to Marshall before he could protest. "I'm sorry for the inconvenience, Marshall, but you wouldn't want to interfere with official sheriff's department business . . . would you?"

Marshall's ice-blue eyes seemed to glitter for an instant in the morning sunlight, and Joanne felt a mild sensation of pressure inside her head. But the feeling quickly passed, and Marshall's gaze returned to normal. If it had ever been anything *but* normal, that is.

He sighed, the sound a frustrated admission of defeat. "Very well. But can you at least keep the car out of sight?"

Ronnie was still in the process of taking photos of Debbie's car. So far, he'd only snapped two, not because he was dawdling, Joanne knew, but because he took his time setting up his shots so they were perfect. Ronnie only hurried in an emergency, and even then only if it was a *life-and-death* emergency. But now Ronnie paused in his work and glanced over at Joanne, as if waiting to see how she was going to respond.

"We'll park it in the garage at the county building," Joanne said. "Will that do?"

"I suppose it'll have to, won't it?" Marshall's lips formed a humorless smile. "To be honest, it's not so much you or your people I'm worried about. I trust you to perform your duties with due diligence."

Right, Joanne thought. *That's why you made it a point to get here before I did.*

Ronnie—reassured that his work wasn't going to be rushed, Joanne guessed—stopped paying attention to the conversation and returned to choosing his next shot.

Marshall continued. "It's Dale that concerns me. I'd rather not see a photo of Debbie's redecorated car splashed on the front of that bird-cage liner he calls a paper." His brow crinkled into a slight frown. "Speaking of Dale, where is he? I thought surely your *good friend* would have gotten here by now."

Joanne had been thinking the same thing, but she didn't want to tell Marshall that, not after the way he'd stressed the words *good friend* as if to imply that Dale was quite a bit more to her than that. She doubted Marshall really believed there was anything romantic between Dale and her. Insinuating otherwise was simply one more way for Marshall to try to get the better of her.

She shrugged. "He'll be along sooner or later, I'm sure. But he won't print anything that will compromise an investigation, you know that. He's too much of a professional."

Now it was Marshall's turn to shrug. "Maybe. But Dale's been stuck in Cross County for a long time. It would be tempting to make the most out of a story like this, use it as a ticket back to the big time. It might not get him all the way back to Chicago, but maybe Cincinnati or Cleveland."

"Don't be ridiculous. A story about a vandalized car wouldn't . . ." Joanne trailed off as the full implications of Marshall's words sank in. "You know about last night."

Marshall gave her a smile that was just a degree or two a way from a smirk. "Does that surprise you?"

"Not really." She mentally kicked herself for not realizing this sooner. She'd had too little sleep last night, and her brain was sludge this morning. Not that it was a good excuse. It just meant that she would have to work all the harder to focus.

Debbie had been silent all this time, merely listening while Joanne and Marshall verbally jousted. But now she spoke up.

"What are you two talking about? Did something else happen last night? Something . . . bad?"

Joanne knew Debbie would have to be told about the murder, and she could well imagine the poor woman's reaction when she heard that someone had killed a boy last night using her son's M.O. But this was neither the time nor the place for that conversation—especially not with Marshall Cross present.

"I'll tell you in a bit, Debbie. Okay?"

Debbie's mouth twitched, and she looked from Joanne to Marshall then back again. "Oh, God . . . it's about Carl, isn't it?"

Before Joanne could reply, Debbie turned and ran toward the café's entrance.

"Go ahead," Marshall said. "You need to keep her from disturbing any evidence inside. Don't worry about my touching the car while you're gone. I'm sure Ronnie will keep a close eye on me. Right, Ronnie?"

The deputy had taken a grand total of one additional shot since resuming his task. Now he looked away from the camera's viewfinder, and while only his eyes were visible above his surgical mask, Joanne could see the uncertainty in them. Still, when he spoke, his voice was firm enough.

"That's right, Sheriff. I'll see to things out here."

For a moment, Joanne was torn. She didn't like the idea of leaving Ronnie alone with Marshall, but she couldn't let Debbie be alone inside the café, either. Finally, she nodded to Ronnie and gave Marshall a last look.

"We'll talk again," he said.

Joanne's jaw muscles bunched tight as she replied. "Yes, we will." Then she turned and headed for the café.

■ ■ ■ ■ ■

"Hello, Tyrone. What've I missed so far?"

Tyrone Gantz didn't jump at the sound of Dale's voice, though the reporter had approached from behind as quietly as he could. It was a little game Dale played, seeing if he could sneak up on Tyrone. Though he'd been trying for years, he always failed.

"Not much. Ronnie just got here a couple minutes ago. He's taking photos of Debbie's car." Tyrone's voice was soft and whiskey-rough, and if Dale hadn't known the man for years, he might've thought him ill. But Tyrone always sounded like this, and Dale figured it was because he didn't get the chance to talk very often. Dale wondered if anyone ever spoke with Tyrone besides him. Maybe not, he decided.

Tyrone stood near the mouth of the alley between Holloway's and Mitch Phillips' dental clinic, Nothing But the Tooth. He wore a gray trench coat that was at least as old as he was, and which probably hadn't been cleaned since the day it was purchased. Dale knew this wasn't due to neglect on Tyrone's part. The multitude of faded stains and ground-in dirt made for effective camouflage, helping Tyrone to blend in with his surroundings. It helped that the man could be as still as a corpse when he wished, barely seeming to breathe.

Tyrone was a short, stout man who could've been anywhere from fifty to eighty. His white hair was long and unkempt, his beard likewise, though both were clean. Beneath the trench coat he wore a white t-shirt—which Dale knew from their long acquaintance would be freshly laundered—along with jeans and tennis shoes. He looked every bit the stereotype of a homeless person, and as far as Dale knew, Tyrone might well live on the streets. But there was nothing stereotypical about this man.

Dale didn't ask Tyrone if Joanne had spotted him. Not only did he already know the answer, but the question would've been an insult to Tyrone's pride.

Dale moved up close behind Tyrone so he could look over the man's shoulder. The trench coat smelled of decades' worth of mildew, and Dale was forced to breathe through his mouth if he wanted to remain in proximity to Tyrone. He didn't want to get any closer to the mouth of the alley, though. Dale was good at what he did, but he knew he was nowhere close to Tyrone's league when it came to staying out of sight, and he didn't want Joanne—or worse, Marshall Cross—to know he was watching them. Besides, he didn't want to block Tyrone's view. That would be rude.

There wasn't much traffic this time of morning, but even so, Dale wasn't able to make out any of the conversation taking place across the street. His hearing had never been the greatest, and it only seemed to be getting worse as the years went by. But that was all right. He could always get Joanne to fill him in later. He was here for a different reason.

"I was here last night," Tyrone said. "Well, technically I wasn't *here*. I was sitting in Holloways' doorway."

"You saw what happened." It wasn't a question.

"Yes. But I've told you before, Dale. It's my job to witness. Not to interfere."

"I'm not asking you to interfere. I'm asking you to share what you know. Isn't that what being a witness is all about?"

Tyrone didn't respond right away, and while Dale couldn't see the man's facial expression from where he stood, he knew Tyrone was smiling ruefully.

"You always use the same argument."

"That's because it always works."

Tyrone chuckled, a hoarse, almost tubercular sound. "We're two of a kind, aren't we? Though I watch in hiding and you in plain sight. We're like the blind men and the elephant. We each see pieces of the whole. So how did you find out about Debbie Coulter's car? Police scanner? Or did Sheriff Talon call and give you a head's up?"

"This is embarrassing to admit, but as I walked out of the *Echo* office today, I saw Marshall Cross drive by. I followed on foot and saw him meet Debbie outside the café. I figured you'd be around somewhere—you always are when something interesting is going on—so I decided to poke around in some likely hiding places until I found you."

Across the street, something had upset Debbie. She turned and ran inside the café. Joanne spoke with Marshall for a moment before following Debbie inside. Marshall didn't leave, though. He kept standing there, watching as Ronnie continued his laboriously meticulous photography of the defaced Ford.

"You wouldn't have found me if I hadn't wanted you to," Tyrone said. There was no braggadocio in his voice. He was simply stating a fact.

"I know. So . . . what happened?"

"You go first," Tyrone said. "Despite your flattering portrayal of me, I can only get so far so fast on foot. I know something happened outside town last night. I saw the paramedic van leave the county building at 2:58 a.m."

Dale had never seen Tyrone wear a watch, yet he somehow always knew the precise time.

Dale told him about the murder. Though he knew Joanne wouldn't approve, he didn't hold back a single detail. It was the only way to make sure Tyrone would do the same when it was his turn.

Just as Dale finished with his story, he saw Ronnie Doyle drop his camera onto the asphalt, watched plastic fragments break off the casing. Ronnie himself quickly went down after it, falling first to his knees, then pitching forward onto his hands. He crouched there on all fours, head lowered, shivering as if caught in a blast of winter air, features twisted into a mask of utter revulsion.

Marshall Cross stood with his arms folded, impassively regarding Ronnie. And then, though Dale hadn't been able to make out anything else that had been said across the street that morning, he quite clearly heard Ronnie whisper a single word.

"Yes."

· · · · ·

Ronnie tried to go about his work while pretending Marshall Cross wasn't standing there watching. He didn't glance in Marshall's direction, made sure that the man wasn't visible through the camera lens as he lined up his shots. But it didn't help. Ronnie could feel Marshall's gaze on him, tracking his every move, like a hawk perched on a telephone pole, eyeing a field mouse he's considering making a quick snack of. Ronnie felt a slight pressure in his head, and then his skin began to itch, as if hundred of tiny insects were lightly crawling over the surface of his body. He told himself he was just feeling anxious, that the sensation was all in his mind, and he did his best to try to ignore it. But the itching grew in intensity until it became a fiery pain, as if the insects— thousand of them, now—were sinking hook-like pincers into his flesh and tearing away tiny chunks of meat.

Ronnie gritted his teeth and a soft whine escaped his throat. It was the kind of sound a small, frightened dog might make just before it squirted a stream of urine onto the ground. Sweat-beads formed on his forehead and began sliding down the sides of his face, trickling down his neck. He *hated* sweating, couldn't stand the way it made his clothes cling cold and damp against his body. He wanted nothing more than to drop the camera onto the ground and start scratching, raking fingernails over his flesh to dislodge the maddening biting things that he knew couldn't be real, but which he felt nevertheless.

But instead he gritted his teeth harder until his fillings started to ache, and he forced himself to breathe evenly as he struggled to concentrate on taking the next photograph. Sheriff Talon was depending on him to do this job, and Ronnie had never let her down before, and he sure as hell didn't intend to now.

"Something wrong, Ronnie?" Marshall asked. Underneath the man's tone of cool detachment, Ronnie thought he heard dark amusement. "You seem a trifle uncomfortable."

The burning sensation increased, and Ronnie ground his teeth together so hard one of the fillings in his back molars cracked. A tiny lance of pain shot through his tooth, but it was nothing compared to the agonizing fire blazing across his skin. The camera shook in his trembling hands, making the world seen through the viewfinder appear as if it were caught in the throes of an earthquake. His breath now came in ragged gasps. It felt as if he'd been coated head to toe in liquid flame.

"I can make it go away."

Ronnie heard Marshall's words as if they came from a great distance, and though he had no rational reason to believe them, he did. Ronnie's family had moved to Cross County when he was eleven. He was a clean boy even then. An *especially* clean boy. But he hadn't yet taken to washing his hands so many times a day that the skin became red, chapped, and fissured with cracks. Hadn't yet started wearing the surgical mask when he went outside, the mask that would become his second—and in some ways truest—face. After he started school, it wasn't long before the other children began telling him stories about the Crosses with ghoulish enthusiasm. They lived in a castle outside town, their kids were all home-schooled, they didn't attend any of the churches in town, and some folks said they had a family chapel of some sort in their fortress home. But to whom—or what—they prayed to, no one knew. Warnings came with the tales as well, passed along with none of the mischievous glee of the stories. The kids turned dead serious, and their hushed tones and furtive glances around as they spoke—as if they feared someone, the *wrong* someone—might overhear, frightened young Ronnie more than all the lurid rumors about the Crosses combined.

When a Cross asks you to do something, you should. But when a Cross tells you to do something, you've got to.

There would be a pause then, and the advice-giver's voice always fell to a whisper.

They can make *you.*

And so now, over forty years later, Ronnie believed Marshall could do as he said, believed from the top of his flaming scalp to the bottoms of his fire-seared feet.

"Something's happening, Ronnie. Something that involves Family business."

Though it was difficult for Ronnie to make out Marshall's voice through the red haze of pain that enshrouded his mind, he was still able to hear the way Marshall stressed the word *Family.*

"Joanne's good at what she does, and normally we're content to let her go about her job without any interference on our part. But whatever's going on is too important for us to stand by and wait for the wheels of justice to turn on their own. Joanne won't like us taking an active hand in her investigation, and because of this, she will no doubt be reluctant to share whatever information she discovers. That's where you come in, Ronnie."

Ronnie's breath was coming in ragged bursts now—*huh-huh-huh-huh-huh!*—and a far-off corner of his mind that wasn't consumed by pain and terror wondered if he were on the verge of hyperventilating.

"I need someone to keep me apprised of Joanne's progress. Someone who'll tell me everything—and who will of course keep our arrangement secret from the good Sheriff. Do that for me, and the pain will go away. It won't even be a memory."

Ronnie wanted to tell Marshall yes, wanted to cry out that he'd do anything, anything at all, if Marshall would stop the pain. But Marshall Cross didn't understand who he was dealing with. Ronnie lived a life of complete control: ordered, regulated, sterilized . . . as germ-free, contact-free, and disturbance-free as it was possible for a human being to get. Ronnie wanted to say yes and end the agony, but he wanted to do right by Sheriff Talon even more.

And he understood control.

And so he fought to ignore the pain that held him in its blazing grip, and he managed to gasp out a single word.

"Nuh . . . No."

Marshall's gaze filled with regret. "I'm sorry you feel that way,

Ronnie. I truly do. I'd hoped it wouldn't come to this."

Ronnie felt that odd pressure inside his head again, and suddenly as if a switch had been thrown somewhere inside his brain, the pain ceased. The sudden absence of sensation was so startling that he drew in a gasping breath. He stood stunned for a moment, not quite able to bring himself to believe it was really over.

And it wasn't.

His hands were ungloved, his face unmasked, and he stood naked in the morning sun. But his skin wasn't completely exposed to the air. He was covered with thick, foul-smelling, brownish-green muck, and with horror he realized he was slathered in feces. And that wasn't the whole of it. Wriggling white things that could only be maggots crawled in and out of the filth, and Ronnie could feel them writhe against his skin. He held his breath to keep from inhaling the stench, and he squeezed his eyes shut to keep the maggots from getting at his eyes. He tried not to think of the millions . . . no, *billions* of germs that were crawling all over him right now, furiously seeking a way to get inside his body where they could begin to multiply.

The pain had been agonizing, but Ronnie could deal with pain. After all, it was just a sensation, and sensations could be ignored. But *this* . . . this was too much for him. He started shuddering and couldn't stop. Tears streamed from the corners of his eyes, their moisture doing little wash the muck from his face. The camera, which he hadn't realized he was still holding, slipped from his fingers and fell to the ground. Seconds later, Ronnie was down on his hands and knees. Another few seconds after that, he whispered a single word.

It turned out Ronnie had been wrong about Marshall Cross. He'd known precisely what sort of man he'd been dealing with.

CHAPTER SIX

Joanne found Debbie standing behind the counter, wiping her eyes with a handful of napkins. She tried not to think about everything Debbie might've touched on her way inside—the front door handle, the counter, who knew what else—and the evidence she might've destroyed by doing so. Instead, she walked over to the counter and sat on a stool directly in front of Debbie.

"You okay?"

Debbie dabbed at her eyes one more time before nodding.

"Tell me what else happened last night," she said. *"Please."*

Joanne knew she shouldn't, that she should first question Debbie about what had happened here at the café so that her memory wouldn't be compromised. She would undoubtedly interpret what happened here at the café differently once she learned about the murder. Maybe only in some small, unimportant ways, but maybe in some major ones. It was a mistake, and Joanne knew it, but she decided to tell Debbie what she wanted to know. The woman had suffered so much over the years, and Joanne couldn't bring herself to add to that suffering, even if only for a few moments.

She thought Debbie might start crying again as she listened to the details of last night's murder, but instead the woman grew calmer the more Joanne spoke. When she finished, Debbie regarded her silently for a moment, her expression unreadable.

"You don't know who the boy is . . . was?"

"Not yet. And so far no missing persons reports have come in."

"And he had Carl's mark on him. But he wasn't found on the Deveraux Farm."

Joanne didn't respond, as she sensed Debbie wasn't asking questions so much as thinking aloud.

"It's sad," said Debbie. "I mean, someone died last night, and I should feel sorry for him, but my first reaction is to hope that maybe Carl wasn't a killer after all. That someone else was responsible and my baby was innocent. I know he was guilty. He told me so, and I believed him. But here I stand, ready to forget all of that on the slim chance my boy's memory might be redeemed." Debbie gave Joanne a small, sad smile. "Pretty goddamned pathetic, huh?"

"Not at all. It just means that despite everything, you still love your son." Joanne paused and took a breath as she prepared to shift gears. "I hate to do this right now, but I have to ask you some questions about what happened here last night."

"Sure, I understand. You want me to brew some coffee?"

Joanne wanted to say that Debbie shouldn't touch anything else in the café, but then she figured what were the odds that whoever had broken in last night had messed with the coffee machine? Besides, given how little sleep Joanne had last night, she needed all the caffeine she could get.

"Sounds good."

Debbie went to work and a few minutes later the two women sat side by side at the counter, two steaming mugs of coffee in front of them, the rich aroma hanging pleasantly in the air. The atmosphere seemed far too cozy, too *normal*, considering what they were about to discuss. Joanne started with the question that had been foremost on her mind since the moment she'd received Ronnie's call.

"Why did you wait until this morning to report the break-in?"

Debbie held her mug cupped in her hands, and she gazed down at its contents as if she might find answers, or at least a measure of reassurance, in its black depths.

"I'm embarrassed to admit it, but I was scared. So scared that I guess I didn't want to face it, you know? It was easier to tell myself that it was just another cruel practical joke that had gone too far. By the time I walked home, I'd convinced myself that it was no big deal, and I decided to come in early today and clean up the mess before opening."

Debbie had lived out in the country for decades, but a couple years ago—after one too many rubber knives coated with red-paint blood had been left in her mailbox—she'd sold her house and moved into another on the south side of town, where there were neighborhood watch programs and more regular sheriff patrols. A longish walk, but still doable for an out-of-shape middle-aged woman, especially if she was wired from adrenaline.

"What changed your mind about reporting the incident?" Joanne asked.

"After I got home, I couldn't sleep. I just lay in bed and stared at the ceiling, going over what happened, and the more I thought about it, the more it seemed different than all those other times. It probably sounds stupid, but even though I never saw anyone during the break-in, I could *feel* their hatred. It was like the air was thick with it, you know? Like the way it gets when a storm's rolling in."

Joanne couldn't have put it better herself. A storm was indeed descending on Cross County—a goddamned big one. And she wondered if there was anyplace where its citizens could find shelter.

• • • • •

Dale started to move past Tyrone, intending to leave the alley and rush across the street to Ronnie's aid. But Tyrone grabbed hold of his arm and held him back.

"Wait," Tyrone whispered.

Dale hesitated long enough to see Ronnie push back onto his heels. The deputy sat like that for a moment while he got himself together, and then he gathered up the camera he'd dropped, along with the pieces that had broken off. He stood, swaying for an instant as if he might collapse again, but then he grew steadier, and it looked like he was going to be able to remain on his feet.

"What happened?" Dale asked.

"You know. Marshall did something to him."

It was a simple declaration, but one fraught with meaning. Tyrone was right. Dale did know, better than almost anyone—anyone whose surname wasn't Cross, that is. But as intrigued as he was to know the precise nature of what had been done to Ronnie, he needed some information from Tyrone first.

"You were about to tell me what you saw last night."

Tyrone smiled. "I was?" But then he went on to tell Dale what he had witnessed from his vantage point sitting in the doorway of Holloway's Cards and Notions.

Dale listened as Tyrone talked, but he continued watching what was happening across the street. Ronnie put the damaged camera back in his cruiser and removed the evidence kit from the trunk. As the deputy started to work on gathering evidence from the vandalized Ford, Marshall climbed into his Hummer, started the engine, and pulled out of the parking lot. Marshall gave Ronnie a last look before driving away, but the deputy ignored him and continued with his work. Dale wondered how much effort it had cost Ronnie to do that.

When Tyrone finished, Dale turned to him and said, "And that was the last time you saw the person who broke in?"

"It was a quiet night after that. Until the paramedics left the county building and headed out for the murder site, that is."

Dale thought about Tyrone's description of the person he'd seen break into the Caffeine Café. Medium height, slender build, dressed in a gray hooded sweatshirt, jeans, and running shoes. Head and face obscured by the hood and the night's shadows. It didn't occur to Dale to question any of the details Tyrone supplied. He knew the man's attention to specifics was scrupulous, and his memory unimpeachable. If any human on the planet had a brain that was the equivalent of a security camera, it was Tyrone Gantz.

The description wasn't especially helpful, but it was something to start with. Beyond the fact that it wasn't someone tall or fat, there wasn't a lot to go on. Even the person's gender was indeterminate. And of course there was no guarantee the person in the hoody was the same one who'd later killed that boy out on a country road. Though whoever it was would've had ample time after scaring Debbie to commit the murder. A couple of hours, at least.

A thought occurred to Dale then. Maybe whoever it was had wanted to do more than simply frighten Debbie. Maybe he or she had intended to kill Debbie and had muffed the job. In which case, maybe the boy had been only a substitute, someone on whom the killer could take out the frustration of botching the attempt on Debbie. But if the boy had been simply a target of opportunity, why had the killer taken his wallet? To pick up a few extra bucks or to delay having the boy identified? Dale was certain Joanne would find out who the boy was eventually, but if the killer wanted to keep the boy's identity a secret, then the sooner they discovered who he was, the better. If there was only some way to speed up the process . . .

There might be one way, he realized. It was something of a

longshot, especially since all he had to go on was a physical description of the victim, but it *might* be enough.

"I can hear the wheels turning in your head," Tyrone said. "Care to share?"

"Not yet. It might be nothing, but if it turns about to be important, I promise I'll let you know."

"Fair enough."

The two men were silent for a several minutes after that. They watched Ronnie spread fingerprint powder on the door handles of Debbie's Ford, and even from across the street, Dale could see the deputy's hands were still shaking from his encounter with Marshall Cross.

"Looks like the fun's over," Tyrone said. "I think I'll be moving along to see what else might be transpiring in Rhine this morning. You?"

"I'm a reporter, aren't I? I suppose it's time I went to work."

Tyrone gave Dale a final nod before turning around and heading down the alley. Dale walked out onto the sidewalk, stepped off the curb, and headed across the street to the Caffeine Café.

· · · · ·

Joanne drove down Route 33, past fields of dry cornstalks swaying in the wind. Though the cruiser's windows were up, Joanne could imagine the rustling sound the stalks made as they rubbed against each other, a chorus of whispers, as if the fields were trying to tell her something but she couldn't quite make out their words. It wouldn't be much longer before the stalks were cut down and used to make Mummers for the Harvest Festival. The cornstalk men were a tradition in Cross County, but while most folks found the Mummers quaint and charming, Joanne thought they were creepy as hell. She'd never made one as a kid, and every year she'd begged her parents not to buy one, though her dad

TIM WAGGONER

68

usually had. *Wouldn't be Harvest Festival without one,* he'd say.

"I'm trying to think of a word to describe your expression right now. I'm torn between *pensive* and *brooding.*"

Joanne glanced over at Dale and smiled. "Just thinking."

"I don't suppose you're about to have a dazzlingly brilliant insight that will solve both the murder *and* the break-in."

"I wish."

Dale smiled at her and Joanne had a memory flash of the first time she'd seen that smile. She'd been nine years old . . .

• • • • •

She must've been asleep or something, because one moment there had been only darkness, and the next she was looking up at a kind face smiling down at her through a neatly trimmed black beard flecked with gray. The face was so close that at first she thought the man was leaning down over her, but then she realized she wasn't lying down. The face was so close because the man it belonged to was carrying her. His smile was gentle and reassuring, and she was cold, so she nestled her head in the crook of his shoulder. He was warm and smelled of aftershave and deodorant. Comforting male scents that made her feel cared for, protected.

"How are you feeling?" The man's voice was rough, but his tone held only concern.

"Okay, I guess. Sleepy." She yawned then as if saying the word reminded her of how weary she was. Her body felt heavy, and it was all she could do to keep her eyes open. She was glad the nice man was carrying her, for she was certain she was far too tired to walk.

"I'm not surprised. You've been through a lot these last few days. But it's over now, and I'm going to take you home."

Home . . . it seemed like so long since she'd been there. She tried to picture it, but no image came into her mind. Just a feeling of longing, a need to be there as soon as possible. Once there, she would be able to sleep . . . finally.

The man was wearing a suit and tie, and Joanne thought of another man she'd seen at the bank once, when Mommy and Daddy had taken her with them when they'd applied for a loan. She almost asked the nice man if worked at the same bank, but then she gazed upward and saw the canopy of lush green leaves above them. She heard them whisper softly n the breeze, heard birdsong, and the cracking of twigs as small animals moved through the undergrowth.

"Where"—she yawned again—"are we?"

"In the woods. This is where I found you."

Joanne had a child's awareness of when adults were lying to her, and she thought this man was doing so now. Maybe he thought it was for her own good. Wasn't that why adults usually lied? But he was nice, so she decided not to hold this lie against him.

"Who are you?" she asked.

His smile widened. "My name's Dale. And don't worry, Joanne. I'm a friend."

She knew he wasn't lying this time, and she smiled back.

 . . . . .

"Either you're putting your vast powers of deductive reasoning to work, or you're simply ignoring me. Which is it?"

Joanne turned to look at Dale. "What?"

He grinned. "I've asked you the same question twice, and you didn't answer either time."

She faced forward again. "Sorry. Guess my mind wandered for a moment."

"Apology accepted. But not that I've finally managed to snag your attention, I'll try again. What now? Back to town?"

After Dale had hooked up with Joanne at the Caffeine Café, she'd decided to go take a look at the murder scene in daylight. Dale had asked if he could ride along, and she'd said sure. Not only was she grateful for his reassuring presence—for part of her was still the nine-year-old girl he had rescued years ago—but he made an effective sounding board for ideas. She always seemed to think better when he was around.

Their stop at the murder scene had been a bust, though. The location looked no different in the light of day, and they'd found no evidence that had been overlooked last night. Joanne hadn't really expected to find anything, but it had been worth a try, for the sake of being thorough, if nothing else. But Dale's question was a good one: what next?

"I *would* like to get an official statement from Tyrone Gantz," she said.

"As much as I sympathize with you desire to cross your t's and dot your i's, you know you won't be able to find Tyrone unless he wants you to."

Dale had a tendency to exaggerate and over-dramatize, and he sometimes acted as if Tyrone had almost preternatural skill at remaining hidden. Still, he was right. Finding Tyrone wouldn't be easy, and she could put her time to better use than running all over the county looking for him. She'd ask one of her deputies to track down Tyrone and take his statement. Maybe Ronnie, although he wouldn't be thrilled to talk to Tyrone, not with that ratty trench coat he always wore.

Thinking of Ronnie reminded her of something she'd noticed before she and Dale had left town.

"Back at the café, did Ronnie seem normal to you?"

Dale smiled. "You're talking about a man whose lower face I've rarely seen. I'm not sure he's ever seemed *normal* to me."

"When he came into the café to process the scene, he seemed . . . I don't know. Distant, somehow. Guarded. He avoided looking me in the eye, and he hardly said a word. Didn't you notice?"

Dale hesitated a moment before answering. Not long, but long enough. "No, but like I said, Ronnie's behavior has always struck me as a little off. I wouldn't read too much into it if I were you."

"Maybe you're right." But she couldn't escape the feeling that something had been bothering Ronnie, and she wouldn't have been surprised to learn that Marshall Cross had something to do with it.

She thought of Dale's hesitation, and she wondered if once again he was lying to her for her own good.

"There's something else I've been wondering about," she said. "It seemed as if Marshall and Debbie knew each other. Not like they were old friends exactly, but definitely more than acquaintances."

"Now *that's* interesting. You know, in the weeks after Carl Coulter was arrested, it was rumored that Marshall paid several visits to Debbie. I heard he did the same again during Carl's trial. I figured it was simply a case of the local lord looking after one of his vassals. But now that I think of it, I've never known Marshall—or any of the Crosses, for that matter—to take such an ongoing personal interest in a townsfolk problem."

"It *was* a high-profile case," Joanne said. "There was a lot of media attention, right?"

"A goddamned circus is what it was."

"So maybe Marshall just wanted to make sure the situation was handled in such a way that it didn't make the family look bad." *Just like he wants to do now.*

"Is that what you really think?" Dale asked.

"Honestly, I don't know what the hell to think right now."

Dale glanced out the windshield. "Well, your conscious mind

might be spinning its wheels at the moment, but it looks like your subconscious has an idea or two." He pointed.

Joanne looked and saw the less than a quarter mile ahead of them was the dirt road turn-off that led to the Deveraux Farm.

She supposed on some level she *had* been heading this way on purpose. Both of the crimes that had taken place last night had connections to the murders committed by Carl Coulter. It only made sense to check out the location where Debbie's "baby" had slaughtered four people.

"Got your digital camera on you?" she asked.

Dale patted the right pocket of his suit jacket. "Always."

"Then let's go take a look." And though there were no other vehicles in sight, Joanne put on her signal before slowing and turning onto the dirt road. As she did, the first stirrings of cold nausea blossomed in her gut, and she knew she'd made the right choice.

Her face must've shown how she felt, for Dale asked, "Feeling sick?"

"Yep."

He grinned. "Good."

CHAPTER SEVEN

Joanne parked the cruiser at the edge of an overgrown field. The gravel driveway that had once led to the farm had long ago disappeared beneath grass and weeds, but the teenagers who came out here to make out had worn this alternate path. The farm was on the usual patrol route for the sheriff's department as well. Joanne wasn't the type to leave all the scut work to her deputies, and she put in her fair share of patrol hours. But though she made sure to check on the Deveraux Farm whenever she was on patrol, she never lingered. The fact that four people had been killed and mutilated here was bad enough, but whenever she came here her stomach clenched and her head started to ache. Not as bad as when she had one of her Feelings, but bad enough to be uncomfortable, and the physical effects would last for a couple hours after she left. Her stomach was already bugging her, and she could feel the beginnings of a headache behind her eyes.

She turned off the cruiser's engine and she and Dale just sat for a moment looking out the windshield at the abandoned farmhouse. Kids in Cross County—and more than a few adults—thought this place was haunted. Joanne was too sensible to believe such crap, but every time she visited the farm, she understood a little better why some folks did believe.

"Don't get any ideas about making a move on me," Dale said. "I'm not that kind of guy."

Joanne grinned. "Duly noted."

They got out of the cruiser and started walking toward the Deveraux place. Dale took his camera out of his jacket pocket and held it ready at his side, as if it were a weapon and he a soldier heading into battle. The thought reminded Joanne to undo the snap on the side holster that held her 9 mm. They knew there was a murderer on the loose, and while she didn't expect some masked backwoods maniac to come rushing at them with a roaring chainsaw, she was too much a professional to take any unnecessary chances.

The weeds were nearly waist high, and though Joanne looked closely, she saw no sign that anyone had been through here recently—no stems bent or broken, no plants flattened. Of course, that didn't mean much. There were any number of ways to approach the farm. Just because there were no visible signs of trespass didn't mean someone hadn't been here. Someone who even now might be lurking in the house or hiding crouched inside the barn, listening intently as they approached.

But the morning refused to cooperate with Joanne's sinister imaginings. The sky was a cloudless robin's egg blue, and a gentle breeze wafted across the fields. The breeze carried a hint of not-so-far-off winter, but the slight chill was offset by the warming rays of the sun. It was a pleasant, almost cheerful day, wholly inappropriate for a setting where people had died in agony and terror. It seemed almost an affront somehow, as if the world had forgotten what had happened here or—if it did remember—refused to acknowledge the events by providing a cloudy gloom-enshrouded atmosphere.

"Been a long time since I've been out here," Dale said as they continued making their way across the field. "Can't say I've missed it. But I suppose it's useful to refamiliarize myself with the place—the sights, sounds, smells . . ."

"Spoken like a true reporter." Joanne remembered then what Marshall had told her in the parking lot of the Caffeine Café. *Dale's been stuck in Cross County for a long time. It would be tempting to make the most out of a story like this, use it as a ticket back to the big time.*

"You ever miss working for a big city paper?" As soon as she asked the question, she wished she could take it back. Partly because she was ashamed at the lack of faith in Dale that it implied, and partly because she was angry at herself for allowing Marshall to get to her.

If Dale thought her question odd, he gave no sign as he answered. "It would be nice not having to worry about printing the bridge scores from the nursing home in the sports section every week. Those old folks get testy as hell if I'm even a single point off."

Joanne smiled at the joke, but she noticed Dale avoided directly answering her question. She wanted to leave it at that, but Marshall's insinuations—damn him, anyway!—had gotten her to thinking. She was about to press Dale further when her cell phone rang.

"I hope it's Terry," she said as she removed the phone from her belt carrier. Maybe he'd already finished his autopsy of the murdered boy and had the preliminary results for her. Better yet, maybe he'd somehow learned the boy's identity.

"Sheriff Talon."

"I'm finished with the diner, Sheriff."

Ronnie, and his voice was oddly toneless, almost as if he were reading from a script and his heart wasn't in his performance.

"Find anything of interest?"

"Not really. Got some prints, but it's hard to say if they'll come to anything. I printed Mrs. Coulter for comparison, too."

Joanne knew there was no way to print all of Debbie's customers, especially since some of them just stopped in as they were passing through. Any prints Ronnie got might well prove useless when it came to either identifying *or* eliminating suspects. Still, they had to try.

"Anything else you'd like me to do?" Ronnie asked, tone still flat and mechanical.

She was starting to worry about him. What if his neurosis was getting worse and he had the beginnings of a full-blown psychotic breakdown? She hated to think so selfishly, but she couldn't afford to lose him, not right now with a murder case on their hands.

"Why don't you head back to the office and get the prints ready to travel to the state crime lab? I want them to go out ASAP."

One of them—Ronnie or Joanne herself—would drive the prints to Columbus and deliver them personally to maintain the chain of evidence. Not for the first time she wished Cross County had its own crime lab. The state lab usually had a backlog of evidence to process, and it could well be some time before they got any results back to her. She'd make a few calls, see if she could get them to expedite her material, but she doubted it would help speed things up significantly. She supposed she could ask Marshall to see what he could do. Rumor had it that the Crosses had connections in the statehouse. She didn't like the idea of asking Marshall for help, and she sure as hell didn't like the idea of being beholden to him for a favor. Still, she'd consider it.

"Will do, Sheriff. Anything else?"

"I've got reason to believe that Tyrone Gantz may have witnessed the break-in at the café last night. We'll need to get a statement from him. I'm poking around at the Deveraux Farm right now, and I may be here for a while, so I need someone to track him down and talk to him. When you get back to the station, see if you can find someone to take care of it." She thought of who was on duty today. "Kelly, maybe. Or if she's too busy, ask Harley." She wasn't about to ask Ronnie to do it. The way he was acting, the last thing she wanted to do was put anymore stress on him.

"Sure thing, Sheriff."

Joanne told Ronnie to keep her posted, then she disconnected and slipped her phone into its carrier. She and Dale had continued walking while she'd spoken with Ronnie, and they now reached the Deveraux house. Most of the white paint had flaked away over the years, exposing dull gray wood. The windows—those that hadn't been shattered by stone-throwing teenagers eager to prove their bravery—were streaked and grimy. Half the shingles had peeled off the roof, and Joanne thought it was only a matter of time before the elements weakened the roof to the point of collapse. The barn didn't look any better. Joanne assumed it had been painted once, but not a single flake remained to indicate the color it had been. It was a gray, lopsided structure covered by a rusty corrugated tin roof. It had no windows to break, so the local daredevils had been forced to carve graffiti into the soft wood. Most of it has simple and banal—people's names, profanity, and names of bands followed by *rocks!* or *rules!* And in more than few cases, those words had been scratched out and *sucks!* etched beneath. But a few of the messages were more original and some were downright enigmatic. *Jizbo seeks solace* and *They came in through the out door.* The strangest was a smiley face with two X's in place of eyes, and above it the words *Only the dead.* Considering what had happened behind these walls, she couldn't help shuddering when she saw it.

They stopped at a point halfway between the house and the

barn. Dale took a picture of the former and continued to look at it when he was finished.

"It wasn't all that different twenty years ago," Dale said. "The yard was better kept, though it needed mowing, and both the house and the barn could've used fresh paint. Maggie Deveraux had lost her husband Bill only six months earlier, and she was still grieving him. She was Carl's first victim, you know."

Joanne *did* know. Carl the Cutter was local legend, and even if she hadn't been sheriff, she'd have been familiar with the details of the case. Still, she didn't want to interrupt Dale. He'd accompanied her predecessor, Sheriff Manchester, when the bodies had been discovered, and she wanted to hear about Dale remembered about the crime scene.

"Carl never did explain why he chose Maggie. 'I had reason,' was all he'd say whenever asked why he'd picked any of his victims. He drove out here one night, parked his pick-up, calmly walked up to the door and knocked. It was close to midnight, but even so, Maggie answered the door. This is the country, and if someone's at your door late at night, it usually means someone's in trouble. Unfortunately in this case, that someone turned out to be Maggie. Carl forced his way in, slashed her throat, and then carried her body out to the barn. It was there that he carved his signature design into her abdomen."

To anyone else, Dale's recitation of these events would've seemed detached and unemotional, but Joanne could hear the underlying tension in his voice as he fought to keep a firm hold on his revulsion.

Dale turned to take a picture of the barn and then, as if by unspoken agreement, the two of them started walking toward it. Joanne kept her gaze on the ground, looking for any evidence that someone had been here recently, but she saw nothing. Her rational mind was beginning to think this was going to turn out to be a wasted trip, but the mild nausea roiling in her stomach and the vague tingling at the back of her skull said different.

Dale continued his story. "There was a padlock on the outside of those doors." He pointed to the barn's main entrance, a pair of large doors that were designed to swing outward. The wood had become warped over the years, and the doors didn't quite align anymore, leaving a three to four-inch gap between them. "Carl never used them, though. There's a regular-sized door in the back, but Carl never kept it locked. It was like he didn't care if anyone discovered the bodies—or maybe *wanted* them to be discovered."

"That might not mean anything," Joanne said. "Carl wasn't exactly a poster boy for mental health. His mind might've been so far gone it never occurred to him to try to conceal his crimes."

"But he took over Maggie's farm after killing her and used it as his base of operations. Seems like the act of someone who wants to carry out his work undisturbed."

"That's not the same as wanting to avoid capture," Joanne pointed out. "And what was left of his sanity probably degenerated pretty quickly as the bodies began to pile up."

"Maybe," Dale said. "But it struck me as strange back then, and it still seems that way to me now."

They reached the barn and stopped before the warped double doors.

"The smell was really strong this close," Dale said. "I hadn't lived in Cross County very long at the time, but even a city boy like me could tell that we weren't smelling moldy hay and cow shit. It was late spring, which was the only saving grace. I don't even want to think how bad the stench would've been in summer."

Joanne's queasy stomach gurgled at the thought, and she pressed a hand against her abdomen to quiet it.

Dale inhaled through his nose. "No smell now, though. That's a good sign, right?"

Joanne didn't answer. The fall weather was cool enough to keep a dead body from getting too rank—especially if it was fresh. But she didn't see a need to tell Dale that.

"I assume you and Sheriff Manchester entered through the back," she said.

Dale nodded. "Stan didn't want to mess with breaking the lock on the main doors. Thought it would make too much noise. 'Better to get in as fast and quiet and you can,' he told me later."

"Wise man. I think we'll do the same."

They walked around to the rear of the barn, seeing nothing along the side of the structure but more weeds and graffiti. There was nothing particularly remarkable about the back door, save for its smooth, clean surface. Perhaps the graffiti artists hadn't gotten around to leaving their mark on this door yet. Or maybe the thought that Carl the Cutter had once used the door made them leave it alone out of a strange sort of respect—or perhaps fear.

Dale reached for the rusty doorknob, but Joanne grabbed hold of his wrist before he could touch it.

He gave her a sheepish smile. "Sorry. You'd think I'd know better by now."

Joanne released her grip and Dale lowered his hand to his side.

"Don't worry about it," she said. "Your mind's twenty years in the past right now."

She removed a rubber glove from her pocket and slipped it over her left hand. She wanted to keep her right uncovered in case she needed to use her 9 mm. She bent close to examine the doorknob and saw nothing special. No sign of forced entry, no sign the reddish-brown rust had been recently disturbed. She gently took hold of the knob and turned. It moved more easily than she expected, and she pushed the door open. The hinges creaked, the sound loud as a gunshot in the silence.

But not loud enough to cover the sound of something moving inside the barn.

Joanne froze, left hand still gripping the doorknob. She felt her pulse speed up, and she rested her right hand on the butt of her weapon, though she made no move to draw it yet.

"Stay back," she whispered to Dale. She didn't know if he'd heard the sound, but she didn't have time to explain. Either way, she hoped he'd listen to her and do as she said. She then stepped across the barn's threshold into shadow.

She immediately stepped to the side so she wouldn't be backlit by the light filtering in through the open doorway. The barn's tin roof kept the light out, but the planks, like the large double doors, had warped over the years, creating numerous spaces for sunlight to penetrate. The interior of the barn remained dim and shadowy, but there was enough light that Joanne's eyes quickly began to adjust. She swept her gaze from right to left then back again. She saw the bulk of an old tractor, a jumble of gardening tools, a rototiller, and the like. Evidently Bill Deveraux hadn't kept any animals in the barn and had only used it for equipment storage. Joanne didn't like it. Too many places to hide in here.

Joanne unclipped the flashlight from her belt, thumbed the switch to activate it, and held her breath as she shined the beam where the mass of junk was the thickest. If there was anyone in here and they were armed, she'd just made herself the perfect target. There was another reason she held her breath, though: so she could listen better. She strained to hear the slightest sound that would indicate someone was hiding in the barn—a foot sliding across the dirt floor, the rustle of clothing as someone shifted position, the too-loud respiration of excited breathing. But she heard nothing.

"Cross County Sheriff's Department!" she called out. "Anyone in here?" She waited for a count of ten as she panned the flashlight beam around the barn. Still nothing.

One side of the barn was relatively clear of clutter, and as the flashlight beam passed over it, Joanne had the impression that a shadowy form was standing there. A thrill of adrenaline surged through her, and she swung the beam back as she drew her 9 mm from its holster.

But no one was there.

"Sheriff's Department!" she repeated. "Come out with your hands in the air!"

She moved the beam rapidly back and forth, searching for whoever it was because goddamnit, she'd seen someone! But once again the light revealed no one, and Joanne knew that there wasn't enough cover on that side of the barn to allow someone to hide so swiftly and silently.

The noise she'd heard was probably an animal of some sort—a raccoon or a feral cat—that had been spooked when she'd opened the door. Whatever it was had most likely fled the barn and taken refuge in the high grass outside. She was angry at herself for allowing her imagination to run away with her like a damned rookie. It was one thing to react cautiously when one heard a noise, but quite another to imagine seeing someone that wasn't there. Even worse, the figure had resembled Carl Coulter: stocky, thick-necked, shaved head, black muscle shirt, and ratty jeans. It was the way he'd looked when Sheriff Manchester and Dale had caught him right here in this very place. She knew, because she'd seen the photos Dale had taken. In the pictures, Carl's hands had been coated with blood, for he'd just finished working on the corpse of his latest—and as it would turn out last—victim, Marianne Hendrickson.

Had her imaginary Carl had bloody hands? She'd tried to remember, but the vision, if that was the right word for it, had lasted only a fraction of a second. She decided it didn't really matter. It hadn't been real, so who cared about specifics? Still, she thought maybe she *had* seen smears of crimson on his hands. Red, wet, and fresh.

She replaced her weapon in its holster. "All right, Dale. You can come in."

Dale entered and walked over to join her. "All clear, I presume."

"I make no guarantees that there aren't any bats hanging from the rafters, but I'm fairly confident there are no murderers hiding in the shadows." She decided not to mention her "vision" of Carl to Dale. Not only because it was embarrassing, but because he had a tendency to place far more stock in such occurrences than she did. The last thing she needed was for him to start theorizing about why she'd seen Carl and what it might mean. She knew *exactly* what it meant. She was running on too little sleep today, simple as that.

She realized then that she was trying awfully hard to convince herself it was nothing. She also realized it wasn't working.

"At least there are no other bodies here," Dale said. "After seeing Carl's mark on that boy's belly last night, I was afraid we'd find corpses stacked halfway to the ceiling." He looked around. "Nothing's changed. By now, you'd think vandals would've left their mark inside as well as out."

"Probably too afraid to come inside," Joanne said. "I bet even the bravest—or should I say drunkest—only ever manage to open the door and poke their heads in before getting so close to pissing themselves that they turn tail and run."

Dale clucked his tongue. "You're getting awfully cynical in your old age, my dear. I bet you're right, though." He grew thoughtful once more. "It was night when Stan and I got here. Did I tell you that? The electric was still hooked up then, and Carl had the lights turned on. There were only a couple in the ceiling, and neither was all that bright. They gave the inside of the barn an eerie half-lit look, like something out of a dream. Carl looked up when we burst in—he was crouched over Marianne's body—he'd just finished carving that strange symbol of his onto her belly. He never did tell anyone what the damned thing signified, and I've been unable find anything close to it in all the research I've done over the years. People started talking after the story broke, saying Carl was in some kind of satanic cult, and that's where the symbol came from. Stan and I came to believe it was just something Carl had made up, and its meaning was personal to him—assuming it held any meaning at all and wasn't just a psychotic's version of doodling."

"He arranged the other bodies against the wall, didn't he?" Joanne said.

Dale nodded. "So they were facing the back door. They were sitting with hands at their sides, legs stretched out in front of them. They were naked and covered with dried blood from their throat and stomach wounds. Small chunks of flesh were missing here and there. At first we thought Carl had eaten parts of his victims, but Doc Lahmon—he was the coroner back then—said rats had been at the bodies, probably while Carl was away." Dale closed his eyes and gave his head a little shake, as if trying to dismiss the memory.

"Where was Carl exactly?" Joanne didn't worry that Dale wouldn't remember. He had a reporter's recall, and besides, no one could forget a detail like that—not after living through it.

"Right over there." Dale pointed without hesitation, and a chill shuddered down Joanne's spine. Dale indicated the exact spot where she'd briefly glimpsed Carl's image. Dale frowned. "What's that?"

Joanne trained the flashlight's beam on the ground where Dale pointed. The light revealed an object that was small, square, flat, and black.

"Looks like a wallet," she said.

They walked over to the object—both watching to make sure they didn't inadvertently trample any evidence. Sure enough, it was a wallet.

"Maybe one of those drunks you mentioned before managed to find the courage to come inside all the way and dropped it," Dale said.

"You don't really believe that."

"No, I don't."

Dale took a couple pictures of the wallet, and then Joanne handed him a flashlight. He held the beam steady while Joanne crouched down and carefully picked the wallet up with the thumb and forefinger of her gloved hand. She flipped it open and there, stored inside a laminated flap, was a driver's license with a familiar photo. It was the boy who'd been murdered last night.

"Ray Porter," she read aloud.

Her stomach twisted, her head throbbed, and though she knew it wasn't real, out of the corner of her eye she thought she saw something—a man-shaped something—withdraw into the shadows and be swallowed by darkness.

CHAPTER EIGHT

Joanne dusted the barn's door knob for prints, but it was too rusty to yield anything. She bagged the wallet, and since it was a key piece of evidence, it would have to go to the state crime lab for processing. She and Dale found no other evidence, but she decided to have Ronnie come out here and give the place a once-over as soon as possible. She hated to overwork him, but if she'd missed anything, she was confident only Ronnie would find it.

She drove Dale back to town. They were quiet for much of the drive, each lost in their own thoughts. Eventually, Dale broke the silence.

"There was no sign Ray Porter had been in the barn."

"It's a bit early to come to that conclusion," Joanne cautioned. "While it's certain that he was killed at the location where his body was found, he could've been in the barn before that."

"And he just happened to drop his wallet there?"

"Maybe the killer found Ray in the barn and abducted him. Or maybe he already had Ray and took him there for some reason before taking him to the murder scene. The wallet could've been dropped then."

"There were no indications of a struggle at the barn," Dale said.

"Hard to tell with all that junk there. If something had been knocked over or disturbed, how would we know? Still, the dirt floor showed no signs of a scuffle."

Dale thought for a moment and then shook his head, lips pursed in distaste. "Maybe, but I don't like it. It seems too convenient, like the wallet was purposely left there for us to find."

"The scene might've been staged," Joanne admitted. "Theatre is a big part of a murder like this. Copying Carl's MO, terrorizing his mother, spray-painting Carl's symbol all over her car . . ."

"Assuming the two incidents are linked. A safe enough assumption, I'll grant, but still only an assumption at this point."

"Agreed."

They fell silent again for a few moments before Dale continued.

"I assume you're going to pay the poor boy's parents a visit."

"Yeah. It's not the kind of news you can deliver by phone. Besides, I'll have to bring them in to identify the body." That was a chore Joanne definitely wasn't looking forward to. "Nothing personal, Dale, but it's the sort of thing I should do alone."

"I understand completely. I have an errand of my own to run anyway."

"Oh?"

"I'm going to drive out to the lake and talk with Sadie Muir."

She gave him a disapproving glance. "Dale . . ."

"When you use that tone of voice, you sound like my mother. I was already planning on talking to Sadie before we found the wallet. I'd hoped she might be able to help identify the murdered boy. She knows more about the genealogy of the county's families than anyone else. I've heard that even Althea Cross relies on her expertise from time to time."

"And you thought she could identify the boy from just a description?"

"I do have photos of the body, too, but yes, I did."

Joanne wanted to tell Dale it was a foolish idea. Cross County had more than its fair share of residents who contributed to what was euphemistically described as the "local color," but Sadie Muir was more than merely eccentric. As far as Joanne was concerned, the woman was downright certifiable. But she had to admit that Dale had a point. Sadie might well have been able to identify Ray Porter from his photo—and she probably could've traced his ancestry all the back to before his ancestors first came to America.

"We know who Ray is now," Joanne said. "So why go see Sadie?"

"To learn if there's any connection between Ray Porter and the four people Carl Coulter murdered." He shrugged. "It'll probably turn out to be a waste of time. After all, no connection was ever established between Carl's victims. But I figure it's worth a shot." He grinned. "Besides, it's not like I have anything better to do. My social calendar is inexplicably empty for the rest of the day."

Joanne smiled. "All right, go see Sadie. But if you learn anything interesting, let me know."

"Don't I always?"

. . . . .

After dropping Ray off at the *Echo* office, Joanne stopped by the county building to put Ray Porter's wallet in the evidence locker. She then went into the main office to look for Ronnie and found him at his desk, sitting in front of his computer and typing reports. Since he was inside at his work station—an environment he completely controlled—he wasn't wearing his surgical mask or rubber gloves.

"You think you could take the evidence we've gathered in the murder and Debbie's break-in and run it up to Columbus?"

Ronnie frowned. "After I finish my reports, I was planning on going out to look for Tyrone Gantz."

"Getting the evidence to Columbus is more important. Get someone else to find Tyrone. In fact, tell everyone on patrol to look for him. Whoever finds him first can bring him in and take down his statement." Besides, a road trip might give Ronnie the break he needed, give him a chance to relax a little.

"Sure thing, Joanne."

She nodded and was about to explain to Ronnie that while the trip to Columbus normally could've waited until tomorrow, she wanted to get things moving on the dual investigations as fast as possible. But then she realized something. "You called me by my first name."

Ronnie frowned, and she saw a bead of sweat trickle down his forehead and through the crease in his brow.

"I'm sure I didn't, Sheriff." His tone was one of honest puzzlement.

"It's no big deal. You know you're welcome to call me by my first name."

"You've made that perfectly clear on many occasions, Sheriff. And while I always appreciate the offer, I still prefer to address you as Sheriff . . . Joanne."

Joanne searched Ronnie's face for any hint he was teasing her. Ronnie wasn't a big joker, but he wasn't entirely humorless. But again she saw nothing but confusion this time. Ever since Emily Davis, their administrative assistant, had gone on maternity leave a couple weeks ago, they'd all been picking up the slack, but Ronnie, most likely due to his compulsive nature, had taken on more of her duties than anyone else in the department. He was doubtless overworked and overstressed. She tried to remember when Ronnie had last taken a vacation, and she realized that he hadn't, not since she'd become Sheriff, anyway. He was way overdue, but she decided this wasn't the best time to bring it up. She'd say something to him later.

"All right then, Ronnie. Whatever you're most comfortable with."

"I'll finish up here, check out the Deveraux place, and—if I don't have time to do it myself—I'll see about finding someone to track down Tyrone Gantz and get a statement. I should be able to leave for Columbus around dinnertime, maybe a bit later, if that's all right."

"Sounds good. I'm going to go check to see if Terry's started the autopsy of the Porter boy yet, and then I'm going to head over to the parents' house and break the news to them. If any reporters call, you know the drill. It's too early in the investigation to release any information, but we're working on pursuing all leads, and so forth. Okay?"

"Yes, Sheriff."

"Great, Ronnie. Thanks."

She turned to go, and as she headed away from Ronnie's desk, she heard him softly say, "You're welcome, Joanne."

· · · · ·

As soon as Joanne left the office, Ronnie's gaze fell to the telephone sitting on his desk. There was nothing remarkable about the device—bland off-white plastic, rectangular buttons for selecting different lines or transferring calls. He cleaned it with bleach wipes ever morning, after each use, and then a final time before leaving for the day. It was just a normal office phone, nothing special. But he could swear it was whispering to him right now, its voice a soft electronic hiss of static forming inaudible syllables. Even so, he nevertheless understood what it wanted him to do. He had something to report, and he was supposed to pick up the receiver and punch in the number for Marshall Cross's cell phone.

The fingers of his right hand twitched, but he did not reach toward the phone. He felt a pinprick of pain behind his forehead as if a long sharp needle was slowly being driven through the bone and into the soft flesh beneath. He wasn't going to betray Jo— *Sheriff* Talon. He wasn't!

The static-hiss grew louder, more insistent, and the needle penetrating his brain now felt like a blunt carpenter's nail. He felt a squirming-itching sensation on his right hand. He didn't want to look at it, told himself that he wasn't really feeling anything, and even if he was, it wasn't anything to worry about. The rubber gloves he wore so often sometimes caused the skin on his hands to dry out. He just needed to moisturize more, that's all. He kept a bottle of hypoallergenic hand cream in his desk, along with a mini-pharmacy of healthcare and hygiene supplies. His rationalizing did little good, though. His head continued to throb, the pounding intensifying the itch, which in turn only served to intensify the pounding.

He gritted his teeth against the mounting discomfort and told himself to forget about picking up the phone to call Marshall Cross. All he needed to do was take care of his itching hand and everything would be all right.

With his left hand—which felt perfectly normal—he reached for the drawer where he kept his cream. He forced himself to look in the opposite direction so he wouldn't catch a glimpse of his right hand, not that there was anything to see, not if his problem was just dry skin. As he groped for the drawer handle, he heard something hit the floor with a soft, moist plap. Something that had fallen from his right hand.

Icewater flooded his bowels and, unable to stop himself any longer, he looked at his right hand.

It was covered by a mass of wriggling creatures, so many that his flesh was no longer visible. Two-inch long greenish-gray gelatinous blobs, roughly ovoid in shape. Their writhing bodies lengthened and compressed like caterpillars as they moved, but they weren't insectine. Ronnie understood instinctively what he was looking at, for he'd been battling the goddamned things his entire life. They were bacteria, germs, viruses … they were *filth*, somehow grown from microscopic size.

All the better to feast on your delectable flesh, my dear.

With his left hand he opened the desk drawer, then gripped the front of it with his right hand so his fingers were hanging over the top. Then with his left he jammed the drawer closed as hard as he could. Pain exploded in his hand. It was almost enough to drown out the static-voice of the phone and the hot agony drilling into his brain.

Almost.

He closed the drawer again, a third time, and a fourth, gritting his teeth to keep from crying out. He was alone in this part of the office, but he didn't want to alarm Doris in the dispatcher's room or the deputies in the jail division down the hall. Tears streamed down his face, slid down his neck, soaked into the collar of his uniform.

He opened the drawer one last time and removed his hand. The fingers were bent and twisted, and there was blood where the skin had torn. But there were no more gray-green wigglers on his flesh. The filth was gone. Still, he knew it could return anytime, and would—if he didn't do what was expected of him.

The phone was shouting now, its voice nearly deafening, and a red-hot railroad spike was lodged in his skull. Sobbing, broken fingers shaking, Ronnie reached for the phone.

. . . . .

Coroner was an elected position in Cross County, and Terry had a regular medical practice in town. But when he needed to perform an autopsy, he did so in the county morgue facility housed within the county building. That's where Joanne found him, already gowned and gloved, wearing a clear plastic face shield. Ray Porter lay spread out on an aluminum table with faucets and drains for washing away and collecting blood. The boy was naked, no trace of blood on his body.

The room was small, colors institutional pistachio and tan, tiled floor, and fluorescent lights. One autopsy table, a counter with hose, sink, drain, surgical tools, hanging scale, bottles of chemicals, and a half dozen freezers for cadavers built into the wall. The facilities were modest, but they usually served the county's needs well enough. And if for some reason they didn't—like the after the fire in the historic district a few years ago—Terry would use the morgue over at Resurrection Hospital, near the county line.

Terry looked up as Joanne entered, and despite the morbid surroundings, her heart warmed when he smiled at her.

"I just finished washing him off and was about to start cutting."

"His name is Ray Porter," Joanne said. "We found his wallet out at the Deveraux Farm."

Terry frowned. "By *we*, I assume you mean you and Dale."

She smiled. "Jealous, table for one."

Terry smiled back. "Very funny." He turned to look at Ray's body. "Nice to meet you, Ray Porter, though I wish to hell it had been under better circumstances." He faced Joanne once more. "What was his wallet doing at the farm? That's weird."

"Tell me about it. I'm going to talk to his parents. How long until you finish and get him sewn up so I can bring his folks in to identify him?"

"If you like, I can just do a preliminary examination now, and then wait until after the parents have been here to do a full autopsy."

Joanne considered a moment. "No, the sooner you start, the better. Plus that way you can also sew up the gash in his throat so it doesn't look so bad, and we can cover the design on his stomach with a sheet. It's bad enough his folks are going to have to see their son's corpse this afternoon. No need to make it any worse for them."

"Right." Terry glanced up at the clock on the wall. It was closing in on noon, and Joanne realized she hadn't anything to eat since breakfast. She looked at Ray's lifeless body and decided to skip lunch.

"I should be finished by three. You can have the parents stop by any time after that. But call first, just in case I'm running late."

Joanne nodded. "So . . . what's your schedule look like later this evening, Dr. Birch?"

"I had to cancel my morning patients so I could be here, and a few of them are going to see me after five. But I should be free as the breeze around seven." He removed his face shield and set it down on the counter. "Got anything in mind?"

She stepped close, put her hands on his shoulders, and leaned up to kiss him. He slipped his hand around her waist and drew her tight against his body. His lips parted and the tip of his tongue sought hers, but she gently pushed him away.

"Sorry, but this isn't exactly the most romantic of settings."

He grinned. "I guess not. How about I come over to your place around eight or so? We could have a late dinner . . . or whatever." He comically waggled his eyebrows and Joanne laughed.

"*Whatever* sounds good. I'll call you if anything changes, okay?" She gave him a last quick kiss, studiously avoiding glancing at Ray Porter. But she did give the boy's corpse a final look as she turned to go. She was not looking forward to what she had to do next.

• • • • •

Marshall stepped into the coroner's office just as Terry Birch was using a scalpel to make a deep incision from Ray Porter's right shoulder down to the boy's breast bone. He was glad to see the autopsy was just beginning in earnest. Ronnie's call had been well timed.

"I apologize for interrupting, but I doubt your patient will mind very much."

Terry looked up, startled, but Marshall noted the hand holding the scalpel remained rock-steady. He approved. Power was useless without control.

"Believe it or not, Mr. Cross. There are some places even *you* aren't allowed to go. As you can see, I'm in the middle of an autopsy. You need to leave. *Now.*"

The only person Marshall took orders from was his mother— and only then because it was his duty. His eyes narrowed and his nostrils flared, and he imagined his hand shooting forward, fingers digging into the soft flesh of the coroner's neck, and squeezing until the man's windpipe collapsed. But he maintained iron-clad control of his anger, and the most his hand did was twitch once then fall still. When he spoke, his voice was calm and relaxed, even if he himself was not.

"I've come to pay my respects to the young man."

Behind his face shield, Terry raised an eyebrow. "This is rather an odd time for it, don't you think?"

"Not at all. My family often performs such tasks in private. We ... have a tendency to draw much attention when we're in public, and we have no wish to diminish the loss of the boy in any way."

Terry looked at Marshall for several seconds, as if the coroner was attempting to gauge the sincerity of his words.

"Very well. You've paid your respects. Now leave and let me get on with my work."

Marshall took several steps closer until he stood within six feet of the autopsy table. He saw the line of blood where Terry had cut Ray Porter's chest, but there wasn't a lot of it. Blood didn't well forth very strongly when one no longer possessed a beating heart. Marshall could smell the blood too, an acrid slightly spoiled scent just beginning to filter into the air. It was the odor of blood with no life left in it. He found the stench offensive, but he kept his facial expression neutral. Control was everything.

"I would appreciate it if you could share with me any preliminary impressions you've gleaned so far from your examination of the body. As you might imagine, my family is shocked by this brutal and senseless crime, and we'd like to do whatever we can to help."

"You sure you're not just getting off on being this close to a dead body?" Terry asked. "You wouldn't be the first."

Marshall allowed his lips to form a smile, but his gaze remained cold. "I could ask you the same thing, *Doctor*, but my manners are better than that." His lips drew back from his teeth. "Besides, I've been in the presence of the dead before. So often, in fact, that the experience long ago lost whatever novelty it may have once held for me."

Terry opened his mouth, his facial expression indicating he was about to ask Marshall exactly what he meant by that. But the coroner closed his mouth fast, his teeth clacking together as he did so.

Wise man, Marshall thought.

Marshall took another step forward and inhaled deeply. Mixed in with the smell of dead blood was something else, something familiar. And it wasn't coming from the boy's corpse.

He looked at Terry. "You've got Cross blood in you. I can smell it. Not a lot and"—he sniffed again—"a generation or two back, but it's there."

Terry lifted the scalpel from Ray's body, a small dark ruby of blood clinging to the instrument's tip. He made no move to put the scalpel down, though. "Don't think your amateur magician's tricks are going to impress me. It's not generally known, but my great-grandmother was a Cross. Her name was Thelma."

Marshall thought for a moment. "If I recall correctly Thelma Cross married a local barber, and the two of them moved out of state."

The coroner might put up a good front, but Marshall could tell Terry was both impressed and disturbed by his knowledge.

"That's right. But they didn't move by choice. Your family drove them out because you thought she'd married beneath her and tarnished the Cross name."

Marshall took another step forward. Now he was within arm's reach of Terry—which meant he was in range of the coroner's scalpel should the man decide to use it as a weapon against Marshall.

"And now, two generations later, you've returned to you ancestral home. How commendable. So . . . as a member of the family, I'd appreciate it if you call tell me what you've learned so far."

Terry looked at Marshall, gaze clouded with confusion. Marshall gave a little mental push—not too much—but it was enough to at least loosen Terry's tongue.

"I haven't learned anything beyond what you can see. The boy's throat was slashed and a design carved into his stomach. A design resembling the one Carl Coulter cut into his victims. But I imagine you were already aware of those details." Terry hesitated. "We do have a name now . . ."

"Ray Porter. Yes, I know." *Thanks to Ronnie.* "If you wouldn't mind, Terry, I'd like a few minutes alone with the poor boy."

Terry blinked several times, and his cooperative manner of a moment ago vanished.

"You can't be serious! I can't leave you alone with a body. Not only are you no relation to the boy, I've already started my autopsy. If you don't leave right now, I'm going to call Joanne and have her come here and throw you out."

Marshall smiled tightly as he took a final step forward. Now he stood only inches from Terry.

"Hiding behind your woman like a coward? I'm not surprised. Joanne is twice the man you'll ever be."

Terry raised the scalpel, and for an instant Marshall thought he'd goaded the man too far and that he was going to attack. Marshall almost hoped he would. But the coroner lowered his hand to his side and in a low, dangerous voice said, "Get the hell out of here."

Marshall considered his options. He could try pushing Terry further, but the man had a strong will. It would take a significant effort to make him give in, and Terry's mind might well suffer damage in the process. If this was the only time Marshall could get access to Ray Porter's body, he'd have gone ahead and risked damaging the coroner's mind. But there would be other opportunities. Perhaps he could make use of Ronnie again.

"Very well. I understand your position and accept it. Take good care of the boy. He's suffered a great deal."

Before Terry could respond, Marshall turned and headed for the door. He'd be back and he'd find a way to get some time alone with the corpse. And then he could do what *he* needed to do to take care of the boy.

Once out in the hall, Marshall considered going to speak with Ronnie, but his cell phone rang. He took the call, and when the short communication was over, he forgot about Ronnie. He walked out of the building, got into his Hummer, and drove out of the lot.

. . . . .

Ray Porter's parents lived on the north side of Rhine. When Joanne was a child, this had been one of the nicer, if somewhat generic, neighborhoods in town. Ranch homes, spacious well-landscaped yards, new sidewalks and freshly blacktopped roads. But in the decades since Rhine's economic health had declined, property values began to fall, and people moved out in droves. Before long, what had once been an upper middle-class neighborhood became only a step or two above poverty level. Houses in need of repair, yards overgrown or dotted with bare patches of earth, streets and sidewalks cracked and uneven. Dented, rust-nibbled cars were parked in driveways or in yards, usually several vehicles per property, and groups of people who were either malnutrition-thin or swaddled in multiple rolls of fat gathered on porches. The men wore jeans and nothing else as long as the weather was halfway warm, the women dressed in too-tight t-shirts and shorts. Alcohol, substance abuse, and domestic violence were daily occurrences on the Northside, and the Sheriff's Department spent a lot of its working hours here. Sometimes Joanne thought she spent more time on the Northside than she did in her own home.

Joanne should've been surprised to see Marshall Cross's Hummer parked on the street in front of Isaac and Georgia Porter's home, but she wasn't. She was, however, royally pissed. It was one thing for Marshall to show up at the Caffeine Café this morning, but to intrude *now*, when she had come to inform the Porters about their son's death . . .

It was inexcusable.

She pulled her cruiser in behind Marshall's vehicle, resisting the urge to bang his back bumper only through a supreme act of will. She parked, turned off the engine, and got out of the car, mind filled with images of what she intended to do to *Mr. Cross* when she got hold of him.

She had settled on either a punch to the windpipe or the classic kneecap to the testicles by the time she reached Marshall's driver's side door. The glass was tinted and she couldn't see inside, but she knew the sonofabitch was in there, getting off on seeing how worked up she was. She reached out, intending to rap her knuckles on the window, but before she could make contact, the glass lowered with an electronic hum.

"Is there a problem, Officer?" Marshall held up a hand before Joanne could start yelling. "Sorry, I couldn't resist."

"I don't give a damn why you're here, and I don't give a damn how you learned Ray Porter's name. All I want you to do is leave. *Now.*"

"Don't worry. I have no plans to speak directly with the boy's parents. I would never do anything so crass. But I wanted to speak with you before you went inside. First, I want to warn you. I received a phone call from an acquaintance of mine who works for a Cincinnati television station. He told me reporters have finally gotten word of last night's murder, and they're on their way to town even as we speak. They will undoubtedly be at the county building before you get there with the Porters. I imagine identifying their son's remains will be hard enough on them without a mob of idiots shoving microphones and cameras in their faces. So if there's anything you can do to spare them that indignity, I urge you to do it."

Intellectually, Joanne understood what he'd said, but her anger still roiled inside her, and it took a moment before she could trust herself to reply.

"Thanks, but you could've just called to tell me that."

Marshall smiled. "What makes you think I have your cell phone number?"

"You seem to know everything else that goes on around here." She took a deep breath and released it. Her anger had subsided for the most part, but traces yet remained. "You said *first*. That implies there's something else you want to say."

"The Porters are going to have much to deal with over the next few days, and I don't want them to worry about money. If you get the chance—whenever it seems most appropriate— would you let them know that my family intends to pay their son's funeral expenses?"

Joanne looked at Marshall for a long moment. His expression grew harder the longer she scrutinized him.

"Do you doubt my sincerity?"

"Not at all. But I do wonder about your motives. Your family's known for many things, but selfless generosity isn't one of them."

"You find it difficult to believe that we simply wish to help out another family in a time of tragedy?"

"It's the *simply* that's giving me trouble. I do believe you want to help the boy's parents, and it's not like you don't have the money to spare. But I can't believe that's *all* you want."

Marshall looked at her, his ice-blue eyes giving no hint to what he was feeling.

"Think whatever you wish. Just please deliver the message."

He turned forward and his window hummed as it closed. A second later the Hummer's engine came to life, and Marshall pulled away from the curb and drove off down the road, scrupulously adhering to the speed limit. Joanne watched him go. She'd struck a nerve, she was sure of that, but she couldn't figure out what the Crosses' angle was in offering to pay for Ray

Porter's funeral. She decided not to worry about it right now. She had an unpleasant duty to perform, and the sooner she got it done, the sooner she could get back to trying to find out who killed Ray Porter.

Sometimes she really hated her job.

She started walking up the Porters' driveway.

CHAPTER **NINE**

It was midafternoon by the time Dale reached Lake Hush. It had been some time since he'd been here, and he was tempted to drive all the way around the lake. It was something he used to do when he first moved to Cross County. No matter the season, a drive around the lake had always lightened his mood. He supposed it reminded him of Lake Michigan back home in Chicago. Sweet Home, Chicago, as the song went.

Lake Hush was hardly on a par with one of the Great Lakes, but circling it had made him think about driving down Lakeshore Drive with his wife and daughter. He wasn't sure when it had happened or even exactly why, but eventually he'd stopped coming out here. It wasn't because he'd forgotten about Marianne and Alice. He'd spoken to other people who'd lost loved ones, and they told of memories blurred by the passage of years, faces only half-recalled, voices and laughs lost forever. But that hadn't happened to him. For the last twenty years, he'd worked everyday to maintain the clarity and sharpness of his memories. He was sure many would've thought him morbidly obsessed, unable to follow the well-intentioned but patronizing advice so many of his friends in Chicago had given him in the weeks after the funerals.

You have to start letting go, Dale. You have to get on with your life.

Dale's response was always simple and direct. *Screw that.*

Maybe he couldn't bring his wife and daughter back to life, but he'd be damned if he'd allow what remnants of them that lived in his heart and mind to perish.

And yet . . . he didn't drive around the lake anymore, did he? And could he say for certain that the images in his mind were true memories, or were they rather memories of memories? Distorted and degraded, like a picture that's been photocopied one time too many. And their voices . . . he could close his eyes, concentrate, and hear them speak, hear them laugh. Marianne's delighted giggle, Alice's hearty guffaw. Were those their actual voices or were they merely imperfect recreations, like a mediocre comedian mimicking the voice of a famous celebrity? You knew who it was, even though the comic didn't *really* sound all that much like the person.

Maybe that was the true reason he'd stopped taking leisurely drives around Lake Hush. Not because he was starting to forget about Marianne and Alice, but because despite his best efforts to delude himself otherwise, he already had, and seeing Lake Hush—which, like Lake Michigan, never changed—only made him aware of his fading memory.

The western shore of Lake Hush bordered the edge of Mare's Nest Woods. Towering oak and pine trees formed a solid wall of green. Autumn browns, yellows, and reds were still a few weeks away. Summer may have been on its way out the door, but it was determined to linger at the threshold a bit longer.

Dale pulled onto Limberlost Road and headed east. He'd tried calling Sadie Muir from the *Echo* office several times, but he'd only gotten her machine. He'd tried e-mailing her because he knew she spent a lot of time online. She did most of the genealogical work for her clients via computer, and it was also how she bought groceries. He hadn't expected her to reply, but he wanted to make sure she knew he was coming. Sadie wasn't completely antisocial, but she didn't like surprise visitors. And since he'd never heard of her inviting anyone to her place, *all* her visitors were surprises.

He was halfway around the lake—well past the dock and beach area—and almost to Barrow Hill Park before he spotted Sadie's houseboat. He pulled over to the side of the road, parked his Jeep, and walked down to the edge of the water to get a closer look.

Dale had no idea how Lake Hush had gotten its name, but he wouldn't have been surprised if it was due to the water's stillness. Regardless of the weather conditions or the time of year, the surface of the lake remained calm and smooth as glass. Even when the prow of a motorboat cut through the water, the wakes were never very large, and they died away quickly. And if you stood on the shore looking out across the water, you could almost feel the lake pulling sound toward it, stifling it, as if it were determined to draw all noise into its depths and drown it. The whisper of the wind, the trill of birdsong, footfalls on grass, your own breath and heartbeat, all were muffled at the water's edge. While he found it soothing to drive past, he didn't like being outside his Jeep and close to the water. He found the silence eerie and isolating.

Sadie's boat sat in the middle of the lake, and it showed no sign of coming toward shore. She was likely anchored there and determined not to budge. She wasn't going to make this easy for him, but then he didn't expect her to.

He headed back to his Jeep and removed a heavy block of wadded-up plastic and an aluminum oar from the back. As he carried the self-inflating raft back toward the water, he felt a crawly sensation on the back of his neck, as if he were being watched. At first he thought that Sadie must've been watching him from his boat through a pair of binoculars. But the farther he walked, the more he realized it felt as if someone was watching him from behind. He stopped and glanced back over his shoulder. He saw nothing but his Jeep, the road, and beyond it a gently sloping grass-covered hill dotted with a few medium-sized elm trees. He faced forward and continued walking, but the feeling of being watched remained.

When he reached the water once more, he laid the raft and the oar on the ground, and then he turned to look across the road again. Still nothing there. He saw no hint of movement, heard no noise . . . not that he could hear much of anything this close to the lake. He pulled the ring to activate the raft's self-inflation device and stepped back as the orange block unfolded and expanded, the hiss of air—which normally would've been loud—muted near the water.

He kept his gaze fastened on the elms across the road the entire time.

When the raft was fully inflated, he grabbed the oar, put the raft into the water, and boarded with as much grace as he could muster, which meant he succeeded in not capsizing the damned thing. He used the oar to push away from the shore and then began paddling, trying to go as fast as he could without tipping over. He wasn't the most experienced mariner in the world, and his strokes were awkward and used too much energy. He splashed a great deal, not that it made much noise, and soon his suit was wet. Some lakes smelled of dead fish and decaying plant matter, but the water in Lake Hush had a coppery scent with a hint of something like ammonia. Dale wondered if some sort of industrial waste was being piped into the lake, but there were no factories within miles of here.

By the time he was halfway to Sadie's boat, he was sweaty, breathing hard, and his right shoulder felt as if it were on fire. He heard the muffled growl of the houseboat's engine starting up, and the craft began heading toward him at a leisurely pace.

Grateful that Sadie had decided to take pity on him, Dale stopped paddling and waited for her to reach him. She cut the engine when she was within a dozen yards and drifted the rest of the way to him.

She appeared on deck and hooked a metal ladder over the rail. She was a reed-thin woman in her early seventies, with short white hair and wire-frame glasses. She wore a flannel shirt that was too large for her, unbuttoned, sleeves rolled up, over a white blouse. Dale knew the shirt had belonged to her husband. As far as he knew, she always wore his clothes.

"Permission to come aboard?" Dale asked. He tried to sound cheerful, but his voice came out as a near gasp. *Getting old*, he thought. It was a thought that occurred to him more often than he liked these days.

Sadie didn't answer at first. She stood near the ladder, hands gripping the railing, gaze trained on the shore. After several moments she said, "It's out there, you know. It's *always* out there." She turned and walked away from the rail.

Dale decided that was the closest thing to an invitation to board he was going to get. He tied his raft to the ladder's bottom rung, then began climbing, still feeling as if something was watching him from shore.

. . . . .

"Hope you like your coffee strong."

Sadie hadn't offered him coffee and Dale hadn't asked for any, but she nevertheless set a steaming mug down in front of him. He tended to avoid caffeine on general principle since he figured he was naturally wired enough. But he didn't want to be an ungracious guest, so he nodded his thanks.

Sadie put a mug for herself down on the table opposite Dale then took a seat. Her kitchen—or galley, since they were on a boat—was small, he supposed, but the one in his apartment wasn't much larger. It had all the basic necessities: stove, sink, countertop, full-sized refrigerator, and a dining table with four chairs. It was the masses of lopsidedly stacked notebooks and tottering towers of print-outs that made the kitchen seem smaller than it really was. They were everywhere—piled on top of the fridge, the counter, on the chairs they weren't using, on the floor. This much paper, a great deal of it yellowed and curling at the edges, had to be a fire hazard this close the stove. Dale found his gaze wandering about the kitchen, searching for a fire extinguisher. Sadie had been a long-time member of the Cross County History Society, and genealogy had been her hobby. Perhaps, Dale had always thought, because she'd never had children of her own. But after her husband's disappearance fifteen years ago, what was once merely a pastime had become her life. She did genealogical research not only for clients in the county, but—thanks to the Internet—from all over America, and even other countries.

Sadie gave him a smile. "Probably should get me a filing system, huh?"

"This is nothing. You should see the mess I have at the paper."

She took a long sip of her coffee, though from the furious way it was steaming, it had to be near boiling. She swallowed, put down her mug, and said, "What can I do for you, Dale?"

Dale eyed his coffee considering whether to risk taking a sip. If his mouth had been insulated with asbestos, there'd be no problem. As it was . . .

"I need some information."

Sadie burst out laughing. "No shit. You're a *reporter*, Dale. Why the hell else would you come see me? The last time you were here was . . . six years ago last May. When the graves of the

O'Brien family were dug up and the coffins switched from one plot to another."

"I remember." It wasn't exactly the sort of thing one forgot. When the switch had first been discovered, everyone assumed it was some sort of sick joke. But it turned out the sole surviving O'Brien—a spinster cousin—suffered from obsessive-compulsive disorder and had paid a handyman to, as she later phrased it, "Put everyone in their proper places." Dale had been the one to discover the existence of the cousin, whose last name was Morris, with Sadie's help. Dale had tracked down the woman to interview her, only to have the handyman attempt to kill him to prevent Dale from exposing what he'd done. It had been a near thing, but in the end Dale survived, and the handyman went to jail for attempted murder. The O'Brien cousin avoided being charged with grave descrecation, mostly due to her age, and since she was the only living relative, it was decided that she could arrange her kin any way she liked. The O'Briens had remained in their new resting places ever since.

Dale was about to ask how much Sadie was going to charge him today when she learned forward, her eye shining.

"You saw it, didn't you? I was up on deck, watching."

Dale reached out and took hold of his mug. It was still hot enough to hurt his hand, but he didn't let go. He was tempted to lie to Sadie, to feed into her obsession to keep her in a cooperative mood. But the desperate hope in her eyes forced him to tell the truth.

"I didn't see anything, Sadie. I thought I *felt* something watching me, but I'm sure it was just my imagination."

She slammed her hand down on the table so hard the noise made him jump, and he splashed burning-hot coffee onto his hand.

"I knew it! You *did* see it!"

Dale didn't see any point in correcting her, so he said nothing. He knew from experience that he was going to have to let this play out before he could have a productive conversation with her.

"It's always there, on the shore, watching, waiting. Doesn't matter where I drop anchor. The middle of the lake, west end, east end, north or south. It follows me."

She took a great gulp of her coffee this time, and Dale wondered if she hadn't opened her throat wide and poured the hot black stuff straight down into her stomach.

"Truth to tell, I've never seen it up close. Couldn't even tell you exactly what it is. Jeffrey saw it, though. Close as you could get."

Despite his decision to let her talk, Dale couldn't remain silent while she ran through the whole morbid story.

"No one knows for sure what happened to Jeffrey."

She scowled. "That's what Sheriff Manchester said. No body, no crime, right?" Her voice was bitter, and despite the delusion she lived with, he couldn't blame her.

"Not necessarily. But just because Jeffrey disappeared is no reason to believe he was killed by some kind of . . . monster."

"Don't you patronize me, Dale Ramsey." She finished the last of her coffee, then stood and went over to the sink. As she rinsed her mug out, she said, "You've lived in this goddamned place long enough to know better."

Dale opened his mouth to reply, but then closed it. She was right. He decided to shut up for real this time and just listen, even though he'd heard the story before. He wondered how many other clients of hers had sat here at this table, a mug of blazing-hot coffee on front of them, listening to Sadie recite the same tale. He wondered if she told it the same way word for word every time.

Sadie took a sponge from the counter, squirted a glob of dishwasher liquid on it, and began washing the mug.

"Jeffrey liked to hunt. He wasn't a fanatic about it or anything. He didn't get his kills stuffed and mounted, didn't go around bragging about all the animals he'd shot. For him, hunting was a chance to spend some time outdoors, getting in touch with his primal side, you know?"

The mug had to be clean now, cleaner than clean, but Sadie continued washing it.

"One afternoon he was out in Mare's Nest Woods. It was November, just before Thanksgiving. He was out for deer, but while the woods were usually thick with them, he hadn't seen one all day. He was about to give up and come on home, when he heard something moving in the brush. He was usually a cautious hunter, always made sure of what he was shooting at before pulling the trigger. But it had been a long, disappointing day and he was tired, frustrated, and jumpy. Without thinking, he pointed his rifle in the direction of the noise and fired. He waited for the last echo of the gunshot to die away before going forward to check and see if he'd hit anything—or any*one*. In the back of his mind was the fear that because he hadn't waited to visually verify his target, he might've shot another hunter."

She put the sponge down, rinsed the mug again, and this time put it in the dish rack to dry. She returned to the table and sat down once more. She eyed Dale's mug, which he still held but hadn't drank out of.

"You going to drink that or just sit there and fondle it?"

He pushed the mug toward her, and she lifted it to her lips and drained half of it in a single gulp. Then she continued.

"As Jeffrey walked forward, rifle held at the ready, he listened hard for any sound ... wounded animal thrashing, a person moaning in pain, but he heard nothing. He was beginning to think he hadn't heard anything in the first place, that he was so tired he'd shot at nothing but some bushes. But then something came bursting through the brush toward him. It moved so fast that Jeffrey didn't get a good look at it. He saw black fur, four legs, a snout, sharp teeth, and eyes ... he said the eyes were the worst, because they looked so human. And he saw blood, lots of it, smeared all over the thing's side where Jeffrey's bullet had struck. The thing slammed into Jeffrey's side as it ran past, hitting him so hard that he spun halfway around before falling to the ground. The thing kept on going, and it quickly vanished into the woods.

"Jeffrey sat up and checked his side, afraid the animal—whatever it was—had bit, clawed, or gored him as it ran past. He was banged up pretty good. You should've seen the bruises on him a couple days later, but he wasn't bleeding. He'd dropped his rifle when he fell, and he grabbed hold of it then, just in case the animal decided to come back and get even. But it didn't return.

"Eventually Jeffrey got back on his feet, sore as hell and twice as scared, but he was alive, and he figured that was all that counted. The animal had left a trail of blood when it ran, but even though a responsible hunter is supposed to track down an animal he's wounded and put it out of its misery, Jeffrey wasn't about to go after the damned thing. When he told me the story later, he said that when the animal sped past him, he heard it sobbing in a human voice."

She paused and polished off the rest of Dale's coffee. He thought she might take his mug to the sink and wash it multiple times as she'd done with hers, but she made no move to rise from the table. He waited for her to continue, but she didn't say any more, just stared down into the empty mug in front of her.

"Why don't you finish?" Dale gently prodded.

"Why bother? You know the rest of it. I was just talking to hear myself talk, I guess." She glanced up and gave him a tentative smile. "Gets lonely out here sometimes, you know? The phone and e-mail are nice, but they aren't like having a real person to talk to."

Dale thought of how many nights he'd spent sitting in his apartment when books, TV, and the radio weren't company enough to fill the long hours until he couldn't resist sleep any longer.

He did know the rest of Sadie's story. Jeffrey returned home after his bizarre experience and swore off hunting for good. A year later, deer season rolled around again, and by that time he'd convinced himself that he'd wounded a coyote or maybe even a wolf. And he'd decided not to let fear stop him from enjoying his "primal side," as Sadie had put it. He went back into Mare's Nest Woods and was never heard from again. Sadie called Stan Manchester that evening, but the Sheriff figured Jeffrey had probably had one too many beers while he was out and would be home when he sobered up. Sadie told Stan that Jeffrey didn't drink when he hunted, but Stan figured Jeffrey just told his wife that to keep her from bitching at him. And maybe that was so, but when Jeffrey still hadn't returned home by the next afternoon, Stan got a search party together—Dale included— and went out into the woods to look for the wayward hunter.

The search lasted the better part of a week, but when no sign of Jeffrey was found, not even his car, Stan figured that either Jeffrey had been killed and his car stolen or, more likely, he'd taken the opportunity to step out on his wife. He wouldn't have been the first husband in history to do so, and Stan called off the search. But Sadie had a different theory. She figured that the creature Jeffrey had wounded the previous year had survived, healed, and finally gotten its revenge. That, or it had died and its mate had killed Jeffrey. Whichever the case, the thing that had slain Jeffrey evidently hadn't been satisfied that its vengeance was complete, for it began to stalk Sadie.

She began to hear it padding around her house at night, scratching at the door—though it never left any marks—and crying softly outside her bedroom window at night while she lay in the bed she'd shared with her husband. But whenever Sadie mustered the courage to push apart the curtains and look outside, she saw nothing. Sadie became so afraid that she stopped leaving the house. But she still didn't feel safe, and eventually she decided to leave solid land altogether, and she sold her home, bought a houseboat, and took up residence on the lake.

Dale wasn't certain how she thought this move would thwart her *bête noir*. Couldn't the animal just swim out and get her? But she said it was a creature of land, not water, and as long as she never set foot ashore for the remainder of her life, she'd be safe. The closest she came to shore was when she moored at the marina's dock to pick up her mail and the groceries she ordered online. But she always remained aboard her houseboat during these transactions, carrying a loaded rifle just like her husband's.

Dale didn't believe that some sort of monster endlessly prowled the shores of Lake Hush, waiting for the opportunity to slay the widow of Jeffrey Muir, Great White Hunter. But then again, considering some of the things he'd seen in his life, he couldn't say he *dis*believed it, either. Especially not when he recalled the sensation of being watched back on shore.

"Well, now," Sadie said. "As I started to say earlier, how can I help you?"

Dale smiled. "I need you to do some research on a boy named Porter."

. . . . .

For the next two hours Dale hung out in Sadie's cramped office aboard her houseboat, sipping coffee as he watched her go about her work. Sadie's office was crammed with even more stacks of papers and books than her kitchen. She had a state-of-the art PC and printer on a desk made out of an old door laid across two small filing cabinets. The only chair was the one at her computer, and Dale was forced to sit on a pile of three-ring binders.

Sadie surfed the Net, consulted homemade genealogical charts, made phone calls, sent e-mails, and, he was certain, broke more than a few privacy laws in obtaining the information he'd requested. It was like watching a world-class conductor lead an orchestra, or a phenomenally skilled surgeon perform a life-saving operation. Sadie might not have been the pinnacle of mental health, but she knew her shit, that was for sure.

At the end of two hours—during which Dale had observed without saying a word—Sadie's printer began churning out pages. She pushed her office chair away from her workstation and stretched her arms over her head with a groan.

"All finished. I'm not sure I came up with anything you'll find useful, though."

Dale eyed the documents coming out of the printer with barely restrained greed. It was all he could do to keep from snatching up the pages as they were completed.

"Can you hit the highlights for me?" he asked.

"Sure thing. But first, let's settle up." Before Dale could reach for his wallet, she said, "You checking account number still the same as last time?" When he said it was, she attacked her keyboard again, and after a few mouse clicks, she said, "There. I've transferred the funds from your checking to mine. You should change your password periodically, you know. You're still using the same one as the last time we did business."

Dale would've liked to have known exactly how much today's "business" had set him back, but he supposed it didn't matter much right now. At the moment, all he cared about was what Sadie had discovered.

"No links between Carl's victims were found during the original investigation, if I remember right," Sadie said.

"You do. But I thought with all the advancements in computer technology since then . . ."

"Sorry. Nothing's changed. I couldn't find any significant connections between Carl's four victims, and believe me, I tried everything I could think of. Two were distantly related by marriage a few generations back, but I doubt either of them knew it." She nodded toward the printer. "It's in the report."

Dale had been in the newspaper game more than long enough to know better than to get his hopes up, but that's exactly what he had done. Now he felt those hopes fade, and he realized Joanne had been right. This trip had been a waste of time and, unfortunately for his bank account, a waste of money too.

"I found nothing of particular interest regarding Ray Porter. One of Carl's victims was distantly related to the Porters, but her connection to Ray is so distant that to anyone not obsessed with genealogy, they might as well not be related at all. Sorry."

Dale's hopes had been on life support, and Sadie had just pulled the plug.

"I did find one interesting tidbit, though," she added. "I called a friend of mine who works at the records department over at Resurrection Hospital. I had her check the birth records to see if any of the victims were born there or ever had been admitted as patients. Three were born there, and two were patients. One for a broken elbow, the other for a severe allergic reaction to an antibiotic."

Dale's hopes were officially deader than a road-pizza possum. Not only was this information unimportant, it was downright dull.

"On a whim, I asked her to look up Carl Coulter's records. He was never a patient at the hospital, but he was born there."

"Anyone who's native to Cross County is born there," Dale said.

"True enough," Sadie agreed. "But that's not the interesting part. Turns out Carl's birth certificate doesn't list a father."

Dale frowned. "Really? But Lester Coulter was his father. He and Debbie had been married several years before Carl's birth." Dale hadn't lived in Cross County back then, but he'd thoroughly researched Carl's background during the time of the murders. Even so, he hadn't discovered Sadie's "tidbit" at the time.

"Now before you go getting too excited, keep in mind that it might have simply been a mistake. Things like that happen sometimes, even with computers. Hospitals are busy places and the birth of a child can be a confusing time."

Dale thought of Alice's birth. Marianne had been in labor over thirty-six hours before their daughter was born, and he'd been up with his wife the entire time. He'd been so exhausted when the baby arrived that it had taken him a good half hour to remember whether it was a boy or girl. A confusing time, indeed.

The printer spit out the final page of Sadie's report and fell silent. She gathered the pages and stapled them together before handing them to Dale.

"I hope it's at least some help to you," she said.

"Information is always helpful, one way or another," he said. "The trick lies in figuring out just how."

"Not that I'm trying to drum up business for the competition, but you know I'm not the only source of information in the county," Sadie said. "You might think about paying Eve a visit."

Eve owned and operated the House of Unearthly Delights, a brothel near Somerset where, as county legend had it, any and all desires could be fulfilled—for a price. Prostitutes were excellent sources of information since their customers often talked as much, if not more, than they did anything else. But upon hearing Sadie's suggestion, Dale felt a cold, clenching sensation in his gut, as if a giant hand of ice had grabbed hold of his stomach and squeezed. "In all the years I've lived and worked in Cross County, I have never once consulted Eve, and I don't intend to do so now."

Sadie's eyes narrowed in an appraising look. "Don't tell me you're afraid of her."

"No, but I *am* afraid of what she can do," Dale said, then in a softer voice added, "As valuable as information is, sometimes the price is simply too high."

· · · · ·

Sadie took pity on Dale and dropped him off close to shore so he wouldn't have so far to paddle his raft. She didn't stick around to make sure he reached land safely, though. The instant he untied his raft from the boarding ladder, she engaged the engine and headed back toward the middle of the lake.

Dale managed to get to shore without overturning his rubber raft. He pulled it onto land, deflated it, shook it a couple times to get the water off, then folded it up. He started back toward the Jeep, the raft and paddle under one arm, Sadie's report tucked away in a pocket of his suit jacket. As he walked, he told himself that he didn't feel himself being watched, that there was no shadowy movement between the trees on the other side of the road. Nevertheless, the skin on the back of his neck crawled as he tossed the deflated raft and paddle in the back of his Jeep, then climbed behind the wheel. He forced himself not to look toward the trees as he started the engine and pulled onto Limberlost Road.

As he accelerated, he checked the rearview mirror out of habit. He couldn't be sure, but he thought he caught a glimpse of something black following at a distance, running sleek and low to the ground. But when he blinked, whatever it was—if indeed it had been real at all—was gone.

Dale increased his speed, though. Just in case.

Still, the itch on the back of his neck remained, and a disturbing thought occurred to him. What if Sadie's Black Beast had gotten tired of waiting for her to make landfall and had decided to seek out other prey? Like a reporter who should've retired by now. He forced a laugh and told himself it was a foolish notion. But he didn't look in his rearview mirror again all the way back to town.

⬛ ⬛ ⬛ ⬛ ⬛

Tyrone Gantz sat on a bus-stop bench across the street from the Burrito Bungalow. A sheriff's cruiser was parked next to a Camaro. A '78, Tyrone guessed, though by no means was he an expert on cars. A deputy he recognized but whose name he didn't know—probably one of the newer additions to the department, he figured—stood next to the vehicle, talking with the Bungalow's manager, a skinny kid with an acne-scarred face who looked ridiculous wearing the large floppy sombrero that was part of his uniform. There was enough traffic going by that Tyrone couldn't hear what they were saying, but he had a good idea.

He sensed someone approaching from behind, and he steeled himself for what was to come. He doubted it was Dale again, not so soon. That meant it most likely was another deputy, maybe even Sheriff Talon herself. Dale had doubtless told the sheriff what he'd learned from Tyrone, and the sheriff would

CROSS COUNTY

123

want him to make an official statement. Tyrone didn't want to be bothered. He didn't mind doing his civic duty, but he didn't want to waste time that could be put to better use observing. He supposed there was no avoiding it, though, and if he'd really wanted to, he wouldn't have sat here in plain sight. Better to get it over and done with so he could return to his sacred work of bearing witness.

Tyrone didn't take his gaze off the scene across the street as the newcomer took a seat on the bench next to him.

"Good afternoon, Tyrone."

The voice startled him so much that he almost sprang off the bench. With an effort, he kept his seat and turned to face Marshall Cross.

Tyrone tried to respond, but his voice refused to work. He swallowed and tried again. "The same to you."

"It's shaping up to be a lovely day, don't you think?" Marshall looked up at the sky. "The forecast said there was a chance of rain, but I think it's going to hold off until tonight." Marshall turned to Tyrone and showed his teeth in what could only nominally be called a smile. "What do you think?"

"Hard to say."

Marshall nodded as if Tyrone had just uttered a profound piece of wisdom. "True, true."

They sat quietly for the next several minutes, watching as the deputy across the street continued questioning Mr. Sombrero.

"I've never eaten there myself," Marshall said after a time. "I don't imagine the food's any good."

"Not really. But you didn't come here to discuss the culinary merits of fast food. What do you want?"

"No need to be so defensive, Tyrone. I only want from you what everyone else does: information."

"You want to know about what I saw happen at the Caffeine Café last night."

"Not unless there's anything you neglected to tell Dale this morning."

For an instant, Tyrone feared Dale had passed along what he'd learned to Marshall Cross. That Dale had told Sheriff Talon didn't bother him. He knew how close the two of them were. But for Dale to tell Marshall . . . then he realized there was no way Dale would've told Marshall anything. The reporter had no more love for the Crosses than Tyrone did.

And then it hit him. "Ronnie Doyle. We saw you do something to him in the Café's parking lot."

"I don't know what you're talking about. If you were observing closely—and I'm certain you were—you saw that I didn't lay a hand on him." Marshall leaned closer, and his ice-blue eyes seemed to glitter for an instant. "But if I *had* done something to Ronnie to make him more cooperative, I'd wager it would've been something you'd rather not experience firsthand."

Tyrone averted his gaze so he wouldn't have to look into Marshall's piercing eyes. "What do you want to know?"

"Anything else that might shed light on what happened last night. You see many things that others don't, Tyrone. But I know you only give out the information you wish to. Perhaps you held something back from Dale." Marshall nodded toward the scene taking place across the street. "For instance, do you have any idea what's happening over there?"

Tyrone focused his attention on the deputy and Mr. Sombrero, grateful to have something other than Marshall Cross's eyes to look at. "Dale only asked about the Café. He didn't ask about the Burrito Bungalow."

"Ah! So you *do* know something!"

Tyrone certainly did. He also knew that Marshall Cross wasn't going to be happy when he heard what it was. But he also knew that if he didn't tell Marshall what he wanted to know, the man would attempt to force him, just like he had Ronnie. And Tyrone knew what happened to folks the Crosses tried to persuade in their special way. That was something he wanted to avoid at all costs. He needed his mind to remain sharp and clear if he was to carry on his duties as the county's witness.

"I'm only guessing," Tyrone began, "but I'd say that Camaro belongs to the boy who was murdered last night."

"His name is Ray Porter," Marshall supplied. "And that was my guess too. I don't suppose you happened to observe anything here last night?"

Tyrone wanted to lie, but it wasn't his way. If someone asked him a straight question, he always answered it honestly—even if that someone was a Cross.

"As a matter of fact, I did. After I saw what happened at the Caffeine Café, I started walking in this direction. The Bungalow is one of the few places open late in town, and I thought if anything else interesting was going to happen last night, there was a good chance it would be here."

A predatory gleam came into Marshall's eyes. "Sounds as if you guessed right. Tell me what you saw."

"I didn't think much of it until today when I saw the boy's Camaro was back. The deputy was already in the parking lot when I arrived." He knew he was stalling, but he couldn't help himself.

"Back in the lot?" Marshall asked. "You saw it here last night?"

Tyrone nodded. "The boy stopped in at 11:08 p.m. He met a young woman, she got into his car, and they drove off together. I didn't hear anything they said to one another, but from their body language, I had the impression that they already knew each other."

"Interesting. Can you describe the girl for me?"

"I can do better than that. I can tell you her name."

Tyrone paused, and after a moment, Marshall said, "Well?"

Tyrone sighed. He knew he couldn't put this off any longer. "Lenora Cross."

CHAPTER TEN

Marshall stopped back at the county building later in the afternoon. Neither Joanne nor Terry was in, and thankfully the media had come and gone. Ronnie was still there, though, and he was all Marshall needed. Ronnie let him into the coroner's office, and Marshall spent several undisturbed moments alone with the body of Ray Porter. When he was finished, he gently slid the boy's table back into the freezer and departed. He didn't thank Ronnie on his way out. One didn't thank tools. One merely used them as needed.

It was close to five by the time Marshall drove his Hummer up the long winding driveway that led to Sanctity. Huge oak trees lined the driveway on both sides, their long shadows merging to create a dark passage between the outside world and the ancestral Cross home. The ironic effect was not lost on Marshall.

He didn't feel like letting one of the servants park his vehicle. He was doing his best to control his anger, but he didn't want anyone to see him like this. More to the point, *he* didn't want to see anyone. Not until he'd spoken with Lenora. So he drove past the main house, circled around to the back, and pulled into a garage the size of a small aircraft hangar. As he parked his Hummer, he noted the number of cars—all high-class, all expensive— already parked there. Though only Althea Cross's immediate family resided at Sanctity, the mansion was technically home to all within the family, and Crosses came and went as they pleased.

Many lived elsewhere in the county, working as doctors, lawyers, real estate agents, and such. If they felt like working at all, that is. Every Cross had access to more money than could be spent in a single lifetime, provided they remained in Althea's good graces. But Sanctity was Mecca for Crosses that lived farther away, and Marshall noted license plates from Pennsylvania, Indiana, and Kentucky. Undoubtedly a number of the other vehicles in the garage were airport rentals, used by family members that lived too far away to drive.

Normally, the prospect of seeing so many visiting relatives upon coming home would've filled Marshall with a mixture of anticipation and pride. But now he was just irritated. As the current head of the household—below Althea herself, of course—it was his job to greet the guests, spend a few moments making small talk, and in the process reassuring them that their current status in the family was not only intact, but dangling the possibility before them that their fortunes stood a halfway decent chance of rising, should they play their cards right. Althea herself wouldn't come down from her room—she rarely did—though she would receive a handful of visitors, if Marshall approved of them. Important if not especially pleasant duties for the man whose license plates read CROSS2. But he had more important fish to fry tonight.

He walked across the immaculately kept grounds between the garage and the main house, past the flower garden, the gazebo, topiaries shaped like mythical creatures, and a marble fountain in the middle of a mosaic tiled courtyard. Even as he struggled to maintain control of his anger, he noted with satisfaction that everything looked perfect, just as it should.

He reached into the main pocket of his suit jacket and touched the grainy surface of the small stone carving within. The figure's crude features were roughly human, and the object was warmer than could be accounted for by simply absorbing Marshall's body heat. He knew he should take the icon to the Reliquary right away, but he feared he was too furious with Lenora to achieve the proper state of mind. He supposed the task could wait a bit, though the sooner he attended to it, the better.

He entered the main house through the kitchen entrance, startling the coterie of chefs preparing the evening meal. They turned to face him as he moved past, like troops presenting themselves for their commander's review. Marshall ignored them and continued on. He sniffed the air and was glad to discover that tonight's main course was going to be lamb, one of his favorites. That was something to look forward to at least.

He left the kitchen and continued down a long corridor. He checked the library and the gallery, nodding perfunctory greetings to the relatives that were there, sipping mixed drinks and nibbling hors d'oeuvres from trays carried by unobtrusive servants. He finally found Lenora in the Solarium, sitting on a marble bench and drinking a mojito with a handsome blonde-haired, tanned young man in a polo shirt and designer jeans who was doing his best to impress her with how charming and witty he was. They were the only two people in the room.

The Solarium was one of the most beautiful rooms in Sanctity. It had a tiled floor, glass ceiling, and marble benches, along with an indoor garden comprised of palm trees, hibiscus, and orchids. Tiny songbirds perched on leaves or flitted about the room, and their singing combined with the soft trickle of water from the Solarium's centerpiece, an artificial waterfall on the far side of the room, to create a soothing soundscape.

Marshall felt no real resentment toward the lad for chatting up his daughter. Lenora was beautiful, even by Cross standards, and she looked especially fetching tonight in a black mini dress and high heels. For a moment he stood in the doorway and just looked at her. She might not have been the mirror image of her mother—her forehead was too high, her blue eyes too large—but she still resembled Charlotte so much that sometimes it took his breath away.

Though he made no movement or sound to draw her attention, Lenora tore her gaze from the pretty boy's face and looked at Marshall. Her eyes narrowed and her lips tightened. She obviously wasn't thrilled to see her father, which worked out well, as he wasn't particularly happy at the moment either.

Marshall entered the Solarium, walking at a measured pace. He kept his gaze fastened on Lenora, all but ignoring the boy. The boy, however, was too much of a go-getter to let a little thing like an elder's indifference stop him from trying to make a favorable impression, and thereby gain a bit of added status in the family.

"Hello, sir. I'm Sebastian Cross, from Atlanta." His southern accent was noticeable, but not overdone. Carefully honed to be charming and not off-putting, Marshall guessed. The boy stuck out his hand for Marshall to shake, but Marshall didn't bother to look at it, let alone reach out to clasp it.

"I'm sorry to be so rude, Sebastian, but I have a very important matter to discuss with my daughter. Dinner will be served shortly. Why don't you start making your way toward the dining room?"

The boy flicked his gaze to Lenora for a hint how to respond. She looked at Marshall, trying to assess her father's mood. Finally she jerked her chin in the direction of the door and the boy, through clearly disappointed, got the message. He smiled, trying to at least appear gracious about being dismissed.

"I understand completely, sir. It was an honor to meet you, and I hope we have a chance to speak at more length some other time."

He gave Lenora a last look before heading toward the Solarium's door. Though the boy's mojito was still half-full, Marshall wagered it would be empty before Sebastian had gotten very far down the hall, and he wouldn't be surprised if the boy went off in search of a refill.

When Sebastian was gone, Lenora said, "That was classy of you, Father. You should write a book on etiquette."

She raised her glass to her lips, but before she could take a sip, Marshall's hand shot out fast as a striking snake and grabbed hold of her wrist. Her gaze hardened and the hatred in her eyes hit him like physical blow.

"Did you grab Mother like this?"

Marshall was ashamed at his loss of control, but he didn't release his hold on Lenora. "I know where you were last night."

Lenora's eyes widened and her anger gave way to fear. Still, she tried to put up a brave front. "I went into town last night. So what?"

"You met a boy named Ray Porter at the Burrito Bungalow around eleven o'clock. You got in his Camaro and rode off with him."

"Once again, so what?" She'd regained some of her self-assurance, enough to pull free of Marshall's grip. He let her go without a struggle and didn't try to stop her from taking a sip of her mojito this time. The pause gave him a chance to regain some of his own self-control.

Lenora went on. "We just went for a ride. It wasn't like we were running off to elope or anything. He seemed nice at first, but he turned out to be a jerk in the end." A measure of her former hatred returned to her gaze. "Just like all men."

Marshall ignored her gibe. "What happened? Tell me everything."

She shrugged. "There's not much to tell. We went for a drive. I convinced him to take me to the Deveraux Farm. We parked, he put the moves of me, and he got pissed when I wouldn't spread my legs for him. *I* got pissed then, and I drove his Camaro back to town, leaving him to walk home. I parked the Camaro back at the Bungalow so he could find it, and I got back into my car—I took the Beemer last night—and then I came home. I ate a pint of Cherry Garcia, and then I went to bed. Happy?"

Marshall detected no deception in Lenora's tone, but he knew that didn't mean much. Crosses learned to lie as soon as they learned to speak. He reached out with his mind, intending to give her a gentle push, little more than a mental nudge, really, to urge her to tell the truth.

Her eyes widened and she took a half-step back. Surprise swiftly gave way to anger, and he felt her push back, far more strongly than he thought her capable of. He withstood her counterassault, though it took more effort than he expected.

"I didn't realize you'd grown so strong. I'm impressed. I am, however, disappointed that you could be goaded into revealing the measure of your power so easily. You lose an important advantage against an opponent if you lay all your cards face-up on the table during the first hand."

"Spare me your Las Vegas version of Sun Tzu. What the hell were you thinking of, trying that on me? I'm your daughter!"

Marshall gave her a grim smile. "Which is the only reason I allow you to speak to me with such disrespect—up to a point."

"Funny. I thought the reason you cut me so much slack is because you feel guilty for driving Mother away."

The words were delivered coolly, but they struck Marshall with far more impact than Lenora's push-back had. He understood how Lenora felt and wished he could tell her the truth, but he kept his expression impassive. He'd spent a lifetime concealing his emotions from potential enemies—which to a Cross meant everyone. He couldn't change now, not even for his child.

"I apologize for trying to push you, but it's vital I know the truth about what you did and where you went. Ray Porter was killed last night."

Marshall observed Lenora's reaction closely, alert for the slightest hint of guilt. Whether or not she was capable of murder was a question that didn't even occur to him. She was a Cross and his daughter. The question was whether she'd had anything to do with *this* murder. But he saw only shock and disbelief on her face. Either Lenora was better at masking her true feelings than he'd thought, or she'd truly been unaware of Ray Porter's death.

He quickly told her the details of the boy's murder. When he was finished, she said, "Why haven't I heard about it before now? I mean, I know why *you* didn't tell me. You didn't know I was with Ray last night. But I haven't heard anything on the news and nobody here is talking about it."

"I've done my best to stall the reporters. You can imagine how they're going to sensationalize the story, especially with the connection to the Coulter killings. But they've gotten wind of it now, and you can bet it'll be all over the evening broadcasts."

Lenora's eyes narrowed. "It's driving you crazy that you can't manage this, isn't it? It doesn't matter how strong you are, you can't make everyone do what you want, and that just pisses you off to no end . . . especially in *this* case, huh?"

Marshall felt something then that he hadn't experience in a very long time. Fear.

"What are you implying?" That's what he said. What he thought was: *How much does she know?*

She shrugged. "Nothing. The bigger the problem the harder

it is to control. The harder something is to control, the more it makes you angry. That's all."

Marshall very much doubted that *was* all, but he decided to let it go. For now.

"Did you push the Porter boy?"

"Why? Do you think it had something to do with his getting killed?"

"*Did* you?" he repeated.

"A little." She answered in a soft voice and lowered her gaze to the floor. No longer was she a self-assured woman in her early twenties. She was the recalcitrant little girl he'd disciplined so many times over the years. He didn't want to discipline her now, though. He wanted to comfort her, to hold her and tell her it was all right, everything was going to work out, he'd see to it. But he couldn't bring himself to bridge the emotional gap between them. He wished Charlotte was here. Lenora's mother had been so much better at serving their daughter's emotional needs than he ever could be.

Lenora went on. "Ray didn't want to go to the Deveraux Farm, so I gave him a push to make him take me. Nothing major." She raised her head and met Marshall's gaze once more. She smiled weakly. "It didn't take a lot to convince him. It's not like I need to do much pushing to get boys to do what I want, you know?"

Marshall did. Lenora was heartbreakingly beautiful, just like her mother.

"I doubt your push had anything to do with Ray's murder. It's possible the boy's judgment might've been clouded, his reaction time slowed a bit, but as you said, nothing major. I'm more concerned with why you chose to go to the Deveraux Farm. It seems like quite a coincidence, given how Ray was killed—and what happened at the Caffeine Café before that."

"No reason. I'd never been there before. That's where normal girls go to park with boys. I guess I just wanted to see what it was like to be like everyone else. At least for one night."

"But you're not like everyone else, you're—"

"A Cross. I know. It's not like anyone ever lets me forget it. But if you want the truth, being royalty can get pretty goddamned boring. I don't need to go to college because I'll never need to work to support myself. I don't have anywhere to go or anything to do, except be rich and powerful."

"There's much more to being a Cross than that, and you know it. We have responsibilities." He thought once more of the small stone icon in his jacket pocket. "Important ones."

"Maybe so. But why should that mean we can't have lives of our own as well?" She paused, then asked, "Will I need to speak with the sheriff?"

Marshall understood what his daughter was really asking. *Are you going to take care of this? Will you protect me?*

"Joanne will discover that you . . . *took a ride* with the boy sooner or later. You met him in public. Someone likely recognized you." Left unspoken was the reason—because she was his daughter. "I'll speak with Joanne, but the least she'll want you to do is give a statement. I'll try to convince her to come here to take it, though. To save you the discomfort of going into town."

Lenora's lips pursed in an expression that came dangerously close to a sneer. "To save *you* embarrassment, you mean."

Marshall decided to let that pass, primarily because there was more than a modicum of truth to it.

Lenora looked down at her empty glass. "If you'll excuse me, Father, I need a refill."

She walked past Marshall and out of the Solarium. He stood

alone, listening to the waterfall and the birds as he thought. It was several moments before he realized that not only hadn't Lenora reacted when he'd mentioned what had happened at the Caffeine Café, she hadn't asked him to supply any details. He supposed it was possible that news of the break-in and vandalism had spread through town and reached Sanctity by now. Cross County was big, but it wasn't *that* big.

Maybe he should give Ronnie a call, though. To buy a little insurance, just in case.

·　·　·　·　·

After dinner, Marshall entered a special room on Sanctity's upper floor. The door was locked and only two people had keys: Marshall and his mother. He unlocked the door, entered, and locked it behind him. He crossed the room, which was empty of furniture or decoration of any sort, and stopped before an elevator. He used another key to activate it, and when the door opened he stepped inside. The interior was padded with black leather, and there was only a single unmarked button on the control panel. Marshall pressed the button, the door closed, and he felt the elevator smoothly begin its descent. He then reached into his suit jacket and removed the warm stone figurine he'd carried since his second visit to the coroner's office.

He didn't know what role his family might or might not have played in Ray Porter's death, but if there was even a chance the family had something to do with his death, Marshall's duty was clear.

He looked down at the icon nestled in his palm.

"On behalf of my family, I apologize," he whispered.

The elevator stopped, the doors opened, and Marshall stepped out. Motion-detection sensors caused a light to come on overhead, illuminating a row of small motorized carts. Marshall chose one, climbed in, pressed a button to activate the engine, and then turned on the headlights. The cart hummed as he drove down a narrow tunnel, bearing the spirit of Ray Porter to its final resting place.

CHAPTER ELEVEN

Barrow Hill Mound is one of the major prehistoric Native American features in Ohio. The largest conical-shaped earthwork of its kind in the state, it measures more than eighty feet in height. Archeologists believe the mound was created by the Nadana Indians around 1000 BC. The origin of these advanced people is unknown, but they lived in the Southern Ohio region until about 400 AD, when all traces of their culture disappeared.

The Nadana were the first Indians in the area to domesticate certain food plants and create what, for the time, were sophisticated works of art. They lived in permanent settlements on the shore of what is now called Lake Hush. The Nadana are believed to have developed intricate and elaborate death ceremonies during which they interred their dead within an earthen mound which expanded in size as their culture developed.

Barrow Hill Mound Park is open to the public during daylight hours throughout the year. Picnic facilities are available.

www.crosscountyoh.org

I don't think we're allowed to climb it, Sarah."

"C'mon, Jo!" A ten-year-old girl with short black hair and skin so white it almost gleamed like ivory let out a laugh that was half joyful, half snotty. "Don't be such a chicken!"

The two girls stood at the base of Barrow Hill, bikes lying on the grass behind them on the other side of the metal railing

that encircled the huge grass-covered mound. Joanne had reluctant to climb over the railing, even to placate the girl who was
the only person to stay friends with her after her disappearance.
Almost a year had passed since Mr. Ramsey had carried her out
of the woods, but kids still made fun of her, called her names
like Milk Carton Face and Invisible Girl. That was hard enough,
but some children—and some adults—acted scared of her, as if
they sensed she'd somehow changed during the six days she was
missing. Even her own mom and dad acted different around her.
They were still nice, but they didn't touch her very often anymore
and tried to avoid standing too close to her, as if whatever had
happened to her might be contagious.

So maybe Sarah Rodgers was a brat sometimes, and maybe she
was too eager to get both of them in trouble whenever the chance
arose. But Sarah was her only friend, and that made her Joanne's
best friend, and Joanne was determined to keep it that way—no
matter what she had to do. But climbing up the mound . . .

She wasn't sure why, but she knew there was something *wrong*
about it, something other than the REMAIN BEHIND THE
RAILING AT ALL TIMES sign.

It was early April, jacket weather, and a light breeze was blowing
through the park. There were no trees near the mound. A metal
plaque welded to the railing gave an overview of the mound's
history, and from reading it, Joanne knew the trees had been
cleared when the park was established in 1932. But she couldn't
shake the strange notion that the real reason there were no trees
was because that nothing could grow so close to the mound. But
that was silly. Barrow Hill was covered with grass, wasn't it?

A thought whispered through her mind. *Maybe it's not grass.
Maybe it's* hair.

A shiver rippled down her back, and she felt a chill that had nothing to do with the early spring breeze. She didn't want to be here. Somehow, she knew this was a bad place.

Sarah, as usual not waiting to see if Joanne followed, started toward the mound. The slope was gradual enough that the girl didn't have any trouble scrabbling up, climbing using both hands and feet, hunched over like an animal.

Joanne's apprehension gave way to complete terror, and she called out Sarah's name. Sarah just laughed that laugh again and kept going. Joanne felt weak all over, shaky and sick, like she had the flu, only ten times worse. Her stomach lurched, worse than the time she rode the Beast at Kings Island. She didn't know how, didn't *care* how, but she knew that something was going to happen to Sarah if she kept climbing the mound. Something awful.

Despite how sick she felt, Joanne started to climb after her friend, calling out, "Stop! Come back!"

But before she could get very far, a hand clamped down on her shoulder and stopped her. She was so caught up in her fear for Sarah that at first she barely registered the sensation of pressure on her shoulder. She fought to shrug free of whatever force was keeping her from going after her friend, but when she couldn't break free, when all she could do was watch as Sarah continued moving up the hillside, seeming to pick up speed as she went, Joanne turned around.

"Don't be afraid, Sheriff."

Sallow, desiccated flesh drawn tight to the skull, icy blue eyes sunken deep into their sockets, shriveled lips pulled back to reveal yellow teeth and snail-belly gray gums. Bald head, wire-haired mustache and goatee, and a blue button shirt, navy pants, and black shoes without laces. A prison uniform, she recognized, though she had idea how she should know this.

"I need to show you something."

The corpse-thing's voice was a breathy rasp, a dry wind moving across barren, rocky ground. Its mouth yawned, stretching nightmarishly wide, and a foul stench wafted forth from the cavernous opening. It smelled like shit and vomit and rotting meat. It smelled like death.

Joanne felt hot bile bubble up to the top of her throat, and now she struggled to break free of the corpse-thing's grip so she could start running as fast and far as she could away from there and never ever stop. But the thing's bony claw on her shoulder was too strong, and all she could do was stare into the darkness within the creature's still widening mouth. Soon the darkness filled her vision completely and she could see nothing else, was no longer sure there *was* anything else. But then shapes started to form in the emptiness. Shapes that might be faces, but they were still too unformed for Joanne to tell for sure. The shapes slowly became more distinct while the death-stench continued emanating from the darkness like a wind blown straight from hell. Though it was the hardest thing she'd ever had to do in her young life, Joanne fought to keep from throwing up. She sensed the corpse-thing was attempting to reveal something to her, something important.

But just as the shapes neared the point of clarity, Joanne heard a high-pitched shriek of terror and pain. At first she thought the scream had come from her own mouth, but then she remembered the sensation of danger she'd felt before the corpse-thing's arrival ... remembered Sarah rushing pell-mell up the mound, determined to be crowned Queen of Barrow Hill.

Joanne tore her gaze away from the darkness just in time to see Sarah—like Jill—come tumbling down the hillside. Except, unlike the nursery rhyme character, Sarah had somehow lost one of her legs during her fall. As Sarah rolled toward Joanne, blood sprayed from the stump where her leg had been connected to the knee, and Joanne saw a white knob of bone sticking out of ragged red meat. Sarah came to a stop at the bottom of the hill not five feet from where Joanne stood. She lay there, not moving, sobbing weakly as blood continued to flow from her wound.

Joanne opened her mouth to scream, but dead fingers wrapped over the bottom half of her face, cutting off her voice.

"Thanks for sharing this memory with me, Sheriff. It's the most amusing thing I've seen since Death Row."

She felt a sandpaper-dry tongue rasp across her cheek, followed by laughter brittle as ancient bone shards.

· · · · ·

"Jesus, hon! You all right?"

Joanne felt hands on her bare shoulders. She remembered the touch of dead flesh and she tried to pull away, but the hands grabbed her wrists to keep her from fleeing.

"Joanne, it's just me. Relax. You had a bad dream."

A confused rush of data streamed into her consciousness. She was sitting naked on a bed in a dark room, someone sat next to her holding onto her wrists, his thumbs gently stroking her skin. She inhaled the mingled scents of masculine sweat and post-coital musk. She was in her bedroom with Terry. They'd discussed the latest details of the investigation over dinner, then retired to her boudoir to have each other for dessert. She must've fallen asleep and . . .

"I was dreaming."

"It must've been a hell of a nasty one, too. I almost had a heart attack when you screamed."

For an instant she couldn't recall the details of her dream, but then pieces came tumbling back and swiftly assembled themselves.

"Nasty is an understatement."

Terry let go of her wrists and wrapped his arms around her. They lay back down on the bed and Joanne snuggled close to her lover.

"Want to talk about it?" he asked.

His mouth was near her neck and his soft breath rose goosebumps on her flesh, making her shiver.

"Did I ever tell you about the first time I had one of my Feelings?"

Terry hesitated before answering. He was a doctor, a man of science, and Joanne knew he became uncomfortable when she started talking about this subject—which was why she didn't bring it up very often.

"No. Is that what you dreamed about?"

"Yeah. I was nine. It was only a few months after my disappearance. A friend of mine—Sarah Rodgers—and I were messing around near Barrow Hill Mound. She started to climb and I had the most terrible feeling that something bad was going to happen to her. I shouted for her to come down, but she didn't listen. I wanted to go up after her, but I felt so sick and weak . . . and I was so scared. I stood frozen at the bottom, watching her climb, and then she screamed and came rolling down the hill. Somehow she'd lost her leg."

"She *what?*"

"When she came to a stop, I saw that her left leg was gone beneath the knee. It had been ripped right off. The flesh around the wound was torn and ragged and there was blood everywhere. I'd never seen anyone seriously injured before that, and I had no idea that a person—especially a kid like me—could have so much blood in their body."

"Christ . . . what did you do?"

"I took off my t-shirt and used it to try and staunch the wound. It didn't do much to slow the bleeding, though, and I was afraid Sarah was going to die. She was so pale ... I guess she was in shock, too, because all she did was look up at the sky and tremble while I worked to save her. I gave up on my shirt and tossed it aside. I pulled Sarah's shirt off her and ripped it in two. I remember seeing someone put a tourniquet on a snakebite victim in a movie, and I figured the same technique might stop Sarah's bleeding. I wrapped a strip of her shirt around her knee and tied it as tight as I could. The bleeding slowed finally, but it didn't stop. I twisted the knot with my hand, and the blood flow died away to a tiny trickle. I felt thrilled that I'd stopped Sarah from bleeding to death, but my feeling of triumph immediately gave way to despair when I realized I couldn't leave her to go get help because she'd started bleeding again. We'd ridden our bikes to the park, but no matter how fast I rode, I knew Sarah would be dead before I got back to town."

"What happened? Did she die?"

"We got lucky. A sheriff's deputy was making his usual drive through the park, and he saw us. He stopped and ran over to help. I was so happy to see him. I think that was the moment that I first started wanting to be a cop. He was able to make a much better tourniquet for Sarah and then he carried her to his vehicle and put her in the backseat. I got our jackets, put mine on and helped Sarah into hers. Then I sat with her, holding her hand and telling her everything was going to be all right while the deputy drove like hell to Resurrection Hospital. The doctors told me later that we'd gotten Sarah there just in time. Any longer and it she wouldn't have made it."

"I don't know Sarah. Does she live in the county?"

"We didn't speak much after that. I guess in a way Sarah

blamed me for what happened, though it was her idea to climb the mound. But that didn't matter because I blamed myself. I'd *known* something bad was going to happen, but I'd failed to act on that feeling in time to do anything about it. After that, I vowed never to ignore one of my Feelings again, no matter how vague it might be. And I never have. Anyway, Sarah was in a wheelchair for a while, and eventually she got a prosthetic leg. Soon after that her family moved. Her dad got a job transfer, I think. I never saw her again."

"God, what a nightmare." Terry gently kissed the side of her neck. "You know, you probably did save her life. If you hadn't stopped the bleeding with your tourniquet, she might've died en route to the hospital."

"Maybe."

"Not to be morbid, though I admit it's an occupational hazard, but what caused Sarah's injury?"

"No one knows."

"You're shitting me."

"Not at all. Sheriff Manchester and his deputies scoured Barrow Hill, but they found nothing that could account for what happened to Sarah, and Sarah herself had no idea how she lost her leg. All she remembered was feeling a flash of agony and then falling down the hill. The surface of the mound was smooth—no holes or crevices that she might've accidentally stepped into, no place where animals might've laired. Though what sort of animal could've taken a girl's leg clean off, short of a bear, I can't imagine. And here's the really weird part: they never recovered her leg."

"What happened? Did some animal find it and carry it off?"

"I've read the Sheriff's original report. According to him, they found nothing to indicate the leg was taken from the scene. No tracks, no blood trail."

"Maybe Manchester just did a sloppy job of investigating."

"Could be. But I'll tell you something I've never told anyone else. I've never gone back to Barrow Hill Mound. I drive through the park whenever I'm on patrol, but I don't get out of my vehicle."

"Poor baby." Another kiss on the neck, this one including a tiny flick of Terry's tongue on her flesh. The sensation sent an electric jolt running through her body and down into her sex. She felt herself moisten, and she was tempted to see if Terry had rested enough by now to go another round.

"That wasn't the worst part, though. Of the dream, I mean. My memory got mixed with the investigations I'm running now, I guess. I saw Carl Coulter."

She felt Terry stiffen, and not in the good way.

"Something wrong?" she asked.

"No . . . well, yeah. You know I don't put much stock in psychic phenomena or however you want to classify your Feelings. But I can't help thinking there's something ominous about your dreaming of Carl."

She grinned in the dark. "Ominous as in omen? That sounds like you believe in my Feelings more than you want to admit."

"You know what Emerson said about foolish consistencies. So, what was Carl the Cutter doing invading your dream?"

Joanne told him about Carl's role in her nightmare. When she finished, Terry said, "And you have no idea what he was trying to show you?"

"Faces, I think. A pair of them. What does it matter? It was just a dream."

"Oh, so now *you're* a skeptic!"

"I believe in my Feelings because I've experienced them. I've never received dream messages from the spirit world."

"Maybe this is the first time."

That thought hadn't occurred to her before, and now that she contemplated it, she wished Terry had kept it to himself. Especially after the eerie experience she'd had out the Deveraux Farm earlier in the day, when she thought she'd seen someone—or something—resembling Carl Coulter.

Several moments of silence passed before Terry spoke again. "There's something I always wanted to ask you, Joanne, but I've never been able to bring myself to do it."

Her breath caught in her throat, and she could feel her heart pound in her chest. Surely he wasn't going to ask her to marry him. Their relationship was more along the lines of friends with benefits than deeply committed lovers. At least, that's how she viewed it and how she thought Terry did too. But what if she was wrong, what if he *was* going to ask her to marry him? How could she say no in a such a way as to avoid hurting his feelings? And she *would* turn him down . . . wouldn't she?

She forced a smile, though it was a nervous one. "Just go ahead and ask."

Now it was his turn to look nervous. "All right. I know about what happened to you when you were a kid. I guess everyone in the county does. It's a local legend."

It sounded like Terry wasn't going to discuss marriage, and she surprised herself by experiencing a brief pang of disappointment. "A legend, huh? Kind of makes a girl feel important."

"You really don't have any memory of what happened?"

"None. I was riding my bike in front of my house one morning, and the next thing I knew it was six days later and Dale found me in the woods. He said I was just sitting on the ground, but I don't remember that part." She'd been naked too, but she decided not to share that tidbit of information with Terry. She wasn't comfortable with the thought of Terry imagining Dale carrying her like that. It was something intimate—though in no way sexual—between Dale and her. A private moment not to be shared, not even with a man she'd just made love to.

"And you weren't . . . *hurt* in any way?" he asked.

She could tell by how Terry had paused before saying *hurt* that he was asking more than if she'd been injured. "I was examined at the hospital soon after Dale found me. I was uninjured, and the doctors said there was no evidence that I'd been sexually abused." And despite the fact she'd been naked when found, she'd shown no signs of exposure.

Terry looked embarrassed, and Joanne found it endearing. Considering all that he'd seen and done as both a doctor and coroner, he should've been a model of clinical detachment, but she was very glad he wasn't.

"Doesn't it get to you sometimes?" he asked. "Not knowing? You lost six whole days of your life. *Anything* could've happened during that time."

Terry's words caused a cold flutter of panic deep in Joanne's belly, but she suppressed it. She'd had lots of practice over the years. "It didn't bother me much at first. I was so happy to be home that I just tried not to think about it. But I kept having bad dreams, and my parents made me start seeing therapists. By that point, I figured something must've been wrong with me, and I began obsessing over those six days, trying to *make* myself remember where I'd been and what had happened. With time and counseling, I got over that. I adjusted and got on with my life. Now whenever I start to think about it, I remind myself that there's a lot about my childhood that I don't remember. Who does? We remember some things with crystal clarity, sometimes weird and insignificant things. Like I can remember the very first time I managed to blow a real bubblegum bubble. But the day-to-day moments of our lives fade from our minds almost as soon as we've lived them. Memories are echoes, and some are louder and last longer than others, that's all."

Terry looked at her for a long moment before saying, "You're a remarkable woman, Sheriff Talon."

She grinned. "Tell me something I don't know."

"The capital of Paraguay is Asuncion."

It was an old joke between them, and though it had long ago ceased to be funny, it always made her smile. Before either of them could say anything more, however, Joanne's cell phone rang on the nightstand.

"I wish you'd turned the damned thing off, or at least left it in the living room," Terry muttered.

Joanne didn't bother replying. Terry knew what her job was like. She rolled out of his arms and toward the nightstand. She grabbed the phone and answered it.

"Sheriff Talon."

"I assume you saw the news tonight." It was Dale.

She glanced at the clock radio on the nightstand and saw it was only 8:17. She'd thought it later than that.

"I hate seeing myself on TV. They say the camera adds ten pounds, but I think it's more like twenty."

"Who is it?" Terry whispered.

When she said Dale, he made a displeased grunt, got out of bed, and headed for the bathroom. He turned on the light, giving Joanne a nice view of his toned backside before he closed the door.

"I take it that the estimable Dr. Birch has paid a house-call this evening?"

"I'd say that was none of your business, but you'd just ignore me."

"You're right. Sorry it's been so long since I checked in. I wanted to give you some time to deal with the media vultures . . . and to talk to the Porter boy's parents. How did it go?"

She sat back against the headboard and drew the sheet up to her chest to cover herself. She knew it was stupid, but she felt awkward talking to Dale naked. It was like having your father accidentally see you without any clothes on.

"As well as it could. His parents hadn't even realized he didn't come home last night. They figured he got in late and left again before they got up this morning. That, or as Mr. Porter put it, Ray got lucky and slept over at some girl's place. They gave me some names of friends Ray hung out with and we're in the process of tracking them down and questioning them. Maybe we'll learn something useful. Maybe not."

"How did the Porters react to seeing the son's body?"

From anyone else, it might've seemed like a ghoulish question, but Joanne knew why Dale was asking. "They were shocked, and both husband and wife broke into tears. If they had anything to do with Ray's murder, then they both deserve Academy Awards for their performances." Remembering how the Porters had broken down in the coroner's office filled Joanne with sympathy. Their grief had been palpable, so strong she'd almost experienced it as a physical force. She was certain they had no involvement in their boy's death.

"I've had a lot of calls from other reporters, wanting me to give them background information about the infamous Carl the Cutter," Dale said. "I of course responded like the consummate professional I am."

"You told them they could screw you."

"Sideways, as a matter of fact."

"To be fair, the coverage I've seen so far has been more restrained than I expected."

"I imagine you have our friend Marshall to thank for that. But even his influence only extends so far. The coverage will get more lurid tomorrow as the vultures start fighting to hold onto the public's attention. Just wait and see."

Joanne had no doubt Dale was right, but she was grateful for small favors, wherever they came from.

She heard the toilet flush, followed by the faucet running.

"Speaking of Marshall, he met me at the Porters' home," she said. "He told me to tell them he'd pay for Ray's funeral."

"Really? That's odd."

"I thought so too. I did tell the Porters, and they were surprised. But they accepted."

The bathroom door opened and Terry came out. He left the light on, and Joanne could see the disapproving expression on his face. Before she could say anything, he bent over—giving her another great view of his ass—and began picking up his clothes. The two of them had been in a hurry to get naked earlier, and their clothing had been discarded in haste and left to lie wherever it had fallen.

"I wonder why Marshall offered to do that," Dale said.

Joanne shrugged, watching Terry as he began to get dressed. *So much for round two*, she thought.

"He acted like it was almost a matter of honor or something."

"Interesting."

Even over the phone, she could almost hear the wheels turning in Dale's mind.

"You learn anything from Sadie?" she asked.

Dale was silent for a moment before answering. "I think I picked up a thing or two."

There was something strange about his tone, but before she could ask about it, he gave her a quick summary of his afternoon visit to Sadie Muir's houseboat.

"So there's no connection between Ray Porter and Carl Coulter's victims, and Carl had no father on his birth certificate," she said for Terry's benefit. He acknowledged her words with a nod then returned to getting dressed.

"I spent the rest of the afternoon trying to find out why Carl's father wasn't named on his certificate. I checked with some contacts of mine at the hospital, went through my files, even tried to track down Tyrone, but I guess he's tired of talking to me because I couldn't find him. Didn't find anything on the Net, either. The only thing I didn't do was check with Debbie. I figure she's got enough to worry about right now. You talk to her recently?"

"After I was done with the Porters I had Ronnie take them out the back to avoid the reporters, then I went out to talk to them and be made to look fat on TV. After that, I stopped in on Debbie to see how she's doing. She stayed home all day and kept the curtains closed and the phone turned off. A few reporters came by and knocked, but she didn't answer the door. Hell, she almost didn't answer it for me, even after I called out to her. She said she'd been sleeping on and off. I think she'd probably taken a tranquilizer, but she didn't say anything about it. She's worried that whoever broke into the café last night might come after her at home tonight. I suggested she go stay at a friend's house, but she said she didn't have any friends. I told her I'd assign someone to watch her place tonight, and I'd step up patrols in her neighborhood."

Terry had finished dressing and now sat on the edge of the bed, listening, brow furrowed in a slight scowl.

"Do you think she's in any danger?" Dale asked.

"At this point, I don't know what to think. But I'm not going to take any chances. Did you hear we found Ray's car at the Burrito Bungalow?"

Dale hadn't and so Joanne filled him in.

"Witnesses say he met a girl and drove off with her," Joanne said. "A Cross girl in her twenties, blonde hair, gorgeous."

"Naturally. Anyone give a name?"

"One person did, the manager who was on duty that night. He said he thought it was Lenora Cross."

"Now that is *damned* interesting," Dale said.

"Isn't it, though?"

"Have you spoken with Marshall yet?"

"I called him at home. He didn't seem surprised when I told him about Lenora, but you know Marshall. He never gives anything away. I asked him to bring Lenora in for questioning, but he said he'd rather I come out to Sanctity and talk with her there. 'To spare her the embarrassment of going to the station,' he said. He also requested that I arrive at ten o'clock because he had a 'very full schedule' this evening. From his tone, he sounded as if he thought he was being more than accommodating. I didn't like it, but I agreed. You want to come? I like to have another person else present when I question someone. I'd ask Ronnie, but he's driving the wallet to the state crime lab in Columbus tonight."

"Do you have to ask?"

Joanne grinned. "How about I swing by and pick you up around 9:45?"

Dale paused. "It might work better if I meet you there. Okay?"

There was something about his tone that bothered her, as if he were trying a bit too hard to sound casual.

"Something wrong?"

"Not at all. It . . . will just be more convenient."

Marshall Cross wasn't the only man she knew who played things close to the vest. "Sure. Whatever works."

They said goodbye, then Joanne disconnected and put her cell phone back on the nightstand.

"I'm not trained in law enforcement," Terry said, "but it seems to me that taking a reporter along during questioning isn't exactly standard procedure."

There was an edge to Terry's tone, and Joanne responded to it with a surge of irritation. She got out of bed and started getting dressed.

"Dale might not be a cop, but he's got the sharpest instincts of anyone I've ever met." She slipped on her panties then started to put on her bra. "You really do sound jealous now."

He fixed her with a penetrating glare. "Should I be?"

She finished hooking up her bra then turned to look at Terry. "Dale and I are friends. Since my parents divorced and moved out of the county, he's the closest thing to family I have here. He's like an uncle or an older brother."

"*Much* older," Terry said, almost sneering.

"I don't like what you're implying,"

They glared at each other for a moment, and then Terry looked away and let out a long sigh. "Sorry. I guess I am a little jealous." He looked at her again and gave her a sheepish smile. "I'll work on it. While you were talking with Dale, I remembered that there's something I forget to tell you—about Marshall."

Terry went on to tell her about Marshall's visit to the coroner's office earlier. When he finished, Joanne frowned. Still wearing only her bra and panties, she sat down on the bed next to Terry.

"That's weird. Why would he want time alone with Ray Porter's body?"

"Why do the Crosses ever do anything? Because they have the power, that's why."

Joanne knew Terry held no love for the Cross family—few

people in the county did—but she was taken aback by the sudden venom in his voice. Her surprise must've shown on her face, for Terry said, "Sorry. I'm territorial when it comes to my office, I guess. I hate the idea that Marshall thinks he can just barge in when I'm about to begin an autopsy and ask to pay his 'respects' to the body. Since when did the Crosses become so pious anyway?"

Joanne was about to respond when she realized she had no idea if the Crosses practiced any type of religion. She'd never known any of them to attend the Christian churches in Rhine, or for that matter the Jewish synagogue or Unitarian church over in Somerset.

"When I talk to Marshall tonight I'll ask him about his visit to your office." *And why he neglected to tell me about it.* Joanne leaned over and gave Terry a kiss. When she drew back, she said, "Now if you don't mind, it's time for you to go home. I need a shower before I head out to Sanctity. It wouldn't do to enter the hallowed halls of the Cross family manor smelling like a twenty-dollar whore."

Terry grinned. "Don't sell yourself short, love. You're worth fifty dollars at the very least."

She punched him on the arm, hard enough to make him wince.

"All right, all right! One hundred dollars and not a penny more."

Instead of hitting him this time, she jumped on top of him and knocked him back onto the bed, laughing and giggling as they wrestled. When Terry began to kiss her, she said, "I suppose you can stick around for a few more minutes."

And that was the last either of them spoke for a while.

■ ■ ■ ■ ■

Dale stood at his living room window, looking out. He saw nothing but an empty street washed in the muted blue-white glow of fluorescent streetlights. There were shadows too, of course. There were *always* shadows, but he told himself there was nothing hiding in them ... nothing that was looking up at the window on the second floor of the *Echo* offices, watching the old man standing there.

He told himself that he'd turned down Joanne's offer of a ride because he hadn't wanted to inconvenience her, not because he feared that whatever had followed him from Lake Hush might decide to forget about him and start stalking her instead.

He glanced at his watch. 8:47. He had a little less than an hour before he needed to leave for Sanctity. He should put the time to good use, maybe go back through his files to see if he'd missed anything, get on the Internet to see what he could turn up. But he didn't step away from the window. He remained standing there, staring through the glass into the night, keeping watch on the shadows below.

CHAPTER **TWELVE**

Route 70 was a straight shot all the way to Columbus. Two hours of the most boring drive imaginable. Nothing to look at except trees and farmers' fields, with only the occasional roadside cross memorial to an accident victim to break the monotony. It was even more boring at night, when all you could see was only what your headlights revealed. As far as Ronnie was concerned, though, it was perfect. Boring meant predictable, predictable meant controllable, and controllable meant safe. And Ronnie was all about safety. It was why he'd become a peace officer in the first place.

A metal case rested on the passenger seat next to him. Inside wrapped in plastic was Ray Porter's wallet, the fingerprints he'd lifted at the Caffeine Café and the Deveraux Farm, and copies of the crime scene photos. He was determined to deliver the evidence to the state crime lab on time and without incident, and not only because that was how Ronnie liked to roll. He didn't want to let Joanne-Sheriff-Talon down. Not again.

At first Ronnie had been worried about how he would conceal his broken hand from the sheriff and his fellow deputies. He couldn't go to the hospital, for word was likely get back to the sheriff. He'd had to set the bones himself.

After taking double the recommended dose of over-the-counter painkillers, he got a fresh pair of gloves and a container of talcum powder from the supply drawer in his desk. He removed a roll of surgical tape from a first aid kit and then, only because he needed privacy, he went to the men's room and hid in a stall. Fortunately, the restrooms in the County building were regularly cleaned, if not up to Ronnie's exacting standards. He bit down on his wallet to give him something to focus his attention away from the pain to come and hopefully prevent him from screaming in agony as he worked on straightening his twisted fingers. The pain was so exquisitely intense that he'd almost blacked out a couple times. Then he set about taping his fingers. Not any easy task to accomplish working with only one good hand, but he managed. But that led to another problem. His co-workers would undoubtedly notice his taped fingers and ask questions he didn't want to answer. But that's what the gloves were for. He normally didn't wear rubber gloves at his workstation, but he did whenever he had to leave it and go to another section of the department. So his fellow officers were used to seeing him with gloves on, and if they even noticed that he didn't remove them while at his desk, it wouldn't matter. He knew they considered him eccentric at best and a full-blown nutjob at worst. So what if Ronnie Doyle started wearing his gloves all the time? What did you expect from a loon like him?

Getting the rubber gloves on was far easier contemplated than accomplished, however. He first sprinkled talcum inside the gloves so they'd slide on better, but even then he had a hell of a time getting the left one on since his broken right hand wasn't much help. But he did it, and then he began slipping on the left glove. In the end he managed to get the fingers where they belonged and the hand appeared normal enough.

He gripped the steering wheel tighter with his left hand—his right was in no condition to steer—and without thinking, he pressed down on the cruiser's accelerator. But as soon as he noticed the speedometer edge toward 70 mph, he eased back on the gas. He was a law-enforcement officer, and it was his duty to obey the speed limit unless there was a good reason for exceeding it. The fact that he'd gone over 60, even if only for a few seconds, spoke volumes about his mental state. He felt guilty as hell for allowing Marshall Cross to have access to the Porter boy's body. He'd tried to turn Marshall away, to tell him that he'd done more than enough to help him and couldn't in good conscience cooperate any further.

But he hadn't said anything. The pain throbbing through his broken hand had flared into a blaze of agony, and he began to feel the crawling sensation of tiny creatures writhing all over his flesh. He'd escorted Marshall to the coroner's office without a word of protest and stood guard outside while Marshall did whatever he'd come to do. It took five minutes at most, and then Marshall came out and departed without a word or backward glance.

Ronnie tried to put Marshall's visit out of his thoughts and concentrate on driving, but the constant fiery pain of his broken hand made it difficult. He'd taken a prescription-strength dose of ibruprofen, but it had done little to dull the pain. He supposed he'd just have to tough it out. After all, he was a cop. He could take it.

Ronnie's cell phone rang, and even with his broken fingers he had it out of his belt carrier and up to his ear before it could ring a second time.

"Deputy Doyle." He winced whenever he answered a call that way. The alliteration sounded comical, and more than a few of his fellow officers had made Deputy Dawg jokes over the years. At least Sheriff Talon had never made fun of him. If she was even aware of the unintentionally amusing alliteration, she'd never let on.

But it wasn't Sheriff Jo-Jo calling.

"This is the third time I've called tonight, Ronnie. I would've thought a deputy of your rank would check his voicemail more regularly." Marshall's voice had a disapproving tone, like that of a teacher sorely disappointed in a promising student.

At the sound of Marshall's voice, Ronnie felt a lance of pain between his eyes, accompanied by a sick twist of nausea in his gut.

"I-I had my phone turned off earlier. I was at dinner." Which was true, but the main reason Ronnie hadn't checked his messages—though normally he was obsessive about doing so—was because he was afraid Marshall Cross might've called. If he hadn't been so goddamned conscientious he would've been able to leave his phone off for the entire trip to Columbus. After all, Sheriff Talon could always get hold of him on the cruiser's radio if she wanted. Still, he hadn't been able to bring himself to leave his phone off, and now he wished to hell that he had.

"It's important that I'm able to contact you when I need to, Ronnie. Make certain you're always available to me, day or night. Do you understand?"

A pinprick of pain stabbed Ronnie between the eyes, and he clenched his teeth as he tried to ride it out. "Yes, Mr. Cross." As soon as he spoke the words, the pain lessened, though it didn't entirely go away.

"Good. Now listen closely. I want you to do me a favor. From the background noise I assume that you're driving somewhere. Where are you going and for what purpose?"

Lie to the bastard! Ronnie told himself. But the thought brought a new burst of pain in his head, and he knew he had to tell Marshall the truth, whether he wanted to or not. So he did.

"How fortuitous. Here's what I want you to do, Ronnie. I want you to pull off onto the side of the highway and dispose of the evidence that you're carrying. I don't care how you do it, just as long as it's never found again. Will you do that for me?"

"I've done a lot for you already, Mr. Cross. *A lot.* But I can't do this. Destroying evidence ... it wouldn't just be a betrayal of the trust that Jo-sheriff-anne has placed in me. I'd be committing a crime! I've never purposely done anything wrong in my life! I've never exceeded the speed limit except in the line of duty, I've never gotten a parking ticket, I've never even jaywalked!" Tears welled in his eyes and began running down his cheeks.

Marshall didn't answer right away, and though Ronnie knew it was foolish, he began to hope that Marshall would understand and relent. But when Marshall spoke next, his voice was cold and quiet, like a winter's frozen midnight.

"I've told you want to do, Ronnie. Now do it."

Marshall disconnected.

Ronnie continued holding his phone to his ear for several minutes afterward, doing his best to drive with tear-blurred vision. Finally he dropped the cell onto the seat next to him and wiped his eyes with swollen fingers.

Just because the high and mighty Marshall Cross wanted him to do something didn't mean he had to. He was his own man, a deputy sheriff yet, with over twenty years of service in. Hell, he could retire if he really wanted to. Maybe Marshall Cross really did have some kind of power, just as the rumors said. How else could Ronnie explain the bizarre hallucinations he'd experienced? But he was miles away from Marshall now and traveling farther away with every passing second. How far could his power extend before it began to weaken and lost its hold entirely? All Ronnie had to do was keep driving and he'd be okay. He wouldn't be forced to obey Marshall Cross's latest order and he could deliver the evidence intact to the state crime lab. He'd no doubt pay a price for his defiance—likely a steep one—but that was all right. All in the line of duty, right?

Relieved and with growing confidence that he'd overcome Marshall Cross's influence, he took deep breaths and forced himself to relax. Slowly the pain between his eyes began to fade, his nausea to subside.

Ronnie drove for the next few miles in relative peace, with only the pain in his throbbing hand for company. A dot of moisture appeared on his windshield. It was soon followed by another, then another, and more after that. Given all the pollution in the air—pollution that the rainwater surely absorbed—it meant he'd have to wash his cruiser as soon as he got back. It irked him because he kept his vehicle spotless inside and out. It was so clean he never wore his surgical mask or gloves when he drove. *Normally* didn't wear gloves, that is. But until he'd delivered the evidence, he'd just have to deal with a bit of dirt. *That's why they pay you the big bucks, Ronnie old boy.*

The rain started coming down more heavily then, and he reached out with his broken hand and slowly, gently activated the windshield wipers. The blades moved across the outer surface of the glass, but instead of clearing the view, they created a brownish-gray smear.

Ronnie frowned. Ignoring the pain in his hand, he turned the wipers to a higher setting. They obediently swished back and forth more swiftly, but it didn't help. The windshield became smeared even worse than before, and now Ronnie couldn't see the highway in front of him. He wanted to tromp on the brake, yank the steering wheel to the right, and pull the cruiser onto the shoulder before he wrecked, but he resisted the impulse. He knew he'd end up crashing for sure that way. Instead he removed his foot from the gas pedal and began to gently apply pressure to the brake. He hit the washer fluid control and kept it pressed down, hosing the windshield with cleaning fluid. The muck cleared long enough for him to see the red glow of brake lights directly in front of him, and he knew he was only seconds away from slamming into another vehicle. The panic he'd been working so hard to restrain broke loose then, and he jammed the brake down and turned the steering wheel hard to the right.

The brake lights vanished then, and Ronnie wondered if he'd really seen them at all, but it didn't matter. The damage was done.

He'd stopped shooting cleaning fluid at the windshield, and the glass was quickly covered by muck-rain again. Ronnie couldn't see as his cruiser left the highway, but he felt his vehicle judder as its tires rolled over gravel, then the car bucked and jerked as it slid onto grass. He felt the cruiser swerve around in a half-circle, and he gritted his teeth in anticipation of the crushing impact as the car slammed into a tree or fence post. But the collision never happened and the vehicle came to a rest.

Ronnie sat there for several long moments, left hand gripping the steering wheel, right hand in his lap, hurting like a sonofa-bitch. The pain in his head and the nausea in his stomach hadn't let up, but he barely registered their discomfort. He was too busy struggling to accept the fact that he was still alive.

The muck-rain continued to fall, striking the cruiser's roof with loud smacking sounds, as if thousands of fat wet frogs were plummeting from the heavens. The cruiser had stalled out when it came to a stop, but the wipers were still going. They weren't doing any better at clearing away the muck than they had when the cruiser was moving, so Ronnie switched them off. He checked the driver's side windows, the passenger side, turned to look out the back, but all he saw more muck, thick and viscous, sliding down the glass in brown-gray lumps like half-solid, half-liquid shit.

"This isn't real," Ronnie whispered. The brake lights, the muck . . . they were just like the maggots he'd seen at the Caffeine Café and the oversized germs that had prompted him to break his hand to get rid of them. Marshall Cross had done something to his mind, and whatever it was had messed him up, making him see things that weren't there. He could prove it, too. All he had to do was step out of the cruiser and into the rain. It would turn out to be water—that is, if there really was any rain at all and the whole thing wasn't a delusion.

Just . . . step . . . out.

Ronnie unlocked the door and took hold of the handle with his left hand. He started to push open the cruiser's door, but he couldn't move it very far. It was like there was something else on the other side, pushing back. An instant later he realized what it was as brown muck began to ooze through the partially open door. The muck splattered onto his hand, slid down his leg, and began collecting on the cruiser's floor in a pile of foul-smelling brown-gray shit.

He realized the cruiser must have come to a stop in a ditch or low-lying area in the field next to the highway and the shit-storm—for what else could it be called—had become so strong, the shitfall so heavy, that it was rising around the cruiser, threatening to bury it.

A bleat of terror escaped Ronnie's mouth, and he frantically tried to close the car door, but too much muck was flowing in too fast, and he couldn't do it. The level of muck in the cruiser was already past his ankles and rising. From the constant pounding on the vehicle's roof, it was clear the shitstorm wasn't letting up. If anything, it was coming down even harder now.

The muck was up to his calves now, and the stench was so bad that every time he took a breath he was seized by wracking coughs. He tried not to think of the trillions of bacteria swimming in the foul stew that poured into his car, but then he realized that it scarcely mattered. If the muck continued rising at this rate, he would drown in it long before any of the bacteria could invade his body and do any damage. If he didn't want to drown in shit, he was going to have to get out of the cruiser and swim for it. And even then, as hard as the muck was falling from the sky, he might well drown anyway.

The shit in the cruiser had made it up to his knees, and still the level continued to rise.

This isn't real! he told himself again. *It's another hallucination!*

Ronnie understood this, he really did. But he was caught by a flood of a far different kind, a deluge of terror and revulsion so intense, so deep, that it threatened to carry away what remained of his rational mind, leaving only a quivering, mewling animal.

The shit had risen above his belly and was beginning to slide up his chest. Its weight made it difficult to breathe, the pressure so great that he felt his ribs strain and begin to crack.

He fought to draw in a wheezing breath of air, closed his eyes, and shouted, "All right, goddamn you, I'll do it!"

The pressure on his chest vanished, as did the ungodly stench that only a second ago had filled the cruiser. Ronnie opened his eyes and saw that the inside of his vehicle was clean. He looked at the windshield and saw only ripples of water sliding down the glass. He still held the door partially open, but all that came through was rain. His hand, sleeve, and pants legs were wet, but that was all. He looked through the windshield, concentrating on seeing past the rain on the glass. The cruiser's headlights revealed a rain-soaked field, confirming that Ronnie had indeed

swerved off the road. It *had* been an illusion, that's all, and it was over now. But Ronnie felt little relief. He knew the shitstorm—or something even worse—would return if he didn't do what he'd promised.

Despite the cruiser's abrupt stop, the evidence case still sat on the passenger seat next to him. Ronnie gripped the handle with his broken hand, ignoring the bolts of pain that shot up his arm. With his left hand he pushed the car door open the rest of the way then stepped out into the rain. It was coming down hard enough that he was instantly soaked, but he didn't care. On the contrary, after the shitstorm hallucination he reveled in the sensation, though no matter how much water fell on him, he doubted he'd ever feel clean again.

He walked around the front of his cruiser, crossed through the headlight beams, and headed farther away from the highway. The ground sloped upward, and he slipped once, dropping the case and catching himself with his broken hand. The agony that flared shot through his entire body, and his scream cut through the night. He got back on his feet and continued on toward a wire fence that no doubt belonged to a farmer. He considered simply heaving the evidence case over the fence as far as he could, but he decided against it. The evidence would be discovered the next time the farmer worked this portion of his land. Instead, he lay the case on the ground, opened it, and removed the plastic bag containing Ray Porter's wallet and the envelope containing the fingerprints he'd lifted from the Caffeine Café and the barn at the Deveraux Farm. He also removed the envelope containing copies of the crime-scene photos and his incident reports. He closed the case so it wouldn't get any more wet inside than it already was, and then he walked up to the fence and knelt before it.

With his good hand he scooped away moist earth until he'd created a large enough hole. He put the evidence inside, pushed it down into the wet soil, then covered the hole once more. When he was finished, he stood, stomped down on the ground to flatten it, then held out his dirty hand so the rain could wash the soil off his rubber glove. Several of the fingertips had been torn during his digging, but he didn't care. It didn't matter if some dirt got in now. All the water in the world couldn't wash away what he'd done, couldn't cleanse his guilt.

He turned and headed back for the cruiser. Halfway there he considered drawing his 9 mm, sticking the barrel into his mouth and blowing off the top of his skull. But by the time he reached his vehicle, he'd abandoned all thoughts of suicide. He knew he couldn't escape Marshall Cross that easily. Besides, if he was dead, there was no way he could make up for what he'd done to Sheriff Jo-Jo. And whatever else happened, whatever hells Marshall Cross had yet in store for him, Ronnie was determined to make things right. Somehow.

He got back in the cruiser, closed the door, and started the engine. It took some work to get the vehicle out of the ditch—a lot of rocking back and forth, a light touch on the gas—but eventually he succeeded and was back on the highway heading for Columbus at precisely 65 mph. He would finish the trip, he would stop at the state crime lab, but he wouldn't go inside. He'd sit in his cruiser for the amount of time he'd estimate it would take him to hand over the evidence, then he'd start up the engine and begin the long drive back to Cross County. He'd pass the time by thinking of as many different ways to kill Marshall Cross as he could, the more agonizing and humiliating, the better.

Ronnie smiled as he continued driving on into darkness.

CHAPTER **THIRTEEN**

It was spitting rain by the time Joanne drove up to Sanctity's main entrance. From the weather reports she'd seen, it was only going to get worse. Rain often hit harder north of Cross County before moving southward. Ronnie was probably already driving through a good-sized rainstorm on his way to Columbus. If she was lucky, Lenora's questioning wouldn't take too long, and she'd be on the way home before the heavy staff started coming down. She loved lying in bed with the lights off and listening to rain pattering on the roof. It relaxed her like nothing else, not even the attentions of the good Doctor Birch. She'd hate to miss even a minute of it.

Joanne had never been to Sanctity before. She'd driven past the gated driveway entrance hundreds of times, but there were so many trees on the Crosses' property that even in winter-time when the foliage was gone, Sanctity itself remained barely visible. Joanne had served as sheriff of Cross County soon after she'd graduated from college with a degree in criminal justice six years ago. Not a long time, maybe, but long enough to settle into the role. She'd dealt with Crosses before, most often with Marshall, and she didn't hold them in the same sort of awe that so many country residents did. As she herself had as a child. But now, driving up to the black wrought-iron gate in her cruiser, she was surprised by how nervous she felt. She experienced an impulse to speed past the driveway and keep going. But she slowed and pulled up to the gate. She thought maybe she'd see

Dale's Jeep parked alongside the road, her friend sitting inside and waiting for her. But Dale wasn't there. Odd. It wasn't like him to be late.

She rolled down her window and looked for an intercom of some sort to let them know she'd arrived, but she saw none. She didn't see a security camera, either. What was she supposed to do—honk? But before she could do anything, the gate began to swing inward. Smoothly, silently. No ratcheting gears, no electronic hum. She thought of how gates like this always opened on their own in cheap horror movies, a not-so-subtle hint that malevolent forces were at work. It was a ridiculous thought. The Crosses had more than enough money to install a silent opener for their front gate. Nothing particularly malevolent about that, right?

She rolled her window up, and when the gate had opened all the way, she drove through. She didn't look in her rearview mirror to watch the gate close behind her, though. The winding driveway inclined gently upward, and as she drove, her nervousness began to fade, replaced by a faint sense of disappointment. The driveway was paved with blacktop, the grounds, though neatly kept, looked like any other well-to-do homeowner's yard. Trees lining the driveway, grounds covered with lush, healthy grass. It was all so . . . normal. The Crosses might be rich and well-connected, but it seemed that they were only human after all.

Then she rounded a curve and got her first good look at Sanctity.

It's a castle . . .

And if the term wasn't entirely accurate in an architectural sense, it certainly fit. The huge stone edifice loomed before her like a chunk of darkness that had detached from the night and taken on solid form. Light glowed in the windows, but it did nothing to leaven the mansion's dark façade. If anything, the contrast only served to make the structure seem more heavily cloaked in shadow. She felt suddenly small, a child again, and she had a better grasp of why Crosses acted as if they were a superior lifeform. Who wouldn't feel like that after growing up here?

But her feelings of insignificance vanished when she saw Dale's Jeep parked before the front entrance. This was the main reason she'd asked Dale to join her tonight, one that she couldn't tell Terry, no matter how much she cared for him. Dale made her feel safe.

She parked her cruiser behind Dale's Jeep, cut the lights, and turned off the engine. Dale wasn't in his vehicle, and she assumed he was already inside. She hadn't told Marshall she'd asked Dale to come along, but it seemed his arrival had been anticipated or at least not surprising. She wondered if Marshall knew how Dale made her feel, and the thought that Marshall might be inside Sanctity right now, amused that her security blanket had arrived before her, pissed her off. As she walked up concrete steps between a pair of towering ionic columns, she decided to do her best to hold onto that anger, whether it was justified of not. It would serve as effective armor in the place she was about to enter.

As she started toward Sanctity's front entrance—light raindrops sprinkling her uniform—she heard a noise coming from the direction of Dale's Jeep. A soft sound, like padded animal feet moving across blacktop. The sound caused the hair on the back of her neck to rise, and she turned to look behind her. She glimpsed a flash of black disappearing into the darkness, then it was gone. She stood motionless, breath held, listening, gazing into the night, searching for any further sign of movement. But she saw and heard nothing else. She waited a few more seconds before facing forward and resuming her approach to Sanctity.

The front entrance was unlit, but as Joanne approached the large black door, a pair of lights on either side came on. Momentarily dazzled, which no doubt was the intended effect, she averted her gaze. She heard the knob turn, the door open. She turned back, expecting to see a butler wearing a glum, funereal expression standing there. But it was Marshall.

"Good evening, Joanne. I appreciate your being so understanding about coming out here." His smile was reserved. Only appropriate given the circumstances of her visit, Joanne thought.

"Just doing my job." A cliché, maybe, but it was all she could think to say, and it sounded appropriately hard-ass.

Marshall's smile didn't waver an iota, but a cold glint came into his eyes. "Of course. Then by all means, let's get started." He stepped back from the open doorway and gestured for her to enter. She almost expected him to say *Welcome to my parlor* in a menacing voice. But he simply stood there, waiting, that cold gleam still in his gaze.

Joanne stepped inside.

· · · · ·

As Marshall led her through the halls of Sanctity, she was surprised by the sheer number of people present. Every room they passed contained groups of men and women of various ages, all well dressed, all carrying themselves with the patrician air that was a defining feature of Cross-hood. The people talked, drank, and more than a few waved at Marshall as he and Joanne walked past. None seemed to notice that he was accompanied by a woman in a sheriff's uniform, let alone care. They had eyes only for Marshall, as if he were their ruler which, Joanne supposed, in a way he was. The Crown Prince of Crosses.

"Do you have any animals that you let run loose on the property?" she asked as they walked. "A dog, maybe?"

Marshall frowned. "Other than the songbirds in the Solarium and some koi in an artificial pond in the flower garden out back, we have no pets of any sort. Why do you ask?"

"I thought I saw something outside. It was probably a raccoon or something."

"Perhaps." But Marshall sounded doubtful, and he changed the subject. "My mother has asked me to proffer her apologies for not coming down to greet you. She's getting on in years and rarely leaves her room. She hopes you'll understand."

"Of course." Joanne hadn't expected to meet the grande dame of the Cross clan tonight. From what she understood, Althea hadn't been seen in public for years. In a way, she was relieved. The idea of meeting Marshall's mother, the only person he was rumored to fear, was more than a bit intimidating.

Marshall continued leading her along corridors, and as they walked, Joanne realized she was surprised—and to be honest, a bit disappointed—by how normal Sanctity seemed. No, *normal* wasn't the right word. The place *was* a mansion. But after growing up hearing stories about the Crosses and the terrible secrets concealed within their creepy castle of a home, she'd expected—consciously or not—something more. Something out of legend, almost. Sanctity might have been huge, but in the end it had turned out to be life-sized after all.

The atmosphere pervading Sanctity didn't disappoint, however. The air seemed to crackle with repressed tension, a sense of power and violence that, while restrained, threatened to erupt any moment. Perhaps it was just her imagination, or her Feelings picking up on the ever-present potential for danger permeating Sanctity. Whichever the reason, Joanne didn't like the sensation. It set her teeth on edge and made her feel like an animal irritated by an ultrasonic signal that humans couldn't hear.

Lenora was waiting for them in the library, as was Dale. The first thing Joanne noticed about Marshall's daughter was that she possessed the same ice-blue eyes as her father. She sat in a leather chair, legs crossed, arms hanging loose over the armrests, head tilted back, face impassive. She was tricked out in a too-tight, too-mini black mini-dress, and a pair of take-me-now pumps. She looked completely relaxed—or like someone trying very hard to seem that way. Dale sat on a couch opposite Lenora, a glass filled with clear liquid and ice cubes resting within easy reach on a nearby end table. Water, Joanne knew. Dale didn't drink alcohol when he was working.

Marshall must have noted where her gaze had fallen, for he said, "Would you like something to drink, Joanne? Coffee, perhaps? I imagine you've had little sleep the last couple days."

"No, thanks." She glanced around the room, quickly taking in its décor. Mahogany shelves lined the walls, filled with leather-bound books. Domed ceiling, with a mural depicting people in old-fashioned dress working a primitive printing press. No windows. Polished hardwood floors. Chair, couches, and reading table arranged throughout the room in various permutations. She noted that Marshall had chosen the only arrangement of furniture where Lenora could face her questioners with nothing between them. Calculated to create an impression of openness and honesty. After all, what could Lenora Cross have to hide?

Well, that was what Joanne was here to find out, wasn't it?

She walked over to the couch and sat down next to Dale. She wanted to see what Marshall would do next. Would he remain standing to assert his authority as male head of the Cross clan? Or would he opt to take the other leather chair, the one set perpendicular to both the couch and Lenora's chair?

Marshall continued standing for a moment longer, maybe still undecided as to the best strategy. But in the end, he took the second chair.

"We need to get one thing straight before we begin," Joanne said. Though she was speaking to both Marshall and Lenora, she kept her gaze fastened on the girl. "Despite the fact I'm questioning you here rather than downtown, this is official sheriff's department business. Do you understand?"

Marshall began to reply, but Joanne held up a hand to forestall him. He scowled but kept his mouth shut.

"I do," Lenora said. A smile played around her lips as well, and Joanne wondered if she enjoyed seeing her father silenced. Probably, she decided. It wouldn't be easy to have Marshall Cross as your father.

"In your own words, Ms. Cross, tell me what happened last night between you and Ray Porter."

Lenora glanced at Dale before speaking. Despite her amusement at seeing her father quieted by Joanne, Lenora turned to him now. He gave her an almost imperceptible nod. Evidently satisfied, Lenora began to tell her story. It was simple and straightforward and in other circumstances, Joanne might've accepted it at face value. But these circumstances were anything but normal and this homicide investigation was hardly routine.

"You say there was no special reason why you decided to go to the Deveraux Farm," Joanne said.

"That's right. Like I told my father, that's where people go to park around here, isn't it?"

Up to this point, Dale had sat and listened without comment, not even taking notes. But now he spoke up. "Teenagers, maybe. But you're a bit old for cheap thrills like that, aren't you?" The question held an edge of mockery that was unlike Dale, but Joanne knew he was attempting to put Lenora off balance, to shake her up and—if she'd practiced her story—get her to deviate from the script and perhaps trick her into revealing more than she wished.

Lenora frowned, but she answered calmly enough. "I'm not *that* old. I never went there when I was a teen, though, and I guess I wanted to see what I missed out on. Turns out it wasn't much."

Joanne exchanged a quick glance with Dale, and an unspoken message passed between them. Lenora didn't seem particularly upset that Ray Porter had been murdered a short time after they supposedly parted company.

"And when Ray put the moves on you," Joanne said, "you tricked him out of the car, took his vehicle, and left him at the Farm."

Lenora's mouth pursed in irritation. "You make it sound as if I stole it. I just wanted to make sure Ray didn't leave me stranded because he was pissed I didn't put out."

"So you decided to strand him first," Joanne said. "And technically, you did steal his vehicle, though I'll let the point slide. Did you see or hear anything suspicious during the drive to and from the farm? Or while you were there?"

"Nothing. We . . ." Lenora's words trailed off. "Now that I think of it, there *was* one thing."

Both Joanne and Dale sat up straighter, like a pair of hunting dogs that had just located a scent. Marshall also seemed to be paying extra-close attention.

"As I was driving away, I had the weirdest feeling like someone was watching—someone besides Ray, I mean. I didn't think too much of it at the time. After all, it *was* the Deveraux Farm, right? That's why people go there, to get a spooky thrill. I figured it was just my imagination, but now . . ." A note of fear crept into her voice. "Do you think the person who killed Ray was there spying on us?"

Though there was no solid evidence to suggest such a possibility, Joanne said, "Maybe," more to see how Lenora would react than anything else.

The girl's eyes widened. "If I'd been the one left there, the killer might've come after *me*." From the half-shocked tone of her voice, the possibility hadn't occurred to her before now.

Of course not, Joanne thought. Lenora was a Cross, and her family was the center of the universe, at least around these parts. How could anything bad ever happen to someone like her?

Then again, maybe she was putting on an act. But if so, she was doing a damned fine job.

Joanne asked a few more questions, getting estimates on time and the like. Liars tended to give too-precise answers—*I left there at 10:17 on the dot, Sheriff, I swear*—but people with nothing to hide had a more vague sense of time. Lenora gave answers like "Around eleven," and "I don't know sometime after eleven-thirty, maybe? Eleven forty-five? I'm really not sure."

Lenora's imprecision actually added to her credibility. But then again, Marshall had likely coached her ahead of time on how to appear credible.

"One last question, Ms. Cross," Joanne began. "Did you kill Ray Porter?"

"No." She answered without hesitation, and without any sign that she was working hard to seem like the answer came easily to her.

Joanne waited a moment to give Lenora a chance to speak further. People with guilty consciences became quickly uncomfortable with silences and began talking just to fill them up, in their nervousness often contradicting something they said earlier.

But Lenora just sat and looked at Joanne, waiting to see what would happen next.

Joanne turned to Dale to see if he had anything he wanted to ask, but he shook his head. Joanne nodded, then stood. As if it was a signal that this meeting was over, everyone else stood as well.

"Thanks for your cooperation," Joanne said. She turned to Marshall. "*Both* of you. If I have any further questions, I'll be in touch."

"Um, *I* have a question," Lenora said.

Marshall, for the first time since Joanne had known him, showed surprise on his face.

Ah, she thought. *Looks like Lenora has decided to ad lib.*

"Do you ... do you think the killer might come after me? I mean, I was there last night. I didn't see anything, but the killer doesn't know that. Maybe he thinks I saw something." She paused and her face paled, as if something awful had just occurred to her. "What if the killer was after *me* in the first place? What if he killed Ray because he couldn't get to me?"

Joanne couldn't provide real answers for Lenora's concerns, so she decided to rely on that time-honored tool of law-enforcement officers everywhere—SOB: Standard Operational Bullshit.

"We have no reason to believe you were ever a target, Ms. Cross. Neither you nor Ray planned to go the Deveraux Farm, so no one could've known you'd be there. Right now it looks like Ray's murder was a crime of opportunity. It's doubtful the killer ever got a good look at you, and you were driving Ray's Camaro, not your vehicle. There's no evidence to suggest you're in any danger."

"But even if you were," Dale added, "all you need to do is remain here. There's no safer place in the county than within the walls of Sanctity." Dale gave Marshall a sideways look. "Safe from outsiders, at least."

Marshall didn't rise to the bait. "It's true, Lenora. Nothing on earth can harm you here."

Joanne thought about the vision of Carl Coulter she'd had at the Deveraux Farm and of Carl's subsequent appearance in her nightmare.

●　●　●　●　●

It was raining harder when Joanne and Dale left the not-so-hallowed halls of Sanctity, though not quite hard enough to qualify as a full-fledged storm yet. Neither of them carried umbrellas, so they hurried to Joanne's cruiser and quickly got in.

"So what do you think?" Joanne asked.

Dale shrugged. "It's hard to know what to think. She seemed to be telling the truth."

"But she's a Cross."

"Exactly. I liked how you reassured her there at the end. 'We have no reason to believe you were ever a target.' We have no reason to believe she *wasn't*, either. Same thing about them not planning to go out to the farm. Someone could've followed them."

"Lenora said they weren't followed."

"She said they didn't *notice* anyone following them. Big difference, but you already know that."

"Yeah. Her story seems to track well enough, and it provides a possible explanation for why Ray's wallet was in the barn. He could've gone inside on his own, or been taken inside by the killer and dropped it then."

"And the killer decided to drive him out into the middle of nowhere, slash his throat, and leave the body in the ditch?"

"No blood evidence at the barn or in Ray's Camaro."

"Why not just kill him in the barn?" Dale argued. "Especially is the murderer wants to emulate Carl's MO. Carl killed all his victims in that barn. It's a perfect place—quiet, isolated, no neighbors close by. Even on a county road at night, someone might drive by and see you. And if they didn't witness you commit the crime itself, then they might see you driving there before or after. It's seems too risky."

"Maybe the killer was worried Lenora might have a change of heart and come back for Ray," Joanne said.

"Maybe," Dale allowed. "But in that case, how did the killer get Ray to the murder scene? From what you told me on the plane, Terry found no evidence that Ray was bound in any way—no rope burns or duct-tape marks—and there was no blow to the head to knock him out."

"Maybe Ray was drugged. We won't know until the state crime lab returns the toxicology results."

"Carl didn't drug his victims. Another possible difference between the killers—depending, as you said, on the test results."

"From the way you're talking, it sounds like you think there's a possibility that Carl himself might've committed Ray's murder." She tried to make it sound like a joke, but here, sitting in the cruiser in the dark, outside the imposing gothic presence of Sanctity, it didn't sound funny. Not at all.

"I'm just thinking in terms of a copycat, that's all."

"Sure."

But neither of them sounded very convincing, she thought.

She noticed Dale kept looking through the cruiser's windows, checking each one in turn—passenger's side, windshield, driver's side, and rear window. He didn't do this in an obvious way, didn't turn his head all the way around if he didn't have to, didn't allow his gaze to linger long. But it wasn't enough to fool Joanne, though that's what he was obviously trying to do.

"Looking for something?" she asked.

"What? Oh, no. Just seeing what I can see. I don't get up this way much, you know. Nice to see how the other half lives, right?"

She didn't buy his excuse for a second. It was too dark to get a good look at Sanctity's grounds. Besides, Dale didn't give a damn about things like that. He was probably the least materialistic person she knew. But there was one part of his reply that she couldn't let pass without comment.

"I didn't know you'd been here before." When he didn't respond right away, she added. "You said, 'I don't get up this way much.' And don't tell me it's a figure of speech. I know you choose your words more carefully than that."

Dale looked out the windshield again, and this time she had the sense that he did so to avoid meeting her gaze.

"I've been a reporter in this county for a long time, Joanne. I've had occasion to come to Sanctity once or twice while I was working. If the Crosses had their way, I'd have been up here a lot more often. They'd love to have complete control over the *Echo*. Unfortunately for them, the owner, publisher, editor, and chief reporter are all stubborn, uncooperative jackasses."

Joanne grinned. "I though you were the only jackass at the paper."

Dale grinned back. "So *that's* why I have to sign my own paychecks. I always wondered."

Joanne knew Dale had avoided giving her a real answer, but she decided not to push it. If he had something to tell her, he'd do so in his own time. She'd been trying to decide whether to tell him about her nightmare, and she almost decided to hold off. She knew at least part of the reason was because Dale was holding back on her. But in the end she decided not to be petty and told him. When she was done, they discussed the dream a bit, but they mutually decided that Carl's nightmare visit really didn't have any significance. A dream was just a dream, nothing more.

Their discussion got Joanne to thinking about something else that had bothered her on and off over the years. The Crosses had their fingers in everything that went on in their county. But they'd never tried to control her. Urge, manipulate, and occasionally intimidate, yes. But they'd never attempted to bribe or blackmail her. Or, if some of the stories county folk told could be believed, the Crosses had never tried to persuade her in their "special" way, whatever exactly that was. If they'd love to control the paper, as Dale had said, then how much more would they desire to control the Sheriff's Department? Sometimes she thought they might well have done just that with her predecessor, though Dale had never said anything to indicate that Stan Manchester had been corrupt.

She liked to think the reason the Crosses had never tried to corrupt her was because they knew how she'd react to any such attempts. But she doubted it could be that simple. Nothing with the Crosses ever was.

"So now what?" Dale asked.

"I'll do my best to get the state crime lab to hurry up, but it's bound to be a while before we get any results back. In the meantime, I'll have my deputies interview all of Ray's friends, see what they can turn up. I'll go back over the evidence we've gathered, see if anything jumps out that I might've missed before. And all the while I'll be holding my breath and hoping that whoever killed Ray Porter doesn't decide to strike again."

"And what do you think the odds of that are?"

"Not good," she admitted. "There's a reason why the killer's copied Carl's methods. A reason why someone—quite possibly the same person—terrorized Debbie Coulter last night. Whatever's going on, it's not over. It's just begun."

"I wish I could say I disagree, but I can't. I may not get Feelings like yours, but my gut instincts tell me you're right."

"How about you? What's your next move?" She didn't bother asking if he was going to keep investigating Ray's murder and the attack on Debbie. Once Dale started working on a story, he didn't stop. It was another way they were alike.

He glanced out the passenger's side window. "I'm not sure. I might go for a long drive. There's something that's . . . been nagging me lately."

Joanne knew Dale sometimes took such drives, especially when he'd been thinking about his wife and daughter. "Good idea. A drive always clears your head."

"It's not so much a matter of clearing something as it is losing it."

Before Joanne could ask Dale to explain, he got out of the cruiser and hurried through the rain to his Jeep, looking around as if to make sure he wasn't being watched. He got inside, turned on the engine, and hit the headlights. He then turned his vehicle around and began heading down the long driveway.

She wasn't sure, but she thought she saw something dark and sleek follow swiftly after him, running behind the trees lining the driveway. Just like she thought she'd seen something lurking about earlier when she arrived at Sanctity.

No, she decided. She hadn't seen anything. She was tired and stressed, and her eyes were playing tricks on her, simple as that. She'd check in with whoever was on desk duty tonight— Anderson, she thought—and see how things were going. If all was well, she'd head home, crawl into bed, and let the sound of rain falling on the roof lull her to sleep.

She inserted the key into the ignition and started to turn it when her cell phone ran. Fearing her plans for sleep were about to go seriously awry, she answered her phone.

"Sheriff Talon."

"Hello, Joanne. It's nice to hear your voice."

Joanne didn't recognize the woman on the other end. Her words were spoken softly, almost whispered, yet there was an underlying strength and sureness to them. Joanne had the impression she was hearing someone old speak, but someone who still possessed a great deal of vitality.

"I'm sorry, but who is this?"

A gentle chuckle, playful and somehow disturbingly intimate, as if the other woman thought she was sharing a private joke with a confidant.

"It's I who should be sorry, my dear. I should've remembered my manners. This is Althea Cross. I was hoping you might have a few moments to visit with an old woman before you leave the grounds."

Joanne was so surprised that she couldn't answer right away, but she did take the key out of the ignition. And though there was no way Althea could've heard her do this, the woman said, "Good."

CHAPTER FOURTEEN

Joanne carried a flashlight in her right hand and an open umbrella in her left. Rain pelted the umbrella's fabric and rivulets ran down the sides. The rain caught and reflected the flashlight's glow, making it difficult to see. But visibility would've been nonexistent without the flashlight's beam, so she left it on. She stepped cautiously through the wet grass, the cuffs of her uniform pants soaked, as were the socks beneath. Joanne hoped the worst of the storm had already moved far enough south so that Ronnie was out of it. This would be a real bitch to drive through.

The grounds behind Sanctity—one did not use such pedestrian terms as front yard and back yard when referring to a place such as this—were unlit, and Joanne had no idea precisely where she was at and, more importantly, what was around her. Why the darkness, she wondered. It wasn't as if the Crosses couldn't afford to illuminate the grounds. Maybe they weren't used to folks wandering the grounds after the sun had gone down. Maybe Althea had turned off the lights so no one would witness her meeting with Joanne. Perhaps the Crosses were simply more comfortable with darkness. She smiled grimly at the thought.

"Darkness of all kinds," she added, speaking softly to herself.

She continued walking, sweeping the flashlight beam back and forth, hoping to spot the grande dame of the Cross family. She began to feel a strange disorienting sensation, like thousands of ants were crawling through the narrow space between her skull and brain. She remembered another time that she was surrounded by darkness and damp. It hadn't been raining in the cavern, but she'd been cold, naked, alone, and hungry. As soon as the memory flash came, it disappeared, but the feelings of fear and abandonment remained behind.

Joanne considered turning around and heading back to her cruiser and getting the hell out of here. But before she could do so, she heard a woman's voice singing a wordless tune. Out here on Sanctity's grounds, in the dark and the rain, the sound was eerie, and Joanne couldn't help shivering. But her voice was strong as she called out, "Is that you, Mrs. Cross?"

The singing stopped, and the woman replied in a voice that, while soft, was firm and confident. "Call me, Althea, child. I'm over here, in the gazebo."

Joanne swung the beam of her flashlight in the direction of the voice and saw a white gazebo, thin vines curled around the supports of the black-shingled roof. A shadowy form sat on a bench inside, partially hidden by a curtain of streaming rainwater pouring off the roof. The figure was small and slight, barely larger than a child. She raised a hand to cover her eyes.

"I'd be grateful if you could avoid pointing your flashlight directly at me. The light's harsh to these old eyes of mine, I'm afraid."

Joanne angled her hand downward so the flashlight's beam no longer shone on the gazebo but still provided enough illumination to guide her steps as she walked toward it. As she entered the gazebo, she kept the flashlight aimed at her feet, but she didn't turn it off. She didn't fear for her safety. If the Crosses wanted to attack her, they could've done so any time. But she wanted to be able to see Althea Cross, not only to gauge the woman's reactions as they spoke, but out of simple curiosity. Joanne thumbed the catch to automatically close her umbrella, then sat on a bench opposite her hostess.

"Thank you for coming to speak with me," Althea said. "I know it's uncomfortable to be trudging around the grounds in the rain like this when we could be inside, warm and dry."

Althea might not be warm out here, but she *was* dry, Joanne noticed. And there was no sign she'd brought an umbrella with her. Joanne was most assuredly *not* dry.

"You could've just told me to meet you in the gazebo when you called, instead of just saying, 'I'll be out back.'"

"Perhaps. But where would be the fun in that? A night like this"—Althea gestured to the night and the rain—"absolutely demands a touch of intrigue, don't you think?"

"Speaking of intrigue, I assume you wished to meet with me out here so that we could speak in private," Joanne said.

"That, and I love listening to the sound of the rain, especially when there's a bit of thunder off in the distance."

Joanne shouldn't have been startled by Althea's words. After all, lots of people enjoyed listening to rain. But hearing the woman echo the thoughts Joanne had been thinking just before her cell phone rang was more than a little unnerving, given the circumstances.

Joanne had expected Althea Cross to be a wizened old woman in her eighties, if not her nineties. A frail thing with sagging, wrinkled skin, bird-boned arms and legs, and wisps of fine white hair clinging to a liver-spotted scalp. But while the woman sitting across from Joanne was petite, she was anything but decrepit. She appeared to be no older than sixty—which was impossible since Marshall, her son, was in his fifties—and she was elegantly attractive. She possessed high cheekbones, patrician nose, regal chin, and eyes the same ice-blue as her son and granddaughter. Her make-up was subtle and understated, and while her hair was silver, it was thick, full, and salon-styled. She wore an expensive brown leather jacket over a black dress, the hemline just above the knee. Her legs were toned and firm, like those of a woman in her thirties. Hell, they looked better than Joanne's did. A pair of black high heels completed Althea's outfit, and Joanne noted they were not only dry, but there was no mud on them, despite the heavy rainfall. The woman was so slender, maybe she slipped between the raindrops, Joanne thought.

Althea offered her hand, and though Joanne wasn't here for a social occasion, she decided it wouldn't be wise to be rude to the most powerful woman in this part of the state, and so she reached out and clasped Althea's hand. The woman's grip was firmer than Joanne expected, almost painful, in fact, and though the skin was smooth, it was dry and too warm, almost hot. Joanne imagined she was touching the hide of some desert lizard, and she was grateful when Althea released her hand. The older woman's eyes glimmered with amusement, as if she were aware of Joanne's discomfort and enjoyed it.

Joanne worked to maintain her professional composure as she spoke, but it wasn't easy. She had just met Althea Cross, and already the woman had her off balance.

"When your son greeted me tonight, he told me that you rarely left your room. If that's true, I'm glad you made an exception for me."

"Marshall's a dear, and I'd be lost without him. But he can be a bit overprotective at times." A thin smile. "I might not be a young, fresh thing anymore, but I'm hardly an invalid."

Joanne became aware of a scent intermingling with the smells of rain and wet grass. It was sweet in a way, but it was too cloying, too faintly repulsive to be perfume. Certainly not any scent a woman of Althea's wealth and taste would choose to wear. It wasn't a smell Joanne usually associated with old people, either—soap, medicine, or musty cloth. Rather it was the scent of cut flowers on the verge of going bad, petals drooping, their edges turning brown. It was probably some scent clinging to the gazebo itself, Joanne told herself, one that had nothing to do with Althea Cross. A person couldn't smell that like . . . could they?

"You know why I came here tonight," Joanne said.

Althea nodded. "I know all about the murder of the Porter boy. Marshall keeps me well informed. I also know my granddaughter saw the boy last night, and that they parted ways before he was killed. And before you say anything, I understand you can't accept Lenora's story at face value. You can't afford to in your line of work."

"What else do you know?"

Althea surprised Joanne by throwing back her head and letting out a hearty laugh. "Child, if I started telling you *everything* I know, we'd still be here until well after sunrise! But of course you're asking if I know anything that might aid you in your investigation. And while you might find this hard to believe, I *do* wish to help. You fulfill an absolutely vital function in our community, Joanne. I will do whatever I can to help perform that function."

Though Althea's words might've seemed overly formal and forced if someone else had spoken them, coming from her, they possessed a sincere solemnity that made her pledge seem believable, or nearly so.

"Do you know who killed Ray Porter?"

"No."

"Do you know who terrorized Debbie Coulter?"

"No. Do you think they're one and the same? That would be my guess, but then I'm not a trained law-enforcement officer."

Joanne hadn't expected Althea to know, or at least admit to knowing, the answer to those questions, but she'd had to ask.

"I don't mean to be rude, Mrs.—Althea, but I'm tired, wet, and cold. Normally I might not mind sitting here and chatting—"

"Just one local legend to another, eh?"

That was what Terry had called Joanne earlier when he'd asked about her childhood disappearance. Once again Althea was echoing something Joanne had heard elsewhere, almost as if the woman was rooting through her memories and picking out tidbits with which to taunt her. But instead of frightening her this time, Althea's carny trick just pissed her off.

She continued speaking as if Althea hadn't said a word. "If you don't have anything pertinent to discuss, I'm going to say good-night, go home, and try to get some sleep before these bags under my eyes turn into suitcases."

Althea's thin lips pressed together in irritation, but when she spoke her tone remained pleasant enough. "I suppose that depends on how you define the word *pertinent*. What do you know about my son's wife?"

Joanne frowned. Of all the turns their conversation might've taken, she hadn't anticipated this one. "Her name is Charlotte, and according to rumor she left your son several years ago and hasn't been seen since. And no one seems to have any idea where she went."

"Sounds suspicious, doesn't it? Especially given my family's reputation—one that I'll admit is fully deserved."

Joanne felt her pulse kick up a notch. One of the rumors she hadn't mentioned was that some people believed Marshall had tired of his wife and killed her—or ordered someone else to do it. It had happened before Joanne had taken over as sheriff, but in looking over Stan Manchester's files, and doing a bit of digging on her own, she'd come to the conclusion that there was no solid proof one way or the other.

So was Althea now sitting here and telling Joanne that her son had indeed murdered his wife?

"When you questioned my granddaughter, you might have detected an undercurrent of tension between her father and herself."

"Undercurrent? More like raging rapids."

"Indeed. This is due in large part to the fact that Lenora blames Marshall for driving Charlotte away. At least, that's all she'll admit to aloud. But I know she suspects Marshall of killing Charlotte. She wasn't one of the family before she married Marshall, you know. The Cross family is widespread enough to permit distant cousins to marry without unfortunate genetic repercussions for their children. But from time to time we need to bring new blood into the fold. Lenora believes that Marshall never truly loved her mother, but rather used her like an animal, for breeding purposes."

"From the way you're talking, that's sure what it sounds like."

"Quite frankly, it was—to me. But not to Marshall. My son truly loved Charlotte. But though the poor girl tried, she wasn't able to adjust to being a Cross."

Joanne remembered the highly charged atmosphere of repressed violence she'd sensed within the walls of Sanctity. "I can imagine."

Althea raised a single eyebrow at the gibe before continuing. "So she left—of her own free will. Marshall wanted desperately to go after her, but I forbade him. I knew it would only make matters worse, you see."

Joanne *didn't* see, but she decided not to worry about that right now. "Why haven't you told this to Lenora?"

"I have. Many times. The child says she believes me, but she doesn't. I doubt she ever will." The woman lowered her gaze, and though there was nothing in her physical appearance to suggest it, Althea Cross suddenly looked old to Joanne, as if the full weight of all the years she'd lived—and more—had settled on her all at once, like dark birds come home to roost after too brief a flight.

"Does Marshall know how Lenora feels?" Joanne found herself in the extremely odd position of feeling sympathy toward Marshall. He always seemed supremely self-possessed, confident, and in complete control of whatever situation he was in. But Althea had shown her a different side to Marshall—assuming the woman was telling the truth, and Joanne's gut said she was.

"Of course he knows. How could he not? But he rarely speaks of the matter, even to me. He's a proud man, my son. Too much so for his own good at times."

"While I appreciate the insight into your family, why tell me all this? I don't see how it relates to either Ray Porter's murder of the break-in at the Caffeine Café."

Althea shrugged. "Perhaps it doesn't relate. But then your friend Mr. Ramsey would say that all information is useful, one way or another, would he not?"

This time Althea's mentalist act didn't phase Joanne in the least. She'd almost come to expect it.

"Maybe so." Joanne stood. "If there's nothing else . . ."

Althea turned to look out into the dark and the rain. "I wish I could be of more help to you, child. But in many ways Cross County is like a house of cards. Unless one moves with exacting precision and has a light touch, the whole structure will collapse."

She turned back to Joanne and smiled. "But that's why we have you, my dear, isn't it?"

Of everything Joanne had seen and heard since driving through Sanctity's main gate, this statement chilled her like nothing else, though she had no idea why.

Joanne wasn't able to form a reply, so she merely nodded, opened her umbrella, and stepped out into the rain. As she walked away from the gazebo—moving at a faster pace than usual—she heard Althea call out.

"It was good to see you again, dear!"

. . . . .

The rain had fallen off to a light drizzle by the time Lenora took to her bed. Her quarters were larger than some people's homes. She only lacked a complete kitchen, though she did have a mini fridge and a microwave. She had a full bath, and her closet was practically a room in and of itself. Her bed was a huge four-poster with an overstuffed mattress, silk sheets, and far too many pillows. Her comforter was made of ermine, and though she thought the idea of it was disgusting on principle, she would never give it up without a fight to the death. With such luxuriously comfortable accommodations, Lenora rarely had trouble falling asleep and staying that way throughout the night.

But tonight was different.

She had a great deal on her mind, not the least of which was her interrogation by the sheriff and that tag-along reporter. After they'd left, her father had assured her that she'd done fine and that there shouldn't be any further problems. She wished she could believe him, could *trust* him. But she didn't and never would. So she set her alarm, turned out the lights, crawled beneath her ermine and silk, and stared up at the ceiling. Her thoughts swirled in a confusing tumult, and she wished she could give herself a push to calm her unquiet mind. But she couldn't, so she was forced to rely on other more mundane techniques. She concentrated on breathing slowly and evenly, and instead of trying to reign in her unruly thoughts, she allowed them to roam where they would. Eventually, sooner than she expected, her eyelids began to grow heavy and a pleasantly numbing drowsiness settled on her. She was on the verge of sleep, about to tumble off the edge into nothingness, when she sensed a presence in her room.

Her eyes snapped open and she turned her head to see a dark form standing at the side of her bed.

She felt a surge of fear in the center of her chest, but she immediately fought it down. She was a Cross. Her family weren't simply masters of fear. They *were* fear.

"Father, is that you?"

The possibility that her nocturnal visitor might be an intruder never occurred to her. She couldn't conceive of anyone being able to break into Sanctity—and if by some unimaginable miracle someone *did* manage to gain entrance, he or she would never survive long enough to reach this far. She rather hoped her visitor was her would-be suitor from earlier tonight in the Solarium. Sebastian from Atlanta. But it wouldn't do to call out *his* name first, especially if it *was* her father come to check up on her.

But when the figure spoke, its voice belonged neither to her father or her prospective paramour.

"Hi, Lenora."

The fear came rushing back now, and this time she didn't try to dispel it. She reached out with her mind and pushed at the intruder.

"Get out. *Now*."

But the intruder didn't turn and leave. He just stood there, a shadow among shadows.

"Sorry. That won't work on me." A pause. "Not anymore."

Though she couldn't see the intruder's face in the darkness, she heard the grin in his voice. She drew in air to scream, but before she could release any sound, the figure clamped a hand over her mouth. His flesh was cold and slick, like a serpent's skin.

"I need your help—"

She still couldn't make out his features, but somehow she knew that his grin stretched wider than humanly possible.

"—*Sis.*"

Deep within the farthest recesses of her soul, Lenora silently released the scream that had been building inside her. It was only the first of many.

CHAPTER FIFTEEN

No one was watching the Caffeine Café. Why would they? Not only was it late, but the business had remained closed since the break-in last evening. Evidently the Sheriff's Department put little faith in the old maxim of the criminal returning to the scene of the crime. Too bad for them.

Yellow crime-scene tape stretched across the doorway, forbidding entrance to the world. A single quick swipe of a sharp instrument was all it took to remove the ineffective barrier, and a well-placed kick to the door took care of the lock, just like in the movies. The sharp instrument was tucked back into a pocket, next to a book of matches, and its wielder bent down to pick up a plastic container sitting on the ground. It was heavy and liquid sloshed inside as it was lifted.

A smile, and then the figure in the hooded sweatshirt carried the gasoline inside.

· · · · ·

Tyrone loved the way the streets looked after a night's rain. The streetlights' fluorescent glow painted the asphalt with a liquid shimmer, and the air remained charged by the lingering power of the storm. The whole world seemed renewed, and for a short time he could forget the things he'd seen, forget his self-imposed role as the county's witness and just be a man, out alone in the night, glad to be alive.

Tyrone crouched behind a hedge at the front of the Duvalls'

house—a nondescript ranch in a solidly middle-class neigh-borhood. He had to be careful to stay well hidden whenever he observed anything in the suburbs. He was a fixture in town, part of the local color, and thus tolerated as long as he kept to downtown. But when he wandered into residential areas, he ceased being a local eccentric and suddenly became a prowler or peeping tom, and the phones at the Sheriff's Department started ringing. He enjoyed the challenge of remaining unseen in the burbs, and he sometimes came here just to keep his skills sharp. But he wasn't here for practice, not tonight.

He'd chosen to conceal himself behind a hedge on the east end of the Duvalls' house, as far away from their glowing porch light as he could get and still have a good view of the house across the street. There was nothing remarkable about its outward appearance—another in a long line of ranches on either side of Warwick Lane, this one with white-painted brick, black shut-ters, no trees in the yard, and a small flower bed up close to the house. What made this ranch special was who lived in it: Debbie Coulter.

Through a gap in the hedge, Tyrone could see a sheriff's cruiser parked at the curb, the deputy inside no doubt here to keep watch over Debbie's place, in case her attacker from last night returned. This was also the reason Tyrone was here, even though he ran the additional risk of being mistaken for Debbie's attacker should he be spotted. But that was all right. A bit of extra risk only added to the challenge.

Debbie's front porch light was on, as was the light above the garage door. No other lights were on, something Tyrone found surprising. He'd observed people after they'd experienced traumatic or violent events before, and for at least several days afterward they kept lights on inside their homes, no matter the lateness of the hour. Sometimes they kept all the lights on, often for weeks or, more rarely, months. But Debbie's windows were dark. She was home. He was sure of that. Otherwise the deputy wouldn't be sitting outside her house. Tyrone wondered if Debbie was trying to show the world—and of course her attacker—that she couldn't be intimidated. Or perhaps, being the mother of Carl the Cutter, she was more familiar with violence than most and not so deeply disturbed by it. He wondered if she were asleep, and if so, what dreams might plague her. Or was she awake, lying in bed and listening for the slightest of sounds—a crack of breaking glass, a squeal of a window being raised, stealthy footfalls sounding on her carpet?

Tyrone had no interest in preventing an assault on Debbie or revealing the identity of her attacker. He wasn't here to see justice done. Indeed, he wasn't certain the concept held any real meaning beyond an abstraction school children were programmed to believe in. Tyrone was here to watch whatever occurred, for good or ill. Despite Dale and Marshall Cross seeking information from him earlier, Tyrone preferred to remain as uninvolved as possible. A true observer never—

Before Tyrone could finish the thought he saw the cruiser's headlights flick on and heard the sound of its engine roaring to life. Tires squealed as the vehicle pulled away from the curb, rooftop lights flashing, siren whooping. The cruiser accelerated as it raced down Warwick Lane, and then it was gone.

Tyrone felt a pang of disappointment, followed by frustration. Obviously, the deputy was responding to an emergency of some sort, and that could only mean one thing. Tyrone had chosen the wrong vantage point from which to observe tonight. There was no way he could catch up to the deputy on foot, not in time to witness whatever events had drawn him away from his surveillance, but if he hurried, he might be able to observe the aftermath. He started to rise from his hiding place, but then he heard a soft snap, like the sound of a twig being stepped on, and he froze, breath caught in his throat.

The Duvalls weren't known for immaculate lawn care, and leaves and twigs were scattered about their yard. The sound had come from around the side of the house—the side closest to where Tyrone crouched. He held his breath and listened closely, but he didn't hear anything else. He told himself that it was probably just an animal, a cat or rabbit, raccoon or possum. Even in the suburbs there was an abundance of nocturnal animal life.

But he didn't believe it. He'd lived in Cross County too long and seen too much.

He was up and moving before the hand came reaching toward him. Though his decades as a watcher had taught him to move with silent grace, he wasn't a young man anymore, and he doubted he could run swiftly enough to escape his attacker in the open. Instead he shuffled sideways alongside the house, between the row of hedges and the brick, hoping whoever had made a grab for him was too large to follow—and unless he'd lived a lifetime on the streets without regular meals like Tyrone, he was bound to be.

Tyrone was halfway to the Duvalls' porch when a man-shaped silhouette appeared on the other side of the hedge and made another grab for him. Tyrone ducked and his attacker's gloved hands scraped against brick, eliciting a muffled curse from their owner. Tyrone crouched behind the laughingly inadequate protection of the hedge like a small frightened mammal that knew it couldn't escape and that the best it could hope for was a swift death. Tyrone was a master of concealment and evasion, but he knew those skills wouldn't save his life now. Fighting instinct so deeply ingrained it might as well have been inborn, he burst through the hedge, dashed past the shadowy figure, and ran across the Duvalls' yard toward the street. As he ran he didn't look back to see if he was pursued. He knew he was.

Motion across the street caught his eye, and he saw the curtains part in Debbie Coulter's picture window. He felt a desperate surge of hope. She *was* awake, and she was watching. If he could make it to her house, she'd let him in, and he'd be safe. They'd lock his pursuer out, and she'd call the sheriff, and then—

A hand clamped down on his shoulder with an iron grip, ending his run for freedom before he'd even made it halfway across the yard. As Tyrone was spun around to face his attacker, he opened his mouth to call out for help, though he knew the attempt came far too late. But before he could make a sound, his voice was quite literally cut off as razor-sharp steel slashed across his throat. Blood gushed from the wound and bubbled past his lips in a thick, wet cough. He knew he was dying, and while like anyone, he had a number of regrets, his biggest was that when he was gone, there would be no one in the county left to bear witness.

But he could do so one last time. With what remained of his fading willpower, he focused on the dark form standing before him. He knew everyone in the county, and he was certain he'd recognize his killer the instant he got a good look at his features. But even with the blue-white illumination of the streetlights to help him, Tyrone's vision was blurred and gray around the edges. The gray turned black as it spread, until Tyrone could no longer see a thing. His legs gave out beneath him, and he fell to the ground, slumping over onto his side.

Lying there, his blood soaking into the soil, a faint scent of gasoline in his nostrils, Tyrone Gantz died without seeing the face of his killer.

· · · · ·

Joanne's eyes snapped open, and she understood why when she heard the insistent warble of her cell phone. Her sleep—what little of it she'd gotten—had been blessedly dream-free, and for that reason alone she wanted to reach out, turn her phone off, roll over, and escape into soothing nothingness once more. But she picked up the phone and answered it. The man on the other end was Alec Bernstein, one of the deputies on night shift.

"Just got a call from dispatch, Sheriff. The Caffeine Café's on fire."

Joanne had been expecting to hear news of another murder, and it took several seconds for her to process what Alec had told her.

"Are firefighters on their way?"

"Sure thing, Sheriff. They're the ones who called dispatch."

She could hear the whoop of his siren in the background, and she knew the deputy was already on his way. She put her cell on speaker, placed it on the nightstand, and continued talking as she jumped out of bed and started to get dressed. "I figure it's too much of a coincidence that there should be a fire the night after the break-in and the murder. Maybe the killer set the fire, in which case maybe he'll stick around to watch the place burn. You know how firebugs are. Once you get there, take a good look around. If we're lucky, maybe we'll catch the sonofabitch."

"You got it, Sheriff. Anderson radioed me a minute ago. He's en route as well."

Joanne was in the process of buttoning her uniform shirt and she stopped.

"Danny's left the Coulter residence?"

Her displeasure must've come through in her tone, for Alec said, "Something wrong, Sheriff?"

The deputies on the night shift didn't normally call to clear their every move with her, which was how it should be. The action was at the Café right now, and there was a possibility they might have a chance to catch Ray Porter's murderer there. Still, she didn't like the idea of leaving Debbie unguarded. The thought gave her an all-too-familiar cold sick feeling in her stomach and a tingling at the base of her skull.

She finished doing up her buttons. "You two check out the situation at the Café. I'll go see how Debbie Coulter's doing. Call me if you find anything."

Without waiting for a reply, she grabbed her cell and disconnected. She stuck the phone in its belt pouch, grabbed her gun holster, and ran out of the bedroom without bothering to put it on. She couldn't afford to waste any more time.

She had a Feeling.

. . . . .

Debbie Coulter lay awake on the living room couch, TV and lights off, not thinking, not feeling, just being numb. She'd gotten precious little sleep the night before, and it looked like tonight was going to be a repeat. She wasn't too worried about her safety. Sheriff Talon had arranged for one of her deputies to watch over her tonight, and it was comforting to know that she wasn't alone.

When she heard the cruiser's engine start, she sat up. She rose from the couch and started toward the picture window when the high-pitched wail of a siren cut through the night, and flashing red lights were visible through the divide between the curtains. She ran the rest of way, grabbed hold of the cord, and opened the curtains just in time to see her guardian roar off down the street.

Though she knew there had to be a good reason for the deputy's departure, she couldn't help feeling abandoned. Maybe he'd return once the emergency was over. She hoped so. She didn't think she'd be able to make it through the night without someone—

Her thoughts trailed away as she saw movement across the street on the Duvalls' lawn. She didn't know them well. The couple kept their distance from her and wouldn't let their kids come anywhere near the mother of the infamous Carl the Cutter. But she knew them well enough to realize that the trenchcoated man running across the lawn was not Mr. Duvall, nor was the figure in the hooded sweatshirt pursuing him. She watched in horrified fascination as the first man fled toward the street, trenchcoat flaring open behind him like a pair of wings, the hooded man close behind, moving with the strength and grace of a predatory cat. The hooded man easily caught up with his prey, grabbed him by the shoulder—

Was that Tyrone Gantz? What the hell was he doing here, so far from downtown?

—and spun him around. The hooded man raised his right hand and light glinted off the metal object in his grip. The hand swept across Tyrone's throat—she was certain now that it was Tyrone—and a fountain of dark fluid that could only be blood gushed forth.

"God, no ... please ..." she said softly, not even aware she'd spoken.

Tyrone took a couple staggersteps to the left, then collapsed to the lawn. The hooded man regarded her for a moment before kneeling and rolling Tyrone onto his back. He pulled up Tyrone's shirt to expose his abdomen and began cutting.

A strange sense of unreality washed over Debbie then, and without consciously willing it, she turned away from the window and started walking toward the front door. Her fingers felt nothing as she turned the deadbolt and unlatched the chain. She watched her hand grip the knob, turn it, and push the door open. Cool night air washed over her. Although she wore only a nightgown she didn't shiver, and though her bare feet touched the porch's concrete, the sensation didn't register. She crossed the porch, stepped onto wet grass, and continued walking toward the street.

The hooded figure was still working on Tyrone, but he looked up as she reached the sidewalk and stepped into the rain-slick surface of Marwyck Lane. Though she tried to see the face within the hood, only darkness was visible, and she wondered if maybe Tyrone's killer didn't *have* a face, if instead of bone and flesh the hood was filled with solid shadow.

"Carl?" She spoke her son's name softly, but in the night's silence it sounded loud as a gunshot.

The hooded figure stood and began walking toward her, the instrument he'd used to cut Tyrone still held tight in his right hand. Debbie squinted as she tried to focus on the weapon, but it was difficult to make out details from this distance and in this light. Her Carl had used a hunting knife on his victims, but whatever the hooded figure held was smaller than that. For that matter, she'd never known her son to wear a hooded sweatshirt either. He'd been gone a long time, though, and it was only natural that he'd changed somewhat. She had too. She was older now, heavier, and she feared Carl wouldn't recognize her.

"Carl, honey. It's me. It's your mother."

She stepped to the center of the street, stopped and waited

for her boy to join her. The hooded figure continued walking toward Debbie with a determined stride, and she wondered what he would do when he reached her. Would he embrace her? Cut her throat? Either would be all right with her, just as long as they could be together one last time.

As Carl stepped off the curb, Debbie smiled and raised her arms, beckoning her son to come to her. Everything would be okay now that her baby had returned.

She saw bright lights out of the corner of her eye, heard the sound of a car approaching at high speed. She turned and saw a sheriff's cruiser coming down the street toward them, roof lights flashing an angry red. But instead of slowing as the vehicle approached, it angled toward Carl and accelerated.

"No!" Debbie shouted. "You can't take my boy from me! Not again!" She ran between the oncoming cruiser and her son, determined to do whatever it took to protect him. She'd failed Carl when he was alive, hadn't seen the signs of madness and evil growing within him, hadn't prevented them from taking him over. She wouldn't fail him again.

"Run, honey!" Debbie shouted. She didn't turn to see if her boy heeded her words. Standing awash in the headlights' glare, she squeezed her eyes shut and waited for the impact to come.

· · · · ·

"Shit!"

Joanne yanked the steering wheel hard to the left and slammed on the brakes. Her cruiser skidded on the wet asphalt, jumped the curb, and plowed into the yard of the house across the street from Debbie's place. She held on as the ass-end of the vehicle spun around, rear tires churning up a spray of grass and soil, before finally coming to stop with the grill facing the street. She hadn't felt an impact, but she was relieved to see Debbie standing in the middle of the street, unharmed. She was even more relieved to see the man in the hooded sweatshirt running away from Debbie. As Joanne had approached, she'd seen the body lying in the yard, along with the glint of her headlights reflecting off the blade held in the hooded man's hand. You didn't have to be a trained law-enforcement professional to do the math on this one. She'd intended to ram the sonofabitch with her cruiser to save Debbie's life, but she hadn't counted on the woman turning psycho on her at the last instant and throwing herself into the cruiser's path.

Joanne jumped out of her vehicle and drew her 9 mm. "Are you all right?" she shouted to Debbie. But the woman didn't look at her. Instead she faced her fleeing attacker, hands cupped to her mouth, and yelled, "Run, Carl! Don't let them take you again, baby!"

A chill rippled down Joanne's spine upon hearing Debbie's words, but she dismissed it. The man in the hooded sweatshirt was more slender than Carl Coulter. She realized then that for an instant she had actually considered the possibility that the attacker might be Debbie's dead son. *Maybe Debbie isn't the only one going psycho around here,* she thought.

"Get back in your house and lock the door until I return!" Joanne had no idea whether Debbie was lucid enough to obey her order, but she appeared to be uninjured, which was a hell of a lot more than could be said for the person lying in the yard. Joanne unclipped the flashlight from her belt as she ran over, but even before she turned the beam on, she knew the man was beyond anyone's help. His eyes were wide and staring, his throat had been slashed, and a triangle bisected by a jagged lightning bolt had been carved into his stomach. She supposed she shouldn't have been, but she was surprised to see the dead man was Tyrone

Gantz. Had he been killed because he'd witnessed the break-in at the Caffeine Café last night, or had he simply been in the wrong place at the wrong time? Either way, she decided, the poor man was just as dead.

Joanne didn't have to consider her next move. Debbie wasn't hurt, Tyrone was very dead, and his murderer—who definitely was not and *could* not be Carl Coulter—was hauling ass out of here. Two people had been killed in her county in the last twenty-four hours, and Joanne was determined that there wouldn't be a third. She took off running after the hooded man.

In the time it had taken her to check on Debbie and Tyrone, the killer had disappeared between two houses, and Joanne headed in the same direction. As she followed, she was well aware that the killer might be lying in wait for her, so she swept her flashlight's beam back and forth as she ran. The light would give away her position, but it would make it damned difficult for the killer to jump out of the dark and ambush her. Of course, if he had a gun in addition to his knife . . .

No. If he'd had a gun he'd have used it on her when she first arrived on the scene. A man like him didn't shy away from bloodshed, but he was the type who preferred to do his killing up close and personal. Shooting her wouldn't have been any fun for him.

Joanne passed between the houses and saw that neither had privacy fences enclosing their backyards. She assumed the killer had scoped out the location earlier and chosen this as his escape route for that very reason. Most likely he had a vehicle parked somewhere close by, probably on the next street over, and that's where he was headed right now. She had to catch up to him fast or he'd get into his car and vanish into the night. There'd be no way she could get back to her vehicle in time to give chase, and her other deputies were at the Caffeine Café, checking out a fire she was now sure had been set to draw away the man guarding Debbie. They couldn't help. It was all up to her.

Breathing hard, sweat cold on her face in the autumn air, she stopped near a concrete birdbath in one of the yards and panned her flashlight beam around, listening for the thump-thump-thump of feet pounding on the ground. But she saw nothing, and the only sound she heard was the throbbing of her own pulse in her ears. No engine noise, though, so she knew the killer hadn't reached his vehicle yet.

She was debating whether to continue searching the yard or run over to the next street and check there when she finally heard the tell-tale rustle of someone moving through the grass—coming from behind her. She started to spin around but it was too late. She felt something hard collide with the back of her skull, saw a bright white flash behind her eyes, then darkness rushed in to swallow her. Her last coherent thought was that it was too bad she'd never get to hear Dale chide her for screwing up so badly.

· · · · ·

Though it was closing in on three in the morning, Marshall still wore his suit. It had been a busy night and he was bone-weary. It took an effort to walk up the steps to Sanctity's second floor, and he thought, *The years must finally be catching up with me.*

After Joanne and Dale had left, he'd been forced to play host to visiting relatives for the remainder of the evening. After-dinner cocktails liberally seasoned with stultifying conversation—most of it from lower-ranking family members desperate to curry favor with him—eventually culminating in a Gathering before the Reliquary. Leading the ceremony always took a great deal out of him, so much so that he'd almost begged off tonight, but considering the current situation in the county, he'd gone through with it. Who knows? Perhaps it would help.

But now that the relatives were bedded down for the night—finally—and the servants had finished clearing away the detritus of the evening's revels, Marshall could get some sleep ... after performing one final task.

He reached the second floor and made his way through the halls without aid of illumination, for no member of the family, even those coming to Sanctity for the first time, needed light to help find their way around. He stopped when he came to Lenora's bedroom and took hold of the doorknob, but he hesitated before turning it. He knew it wasn't locked. No door in Sanctity was. But his relationship with Lenora was strained enough as it was, and he was reluctant to damage it any further by checking up on her as if she were a little girl. Nevertheless, he was the family's Second, the one responsible for seeing to its affairs in the outer world. And most importantly, he was Lenora's father. He *had* to check on her.

But before Marshall could open the door, his cell phone vibrated in his jacket pocket. He stepped back into the middle of the hallway to answer it, already knowing he wasn't going to like what he was about to hear.

"Yes?" he said in a hushed voice.

It was Glenn Gilman, a firefighter who over the years had racked up a truly impressive amount of debt betting on college football—debt Marshall had made disappear in exchange for the man's lifelong service. He listened without comment as Glenn told him about a fire at the Caffeine Café and, though the details weren't clear as yet, some sort of disturbance at Debbie Coulter's house. When the man was finished, Marshall disconnected without saying a word. He slipped the phone back into his pocket, walked up to Lenora's door, turned the door knob, and entered. His fingers found the light switch on the wall, and he flipped it on.

Lenora's bedding was in disarray, but his daughter was nowhere to be seen.

CHAPTER SIXTEEN

Come dawn, only a blackened husk remained of the Caffeine Café. The charred wood still smoldered in places despite having been drenched by fire hoses, and the parking lot was a wet, sooty mess. The air stank of burnt plastic and wiring, and breathing in the acrid stench coated the throat and sinuses with a greasy chemical residue. The firefighters were gone, having done everything they could, and now it was up to the Sheriff's Department to deal with the remains. Though just what they could do, Joanne—as the saying went in law enforcement—hadn't a goddamned clue.

She stood in the café's empty parking lot, almost in the same spot where she'd stood yesterday morning. News vans were parked on the street, and the on-the-scene reporters stood in front of cameramen, hair and makeup impeccable though the sun had barely risen above the eastern horizon. Joanne wouldn't have been surprised to learn that these men and women weren't human, but rather newsdroids that were activated whenever a big story broke. That would certainly explain their always-perfect hair and clothes, along with their empty bright gazes and plastic smiles.

They'd already finished getting a statement from her, not that she had a lot to tell them, and now they were fighting for Marshall's attention—which was just fine with Joanne. For once she was grateful for him showing up at the scene of an investigation. Her head throbbed so much she felt like she'd mainlined a case of tequila last night. The last thing she wanted to do was talk to anyone, especially more newsdroids. The "local community leader" could keep the media at bay so she could do her job.

"What would you like me to do, Sheriff?"

Ronnie spoke in a normal tone of voice, but his words sounded loud as cannon fire to her ears and set her skull to pounding harder.

"I appreciate you coming to work today, Ronnie, but I think the rest of us have the situation in hand."

As soon as she said it, she'd wished she'd chosen her words more carefully. Ronnie's right hand—gloveless for a change—was swollen, fingers wrapped in surgical tape. He wore his arm in a sling, and from what she could see it was his sole concession to his injury.

She hurried on. "I've got people both out here and over at Debbie Coulter's." Not long after she'd regained consciousness, she'd called in every deputy to work the two crime scenes. But once she saw Ronnie's injured hand—the result, he said, of slipping and falling on rain-slick pavement outside the state crime lab in Columbus—she'd started having second thoughts about calling him in. Not only did his hand look awful, she knew he had to be hurting bad because he'd not only shown up without gloves on either hand, he wasn't wearing a surgical mask and, for the first time since she'd met him, he hadn't shaved before coming to work. His hair was unkempt and oily, too, and she thought he hadn't showered. Before today she would've thought it impossible for Ronnie to neglect his hygiene like this. He must be in agony, she thought. It was the only explanation for his appearance.

"Why don't you go to the hospital and get your hand looked at?" she said. "Bad as it looks, something's sure to be broken. You need to get it set." Hell, he'd probably need surgery.

"I went to the ER in Columbus after I dropped off the evidence. The docs said it looks a lot worse than it is. I should be fine, long as I can keep from bumping it into anything. Besides, they gave me some great pain pills." He grinned, displaying yellow-tinged teeth. His breath smelled stale and foul, and Joanne realized he hadn't brushed his teeth.

No big deal, she thought. He'd probably gotten home late last night, taken his pain meds, and conked out. When he'd gotten the call to come in this morning, she figured he'd been too groggy to do anything other than get dressed and stumble out the door. Still, he didn't *look* groggy. His eyes were bright and alert, and there was a gleam in them she couldn't remember seeing before.

"Not to be disrespectful," Ronnie said, "but have *you* been to the hospital yet? A head injury is nothing to mess around with."

"I'm feeling all right," she lied. "If I start to get worse, I'll go get checked out, okay?" She thought for a moment. "If you're feeling up to it, I suppose you could work crowd control." It was so early that not many looky-loo's had arrived yet, but that was sure to change as the morning wore on.

"Sounds good, Sheriff." Ronnie's gaze flicked to where Marshall stood talking with an attractive model-thin redhead from Action Eye News. The gleam she'd detected a moment ago intensified for an instant, and if she hadn't known Ronnie better, she would've described the look he gave Marshall as one of cold hatred. But then the deputy returned his gaze to her, showed his yellowed teeth in a smile once more, then headed off to get to work.

Something wasn't right here, but Joanne's head hurt too much for her to think straight. *Maybe I should ask Ronnie for some of his meds,* she thought.

She turned to look as a Jeep pulled up to join the caravan of sheriff's cruisers, newsvans, and Marshall's Hummer. The newsdroids got excited at the prospect of having a new face to shove their microphones into, but when they saw Dale get out of the vehicle, their interest died. Reporters only interviewed another reporter when they were desperate.

Dale kept glancing around as he walked across the parking lot toward Joanne. At first she thought he was taking in the scene, noting details that he would write about later. But there was a nervousness verging on desperation to his manner that made her think about the way he'd behaved last night when they'd parted company at Sanctity. Was everyone in this goddamned county going crazy?

As Dale joined her, he said, "In my completely unprofessional medical opinion, you look like shit."

"Right back at you."

The flesh beneath Dale's eyes was swollen and dark, and the eyes themselves seemed to have receded into the sockets somewhat since last she'd seen him. His wrinkles were more pronounced, the lines longer and deeper, and the skin hung lax on his face. His hair and beard were in disarray, and his suit was rumpled, his tie loose and hanging askew.

"I got ambushed like a rookie last night and got hit on the head by a rock," she said. "What's your excuse?"

Dale hesitated before replying. "I drove all night. Thinking."

"The *whole* night?"

He shrugged. "I had a lot to think about."

Joanne thought he was telling her the truth—he certainly looked like he'd been up all night—but not the entire truth.

"Look, Dale, you know I try to respect your privacy, but I'm really starting to worry about you. Tell me what's going on. I'm your friend. I can help."

Dale smiled wearily. "I appreciate that, Joanne. More than I can say. But the problem I have right now is one that I really don't want to share—with anyone. I'll find a way to shake it. Somehow."

Joanne was about to tell Dale that she had no idea what the hell he was talking about, but before she could speak, Marshall detached himself from the newsdroids and came toward them. As soon as his back was to the cameras, his smile fell away and a troubled look came over his features. He stopped when he reached them and stared at the café's ruins for a moment.

"This is starting to piss me off."

His voice was low and dangerous. There was anger and frustration in his tone, and Joanne thought she detected a bit of fear as well, though she couldn't imagine he'd ever admit to it.

"Join the club," she said. She saw no point in wasting time, so she asked, "How much do the two of you know?"

The three compared notes and, as she expected, both Dale and Marshall were already up to speed on last night's events for the most part. Dale had his police scanner and Marshall . . . well, Marshall had his own information network spread throughout the county. She quickly filled in the blanks for them.

When she finished, Marshall asked, "Where is Debbie now?"

"At Resurrection Hospital," Joanne said. "I assigned a deputy to guard her room, with strict orders not to leave his post for any reason short of the end of the world."

"A number of the family work there," Marshall said. "I'll make sure they keep watch over her." He took out his cell phone and stepped away from Joanne and Dale to make the call.

"Must be nice to be a puppetmaster," Dale said with a sneer.

"Depends on the puppets," Joanne replied. She glanced at Ronnie. He was walking the perimeter of the scene to make sure no unauthorized personnel came too close, but his gaze remained fixed on Marshall.

"So what do we have?" Dale said. "The person who killed Tyrone and attacked you matches the description Tyrone gave of the vandal who spray-painted Debbie's car and broke into the café."

"Not much to go on. Anyone could wear a hooded sweatshirt. Other than a rough similarity in physical type, there's nothing to prove they were the same person. Tyrone didn't get a good look at the vandal's features the other night, and I didn't see my attacker clearly either."

Marshall had finished his call and now rejoined them. Dale nodded toward the cluster of TV reporters.

"I guess even the vaunted Cross connections couldn't keep the vultures at bay forever."

Marshall ignored him and addressed Joanne. "I overheard what you were discussing."

Joanne didn't bother asking how Marshall could have listened in on their conversation at the same time he was talking on his phone several yards away. It was one more in a number of weird things she was beginning to take for granted about him.

"What about Debbie?" he continued. "Did she get a good look at whoever it was?"

"Hard to say. After I came to I found her still standing in the street. I questioned her, but the stress of the last couple nights must've gotten to her, and she wasn't in her right mind. All she could tell me was that her son had come back to her."

Marshall raised an eyebrow. "She thinks the killer is literally Carl Coulter?"

"As near as I can tell," Joanne said.

"But the descriptions both you and Tyrone gave don't match Carl's physical type," Dale said.

Joanne almost laughed. "You sound as if you believe it's possible for a man executed in prison to come back to life years later and pick up where he left off."

Marshall didn't respond, and when Joanne looked at Dale, he had a thoughtful, worried expression on his face. She wanted to tell them that they were both nuts, but then she thought of how she'd seen Carl in the Deveraux barn and of the dream she'd had of him last night. Suddenly the two men standing with her no longer seemed quite so crazy.

"Last night's events would seem to strongly link Ray Porter's murder and the original break-in at the café," Marshall said. "Let's assume for the moment that it was the same person who committed all of these crimes. The big question before us is why whoever it is didn't kill Joanne once she was unconscious."

"Don't sound so disappointed," she muttered.

"Don't joke like that," Marshall said, then he surprised her by reaching out and gently squeezing her hand. "Your death would be an unbearable loss to the county."

He still had hold of her hand, and she had to resist the urge to squeeze back. "*Just* to the county?"

He held her hand a moment longer before finally letting go.

"At the risk of making a pun," Dale said, "could we please get back to the business at hand?"

Joanne felt her cheeks burn with embarrassment, and she was surprised to see Marshall color a bit as well.

"That's the first question I asked myself when I came to," she admitted. "I didn't have an answer then, and I don't have one now."

"Perhaps the killer feared you'd already called for backup and deputies were on their way," Dale said.

"Maybe," Marshall replied, "but it doesn't take long to cut a throat and carve a simple design into a body, especially when your victim is unconscious." Both Joanne and Dale stared at him, and he quickly added, "Not that I have firsthand knowledge of such procedures."

"Did the owners of the house wake up?" Dale asked. "Did they turn on the back porch light or anything?"

Joanne shook her head and instantly regretted it when the motion made the throbbing worse. "Believe it or not, the Duvalls slept through the whole thing."

"My guess is the killer set the café on fire to draw away the deputy guarding Debbie and to keep the rest of you busy," Dale said, "which means she was the intended target. That makes poor Tyrone what? An unexpected bonus?"

Dale's voice held barely restrained anguish, and Joanne knew what her friend was thinking. If he hadn't gone to Tyrone for information, the man might still be alive today.

"I believe Tyrone went to Debbie's last night hoping to get a look at some action," Joanne said, "and the killer discovered his presence and decided to take out a potential witness."

"He got more than a look," Marshall said. "He got an extreme close-up."

Joanne ignored him. "There's nothing to indicate Tyrone was targeted on purpose. The killer would've had no way to know he would be there." Joanne had hoped to reassure Dale, but she could see that he didn't feel any better.

"Maybe," Dale said. "But it seems like an awfully big coincidence, doesn't it?"

"One too many, if you ask me," Marshall said. He seemed

to debate with himself a moment before adding, "I spoke with Tyrone yesterday afternoon. It was . . . how I learned that Lenora had gone for a drive with the Porter boy." He held up a hand. "And before either of you ask, neither Lenora nor I lied to you last night. The truth needed no alteration."

"Perhaps you told the truth as you believed it," Dale said. "But how do you know Lenora didn't lie to us—*all* of us?"

Marshall glared at Dale for a long moment, but then his anger drained out of him. His shoulders slumped and he averted his gaze.

"My daughter has been missing since last night. I'm not sure when she left exactly, but she took one of the cars—a BMW. No one saw her go, and though I have every eye I own in the county looking for her, so far no one has reported seeing her."

Joanne didn't ask if he had any idea where she'd gone. If he had, he'd have already checked there. Instead, she asked, "You're sure she left alone? There *were* a lot of people at Sanctity last night."

"There are *always* a lot of guests," Marshall said. "But they are all accounted for. And to answer your next question, she left of her own free will. None of the alarm systems in the house or garage were activated, and no one could've forced Lenora to give them the access codes."

Considering what little she'd seen of Lenora last night, Joanne could believe it. "In this case, maybe your daughter going missing really *is* a coincidence." She thought of her conversation with Althea Cross last night, a conversation Marshall was evidently unaware of. "The two of you seemed to have a strained relationship. Did you have an argument yesterday? Maybe she left because she was mad at you."

Marshall stiffened. "I'd know if my daughter was that angry with me."

"You didn't know she'd gone parking with Ray Porter," Dale pointed out. He spoke with more compassion that Joanne expected, but then she realized the two men had something in common. They'd both lost wives. She wondered if Dale knew the truth about Charlotte Cross's disappearance. He must, she decided. "There are many things we don't know about the people in our lives," Dale continued. "Things we often don't want to know, and so we turn a blind eye toward them. There are so many frightening things in this world, but of them all, the most terrifying is the truth."

Marshall regarded Dale for a long moment, then said, "You sound like a man who speaks from experience."

Dale replied with a brief smile. "I wish I wasn't."

"I'll inform my people to start looking for Lenora," Joanne said. "Just in case."

Marshall looked like he wanted to argue, but in the end he merely nodded.

Silence descended on the three of them after that, and for a time they watched Joanne's deputies poke around the blackened ruins of the Caffeine Café.

"This is going to break Debbie's heart when she learns about it," Dale said. "Ever since she lost her husband and son, this place was all she had. It was her whole life, a way she could give a little something back to the community Carl took so much from." He turned to Joanne. "She doesn't know yet, right?"

"I didn't think she was ready to hear about the fire," Joanne said. "Not in the state she's in."

"I've been reconsidering my earlier thoughts on Debbie's situation," Marshall said. "Even with members of the family watching over her, the hospital isn't a safe place for her. The killer may well make another try for her there. The only place in the world where

TIM WAGGONER

226

she'll truly be safe is within the walls of Sanctity. I propose we remove her from the hospital and take her to my home."

"But she needs medical care," Joanne said.

"And she shall receive it," Marshall replied. "Remember, most of the doctors in this county are related to the Crosses in one way or another. I'll have no problem finding an excellent physician to stay with her."

Joanne was reluctant to agree to Marshall's plan, for the simple reason that she'd be turning over control of Debbie's protection to the Crosses. But then again, Debbie *would* be well guarded at Sanctity—assuming Marshall was telling the truth when he said he wanted to keep her safe. Maybe he had an ulterior motive for wanting to house Debbie at Sanctity, though she couldn't imagine what it might be.

"Not to sound callous," Dale said, "but leaving Debbie in the hospital might be the best way to draw the killer out into the open. It could be our best chance to catch him."

"I will not allow you to use her as bait," Marshall said.

Joanne winced as she felt a sensation of pressure behind her forehead that only added to the pain she already felt. Dale must've experienced something similar, for he grimaced and took a step back from Marshall. But Dale quickly recovered and shot back. "Since when did you give a shit about the welfare of anyone not clinging to the highest branches of the diseased growth you call a family tree?"

Marshall's expression became one of poorly restrained fury, and he took a step toward Dale.

Joanne interposed herself between the two men, but before she could tell them to knock it the hell off, her cell phone rang. She checked the incoming number on the display and recognized it.

"If you two can hold off killing each other for a moment, Terry's calling." She stepped away from Dale and Marshall, who continued glaring at one another but kept their distance, and she answered the phone.

"Hi, lover," Terry said. "I don't suppose your day's off to too good a start, huh?"

She sighed. "How did you guess?"

"I'm just lucky like that. Your head still hurt?"

"It's a little better," she lied. She'd let Terry take a look at it when he'd arrived at the scene of Tyrone's murder, and while he said she didn't appear to have a concussion, she should really be checked out over at the hospital. Her reply, *I've never been one to follow doctor's orders. Out of bed, anyway.*

"I've finished a preliminary examination of Tyrone's body, and while I still need to do an autopsy, I can tell you the man was in surprisingly decent shape for someone who lived on the streets. His wounds are exactly the same as those on Ray Porter. I have no doubt the same person killed both men." His voice shifted from detached professionalism to a much warmer tone. "I'm just grateful the sonofabitch only conked you on the noggin."

She smiled. "Anything else?"

"Not yet. How about you?"

She told him about Lenora being missing and Marshall's plan to take Debbie to Sanctity.

"That strikes me as a screwed-up strategy, quite frankly. Can you afford to let him do that? Wouldn't that count as some kind of unprofessional conduct for your department?"

She frowned, surprised by his reaction. "I know you're not a big fan of the Crosses, but I'm inclined to trust Marshall on this." Until she said it, she hadn't known she'd come to a decision.

"I'm glad you and *Marshall* understand each other so well." Terry's voice dripped with sarcasm.

"Look, I don't know what your problem is, but I really don't need this shit right now."

Terry was quiet so long that Joanne thought the call had been dropped. But then he said, "I'm sorry. Neither of us has gotten enough sleep the last couple nights. How about we pretend we didn't snap at each other, and I'll call you later after I finish Tyrone's autopsy?"

She felt like arguing further, but she knew he was right. She was too sleep-deprived and stressed to think straight, and if their conversation continued, one or both of them would eventually say something they'd regret.

"Sure thing. Talk to you later." Joanne disconnected before Terry could reply. As she tucked her phone back into its belt holder, she thought of what Dale had said about how there were many things we don't know about the people in our lives. She'd just gotten a glimpse of a different side of Terry Birch, and it was one she didn't especially like.

She returned to Dale and Marshall, glad to see that both men had refrained from attacking one another, though from the glares they still exchanged, it hadn't been easy. She told them about Terry's initial analysis of Tyrone's injuries, but neither commented. What was there to say? It wasn't as if the news came as any great surprise.

"I'd like to go get Debbie now," Marshall said. "The sooner she's at Sanctity, the sooner she'll be safe."

"What do you think, Dale?" Joanne asked.

Dale continued scowling at Marshall, but he said, "As much as it pains me to say this, I think Marshall's right. It would be wrong to use Debbie as bait, and she would be safest at Sanctity. It's a good plan—provided Debbie agrees to it."

"She will," Marshall said, a bit too quickly.

Joanne didn't like the sound of that, but she decided not to make an issue of it right then. "Okay, but I have one condition. That I go with you to take Debbie to Sanctity." Her deputies could handle processing the two crime scenes—the ruins of the café and the Duvalls' yard. She'd let Debbie down once by not personally protecting her, and she was determined not to fail her again.

Marshall looked for a moment as if he might argue, but then he forced a smile. "Of course. I'd enjoy the pleasure of your company."

"Thanks for the sentiment, but we're not going on a date." She turned to Dale. "What about you? I'd like to hear that you're going to go home and get some sleep, but I know you better than that."

He gave her a tired smile. "Actually, that's precisely what I was . . ." He trailed off and his gaze flicked to the side as if something had caught his attention. Joanne looked in the direction he was staring, but she saw nothing special, just an empty section of sidewalk.

"Is something wrong?" she asked.

Dale didn't answer right away, and she began to worry that the last couple of days had taken a greater toll on her friend than she'd realized. But then he snapped out of his daze and turned his attention back to her.

"I'm fine. I just had an idea about a . . . a possible lead. It might not be anything," he hastened to add. "But I'll check into it and let you know, all right?"

Joanne frowned. It wasn't like Dale to be mysterious like this. Not with her, at any rate. She couldn't help feeling a bit hurt, but she told herself that maybe Dale didn't feel he could speak freely in Marshall's presence. She was just going to have to trust Dale, which wasn't a problem. There was no one on earth she trusted more.

"All right. Give me a call on my cell, okay?"

Dale nodded, but he seemed distracted once more, and he turned again to look at that empty piece of sidewalk.

"Yeah, sure," he murmured.

Joanne waited a second to see if he would say anything more, and when he didn't she turned and started heading toward her cruiser. Marshall accompanied her.

"We'll take my Hummer," he said.

"Like hell," Joanne countered. "As of now this is official Sheriff's Department business. We'll take my vehicle."

Marshall sighed. "If you insist."

She saw Ronnie standing off to the side, keeping a close watch on a couple over-eager TV reporters who were slowly moving closer to the café's remains.

"Just give me a minute."

Marshall glanced in Ronnie's direction, an unreadable expression on his face. "I'll wait here."

She walked over to where Ronnie stood, not far from a blackened pile of debris. He looked over as she approached.

"Yes, Sheriff?"

She was struck anew by his unclean appearance—not to mention his odor—and while she didn't have a Feeling about it, she knew something was seriously wrong here. But she didn't have time to deal with it now. *Later,* she promised herself. *Once Debbie's safe.*

She quickly told Ronnie what she planned to do and asked that he pass word along to his fellow deputies.

"Someone should go out to the Deveraux Farm and take

another look around," she added. "Just in case the killer returned there last night." The killer had left Ray Porter's wallet in the barn. Maybe he'd left something of Tyrone's this time.

Ronnie nodded. "I'll see to it, Sheriff." He looked past her toward Marshall, and his eyes narrowed. "Do you have to go with *him* to get Mrs. Coulter?"

Joanne was puzzled by Ronnie's question. "I don't *have* to, but I'm *going* to. Why do you ask?"

"Just watch yourself. He's not to be trusted."

Before she could ask him to explain further, he turned and headed off to talk to the reporters who had crept even closer to the crime scene while Ronnie and she had been talking. She was definitely going to have to talk to Ronnie soon, and when she did, she'd insist that he take some time off, whether he liked it or not.

"Call me if you find anything," she said, and then she turned and headed back toward Marshall. On the way, she looked for Dale and saw him standing on the same stretch of sidewalk he'd been so interested in a few moments earlier. She knew it was crazy, but it almost looked like he was listening to something . . . or someone.

■ ■ ■ ■ ■

After Ronnie finished shooing the reporters back to where they belonged, he watched one of the deputies taking photos of charred wood and melted wiring. Normally he would've been the one collecting the evidence, but he was glad he wasn't today. It was a waste of time, for whatever evidence they gathered, Marshall Cross would just make it disappear. Make *Ronnie* make it disappear.

He hadn't made it home from Columbus until well after midnight last night. When he got to his house, he walked inside, not bothering to wipe his feet on the doormat, not noticing let alone caring about the mud he tracked in on the carpeting. He went straight to the kitchen, pulled out a chair from the table, sat down, and waited until dispatch had called him in just after daybreak.

He'd reported for duty, not because he believed in his job anymore. Justice wasn't possible as long as a man like Marshall Cross existed. He'd come to work because he didn't want to let Sheriff Jo-Jo down. And because he knew that sooner or later, he'd get an opportunity to take out Cross.

That opportunity had come sooner than expected, and ever since the man—if indeed that's what he truly was—had arrived, Ronnie had contemplated how best to kill the sonofabitch. If Cross had been an ordinary man, it would be simple. Ronnie would just walk up to the bastard, draw his 9 mm, jam the muzzle to his temple and squeeze the trigger. From the moment he'd sat down in his kitchen last night, he'd practiced drawing his weapon—unloaded, of course—with his left hand and firing it. He was hardly ambidextrous, but he was confident he could get the job done. Sheriff Jo-Jo would then have no choice but to take Ronnie in and his career in law enforcement would be over. But he didn't care. If the last act he performed as a deputy sheriff was to take out a monster like Marshall Cross, it would be worth the cost.

But Cross wasn't an ordinary man, and Ronnie didn't know if he'd be able to conceal his intentions from the man long enough to finish him off. If Cross had even an inkling of what Ronnie planned, he'd use his . . . *influence* to stop him. And then Ronnie would be arrested for attempted murder and Cross would still be alive.

Even so, his left hand itched to draw his 9 mm. He almost

did it, too, but he resisted. He needed to wait until Cross was so distracted that he wouldn't see death coming until it was too late for him to do anything about it, even with his goddamned powers.

He watched the sheriff get in her cruiser, while Cross took the front passenger seat. A moment later, they pulled away from the curb, the reporters shooting video of their departure. And then they were gone. Ronnie felt a stab of disappointment that he'd lost his chance to kill Cross, but he told himself to be patient and keep going through the motions of his job and wait for the perfect opportunity to blow Marshall Cross's head off. And he'd start by doing as Jo-Jo had asked. He'd go out to the Deveraux Farm. Who knows? Maybe he'd find something sharp and nasty there to use on Cross instead of his 9 mm. Something more fun. Maybe something rusty.

Smiling, he headed off to let the other deputies know where he was going.

CHAPTER SEVENTEEN

I imagine you're wondering if you've lost your mind," Tyrone said.

"The thought had occurred to me," Dale admitted.

Standing on the sidewalk in front of him, looking very much alive, was Tyrone Gantz. The flesh on his throat was smooth and unmarked, and Dale knew that if he asked Tyrone to lift his shirt and expose his abdomen, his stomach would also display no sign of injury.

"Can I touch you?" Dale asked.

Tyrone shrugged. "If you want."

With a trembling hand, Dale reached out and touched Tyrone's right cheek. He half expected his fingers to pass through the man's face as if it were no more than an illusion, or perhaps to find the flesh hard and cold as marble. But it just felt like ordinary skin.

Dale lowered his hand, amused to find himself disappointed. "I'd ask if you somehow managed to survive the killer's attack, but no one else sees you, do they? Only me."

"That's right. I had the strongest connection to you in life. That connection remains in death."

It was eerie to hear Tyrone speak of his own ghostly state so matter-of-factly. Dale wanted to believe that he'd finally slipped over the edge into insanity, but he knew he couldn't be so lucky. He'd come to accept so many bizarre things since moving to Cross County years ago that holding a conversation with a recently deceased acquaintance seemed relatively normal, all things considered.

"And before you ask, I don't know who killed me. I have no insight to offer into the afterlife, and I can't tell you anything about your wife and daughter."

Dale hadn't gotten over his surprise at seeing Tyrone's ghost to even begin to formulate questions yet, but those were indeed the first ones he would've asked, though not necessarily in that order. He felt a pang of loss for something he'd never quite dared to hope for: a way to connect to the spirits of his lost loved ones.

"Why not?"

Tyrone frowned, as if he were trying to recall a long-forgotten memory. "I don't know. One moment I was lying on the grass, looking up at the night sky, then everything went black and now I'm standing here. I know I'm dead, and I know only you can see me, but otherwise . . ." He shrugged again.

Dale sighed. "Nothing personal, but what's the point of the spirit of a murdered man returning to the world of the living if he can't help bring his killer to justice?"

"I can still bear witness," Tyrone said. "That's the most important thing to me." He smiled. "And who said I can't help? I may not possess otherworldly insight, but I can still think. Sadie wasn't able to tell you the name of Carl Coulter's father, but it occurs to me that there's someone else who might be able to."

"Don't say Debbie. Even if she were inclined to reveal that information to me, she's not in the clearest frame of mind after last night. I couldn't be sure she was telling us the truth."

"I'm not talking about Debbie Coulter. I think you should pay a visit to Eve. No one knows more about the secrets of Cross County, not even Althea—and supposedly they're sisters. But be warned. Eve doesn't reveal her secrets for free."

Dale's gut twisted with cold nausea. Over the years he'd heard rumors about the high price Eve charged for her favors, and as a result, he'd never sought her assistance. Quite frankly, he'd been scared to. But now it looked like he had nowhere else to turn. "Thanks for the suggestion. Will I . . . see you around?"

Tyrone grinned. "You're the only one who ever will." He turned and started to head down the sidewalk. Dale noticed Tyrone cast no shadow and his footfalls made no sound. Now *that* was more like it.

Tyrone stopped walking for a moment and looked back over his shoulder at Dale.

"By the way, your black-furred friend is hiding in the shadows under your Jeep. Be careful. He's hungry."

Dale cast a nervous glance toward his vehicle. The shadows were indeed thick beneath it, and though he could see nothing within the blackness, he didn't doubt Tyrone's word.

"I know you don't have any otherworldly knowledge to share, but do you have any advice on what I can do about that thing?"

Tyrone considered.

"Get into your Jeep fast and pull in your legs before the damned thing catches hold of you." With that, Tyrone resumed walking away.

"Thanks loads," Dale muttered. He took a deep breath and started toward his Jeep.

. . . . .

Kneeling in the dark, eyes closed but still seeing—staring eyes in pale faces, bloody gashes in throats, designs carved into stomachs with a steady, loving hand. Four of them, and she knows their names as well as she does her own. Better, in fact, for she's not quite sure who she is at the moment. But that's okay. She'll figure it out.

Each of the four was dead before he started in with his design work, but he heard their screams nevertheless. Screams of anger, hatred, and violation. Were they real or had they existed only in his mind? She decides it doesn't matter. Either way, their cries are still the sweetest sounds she's ever heard.

The smells were real, though, that's for certain. The four were kept here for days upon days, closed up in the summer heat and allowed to ripen. She takes in a breath and nearly gags on the foulness as it passes into her nostrils, coils down her throat, and assaults her lungs. She read somewhere once that when you smell, you actually take tiny particles of the thing you're smelling into your body. If that's true, then she's just drawn in a double lungful of Death.

Delicious.

There's power here, different than dominating another's mind with a push. Greater. For Death comes to all things, even those that aren't what most people would think of as living—soil, water, air . . . creation itself. In the end, everything must surrender to the ultimate darkness and become Nothing. It's so elegantly profound, so unimaginably beautiful. Why hasn't she ever understood this before?

Because until last night, a voice—a male voice—whispers in her mind, *you didn't have me.*

She smiles in the dark. True.

She hears the sound of the barn door opening and light—harsh, glaring, hated light—penetrates the barn's soothing gloom. She feels a wave of disappointment. She was having *such* a good time.

She grips the hunting knife lying on the ground beside her—a real beauty that she recently purchased at a sports supply store at the Somerset Mall—and turns to see who has come to pay her a visit.

■ ■ ■ ■ ■

"Lenora? Honey, is that you?"

She looked up and saw Terry standing in the barn's open

doorway, backlit by daylight. He had to know it was her. Her car was parked nearby. She guessed his eyes hadn't had enough time to adjust to the darkness inside the barn, and he wasn't sure who the figure kneeling on the floor was.

"Hello, Doctor Birch," she said. It was her voice, but something about it caused him to take a step back, as if he might turn and flee. She supposed there *was* something strange about the tone, rhythm, and cadence of her words. Something that struck Terry as *wrong*.

Not the Doctor Birch part, though. She often called him that, especially when they were in bed, but she always said it in a sexy, teasing way. Not like this, like she was mocking him.

She rose to her feet and started walking slowly toward Terry, moving in an awkward, stiff manner as if the neurons in her brain were randomly misfiring. It felt as if someone else was operating her body, someone who didn't quite have the hang of it yet.

"Are you okay, Lenora? The way you're walking . . . I don't know a lot about your family's psychic abilities. My professors didn't exactly cover that sort of thing in medical school. Is it possible your powers have malfunctioned somehow and harmed you?"

He started forward, as if intending to examine her, but then his gaze fell to the knife gripped in her hand, and he stopped. Her mouth formed a smile. His vision had obviously adjusted to the barn's gloom.

"Don't worry," her voice said. "You don't have to be afraid of me."

Terry didn't respond to that, but he didn't come any closer. "What are you doing here, baby? Why did you leave Sanctity? Did your father do something to you?"

A voice—a man's voice—whispered in her mind. *That's how the two of you bonded, isn't it? I can see it in you memories.*

Lenora's body kept walking toward Terry, knife held casually at her side, as if it were a natural extension of her hand.

You were both at the same bar one night. You liked his looks and gave him a little push to come over and talk with you. You intended just to use him for sex, but something unexpected happened. You found yourself telling him your life story, pouring out your feelings—especially about your father. Terry resented the Crosses, always had, ever since he learned that his grandfather was excommunicated from the family. His grandfather's unfortunate choice of a bride assured that the Crosses would never accept him as one of them. You and Terry found common ground in your hatred of the family, and it didn't take much pushing on your part to get him to start an affair with you.

Lenora stopped when she was within three feet of Terry. Close, but not so close that she was in reach.

"You're behaving very strangely, love," Terry said. "I know the last couple of days have been stressful for you. Let me take you back to my place. You'll be safe there and you can rest."

He took a step toward her. Her body moved so swiftly she was almost unaware of it, and an instant later, the point of her hunting knife dimpled Terry's throat.

"I could just push you to make you back off, but this is so much more fun." It was her voice, but *his* words. The man who whispered in her thoughts. "Besides, she's pushed you a lot over the last few weeks. Far more than you realize. It takes a toll on the mind, you know. Makes you unbalanced at best and insane at worst." Her mouth smiled as she pressed the knife against his flesh hard enough to prick the skin. A line of blood trickled down his throat. "Which are you, I wonder?"

Terry gave her a leering half-smile. "Is this some kind of kinky role-playing? Do you want to do it here in the Deveraux Barn?

You're one sick bitch." He said this last bit in a voice thick with both admiration and lust.

Her grip tightened on the knife handle, and for an instant she thought the spirit in control of her body was going to shove the blade deep into her lover's throat. But her body lowered the blade and stepped back.

"My mother was the only person who was ever good to me, and I've kept watch over her ever since I . . . went away. When I became aware that she was in danger, I tried telling someone about what you and your little girlfriend were up to. But I couldn't get my message through, so I decided to deliver it in person. Now I realize Lenora never intended to harm Mother, just frighten her. So I came here to think, to figure out what to do next." She felt her smile turn dark. "Got any ideas?"

• • • • •

Terry didn't understand half of what Lenora was raving about, but one item caught his attention and caused him to feel a surge of panic. Lenora had wanted to tell someone about what they'd done. If anyone discovered the truth . . . if *Joanne* did . . .

He reached into his jacket pocket and wrapped his fingers around the handle of his scalpel. The blade had been put to a very different use than intended the last couple days, and it looked like he was going to have to use it that way again. But he didn't take the scalpel out of his pocket, not just yet.

"There's only one thing you can do, Lenora. Come with me to my place. Both your father and Joanne know you're missing. They have people looking for you right now. It won't be long before someone comes out here—a deputy, or one of your father's people. After last night—"

"What about last night?" she interrupted, voice harsh, eyes flashing dangerously.

Some instinct told him not to answer, but he felt a familiar pressure inside his skull, and he knew he didn't have a choice. So he told her.

When he finished, she glared at him for a long moment, hand clutching the knife handle so tightly it looked as if her knuckles might burst through the skin.

"You tried to kill my . . . Debbie Coulter?" Her tone was cold, completely devoid of emotion.

"If you had left after spray-painting Debbie's car and taping the poster on the front door of the café . . ." He shook his head. "But you didn't. You had to break in and scare her, didn't you? When you did that, Debbie Coulter became a potential witness. I was afraid she'd be able to identify you eventually. Tyrone Gantz was a witness, too. It turns out he was across the street watching that night."

Lenora cocked her head to the side, and a distant look came into her eyes, as if she were listening to a voice only she could hear. "Why kill Ray Porter then? He didn't witness anything. His only crime was hoping to get lucky with a beautiful Cross girl."

Rage boiled up inside Terry, just as intense and overwhelming as the night he'd followed Lenora to the Burrito Bungalow and watched from across the street as she chatted up Ray Porter at a table outside. He'd been suspicious for a while that she was cheating on him, and while neither of them had ever said anything about their relationship being exclusive—hell, he was still screwing Joanne, wasn't he?—jealousy got the better of him and he'd taken to following Lenora around until he finally caught her with another man. Man? Hell, with a goddamned boy!

After she left, he'd waited for Ray Porter—though he hadn't known the sonofabitch's name then—to leave so he could follow. But the kid kept hanging around the restaurant, and Terry learned why when a couple hours later Lenora returned, got in Ray's car, and the two drove off.

Terry followed.

He'd parked on a country road near the Deveraux Farm and snuck up on Lenora and Ray just in time to see her kick the asshole out of his car and take off, stranding him. Terry almost did him right there, but though he was angry with Lenora, he didn't want there to be any evidence tying her to Ray's murder. So when Ray started the long, lonely walk back to town, Terry followed at a distance, lights off, until he judged they were far enough away from the farm. Then he parked, cut across a field to intercept the boy, and cut his throat.

And then, because he *was* angry with Lenora, he'd called her cell to tell her what he'd done. But before he could say a word, she told him in a breathless rush about the "prank" she'd played on Debbie Coulter.

Terry thought fast. He wasn't worried about getting caught. He knew enough about crime scene investigation to make sure he left no evidence behind—plus he was the goddamned coroner. If necessary, he could falsify autopsy results, no problem. But having two strange events occur on the same night . . . even in Cross County that was straining coincidence. People were bound to think the two events were connected. He was certain Joanne would. He knew how her mind worked—as well as various other parts of her anatomy.

So since there was no avoiding a link, he decided to strengthen it and misdirect Joanne in the process. He carved Carl Coulter's calling card into Ray Porter's abdomen and then—wearing surgical gloves, of course—he removed the boy's wallet, took it back to the Deveraux Farm, and planted it in the barn. When he was finished, he headed back to town and called Lenora one last time to tell her what he'd done, mostly so she could prepare whatever alibi she might need, but also because he wanted her to know that he'd killed for her and that, by tying Ray's murder to her vandalism at the Caffeine Café, her prank would be all the more effective. Lenora hadn't been upset. Indeed, she'd seemed quite pleased, and if it hadn't been prudent for them to avoid seeing each other for a time, he'd have insisted she come over to his place.

Instead, he screwed Joanne the next day. She was nowhere near as good in bed as Lenora—who could use her mental powers to enhance sex in a way normal women never could—but she made an acceptable substitute, like a living blow-up doll.

Terry had thought he'd taken care of everything, but now events were beginning to spiral out of his control. After setting the Caffeine Café on fire as a diversion, he'd tried to eliminate the two witnesses last night: Tyrone and Debbie. But he'd only succeeded in taking care of Tyrone, and in the process he'd nearly been caught by Joanne. Luckily, he'd been able to ambush her and hit her in the head with a rock he'd picked up in the Duvalls' yard, striking hard enough to render her unconscious but not so hard as to cause serious injury. When she'd slumped to the ground, he told himself that he should kill her too, but he couldn't bring himself to do so. He didn't love her, not really. But he hadn't been able to take her life. So he'd fled and, just as he'd done with Ray Porter, he'd returned a short time later to play coroner.

But this morning he'd heard from Joanne that Lenora was missing and that Marshall Cross was insisting on taking Debbie Coulter—who, it seemed, had been in some sort of shock since last night—to Sanctity. How was Terry supposed to get to her there? And now *this* ... Lenora had bought a ticket on the crazy train, and it looked like she was planning on riding it all the way to the end of the line.

"Forget about Ray," Terry said. "All that matters right now is you—and stopping your father from taking Debbie Coulter to Sanctity."

"My father's doing *what?*"

"He's taking Debbie to Sanctity to prevent another attempt on her life."

Lenora regarded him for a moment in silence, but he could see the calculation going on behind those feral eyes. Slowly, her mouth stretched into a sly smile.

"Thanks. I know what to do now."

She walked past him and as he turned to ask her what the hell she was talking about, she swung the knife handle at his temple. The last thing he saw before the blow fell and darkness rushed in to claim him was Lenora's wild eyes and her cold, cold smile.

· · · · ·

Lenora gazed down at the still form of her lover lying on the dirt floor of the Deveraux barn. Enough light came through the open doorway for her to see that he was still breathing.

We can fix that, said a voice inside her head. An accompanying image flashed through her mind: Terry's throat sliced open, a triangle carved into his stomach, bisected by a jagged lightning bolt.

"No," she whispered, her voice once again hers to command.

It'll only take a couple minutes. It'll be fun. Trust me. I know.

"I won't hurt him. You can't make me."

Want to bet?

Her body took a shuffling step forward, and her knees began to bend of their own accord. Her mind was beginning to clear, but her thoughts were still sluggish and confused. But she knew one thing with absolute certainty. She was Lenora Cross and no one—alive *or* dead—could make her do something she didn't want to.

She straightened and took a step backward. The voice that had taken up residence inside her mind howled with frustration.

He tried to kill my mother!

"So what? She's not *my* mother."

Before she could stop it, her hand brought the knife to her own throat. She smirked with a complete absence of fear.

"You won't do it. Not until you've gotten what you came for. So let's quit jerking around and get to it."

The knife remained at her throat for a moment longer, but then the hand was truly hers again, and she lowered the blade.

All right. But if he interferes again, I'll gut him for sure. You too, if you try to stop me.

"Whatever. Let's go."

She turned away from Terry's unconscious form and started toward the doorway.

CHAPTER EIGHTEEN

Dale hit a drive-thru for an extra-large, extra-strong coffee before leaving Rhine. The damned stuff was volcanically hot, but he gulped it down anyway. He'd drank so much hot coffee throughout the course of the night that he'd long ago scalded his tongue and seared his alimentary canal to the point where he could swallow molten steel and not feel it.

But the latest dose of liquid adrenaline hadn't helped much. He supposed he'd drank so much that he'd developed a temporary resistance to its effects. That, or else he was so goddamned tired that nothing short of replacing his blood supply with methamphetamines would help.

He drove down the country roads with his windows down, hoping the cool blast of early morning air would do for him what coffee no longer could. He knew he was leaving himself vulnerable to the Black Beast. He had no doubt the cursed thing was following him, though he could no longer see it. Not long after leaving Sanctity last night, he'd pushed his rearview and sideview mirrors out of alignment so he wouldn't have to keep seeing the creature reflected there, tirelessly loping along behind despite the pouring rain, keeping up easily, almost mockingly, as if it could put on a burst of speed whenever it wished and catch up to him.

After a few hours of playing follow the leader up and down the roads of Cross County—with only an occasional stop for coffee at one late-night drive-thru or another—Dale had started peeing in empty coffee cups to relieve himself of all the fluid he'd taken in and hurling them out the window like urine-bombs at the Black Beast. He had no idea if any of the cups hit the creature, but that was beside the point. Childish as it might have been, it had felt damned good to do it. If nothing else, it had helped him stay awake. But now his eyes remained open only through sheer stubbornness. They felt gummy, as if his tear ducts were oozing sap, and his hands and feet were numb. The only way he could tell without looking that he still gripped the steering wheel was that he hadn't swerved off the road and slammed into a telephone pole.

He wondered if that was the Black Beast's hunting method—to pursue prey until it grew tired and stopped running. Maybe Sadie—by living on her houseboat on Lake Hush all these years—had managed to outlast the creature. Weary of waiting, the Black Beast had chosen new prey to chase.

Dale had plenty of time to think while he drove, and he thought he knew what the Beast was and where it had come from. This knowledge, however, didn't give him any better idea of how to deal with it. Dale considered who he might go to for help. Not Joanne. The last thing he wanted was for the Beast to decide she would make more interesting prey than an old, broken-down reporter. Joanne had enough to deal with right now. He supposed he could always go to Althea, but he didn't want to be indebted to her if he could avoid it. He'd had enough dealings with the Crosses over the years, and he wanted to try to maintain as much independence from them as he could—even if it might cost him his life.

But now he was so weary of the chase that he was tempted to say to hell with his principles and give Althea a call. He started to reach for his cell phone when he saw a green road sign with white letters that said SOMERSET 5 MILES. As he flew past the sign, he saw an unmarked dirt road coming up on his left. He slowed only because if he took the turn too fast, he'd flip his Jeep. Plus the dirt road was undoubtedly muddy after last night's rain, and the last thing he wanted was to get his Jeep mired down in the muck. The chase would surely be over then, and Dale had no doubt who the loser would be. He took the narrow road as slowly as he dared, and even then the Jeep's tires churned up showers of mud, the vehicle sliding back and forth more than Dale liked. He thought for certain that he wasn't going to make it, but then he saw it not far ahead—a large white two-story house resembling an antebellum mansion that looked as if it belonged in the actual South instead of Southwestern Ohio. But there it was, and Dale had never been more grateful to see anything in his life. There were trees all over the property—apple trees, of course. What other kind would a person named Eve grow? A half dozen vehicles were parked in front of the house, for as rumor had it, there were always visitors here, no matter the hour. The vehicles ranged from a rusted-out pickup missing its passenger door to a tour bus for a musician Dale had never heard of to what he thought was a Stutz Bearcat, the latter looking as if it had just rolled off the assembly line yesterday.

Dale parked next to the Bearcat and turned off the Jeep's engine. He sat for a moment, trying to work up the courage to get out, but he was simply too exhausted to feel much of anything.

"Screw it."

He opened the drive's side door and stepped out onto the muddy ground . . .

. . . only to find the Black Beast waiting for him.

The thing stood less than a dozen yards away. It was a clear, sunny day, and for the first time since the damned thing had begun stalking him, Dale got his first good look at the Beast's features. Black as night, its ebon hide seemed to drink in light instead of reflecting it. Roughly the size and shape of a large wolf, its head was closer to that of a wild boar, porcine with jutting black tusks, and its long hairless tail undulated like a serpent. Worst of all were the eyes. Glossy black orbs—cold, calculating, gleaming with malice and hunger.

The reporter in Dale was tempted to pull his camera from the pocket of his suit jacket and try to get a photo of the Beast. But the creature let out a deep rumbling growl, and Dale forgot about taking a picture. He was instantly alert, every nerve alive and on fire, all weariness gone.

A number of strategies flashed rapidly through his brain, techniques and anecdotes gleaned from reading nature articles and watching wildlife documentaries over the years. Meet the creature's gaze and show no fear. Don't look into the creature's eyes. It'll see that as a challenge and attack. Yell as loud as you can—noise will scare it off. Stay silent and don't provoke it. Stand tall and make yourself an imposing physical presence. Fall to the ground and play dead. But in the end, Dale chose a strategy that had served his species well for several million years.

He ran like hell.

He almost tripped going up the wooden porch steps, and though he felt a nearly irresistible urge to look back and see how close the Beast was—for he had no doubt the thing pursued—he kept his gaze focused on the front door, pounded both his fists on the surface and bellowed an inarticulate cry, praying someone would open the door before he felt razor-sharp ebon claws sink into his back.

And someone did.

Dale stumbled across the entryway, shouting, "Close it, close it, close it!"

The woman who'd let him in didn't bat an eye as she shut the door a split second before something large and heavy slammed into the other side. Dale listened for several moments afterward, but there was only quiet. It seemed the Beast had given up—for now.

Gulping air and pulse thrumming, he turned to thank his rescuer. But the adrenaline surge that had saved his life was fast wearing off, and he'd gone without sleep for so long that as the crash hit, it hit hard. His mouth formed words, but he was unable to get any sound out. He felt light-headed, kitten-weak, and his knees started to buckle, as if his legs refused to bear his weight any longer after the abuse he'd just put them through. He almost laughed. Wouldn't it be ironic if, after all this, he died from something so ordinary as a stroke?

But the woman—who he now realized was little more than a girl, really—rushed to his side and took his arm to steady him.

"Let's get you into the parlor," she said, her voice gentle as the first breeze of spring. "You can rest there while I go get Miss Eve."

The girl was sylph-like, but her grip on his arm was strong and firm as a linebacker's. Her hair was raven-black, straight and cut short. Her skin was so pale it was nearly white, and it reflected light in a way that reminded him of porcelain. Her face was round, her features small and delicate. She had black makeup around her eyes that resembled the khol used by ancient Egyptians, and her lips were equally as dark, though there was something about them that made Dale think she wasn't wearing any lipstick, that her lips were naturally that color. Her eyes were a cold, glittering blue, like ice chips mined from some far-off frozen world. She wore a sleeveless red gown that hugged her like it was her own skin, cut

low to reveal the white flesh of her upper chest and the beginning swells of her small breasts. The gown's hem fell to the tops
of her bare feet, and Dale saw that the nails of her tiny childlike
toes were the same black as her lips, though her neatly trimmed
fingernails remained unpainted.

She steered Dale out of the entranceway and into the front
hall. The walls and floors were made of wood so highly polished
that it gleamed. A series of small chandeliers hung from the
ceiling, lighting the way. They appeared to use real candles instead
of candleflame-shaped bulbs, but though their lights flickered
like fire, the white wax of the candles themselves showed no
sign of melting. The air was filled with intermingled scents that
made Dale think of an exotic spice market in some small desert
country with an unpronounceable name. The precise make-up
of the smells changed as they walked—stronger with jasmine
here, patchouli there, now sandalwood . . . with each breath he
took he felt his pulse slow, his breathing even out, his lighthead-
edness recede. Weariness subsided as strength and alertness
began to return. Perhaps it was merely an effect of his relief at
escaping the Beast. But he didn't think so.

They passed no doors as they traveled down the hall, and it
seemed to Dale that they walked a long time until they finally
reached an open doorway near the end of the hall on the right.
He no longer needed the raven-haired sylph's support to walk, but
she didn't remove her hand from his own and he wasn't inclined
to encourage her to do so just yet. She led him into the room,
and as soon as he stepped across the threshold he felt as if he'd
taken a sledgehammer blow to the gut. This wasn't a parlor. It was
the living room of the first house he and Marianne had bought
back in Chicago, right after Alice was born. The same second-
hand couch Marianne's mother had given them, sorely in need of

reupholstering, the same wooden floor, creaky and worn smooth by the previous occupants, nothing like the gleaming wood in the hall outside. Same floor lamp with tacky tassels on the shade—a wedding present from Dale's grandmother—same TV, same picture window with the same hideous red velour curtains inflicted on them by Marianne's great aunt . . .

His thoughts stalled for a minute as he saw through the window not Eve's apple trees, but rather streetlights, passing cars, and on opposite side of the street, the Kolzinskis' house. He suddenly felt light-headed again, and he wondered if that was why the sylph had continued holding onto his arm, because she had known what he'd see in here and how he would react.

She escorted him to the couch and helped him sit. It seemed smaller than he remembered, but the groaning protests of the old springs were the same.

"Wait here. I'll go see if Miss Eve is available." She gave him a parting smile that was half amused, half sympathetic, and then left.

He sat, breathing in the familiar odors of frying bacon and brewing coffee. *Marianne's* bacon and coffee. He heard the sizzle of meat, the burble of water being heated, the sound of a baby whimpering softly, followed by a gentle, "Hush now," spoken in a voice he hadn't heard in twenty years. He turned toward the open doorway that led to the kitchen, tears welling in his eyes, for he knew then that time hadn't blurred his memory, and his wife's voice was just as he remembered it. The living room astonished him, made him question his sanity, but it was still easier to deal with than that doorway. As miraculous as it was, the living room contained only memories in the form of furnishings. But the doorway to the kitchen . . . if what he heard through it was real, then Marianne was in there, Alice too. If he got up from the couch, walked over to the doorway and stepped into the kitchen, where would he find himself? Reunited with his wife and daughter in a world that had been dead for decades, or would he be standing in another room in Eve's house, the illusion of the past dispelled? And if somehow he *could* rejoin Marianne and Alice, would he still be a man in his sixties, or would he return to his young adulthood physically as well as temporally? Youthful once more, his whole life ahead of him, his wife and child at his side.

He started to rise from the couch when the black-haired girl in the red gown returned. He settled back down with a pang of regret as she walked over to the couch and sat next to him. The springs didn't make a sound beneath her, but then she was so petite she probably didn't weigh enough to dimple the cushion, let alone compress the springs.

"I'm sorry to inform you that Miss Eve is engaged in entertaining another visitor at the moment. But I will be most happy to take care of you myself. As we say here at the Garden of Unearthly Delights, your pleasure is our life."

She smiled—not in a lascivious way, but gently, with sincerity—and placed her small doll hand over his. The ivory color of his skin made him think her touch would be cold, but it was surprisingly warm. An event most rare occurred then. Dale Ramsey, lifelong reporter, found himself struggling to find words.

"I . . . how . . . this room . . ."

Her gaze showed understanding. "Everyone reacts like this. It's only natural. But yes, it's real." She nodded toward the window. "All of it. But it's not just the room that's important, Mr. Ramsey. It's the *day*."

At first Dale didn't know what the girl was referring to, but then a numbing terror clasped his heart with icy claws, and he understood. The girl continued talking, and while her voice now seemed far distant, he had no trouble making out every word.

"You left for work early that day, skipping breakfast so you could meet with a source at a diner downtown. The story you were working on wasn't all that important for a big city like Chicago—allegations of financial mismanagement at a small charitable arts organization. Allegations that were unfounded, as it turned out. But there were no small stories as far as you were concerned, were there? You were young and ambitious, a would-be crusading reporter determined to save the world one word at a time."

Dale detected a new scent mixed with the smells of coffee and bacon, an acrid tang that stung the back of his throat.

"You hadn't wanted to get a gas stove, but your wife insisted. She said they were easier to cook on, that food prepared on them tasted better, that her own mother had never used anything but a gas stove. You were very much in love and wanted to please her, but you still had your misgivings. You were a reporter, and even at so young an age, you'd seen much of the darker side of life. One tragedy after another . . . accidents, murders, scandals, betrayals . . . a random series of meaningless events that convinced you the universe was indifferent at best and maliciously cruel at worst. You used to joke that you didn't think the glass was half empty. You weren't even sure there *was* a glass."

The odor of gas grew stronger, until Dale could no longer smell the bacon or coffee. His throat felt thick and swollen, and every breath became an effort.

"If you hadn't left early that morning, you'd have been there when the stove exploded. You might have been able to keep your wife and daughter from dying in the fire that resulted, and failing that, you could have at least shared their fate. But you didn't find out until several hours later, when you stopped in at the office and your managing editor took you aside to tell you what had happened."

The smell of gas was overwhelming now, and Dale felt dizzy and sick to his stomach.

"You can stand up and walk into the kitchen, Mr. Ramsey. You can turn off the burners on the stove before it explodes. You can save Marianne and Alice." A pause, one that seemed heavy with hidden meaning. "If that's your desire."

Dale's gaze was fixed on the kitchen doorway, and though he wanted nothing more than to leap off the couch and run to the aid of his wife and daughter, there was a question he had to ask first. "Is this real? If I go in there, if I save them, will . . ." He couldn't bring himself to complete the sentence.

The girl finished for him. "Will the past be changed? Will the fire have never happened? Will you have continued your life as a reporter in Chicago, watching Alice grow up, Marianne by your side? Yes and no. The past will remain the same in what most people consider the real world. But things will be different for you, Mr. Ramsey. You and you alone."

Dale tried to speak, coughed, tried again. "It won't be real."

"It will *seem* real. Isn't that almost as good?"

Dale was tempted—God, was he tempted!—but how could he abandon Joanne and retreat into an illusion of the past merely to ease his loneliness and guilt? Was that the kind of man he was? The kind of man Marianne and Alice would want him to be?

He looked once more toward the kitchen doorway, suppressed his tears, and turned his attention back to the girl. Dale struggled to choke out a single word. It was the most difficult thing he'd ever done in his life.

"No."

The girl shrugged, and at once the smell of gas was gone, along with the scents of bacon and coffee, and the sounds of Marianne and Alice in the kitchen. The silence came near to breaking Dale's heart. He told himself that they hadn't been real, that none of it had, but it didn't matter. Real or not, losing them again still hurt like hell. But painful as it was, Dale fought to push his feelings aside. He could deal with them later. Right now he had work to do.

His throat felt normal again, and he was relieved to find himself able to speak easily once more. "I came here for information. A friend of mine suggested Eve might be able to help."

"As you wish. Our only purpose is to satisfy your desires, whatever they might be. We can supply the information you seek ... if you can afford to pay the price." She said this last part matter-of-factly, but her ice-blue eyes shone with a cold, calculating light. He'd seen eyes like that before. Marshall had them, as did Lenora. All pure-bred Crosses had them.

"You're Eve," he said.

Much, if not all, of the coldness left her gaze and she smiled with genuine joy. "Very good, Mr. Ramsey. I thought you might guess the truth."

Dale had never visited the Garden before, but he wasn't surprised Eve knew who he was. Gleaning that bit of information had to be ridiculously simple for someone who could see into the hidden recesses of his heart and bring his most secret desire—or at least an illusion of it—to life.

"Why the pretense?" he asked.

"It keeps me from having to explain why a woman as old as I am looks the way I do."

"So it's true. You *are* Althea's sister."

Eve nodded. "Her fraternal twin, actually. She could do all this too, if she wished. But she keeps herself cut off from others for the most part, preferring to implement her convoluted schemes from her mausoleum of a home, using my nephew as her agent. As for me, I just want to make people happy. That's why long ago I left Sanctity and came here. So I could live the way I wished and use my abilities for the benefit of others."

"At a price."

A sly gleam came into her eyes. "Perhaps I'm not quite as self-less as I make myself out to be."

"I saw the vehicles parked outside. Are your other . . . clients being entertained by the rest of your staff?"

"I have no staff. My garden has only one tender. Me. And my other visitors are enjoying themselves elsewhere in the house. Forget about them. We're here to focus solely on your needs. You seek information."

"Yes."

"And you're willing to pay for it?"

Dale didn't like the way she said the word *pay*. It seemed to contain far too many connotations for his comfort. But he answered yes.

"I always tell my visitors the complete cost up front. Nothing hidden, no tricks. Your price is this place, Dale." She gestured to indicate the living room.

He frowned. "I don't understand."

"The memory of it. In exchange for the information you want, you will surrender the memory of the morning Marianne and Alice died. You won't forget that it occurred, of course. But the sensory details—Alice's laugh as you tickled her under the chin, Marianne's lips pressed against yours as you kissed her goodbye for the last time—these will be gone. Forever. No matter how hard you try, you'll never be able to recall these details again."

Dale's gaze flicked to the kitchen doorway. He thought about it, thought *hard*. Eve sat patiently, not speaking, not moving, her too-warm hand still resting on his, but he barely felt her touch. Long ago, he'd made a promise to protect Joanne and help her in the performance of her duty—not her job as sheriff but her *true* duty—and he would not break that promise. Marianne and Alice wouldn't want him to.

"I'll pay."

Eve showed neither approval nor disapproval. She lifted her hand off Dale's and rose from the couch. "Done," she said.

Dale expected to feel a sudden hollowness inside him as his memories vanished, with the room perhaps collapsing into dust around them as a visual metaphor for what he had lost. But nothing happened.

"Don't look so disappointed," she teased. "The room will remain exactly as it is until we leave it." She turned her back to Dale, reached around, and began to pull down the zipper of her red dress.

"Uh, you did hear me say I want *information*, right?"

She didn't reply, and a second later her dress fell to the floor with soft whisper of cloth. Eve stood naked before him, her petite body sleek and well formed. But the most striking feature was the large tattoo stretching from her upper back all the way down to her smooth, rounded buttocks. It was a design done in lines of lines of black, and it began moving, swirling slowly on her flesh, beginning as a mandala, morphing into a spider's web, becoming a pattern of jagged fissures like cracks in a pane of glass. The effect was hypnotic, and Dale felt drawn toward the changing design, almost as if it were trying to pull him in. Without realizing it, he leaned forward until he was sitting on the edge of the couch. He almost reached out to touch the tattoo when Eve's voice broke the spell.

"Tell me what you want to know."

"Who is Carl Coulter's real father?"

As Dale watched, the lines of ink beneath the surface of Eve's skin bent, twisted, and reformed until they resolved into the image of a man's face. Dale stared at it for several seconds before speaking.

"Well, *that's* interesting."

"I take it that you're satisfied," Eve said. Still keeping her back to him, she knelt down to retrieve her dress and slipped it over her small, slender frame.

"Zip me?" she asked.

Dale stood and did as she requested. Now that he knew who and what she was, she remained as beautiful and exotic as ever, but in a cold, remote way, as if she were a magnificent piece of artwork—a statue or painting—instead of a living woman. When Dale finished, she turned around to face him, and he said, "You couldn't see the answer to my question, but do you know it anyway?"

"My sister and I may have different philosophies regarding our roles in the county, but we still talk from time to time."

It wasn't an answer, but Dale sensed it was all the reply he was going to get. But he had the information he'd come for, so he decided not to press the issue. Not that he could've persuaded Eve to tell him more if she didn't wish to.

"We are finished here, and I have other visitors to attend to. I'll see you out." She started toward the parlor's doorway and Dale followed. "One more thing. Don't look back as we leave. Trust me. It'll be easier that way."

She stepped out into the hallway, and as Dale neared the threshold, he sensed more than saw the objects in his old living room begin to deform, to lose shape and substance. Heeding Eve's advice, he kept his gaze focused straight ahead and didn't look back as the Garden of Unearthly Delights accepted his payment.

Eve led him back to the entryway in silence. The halls no longer smelled like spices, and Dale wondered if that was because his visit was over and he was no longer welcome. He grieved for his lost memories of Marianne and Alice, but his grief was leavened somewhat by the knowledge he'd gained from Eve. He was still trying to sort out all the implications of this latest revelation when they reached the front door, and he remembered what waited for him on the other side.

As Eve reached for the doorknob, he grabbed her wrist to stop her.

"I have a problem."

"No, you don't. All my visitors enjoy my protection." She pulled away from his grip and opened the door.

The Black Beast lay on the front porch, head resting on its paws. Its eyes snapped open and it sprang to its feet, a threatening growl rumbling deep within its throat.

"Hush now," Eve said, gently but firmly. "You've had your fun." She stepped onto the porch without hesitation, and Dale wanted to reach out and pull her back to safety. But though the Black Beast continued growling, it didn't attack her.

Eve placed her hand on the creature's head, as if it were no more than a dog that wanted to be petted. The thing fixed her with a baleful glare and displayed long, sharp teeth, but it still made no move to harm her. Eve kept her hand on the Beast's head, and slowly it stopped snarling and the growls tapered away to nothing.

"Beauty hath charms," Dale murmured.

Eve smiled. "You don't know the half of it."

The Beast began to whine, and Dale saw a shadowy substance

begin to flow up Eve's fingers. The black stuff picked up speed, sliding over her hand and crawling up her forearm. As it continued moving onto her shoulder, the Beast's whines became howls of pain and fear, and Dale saw that the creature appeared smaller than it had a few moments ago, almost as if it were losing substance and dwindling away.

She's absorbing it, he thought.

With a final ear-splitting howl, the Beast collapsed into a pool of shadow that was swiftly absorbed by Eve. The remains slithered up her arm, flowed over her shoulder, and disappeared down her back.

Dale now knew where she got the ink for her ever-changing tattoo, and he shuddered.

She smiled at him again, but there was no mirth in her arctic-blue eyes.

"A girl can never have too many pets."

CHAPTER NINETEEN

On the way to the hospital, Marshall insisted they stop at the county building, though he refused to say why. Joanne agreed to do so, mostly out of curiosity. She accompanied him to the morgue, head throbbing in time with her footsteps as they walked, and when they arrived, she was mildly surprised to discover Terry wasn't there. On the phone earlier, he'd told her that he'd finished the preliminary examination of Tyrone Gantz's body. Shouldn't he have been performing the official autopsy by now?

As if their thoughts were running along similar lines, Marshall said, "I need to see Tyrone's body."

It didn't take long for Joanne to find out which freezer was Tyrone's. She slid it open and exposed Tyrone's sheet-covered body up to the chest. The man's skin was pale and waxen, and the blood had been cleaned away from his throat and stomach wounds, but no other incisions had been made. Terry hadn't done the autopsy. Where the hell was he? Had one of his living patients called with a medical emergency?

While she was trying to come up with an explanation for Terry's absence, Marshall pulled something out of his jacket pocket. At first she couldn't tell what it was, but as he stepped past her and pressed the object to the side of Tyrone's head, she could see it was a crude stone carving of a miniature human figure.

"What the hell are you doing?" She reached out to bat his hand away, but Marshall grabbed her wrist with his other hand, fingers wrapping around like a band of steel.

"It's vital you don't interrupt the process, Joanne. It won't take very—" He broke off, frowning. "Something's wrong. It's not here."

"*What's* not here?" Joanne tried to pull free from Marshall's grip, but she couldn't. She felt like a small child unable to break away from a much stronger adult. It irritated the piss out of her, and she was seriously considering going for her weapon with her free hand when Marshall let her go.

"His essence," Marshall said. He pulled the carving away from Tyrone's head and replaced it in his jacket. "You can put the body away. It's useless now."

Marshall turned and started walking toward the door. Her wrist aching from where Marshall had gripped it, she covered Tyrone with the sheet once more and slid his drawer back into the freezer. Then she hurried after Marshall, but no matter how hard she tried to get him to explain what he'd done—or at least tried to do—he refused to answer.

They didn't speak the rest of the way to Resurrection Hospital.

· · · · ·

"You doing all right back there, Debbie?"

Joanne glanced up at the rearview mirror. Through the black safety mesh that separated the front and back seats of the cruiser, she saw Debbie sitting with her hands on her lap, gazing out the side window. She'd exchanged her hospital gown for the clothes she'd been wearing when Joanne had taken her to the hospital last night—blue sweater, white blouse, jeans, and running shoes. She wore no makeup or jewelry and her face looked washed-out and drawn, as if she'd aged a decade in the few hours since Joanne had last seen her.

Debbie didn't reply and gave no sign she'd heard Joanne's question.

"I feel awkward sitting up front," Marshall said. "Debbie should be sitting here."

Joanne grimaced. She'd gotten some ibruprofen at the hospital pharmacy and had taken three times the recommended dosage. It hadn't removed the pain in her head, but it took the edge off enough for her to function. "We've been through this already." She didn't want to say so again in front of Debbie, but given the way the woman was acting, it simply wasn't a good idea to allow her to sit in front. She'd been docile to the point of near catatonia since they arrived to pick her up, but that could change at any moment. If Debbie should suddenly lose it, she might do something to interfere with Joanne's driving. At the very least Joanne would have to subdue and cuff Debbie if she wouldn't settle down. At worst, Debbie could cause the cruiser to wreck. Either way, it was better for Debbie to ride in the back, though it continued to make Marshall uncomfortable, probably because he viewed the back seat of the cruiser as a place for criminals. Marshall was just going to have to tough it out, though. Debbie seemed content enough back there, and it wouldn't be all that long before they reached Sanctity.

Joanne was still concerned about Debbie's condition, however. She hoped they were doing the right thing. Marshall insisted that the physician who'd tend to Debbie at Sanctity was the best in this part of the state, and while she had no reason to doubt him, she still didn't—

Her cell phone rang, cutting her off in mid-thought. She figured it was Dale, and she was right. She listened for several moments as he spoke. When he was finished, she said, "We've got Debbie and we're on our way to Sanctity. Get there as soon as you can." She disconnected and slipped the phone back into its belt pouch.

She continued driving in silence for a time, and after a bit Marshall asked, "Anything important?"

She stared straight ahead as she drove. "You're Carl Coulter's real father."

Marshall didn't respond right away, but from the back seat, Debbie said, "Of course he is, silly. He did his best to be a good father, too, given the circumstances. Marshall would come over sometimes when my husband was at work or off on a fishing trip with his cronies. Sometimes he'd meet us at a park or a playground—in another town, of course. Sometimes we'd go all the way to Cincinnati. You should've seen the two of them together. Carl just loved spending time with his Uncle Marshall. You should have been there last night, Marshall. He would've been so happy to see you." She fell quiet again and leaned her head against the side window. In the rearview mirror, Joanne saw tears begin to run down the woman's cheeks.

Joanne turned to look at Marshall. "Carl didn't really believe you were his uncle, did he?"

Marshall slumped in his seat, no longer looking like the most powerful man in this part of the state. He looked small, defeated, and so very tired.

"He did when he was young. But as he got older, he discovered the truth. I don't know if he figured it out on his own, if Debbie told him, or if he somehow sensed it. It doesn't matter. He knew."

Joanne didn't say anything. Years of experience in law enforcement had taught her to be quiet and listen when someone was ready to talk, and Marshall was ready.

"I met Debbie when she first opened the café. I was . . . looking to marry a woman outside the extended Cross family. To bring in some new blood."

Joanne remembered her conversation with Althea in the gazebo last night. She'd said the same thing about why Marshall had married Lenora's mother.

"At first I saw it as my duty, and one that I found distasteful, for I wished to marry out of love, not genetic necessity. But as I got to know Debbie, I became attracted to her. She was beautiful, but in a real-world way. Nothing like Cross women. They all seem of a kind, like dolls made of delicate china. Pretty to look at, but cold and hollow inside. But Debbie was different. She'd lived a life that had nothing to do with bettering your position within the family hierarchy and fulfilling your ancestral duties. It was a life she'd made herself, built from her own choices. But she was like a Cross in one important way. She possessed a core of inner strength, as strong as any woman I'd ever met, inside the family or out.

"She was married, but I didn't care. I was Marshall Cross. I could have any woman I wanted. Except, as it turned out, Debbie. Though she was attracted to me, she loved her husband and refused to do anything that would hurt him. I admired that, and I tried to respect it, I really did. But I was young and lacked discipline, and I wanted her so badly . . ."

"You did something to make her sleep with you," Joanne guessed.

"I . . . persisted until she gave in," Marshall hedged. "Even so, she was determined to remain with her husband, and by this point I didn't care. As long as I could be with her, I was willing to share her if that's what it took."

"And eventually she got pregnant by you."

Marshall nodded. "Her husband was a good man, but he had

a low sex drive and they didn't make love often. Debbie assumed I was the father, but we weren't certain until after the child was born and we could have a blood test done in secrecy. But I knew the first time I saw Carl's eyes. All babies start out life with blue eyes, I know, but not Cross blue. Besides, we can always recognize our own kind.

"Debbie still didn't want to marry me, but I was determined to do what I could to provide for my child. I gave her money when she needed it, and as she said, I spent time with them whenever I could. But as the years went by it became harder to conceal the truth from the rest of the world, and Debbie's husband was beginning to become suspicious. Debbie told me that I had to stop seeing Carl and her, and though it broke my heart, I told her I understood and would do as she asked. And I did. Aside from an occasional stop at the café, I had no significant contact with Debbie for years . . . until Carl's murders."

Marshall fell silent, and Joanne looked at the rearview to see how Debbie was taking all this, but the woman seemed to be off in her own world and not paying attention to their conversation.

"What caused Carl to start killing?" she prompted.

"I suspect it was a combination of things. He wasn't raised as a Cross and therefore received little training in how to handle his more aggressive tendencies." Marshall took in a deep breath and let it out. "But I'm afraid the main reason was that he was hoping to impress me, be recognized as a Cross, and invited to live with us at Sanctity. I'd feared as much when he was arrested, and he confirmed it for me during the one visit I paid to him in prison. He told me each of his four victims had committed *offenses* against the family. He wouldn't give me any specifics, so I have no way of knowing whether those offenses were major or minor, real or imagined. I do know that I received no reports to indicate any of Carl's victims had done anything to deserve their fate."

Joanne noted that Marshall wasn't condemning murderous retribution, only disapproving of baseless revenge.

"What about the symbol he carved into his victims?" she asked.

"Meaningless. It was just something Carl made up. A way of signing his work, I suppose."

Marshall said this a little too smoothly for Joanne to buy it. But she decided to let the matter pass for now. Besides, the meaning of the triangle-lightning symbol paled in comparison to the rest of what Marshall had told her so far.

He said nothing more after that, and several minutes went by where the only sounds were the cruiser's engine, the tires rolling across asphalt, and a soft humming from Debbie in the backseat. Finally, Joanne spoke.

"I talked with your mother last night. She called my cell phone as I was getting ready to leave Sanctity and asked me to meet her behind the house."

Marshall looked surprised, but he made no comment, and Joanne continued.

"She told me how you felt about Charlotte and what really happened to her. She also told me why you've allowed Lenora to believe that you drove her mother away—or worse."

"I was married to Charlotte by the time Debbie's husband passed away, or else—" He broke off and shook his head. "It doesn't matter now. I loved Charlotte and had no wish to break Lenora's heart by telling her the truth. Better she hate me. After all, since Charlotte came to detest being a Cross, in a way I *was* responsible for her decision to take her own life."

"Your wife *killed* herself?" Joanne said, unable to keep the shock she felt out of her voice.

Marshall looked at her. "I suppose you believed the rumors that I made Charlotte 'disappear.'"

Joanne felt embarrassed. "Not really, but . . . I had no idea what really happened. I'm sorry."

Marshall accepted Joanne's sympathy with a curt nod.

Joanne thought for a moment. "Does Lenora know that Carl is her half-brother?"

"No." But there was a hint of doubt in Marshall's voice, as if he were less than confident in his reply.

"I wish you two would stop talking," Debbie said. "I can't hear myself hum."

"Sorry," Joanne murmured, and they drove the rest of the way to Sanctity in silence, each lost in his or her own thoughts or—in Debbie's case—a lack thereof.

· · · · ·

Ronnie's skin felt coated with a thick layer of grease, and he itched all over, as if the muck oozing out of his own pores was slowly dissolving his outer flesh. For the first time in close to forty-five years, he hadn't bathed in over twenty-four hours. But instead of feeling dirty, he felt good, felt *free*. Free not only from the constraints placed upon him by his own inflexible patterns of behavior, but free from the constraints of society as well. He was free to do as he damned well pleased, free to do *anything*.

To do what must be done.

But before he could get started on his real work, he had one last task to perform for Sheriff Jo-Jo.

As he pulled his cruiser up to the outskirts of the Deveraux property, he saw a vehicle parked at the edge of a field, not far from the barn. It was a Lexus—Dr. Birch's, as a matter of fact. He frowned as he pulled up next to the car and parked. What was the coroner doing out here? Had a body been discovered? If so, why hadn't dispatch radioed to tell him? Why weren't there other deputies here? It made no sense for Dr. Birch to be on the scene first. Ronnie turned off the cruiser's engine and got out. And that's when he saw that all four of the Lexus's tires had been slashed.

He'd been here yesterday and had given the area a thorough going-over, but now he noticed something strange in addition to the state of Dr. Birch's tires. On the other sides of the Lexus he saw new tires tracks in the muddy ground—he thought of last night's storm and shuddered—and he knew another vehicle had been here recently. And he'd bet a month's salary that whoever had been driving the second vehicle had also slashed the coroner's tires.

He looked at the barn and saw that the door in the back was open, the crime-scene tape he'd stretched across it yesterday cut in two. Dr. Birch wouldn't have done that. He would've opened the door without disturbing the tape and ducked underneath it to enter the barn.

During his career as a law-enforcement officer, Ronnie rarely had cause to draw his weapon in the line of duty, let alone discharge it. But he was free now, and he could do whatever was necessary. He drew his 9 mm, flicked off the safety, and held it at the ready as he started walking across the field toward the barn. If someone was inside, they had surely heard him drive up, but Ronnie still didn't call out. He wanted to hold on to whatever surprise might be left to him.

He took up a position against the wall next the door, just like cops did in the movies. Cops did it in real life, too, in order to avoid catching a bullet in the chest by being an over-eager asshole. He held his breath and listened, but he heard no sounds of movement. He drew in a deep breath and entered the barn, ready to blast the shit out of anything that even looked like it was thinking of moving.

Damned good thing for Terry Birch that he was unconscious.

Ronnie hurried to the coroner's side. He laid his weapon on the ground and then placed the fingers of his uninjured hand against the man's neck. Even with the protective rubber barrier of his glove between them, the feeling of his flesh coming in contact with someone else's turned Ronnie's stomach. But he felt a pulse, a strong one.

Terry groaned and slowly opened his eyes. He looked up at Ronnie, but he must've had trouble focusing, for he squinted and said, "Lenora?"

Lenora, as in Cross? What the hell did she have to do with anything? Though Ronnie had nothing against Lenora up to that moment, she was Marshall's daughter, so he decided to begin despising her too.

"It's Ronnie Doyle, Dr. Birch. Are you okay? What happened?"

Terry struggled to sit up and Ronnie helped him. It meant touching the man again, which in turn meant a new wave of nausea. But Ronnie was a deputy sheriff. He would endure.

"Bitch hit me in the head with a goddamned knife handle, that's what happened. Goddamned bitch." He reached up gingerly to touch his head. He expertly probed the wound for several moments before lowering his hand. "I'll live, which is too bad for her. When I catch up to the backstabbing little cooz, I'm going to slice her throat from ear to ear and piss in the opening."

Only a couple days ago, Terry's foul invective would've shocked Ronnie, but now he took it in stride. He was a man who had quite literally been *pushed* too far.

Ronnie helped the doctor to stand. "Wherever Lenora is, do you think Marshall is there, too?" he asked.

Terry frowned. "She's gone to Sanctity. And yes, Marshall's headed there as well."

Ronnie smiled. "Would you like a ride?"

CHAPTER TWENTY

"You must lie down here and rest." Marshall drew back the covers and stepped away from the huge, canopied king-size bed. He looked at Debbie, but she didn't seem to be paying any attention to him. She kept looking around the bedroom, taking everything in. Joanne didn't blame her. Marshall's quarters were something to see.

Globes of various sizes and types filled his chambers, and his bedroom was no exception. There was a large globe on a support base in the corner, and two smaller ones on the night-stands flanking the bed. On the walls were framed mariners' maps, paper crinkled, colors faded. Joanne had no doubt they were original and not reproductions, and she wondered how old they were. In another corner was a glass display case containing nautical navigation tools—sextants, compasses, spyglasses, and the like.

Marshall noticed Joanne's interest. "I've rarely had the oppor-tunity to travel outside the county." For a moment, it looked as if he might add more, but instead he turned to Debbie again. "Please lie down. You need to rest. You'll be safe here. I swear upon my life."

Marshall raised his hand and took a step toward Debbie, as if he intended to guide her to the bed, but the woman shied away. She'd followed them docilely enough from the car into Sanctity, and she'd trailed after them down the corridors of the mansion, head turning back and forth as she gazed at everything with the wide-eyed wonder of a child. But she'd become more hesitant as they approached Marshall's quarters, and she'd withdrawn almost completely after they entered his bedroom. Joanne couldn't blame her. There was an incredible amount of history between the two, and it was only to be expected that Debbie would be uncomfortable being in Marshall's bedroom, even with Joanne present.

"I wouldn't swear an oath like that, Father. Someone might hold you to it."

They all turned as Lenora entered through the bedroom's open doorway. She looked very different from the last time Joanne had seen her. Her hair was tangled and unwashed, and she wore no makeup or jewelry of any sort. She had on a black t-shirt, jeans, and running shoes. She also held a large hunting knife in her right hand.

Joanne reached for her 9 mm, but before she could draw her weapon, she felt pressure behind her forehead, and her hand froze, no longer hers to control.

Marshall's gaze hardened. "Where have you been?" he demanded. He made no move toward his daughter, however.

The left corner of Lenora's mouth pulled upward in a half-smile. "You have no idea how difficult that question is to answer, Father. Let's just say that I've been away for a while, but I'm back now. Back to take care of Mother." She turned to look at Debbie, and her expression softened.

Debbie hadn't reacted when Lenora entered the room, but now she fixed her full attention on the girl. She frowned at first, but then her eyes widened and she broke into a smile.

"Carl? Is that you?"

"It's so good to see you again, Mother." Lenora started to walk toward Debbie.

Joanne didn't know what was going on here—was Lenora also Marshall and Debbie's child?—but Lenora's parentage didn't matter right now. What mattered was the knife clutched in Lenora's hand. Joanne tried to take a step forward, intending to prevent Lenora from reaching Debbie, but she couldn't move. Whatever Lenora had done to stop her from drawing her 9 mm, it seemed to have also affected the rest of her body. She couldn't move at all. But did that she couldn't speak?

"Marshall—the knife!"

He looked as if he might protest, but then he nodded and furrowed his brow in concentration, light sparking deep within his ice-blue eyes.

Lenora paused and confusion moved across her face. But then she grew confident once more and resumed walking toward Debbie.

"You're strong, Father. I'll grant you that. But there's only one of you. Your will is no match for ours."

Joanne didn't understand what Lenora was talking about, but evidently Marshall did, for his eyes widened in shocked comprehension. He moved forward to interpose himself between Lenora and Debbie, but before he could get more than a couple of steps, Lenora held up a hand and Marshall jerked to a stop, as if he were a dog whose owner had just yanked on his leash.

Lenora grinned. "What part of *no match* didn't you understand? Lenora might not be too fond of Mother, but there's no need to worry about her safety. A few months back Lenora learned the truth about your relationship with Mother. You have *so* many relatives, Father, and they all plot against you while at the same time seeking your favor. They hunger for tidbits of information they might be able to use against you, hoarding them like gold nuggets. I'm one of those nuggets, and Lenora found out about me from one of her many sexual playthings. She immediately began thinking of a way to use her newfound knowledge against you. That's why she vandalized Mother's car and broke into the café the other night—not to harm Mother, but to upset *you*. I can't say I'm happy my sister scared Mother so badly, but I understand her reasons for doing so. And I must admit, I like her style."

Joanne felt the pieces of Lenora's bizarre ranting finally fall into place. "Are you trying to tell us that you're Carl Coulter? That you've . . . what?—*possessed* Lenora?"

Lenora turned to Joanne and this time the cold blue eyes the sheriff saw were the same ones that had gazed at her in her nightmare about Barrow Hill Mound.

"Something like that," Lenora—or rather Carl—said.

Despite seeing a flash of Carl at the Deveraux Farm and dreaming of him later, Joanne wasn't willing to accept she was talking to a dead man whose spirit had sublet the body of his half-sister. But one thing she couldn't deny. She was unable to move her body from the neck down. And if that kind of power was possible, what else might be?

Debbie smiled at Lenora and tears of joy began to slide down her face. "My boy. My sweet, sweet boy."

Marshall struggled against the paralysis inflicted on him by his daughter. His jaw muscles were clenched tight, his body shook as every muscle strained, and beads of sweat broke out on his brow. Despite his monumental effort, he didn't budge so much as a fraction of an inch. Like Joanne before him, Marshall resorted to the only weapon he had left. His voice.

"If you want to ensure your mother's safety, you should release Joanne and me and depart. Whatever you are, were, or have become, you're clearly not sane. You're more a danger to Debbie Coulter than either of us could ever be."

Lenora turned away from Debbie and walked over to her father. She stopped in front of him and raised the knife. She placed the tip of the blade against the soft flesh just beneath Marshall's chin. "I came back because of what Lenora did to Mother and because of what Lenora's . . . *associate* did." She gave Joanne a glance filled with dark amusement before returning her attention to Marshall. "I wasn't happy to see my work copied by an amateur. I'm proud of what I accomplished, even though you still refused to accept me into the family."

"Sheriff Manchester and Dale Ramsey caught you literally red-handed," Marshall said. "There was nothing I could do. Believe me, I tried."

Doubt entered Lenora's—or was it Carl's?—gaze, only to depart just as swiftly as it had come. "And where were you when I was strapped down on a table and my veins were pumped full of poison? No one came to claim my spirit, and I was left to drift where I would, alone and unwanted."

"I carved an icon for you the night after you were found guilty of the murders, and I saved it until your execution. But not even my power or my contacts could get me in to see your body before it was embalmed. Once that process has begun, the spirit flees the body and cannot be found."

Joanne thought of the tiny stone figure Marshall had touched to the side of Tyrone's head in the morgue, and of Marshall's reaction. Is that what he had been trying to do—capture Tyrone's soul in the stone doll? Even if such a thing were possible, why do it?

Lenora looked confused now. She began to lower the knife, and Joanne could feel the pressure in her head easing up a little.

But before she could make another try to draw her weapon, the pressure returned, even stronger than before, making her wince.

"Maybe you're telling the truth, maybe not," Lenora said. "It doesn't matter anymore. Now that *I'm* in charge, I'll protect Mother. She's going to keep me company while I go about my new work. I'm going to destroy the Reliquary."

Marshall paled at Lenora's pronouncement. "You can't be serious! You have no idea what will happen as a result!"

Lenora laughed. "You should see yourself, Father! The look of fear on your face right now is priceless! I know exactly what will happen if the Reliquary is destroyed. The Crosses will lose the source of their power, and when that happens, you'll be no different from ordinary humans." Lenora's mouth stretched into a wicked smile. "You're going to come along, too. After all, you wouldn't want to miss the end of everything you and your family have worked for all these long years, would you?"

"Like hell I'll go with you!" Marshall said. "I'll die first! I may not be able to break free of your domination, but I can still use my powers to burn out my own mind."

Lenora regarded her father for a moment. "You know, I think you'd really do it. But what about her?" Lenora pointed toward Joanne. "Is preserving your family's power worth *her* life?"

Marshall avoided looking at Joanne as he answered. "It's not just a matter of power, Carl. If you and Lenora share any consciousness, surely you understand that by now. But you're mistaken if you think there's anything between Joanne and me. Do with her as you wish."

Joanne knew Marshall would respond this way, perhaps the only way he *could*, but it still hurt to hear him speak the words.

"You know, Father, for someone who's had so much practice lying, you're not very good at it. If you willingly come with Mother and me to the Reliquary, I'll spare your friend. If you don't, I'll kill her just for the fun of it."

"Don't help her . . . them. Whatever," Joanne said. "I won't help this lunatic in any way, even if it's just as a bargaining chip." Joanne didn't know why it was important to protect this Reliquary—whatever it was. She just did. Call it a Feeling.

Lenora fixed Joanne with an arctic stare. "I can give you a push and turn your brain into tapioca. You'd be dead before you hit the floor. Not as satisfying as using a knife, but it *would* be neater."

Marshall looked from Lenora to Joanne to Debbie then back to Lenora. His face was impassive, but Joanne knew inside he was furiously calculating odds and exploring various strategies. At last he said, "Very well. I'll do as you say as long as you spare Joanne's life."

"Don't do me any favors," Joanne snapped. "Whatever's going on here, it needs to stop—now!"

Lenora moved close to Marshall, stood on her tiptoes, and gave him a quick kiss on the cheek. "I knew you wouldn't let me down, Daddy." Her voice inflections were different, as if for a moment Lenora was in control of her own body once more. Then she turned toward Debbie, took the woman's hand, and it was Carl who next spoke. "Come, Mother. Father will follow. Now that he's submitted himself completely to my will, he hasn't a choice."

Lenora led Debbie toward the bedroom door, the older woman smiling contentedly. Marshall trailed after, giving Joanne a glance that she interpreted as, *Don't you dare try to follow us.*

Frustrated, Joanne tried once more to break free of whatever strange spell held her immobile, but it was no use. She still couldn't move.

Lenora stopped at the bedroom door just as she was about to step over the threshold. "One more thing." She turned to look at Joanne, her blue eyes gleamed, and Joanne screamed as she found herself plummeting into darkness.

. . . . .

"What did you do to her?" Marshall demanded.

Joanne lay on the floor, curled into a fetal position and sobbing.

"I promised I wouldn't kill her," Lenora said. "I didn't promise not to make her suffer. Forget her. We have work to do." Lenora turned and continued through the doorway, pulling Debbie after her as if the woman were a small child that couldn't be trusted to walk on her own.

Marshall had to follow as well. He'd allowed himself to be mentally dominated by his two children who now inhabited the same body, and he must obey their commands. Whatever they'd done to Joanne, he might've been able to counteract it—*if* he'd been free to use his powers. But he wasn't, and all he could do was give Joanne a sympathetic look as he walked out of the bedroom and left her sobbing on the floor, alone.

I'm so sorry, he thought. He did his best to put Joanne out of his mind then and turned his thoughts to the task of trying to figure out a way to stop his children before they could carry out their mad plan to destroy the Reliquary.

. . . . .

Dale had heard the phrase *screeching halt* before, of course, but until he slammed on his Jeep's brakes in front of Sanctity's main entrance, he'd never actually experienced one before. It felt damned satisfying.

As he got out of his vehicle and started for the front steps, he started to look for the Beast before remembering with relief that the creature wasn't his problem anymore. What *was* his problem was getting into Sanctity. He hadn't been able to call Marshall or Althea on his cell since he didn't have numbers for any of the Crosses, and while he could always fall back on the meddling reporter's old stand-by—pounding on the door and demanding to be let in—that would only result in the appearance of one servant or another, one that had undoubtedly been well trained not to permit near-hysterical old men to enter Sanctity's hallowed halls. He would need one hell of a good excuse to get inside. It wasn't as if he could say, *Pardon me, but if you don't let me in there's a good chance more people will die before morning*—a lot *more*. That would get the door slammed in his face for sure.

As he reached the door and rang the bell, his exhausted mind still hadn't coughed up any usuable lies, and he doubted it would deliver any in the few seconds it would take for a servant to answer the door. The best plan he could come up with was to knock whoever opened the door on his or her ass, dart past them, and run like hell through Sanctity's corridors, shouting Althea's name the whole way and hoping to draw her attention.

He'd already curled his right hand into a fist and was raising it to strike when the door opened.

"There's no need for such foolishness," Althea said. "Eve called to let me know you were coming."

As Dale lowered his hand with no small amount of embarrassment, he remembered something that Eve had said to him. *My sister and I may have different philosophies regarding our roles in the county, but we still talk from time to time.* He was grateful that this was one of those times.

"If Eve called, then you already know—"

"Everything," Althea interrupted, and then smiled. "But then I usually do, don't I?" Her smile fell away, and her eyes caught and held Dale's gaze with an intense, penetrating look, as if she were peering into the deepest recesses of his being and weighing what she found there. "The time we've both been waiting for is finally upon us, Dale Ramsey. Are you prepared to do what must be done?"

He remembered walking among trees, a little girl sleeping huddled against his chest as he carried her, implicitly trusting him to keep her safe, no matter what.

"I won't let Joanne down," he said.

Althea raised an eyebrow. "You made a vow once. Do you still intend to honor it?"

Dale remembered a darkness empty and cold as space, and from within that vast nothingness, a soundless voice asking him a question. He answered now as he had then.

"Yes. As long as it helps Joanne."

Althea considered a moment before replying. "Tonight it will." She opened the door wide and beckoned him to enter.

· · · · ·

It was cold and dark and she was so alone. The stone felt like ice beneath her bare feet, and she held her arms crossed over her bare chest in a vain attempt to shield her sensitive nipples from the air's chill. Her breath came in ragged gasps, and she shivered from head to toe so violently that she feared she might lose her footing and fall to the ground. The stone beneath her feet was jagged, and as much as it hurt to stand on, she figured it would hurt a hell of a lot worse if she fell on it. She tried to will herself to stop shivering, but it was no use. She was too cold, too frightened.

She had no idea who she was or how she'd gotten here. Though she tried, she couldn't recall any details of life outside the dark and the cold. A terrible possibility occurred to her then. What if there *wasn't* an outside world? What if there was only this awful place and she was the only person who inhabited it? If that was true, then she was profoundly, horribly alone.

She drew in a deep breath of frigid air and then released it in an ear-shattering scream. Pain and fear gave power to her voice, and the sound seemed to continue on after she ran out of breath, as if it had taken on a life of its own. Her scream continued to grow, increasing in volume until it seemed to fill the entire universe. She pressed her hands to her ears to try to shut out the scream, but it didn't help. The sound was within her now as much as without, and she knew it would never stop. She couldn't hear her own sobs as she collapsed to the ground, couldn't feel the hurt as the cold, uncaring rock cut and bruised her naked flesh. The scream had become her entire existence, and she knew with numb certainty that she would never be free of it. Never.

She felt a hand on her shoulder and the scream was cut off, drying away without so much as a last echo. Light flooded her vision and she found herself looking into blue eyes that were cold but not altogether unfriendly.

"It's all right, child. It's over."

At first Joanne didn't recognize the older woman kneeling next to her wearing a black dress, silver hoop earrings, and a diamond pendant. But then her memories returned, and they brought along an extra one with them.

"You're the one who found me in the cave," Joanne whispered. "It was your hand I felt on my shoulder."

Althea smiled. "That's right. But it was Mr. Ramsey who found you first. You were frightened and confused, poor dear, and ran away from him. I helped him find you for the second time."

Joanne frowned. She didn't recall running from anyone, let alone Dale. "The next thing I remember after seeing you in the cave is Dale carrying me in the woods."

"I'd do it again, too," said a male voice. "Though I must admit you'd be a bit harder to carry this time."

Joanne looked away from Althea's face and saw Dale standing behind the woman. He was smiling, but his gaze was filled with concern and, though she wasn't sure why, a sense of urgency.

Joanne felt a surge of panic at the thought she was naked, and she started to ask Dale to turn around when she realized she was still wearing her sheriff's uniform.

"What happened to me just now?" she asked.

"My granddaughter used her mental abilities to trap your mind in an illusion, a psychic prison created from your worst nightmare. I set you free."

Althea helped Joanne to her feet, and once again she was impressed by how strong the older woman was. Joanne looked around and saw she was still in Marshall's bedroom.

"How did you find me?"

"I knew what was happening in here," Althea said. "I'm aware of everything that occurs within the walls of Sanctity. It's the main reason I spend so much time alone in my room. All those thoughts . . ." She shook her head. "I know what my granddaughter has become and what she intends to do, but I am unable to go after her. She has grown far stronger than I would've imagined possible, and if two minds such as ours were in close proximity, especially so near the Reliquary, the effects would be more than disastrous."

Joanne's head was spinning, and not entirely due to the after-effects of being imprisoned in Lenora's psychic trap. "What's a Reliquary?"

"No more questions now, dear. Anything else you need to know, Mr. Ramsey can explain on the way. As much as I'd like to give you a chance to rest, we can't afford to take the time."

Althea left the bedroom walking at a brisk pace. Joanne turned to Dale, hoping he'd clear things up, but he stepped to her side, took hold of her elbow, and began leading her after Althea.

"When did you get here?" she asked. "How long was I out?"

"I just arrived, and from what Althea told me, you were unconscious—or whatever the right word is—for a few minutes. They don't have much of a headstart on us, but every moment counts, so we need to haul ass."

They moved through the outer room of Marshall's quarters. The living area was decorated in similar fashion to his bedroom, with globes, maps, navigation equipment, and bookshelves filled with travel guides. Joanne remembered what Marshall had said about rarely getting the opportunity to travel, and while there was much about Marshall Cross that she didn't like, she couldn't help feeling a certain sympathy for him at that moment.

"Haul ass to where?" she demanded.

"Althea already told you. To the Reliquary. The word refers to a shrine where sacred objects are kept, by the way."

As they left Marshall's quarters and entered the hall, Joanne realized that Dale no longer looked as exhausted as he had this morning at the charred ruins of the Caffeine Café. He seemed completely restored, as if he'd had an infusion of vitality since last she'd seen him. Maybe it was just the urgency of the situation lending him energy, but somehow she didn't think so.

Althea was moving swiftly down the hall away from them, almost but not quite running. Joanne's legs were still wobbly, and her head had begun throbbing again, but with Dale's steadying hand to help her, they managed to close the gap between them and the matriarch of the Cross clan. But soon after that Althea stopped in front of a door. She took a key out of her pocket, unlocked it, and gestured for Joanne and Dale to enter. The room inside was completely empty, save for an elevator door set into the far wall. Althea walked past them and used a second key to activate the elevator. When the door opened, Dale led Joanne into its black leather-padded interior. There was a single unmarked button next to the door, and Joanne pressed it.

Althea did not join them in the elevator.

"You're not coming?" Joanne said.

"I cannot," she said. "It would be . . . dangerous for me to be near the Reliquary right now." She looked at them one last time, her expression unreadable. "Whatever else happens, the Reliquary must be protected at all costs. *All* costs."

Dale nodded. "I understand."

Althea nodded back, and as the door began to slide shut, Joanne said, "I'm glad *you* understand, but would you mind letting me in on the joke?"

He gave her a sympathetic look as she felt the elevator being to smoothly descend. "Do I really need to?"

She was about the scream at him to start giving her straight answer when the back of her skull started tingling so hard it felt like her head might explode any second, and intense nausea squeezed her stomach in a sickly cold grip. It was a Feeling with a capital F—the strongest she'd ever had. She understood Dale's response then. The specific details of what was happening weren't important. What mattered was this shit had to be stopped.

Despite her head and her stomach, she pulled away from Dale, straightened, and drew her 9 mm.

"Tell me what we have to do."

And as the elevator continued its descent, Dale began talking.

CHAPTER TWENTY-ONE

The Crosses were among the first families to settle in this area of Ohio," Dale began. "At least, the first of European origin. A Native American tribe called the Nadana had lived here for centuries before that, but they were gone by the time the white settlers came. Or so it seemed. The settlers built homes and began carving out lives for themselves here, and it wasn't long before they discovered what they came to call Barrow Hill Mound. They didn't know what it was exactly, but they could tell it was man-made. One day a girl—a Cross girl—decided to climb to the top of the mound. And the mound took her."

Joanne thought of what had happened to Sarah Rodgers at the mound and suppressed a shiver.

Dale continued. "It swallowed her whole, as if it were a living thing, leaving no sign of her passage into the earth. Her sister had been playing with her at the time—though she'd been too afraid to climb the mound—and she fled home to tell their parents. Panicked, the girl's mother and father summoned help, and the settlers began digging at the spot where the girl had vanished. After six days they'd only managed to dig down a dozen feet, and though they'd found human remains, the bones were old and obviously belonged to adults. But at the end of the sixth day, the girl reappeared. She came walking out of the woods, naked but otherwise unharmed." He smiled. "That part sound familiar?"

The elevator came to a gentle stop and the door slid open. Outside, a fluorescent light flicked on, illuminating a row of electric carts lined against a stone wall. Dale walked out of the elevator and headed for one of the carts. Joanne walked beside him, still holding her 9 mm, surveying the area as they went, alert for any sign of trouble. Her Feeling was even stronger now, but instead of being debilitated by the accompanying sensations, she seemed to draw strength from them. Good. She figured she was going to need all the help she could get.

Dale climbed behind the cart's steering wheel, and Joanne took the passenger's seat. She understood why Dale had chosen to drive, and she agreed with his decision. He was the one who knew where they were going, and this way, her hands would be free if she needed to fire her weapon. Dale thumbed a button and the engine came to life with a soft electric hum and a faint odor of ozone filled the air. He flicked on the cart's headlights, put the engine in gear, and pressed down on the accelerator. With a jerk, the cart took off, and Dale angled the small vehicle to the left, the headlights illuminating a tunnel that looked to Joanne like it belonged to an old-fashioned mining operation, the kind she'd only ever seen in films.

Dale picked up his story where he'd left off.

"There was one big difference between the Cross girl's disappearance and yours. When the other girl returned, she retained her memory of what had happened to her inside the mound—or more accurately, beneath it. She told the other settlers that an ancient godlike being dwelled in the darkness deep in the earth. A creature that was older than the stars, older than time. The Nadana had known of it, and—following instructions given to them by the creature itself—they built Barrow Hill Mound. Not to worship the creature, but to contain it. The being, whom the settlers came to call the Old One, was so unimaginably ancient that, while it still lived, its vast mind had begun to deteriorate. It had a sort of cosmic version of Alzheimer's, I suppose you could say. Once the mound was built, the Old One slipped into a state resembling hibernation, perhaps to slow the decay of its mind, perhaps for some other unfathomable reason. But in this state it dreamed, and from time to time, its dreams would leak out into reality. The settlers had already experienced a number of strange occurrences since they'd come to the area, and now they understood the reason for them. Such manifestations continue to this day. I should know. I spent most of the night being chased by one."

"What?"

"Nevermind, I'll tell you later. Back to the story. The girl told her people that she'd been with the Old One, actually been inside its mind for six days, and during that time she not only learned the truth about the being, but of how the Nadana had buried their dead above it, so that their spirits could help strengthen the Old One's control of its dreams and keep them from spilling over into the real world. In return, the spirits of the dead enjoyed a paradisiacal existence within the mind of the Old One, and those among the living who served the being were rewarded with great powers of the mind. But eventually the Nadana died out, for reasons not even the Old One seemed entirely clear on. It had been without servants for many, many years, and its mind had deteriorated even further as a result. So when the girl climbed to the top of the mound, the Old One drew her in, taught her about it and its needs, and sent her back to her people to offer them the same deal the Old One had given the Nadana. Serve me and I shall give you power beyond that of all other men, and I will ensure you an afterlife of eternal bliss."

"And they went for it," Joanne said.

"Of course they did. Once the girl showed them her newfound powers and convinced them her story was true. Though I suspect she also used those powers to get them to accept the Old One's offer. So the settlers repaired the damage they'd done to the top of the mound, and at the girl's direction began digging tunnels—like the one we're in now—to reach the Old One. And when they finally did, they built the Reliquary, a repository where the spirits of their dead could be housed and their energy added to the mass of souls that help contain the Old One's dreams."

Joanne remembered the small stone figure Marshall had touched to the head of Tyrone's body, his puzzled expression as he said, *Something's wrong. It's not here.* And when she'd asked what, Marshall's reply was, *His essence.* "They capture the spirit in stone carvings, don't they?"

Dale nodded. "They're called icons. The Old One told the Cross girl that the icons would be more efficient than just burying dead bodies in the mound, and she taught her people how to make them. As long as one is touched to the body within a day or two of death, the spirit can be absorbed."

"So right now we're traveling from Sanctity to the Mound?" Joanne asked.

"The Crosses need access to the Old One to deliver icons to the Reliquary, and though they don't exactly worship the creature, they do gather in its presence. Especially when important family members come in from out of town."

Even though it was Dale telling her these things, Joanne knew that she should've been at least skeptical of the outlandish tale he'd woven for her so far. But too many of the pieces fit, and besides, her gut told her that, bizarre as it might be, Dale was telling her the truth.

"So where do I fit into all this?" she asked. "What happened to me during *my* disappearance?"

"You were playing alone near the mound one day when you felt drawn to climb it." Before she could protest, Dale added, "You don't remember this now, but trust me, it happened. Like the Cross girl long ago, you were taken by the Old One, pulled into its mound, and spent six days there. No one knew what had happened to you, and the whole county began searching. Including me. After losing my own little girl . . ." He broke off with a sigh and shook his head as if to clear the thought away. "Not even Althea knew where you where, not at first, but as the days wore on, she began to suspect. I didn't know the whole story of the Old One then, but I'd discovered some fragments here and there over the years. I went to Sanctity and questioned Althea, and though she wouldn't tell me everything, she gave me enough hints so that I decided to go to the mound and check it out. I climbed to the top, and I was drawn in, just as you were.

"I don't remember much. I remember darkness and light and something that was a hybrid of the two, while at the same time being neither." He smiled apologetically. "Sorry. It's hard to explain. But eventually I became aware that you were there, too. I tried to reach out for you, but I couldn't find you. And then I heard a voice. No . . . more like *felt* it in my mind. It told me things—about itself, about the Nadana, and what they and later the Crosses had done to help preserve the remaining scraps of its sanity. The Old One then asked me if I wanted to return you to the world, and I said yes, more than anything. Then it asked that, if it let me have you, would I serve it. Again, I said yes. And then it told me it would be my task to aid and protect the Guardian. The next thing I knew you and I were standing next to the Reliquary. You were naked, but I still had my clothes on—perhaps because

I wasn't in the Old One's mind for very long, or perhaps because it didn't need to do anything to change me. I don't know. But when you saw me, you screamed and ran off into the darkness. I was alarmed that I might have found you—and made a bargain with some sort of ancient god—only to lose you.

"I started searching, and I quickly became lost as well. Both of us might've died in those tunnels, but Althea came looking for us. She found you, then me. She took us to Sanctity and, despite my protests, she used her powers to suppress your memory of what happened. Afterward, you fell asleep. She said it wasn't necessary that you remember and that it would be a kindness to help you forget until the day you were ready to know the truth. Maybe she was right. At any rate, Marshall drove us into Mare's Nest Woods and dropped us off. You were still asleep, and after Marshall drove away, I began carrying you. Eventually you woke up, your memory of the whole experience gone. I told everyone I'd found you in the woods, and with the help of Stan Manchester, not to mention the Crosses' influence, few questions were asked, and my story was accepted."

Joanne looked at Dale with new understanding. "I always knew you were a good man, Dale Ramsey, but you made a literal deal with a devil to save me. There's no possible way I can ever thank you enough."

Dale drove for a few moments more before responding. "I lost my wife and daughter because of a choice I'd made. Afterward, I vowed I would never lose anyone again, not if I could help it, no matter the cost to me personally. You don't ever have to thank me, Joanne. On the contrary, I should thank you. Rescuing you and working at your side ever since . . . it saved *me*."

Even though Joanne now knew the truth, she still couldn't recall any specific details about the time she'd spent with the Old

One. "There's still one thing I don't know. What did the thing do to me? What *am* I?"

"I told you. You're the Guardian. Even with the Crosses' help, the Old One's dreams still escape from time to time, resulting in the strange events that occur in the county. It's your job to deal with the weirdness when it happens. That's why you have your Feelings. They tell you when something is wrong and needs fixing. Plus—and I'm not sure Althea knows this—I believe you're supposed to serve as a check against the Crosses. They might serve the Old One, but the powers they're granted can be abused all too easily. You're supposed to help keep them in line."

"In other words, I'm the Old One's watchdog." She didn't like the sound of that.

"That's one way to look at it, but not the only way. The borders of Cross County roughly correspond to the Old One's sphere of influence. You're the county sheriff, aren't you? Why did you think you were elected, young as you are? The Crosses wanted to make sure the Guardian was in the best position to perform her duty."

"My election was fixed?" After everything she'd learned recently, she supposed she shouldn't have been surprised, but she was.

"Let's just say the Crosses helped your campaign. And I contributed by convincing you to run in the first place. But I didn't do so to help carry out the Crosses' agenda. I thought you'd make a damned good sheriff, and you have. Better than Stan Manchester ever was—and *not* because you were chosen to serve some half-demented god. Because of who you are. Joanne Talon, steady of hand, clear of eye, and stout of heart."

"And you're full of shit," she muttered.

Though they were zooming through a tunnel in an electric cart, heading for a rendezvous with a danger Joanne was only beginning to fully comprehend, she couldn't help thinking of what implications the revelations she'd learned had for her as a person. She'd meant what she'd said when she'd told Terry she'd learned to leave her disappearance in the past and focus her emotional energy on the here and now. But now she knew that she'd been changed during the six days she'd been missing. But the question was, changed into what? The way she'd emerged naked from the Old One's mind, it was as if she had been destroyed and reborn within the depths of its deteriorating psyche. So what did that make her? If she wasn't the same Joanne Talon that had fallen inside the mound, who was she? Some kind of duplicate? Was she even human at all? And everything she'd done in her life, the choices that she'd made, the accomplishments she'd worked so hard to achieve, the good she'd tried to do for the citizens of Cross County . . . was all of it because she was simply fulfilling her role as the Old One's Guardian, following the path the ancient being had mapped out for her, with no more self-awareness or autonomy than a machine carrying out its preprogrammed function?

"I may well be overflowing with shit," Dale said, "but we still have a job to do. Now it's your turn to get me up to speed. Althea told me that Lenora, Marshall, and Debbie are headed for the Reliquary, and that they pose a threat to it. That's all I know."

Joanne spent the next several minutes of their journey through the dark, winding tunnel telling Dale everything she'd learned since they'd last seen one another.

"Let me see if I got this straight," Dale said. "Carl Coulter's spirit was drawn back to the world of the living because he thought his mother was in danger, and he didn't like the idea of someone impersonating him. He tried contacting you in a dream, but when the dream turned nightmarish, you awoke, and he was unable to deliver his message. So when he couldn't get through to tell you what was happening, he tried to communicate with Lenora, his half-sister. But he did more than just talk with her. He *became* her. And now brother and sister are working together to get revenge on Marshall and the rest of the Crosses by destroying the Reliquary."

"I'd hoped it would sound less insane if I heard it from your lips," Joanne said. "It doesn't."

Dale thought for a moment.

"Then who killed Ray Porter and Tyrone?"

Joanne opened her mouth to answer when she realized that out of everything they'd learned, they still didn't know. "Lenora, I assume." But even as she said it, it didn't sound right, didn't *Feel* right.

"Carl tried to show you two faces in your dream. Lenora is only one person—not counting her new soul-brother—and the second person can't be Carl himself."

"So there's someone else," Joanne said.

"Well, it's not me, and I'm fairly confident it's not you."

"Your faith in me is overwhelming. Tell you what—let's worry about figuring out whodunit later . . . assuming we survive to do anything at all."

"Deal."

· · · · ·

Althea watched as the elevator door closed, cutting off her view of Joanne and Mr. Ramsey. She felt a great deal of sympathy for the girl. Not only was she about to face the greatest challenge of her young life, she was going to learn some uncomfortable truths in the process. If Joanne succeeded, she'd come out of this much stronger. But *if* was a small word with gargantuan implications.

Althea wished she could take a more active hand in this

matter, but she'd gone over all possible strategies and outcomes in her mind a thousand times. And given her mental abilities, she could do more than merely imagine possibilities. She could *see* them. Because of this, she knew without doubt that she was doing the right thing by limiting her involvement. But knowing didn't always make doing any easier.

She still had a task to attend to before her part in this drama was over, though. She walked toward the end of the hall until she reached a winding wrought-iron staircase and descended to the ground floor. She continued on to the main entrance now, and she reached the door just as the bell rang. She unlocked the door and opened it. Standing on the porch, both looking somewhat the worse for the wear, were two men she'd never met before, but whom she'd been expecting nevertheless. They were the last two players, and it was about time they arrived.

"Can I help you?" She kept her voice neutral, as if she had no idea who they were or what they were here for.

The man in the shirt and tie smiled, and his eyes gleamed with a mad intensity that even Althea found daunting.

"You can tell us where Marshall and Lenora are."

· · · · ·

"I wonder if you can appreciate how strange this is for me, Father. I've never been here before, yet my sister has known this place almost since from birth. I have access to both our memories, and it's like seeing through two very different pairs of eyes."

The three of them—four, Marshall supposed, if you counted Lenora and Carl separately—stood in a large cave directly beneath Barrow Hill Mound. The chamber was illuminated by globes of soft white light erected on metal poles around the circumference of the cave. The lights had their own power source and were activated when motion detectors registered the presence of visitors. Their cart was parked near the entrance of the tunnel that led to Sanctity. Four other tunnels branched off from the cave, each leading to a different location in the county, but those tunnels were rarely used. In the middle of the cave lay the object of Carl's fascination. The Reliquary.

It had been carved from a gray stone column and remained connected to the ceiling and floor of the cave. Altogether, the Reliquary measured twenty-five feet from top to bottom. The points where the smooth surface of the Reliquary gave way to rough stone resembled nothing so much as wrinkled brain tissue, a touch Marshall had always found appropriate. Small recessed areas had been carved into the column, dozens upon dozens of them, each precisely large enough for an icon to fit inside. Though only the icons closest to the front were visible, there were many more stored one behind the other. Marshall knew the precise number of icons, their exact locations, and whose spirits were housed within.

The air in the chamber was suffused with power on the verge of breaking free, like a dam near to bursting. Only the combined power of the icons kept the Old One's energy contained.

Perhaps it was coincidence, but Lenora stood directly before the most recent addition to the Reliquary—the icon containing the spirit of Ray Porter. Marshall decided not to point out that bit of irony, though.

Lenora stood two feet from the Reliquary, while Marshall stood several feet farther back, next to Debbie. He could feel Carl and Lenora's power wrapped around him like a giant hand holding him in check. It held him loosely at the moment, but not so loose that he could break free. He knew that if he so much as tried to move a step forward or back on his own, the invisible hand would squeeze tight around him, ensuring he behaved like a good little boy.

Lenora looked as if she wanted to reach out and touch the Reliquary but couldn't bring herself to do so.

"This is where the family gathers to worship the Old One," she said. Or rather Carl said using her voice. Marshall wondered if there was any point in trying to differentiate between the two anymore. As time went on, their personalities seemed to be fusing into one, a new individual, greater than the sum of its parts.

"We don't think of it as worship," Marshall said. "More like communing with the spirits of our forebears and basking in the presence of the Old One's power."

Lenora shrugged without taking her gaze off the Reliquary. "Sounds like worship to me." She paused and tilted her head to the side, as if listening to something she wasn't quite sure she really heard. "What's that noise?"

"The spirits in the icons. They whisper to each other constantly, though it's unclear what they're saying. We think it's part of how they keep the Old One pacified. I imagine it sounds louder to you because you're dead. At least half of you is."

"They're not whispering," Lenora said. "They're singing. It's the most beautiful thing I've ever heard."

Marshall himself could only detect the merest hint of the icons' whispering, and even then only on occasion. He strained to hear what Lenora did, but it was no use. The icons' song was not for him, it seemed.

Lenora turned back to look at Debbie. "Do you hear them, Mother?"

"I don't hear singing *or* whispering," she said petulantly, like a child upset at missing out on something everyone else was experiencing. "But there's something else . . ." She frowned in confusion. "It's not a voice, though. It's pictures. They're in my head, so many of them, going by so fast. The strangest things . . . the most *awful* things . . ." She shuddered and squeezed her eyes shut, as if by doing so she might deny the unsettling images access to her mind. Marshall knew it wouldn't work.

Lenora rushed forward and took hold of Debbie's hand. The woman kept her eyes closed, but now she was shaking her head back and muttering, "No, no, no, no, no . . ."

Lenora shot Marshall an accusing look, as if he was responsible for what was happening to Debbie.

"This close to the Reliquary, her fragile mental defenses aren't enough to keep out the Old One's dreams, even with the icons' assistance," Marshall said. "I can help her—*if* you'll release me. If you do, I promise not to interfere with your plan or attempt to escape."

Lenora reached out and touched Debbie's cheek with gentle concern. Marshall could tell she was considering his offer. Once he was free, he would help shield Debbie from the Old One's dreams. Then, despite his promise, he'd turn on Lenora and Carl and do everything he could against his children to protect the Reliquary. Though Marshall doubted Lenora or Carl could read his thoughts—that was a highly complex and delicate skill only a few Crosses had mastered, Althea chief among them—Lenora looked at him and smiled.

"Nice try, Father." She turned back to Debbie and stroked her cheek. "Be strong, Mother. I promise you won't suffer much longer." She walked back to the Reliquary and fear stabbed into Marshall's gut like a blade of ice.

"What are you going to do?" he asked.

He'd hoped that once Lenora and Carl were in the Reliquary's presence, they'd reconsider their plan to destroy it. Power was a heady brew, as the Crosses had known for generations, and once one had a taste of the pure stuff straight from the source, it became addictive. But evidently not for Carl and Lenora.

"What we came for," Lenora said. "To destroy the Reliquary."

She plucked an icon at random from its alcove and lifted it to her face for a closer look.

"That's Ray Porter's spirit," Marshall said, hoping it would stir sympathy in whatever part of his daughter's soul that remained in her body.

Lenora gazed down upon the icon's crude stone features. "Yes, I can tell. They all look the same, but when you touch one, you know who it is, even if you never met them in life. How interesting."

With a sudden swift motion, she lifted the icon over her head and dashed it to the cave's stone floor. The small statuette broke into pieces and a tiny high-pitched voice like a human scream momentarily cut through the air before dying away.

Marshall closed his eyes. Ray Porter had just died for a second time, and the Reliquary had been weakened by one soul.

Marshall opened his eyes. "So that's your grand plan? To break one icon after another until you weaken the Reliquary to the point where it can no longer hold back the Old One's dreams."

Lenora looked back toward Marshall and smiled. "The county will be plunged into the chaos of a mad god's nightmares. But like a raging fire, eventually the Old One's unchecked power will burn itself out, and it will cease to exist. The god of the Crosses will finally die, and the family will die with it."

"What of the innocents who'll also perish?" Marshall asked. "All the men and women in the county who have nothing to do with the family and who haven't wronged you in any way?"

Lenora burst out laughing. "You can't be serious, Father! They aren't *people*. They're lower life forms, little more than animals."

"Like your mother?" Marshall countered. He was speaking to both of his children, for neither Debbie nor Charlotte had possessed any Cross blood.

Lenora scowled but didn't reply. She took another icon from the Reliquary and held it out for a moment.

"Stuart Burgin. Though Stuart was mostly human, his grandfather was one of the family, and he asked for his grandson's spirit to be granted a place in the Reliquary after his early death from cancer. Sorry, Stuart." She hurled the icon to the ground where it broke just like the first. It also screamed as its spirit fled—to where, Marshall had no idea. But whatever happened to it, it could never compare to the paradise to be found within the group mind of the Reliquary.

"Please, Lenora, Carl . . . you can't do this!"

"Of course we can. Watch." She took another icon from the Reliquary and destroyed it, releasing another spirit and another scream.

"That was Anna Cross, a federal judge."

As she reached for another, Marshall drew upon all of his inner strength and focused it on breaking free of Carl and Lenora's psychic hold on him. He couldn't allow his children to destroy everything his family had worked for over all the long years since they'd first discovered the Old One. But his children were too strong, and he could not break free of their mental domination.

A fourth icon crashed to the cave floor. "Nathaniel Cross. He owned several wineries in California, as well as a number of four-star restaurants."

She reached for a fifth icon.

"The pictures are getting worse," Debbie said in a hollow voice. "Stronger, clearer . . ." She shuddered. "Nastier."

Lenora had only destroyed a quartet of icons so far, but the Reliquary was in many ways like a living organism. The destruction of the icons had created the equivalent of a wound in the combined energy field of the Reliquary. In a sense, it was bleeding power and beginning to weaken. How many more icons could the Reliquary stand to lose before the Old One's dreams began to slip through? A half dozen? Less? Marshall honestly didn't know, but he feared it wouldn't take too many more.

He'd hoped that by submitting to Lenora and Carl and agreeing to accompany them he would buy himself time to come up with a way to stop them. But it was too late. He was unable to break free of their power and there was no one else who—

The whine of an approaching electric cart interrupted Marshall's thought. He turned to see the glow of headlights shining forth from the tunnel leading to Sanctity. He smiled. It might not be the cavalry approaching, but it would do.

CHAPTER TWENTY-TWO

Joanne held onto the dash with her free hand while Dale steered the cart out of the tunnel and into a large cave. She took in the scene in a flash—stone column in the middle of the cave, Lenora standing next to it holding an icon, Marshall and Debbie standing several feet farther back. A series of lights positioned around the cave's perimeter lit the cave. The illumination they gave off wasn't too bright, but it was enough. She'd have to remember to aim carefully if she needed to use her weapon. It would be too easy to misjudge distances in this light.

Dale slammed on the brake too hard and the cart lurched up on two wheels. For a moment Joanne thought she was going to be thrown out of the vehicle, but it came back down on all four tires with a jarring thud.

Joanne jumped out of the cart, assumed a firing stance, and aimed her 9 mm at Lenora.

"Don't move or I'll shoot!" she ordered. "Hell, for what you did to me, I should just go ahead and put a couple bullets in you anyway."

Lenora ignored her and threw the icon to the ground. It broke into several large pieces, and Joanne heard a tiny cry that sounded almost like a scream. The pieces of the broken icon joined the fragments of others that were already lying on the ground. Lenora had been busy. Evidently Marshall remained in thrall to Lenora, for he just stood and watched his daughter destroy the icon.

Joanne was about to give Lenora one last warning before firing, but before she could do so, Debbie whirled around and came running toward her, eyes wide with madness, lips pulled back from her teeth in a feral snarl.

"Don't you hurt my baby!" she shrieked. She raised her hands as she came, as if she intended to claw Joanne's eyes out.

Joanne didn't want to shoot Debbie. The woman was an innocent victim caught up in the Crosses' web of intrigue and deception. But Joanne had to stop Lenora from destroying the Reliquary, and she didn't have the time to subdue Debbie in a nonviolent way. Maybe if she could shoot to wound Debbie—

Joanne was about to fire when Dale rushed in front of her and intercepted Debbie. He threw his arms around the woman and tackled her to the ground. Debbie screamed with fury as she thrashed in Dale's embrace, biting, kicking, and clawing at him.

"Don't just stand there!" Dale shouted. "Go!"

Joanne gave her protector a nod and ran toward Lenora.

Lenora flicked her gaze toward Marshall. "Stop the bitch," she commanded.

Moving stiffly, as if he were fighting every step of the way, Marshall advanced on Joanne.

"I can't stop myself," he said. "You're going to have to shoot me." He sounded so reasonable, so normal, that for a moment Joanne hesitated, not able to believe that he was really going to attack her. But then he was close enough to make a grab for her, and she barely managed to jump aside in time to avoid getting caught. Even moving awkwardly, Marshall was damned fast, faster than an ordinary man. Probably stronger, too. She couldn't afford to let him get hold of her.

She feinted right, and when he made another grab for her, she delivered a kick to his right knee cap. Since that was the leg currently bearing his weight, the blow knocked him off balance and he fell. As he went down, he angled his head toward the ground, and Joanne realized he was hoping to knock himself unconscious when he hit. But he landed on his shoulder, rolled, and came back up on his feet with a feline grace he hadn't exhibited a moment ago. It appeared Lenora had strengthened her control of Marshall's body, which was bad news for Joanne.

Before Joanne had time to put any distance between herself and Marshall, he lashed out at her, chopping his hand into the wrist of her gun hand. Joanne was barely able to drawn back her hand in time to avoid having her wrist shattered, but Marshall still managed to strike a glancing blow. Her hand went immediately numb, her fingers sprang open, and her weapon fell to the cave floor. She lunged for the gun, but Marshall was faster. He kicked the weapon away and then slammed his first into the side of her neck. Pain shot down her spine and white fire exploded behind her eyes. She collapsed to her hands and knees, her awareness flickering like a light bulb on the verge of blacking out, and she fought to hold onto consciousness.

She heard a whining sound, accompanied by a sudden wash of light, and for an instant she feared her synapses were misfiring wildly as her brain began to shut down. But then she realized that what she was hearing was the sound of another electric cart approaching. She looked toward the oncoming light just in time to hear Ronnie scream, "Die, bastard!" followed by the thunder of his 9 mm discharging.

Marshall was knocked off his feet, and this time when he went down, he stayed down.

Groggy, Joanne straightened and turned to see Ronnie coming toward her, weapon drawn and aimed. But he wasn't pointing his 9 mm at her, she realized, but at Marshall's prone form. Past

Ronnie she saw Dale still struggling with Debbie, his face marred by deep gashes where she'd scratched him. She also saw another man climbing off the third cart. She thought at first that she was hallucinating, for the man looked like Terry. But when he didn't suddenly vanish, she realized it really *was* him, and she thought that somehow he and Ronnie had learned what was happening and had come to help. She almost called out to Terry, but then Ronnie was next to her and leveling his weapon at Marshall's head, and she realized the deputy was about to kill Marshall execution-style. Marshall struggled to rise, but then slumped back, too weak to do anything but lie there and bleed from the bullet wound in his chest.

Joanne grabbed Ronnie's wrist and forced his arm upward. She gritted her teeth in anticipation of the weapon accidentally discharging, but Ronnie was too well trained and the 9 mm didn't go off.

"Let go, Jo-Jo. I have to do this."

Jo-Jo? What the hell?

"You don't know what he's done to me," Ronnie said, his voice quavering. "The things he made me see . . . made me *do* . . ."

She understood then that Marshall had used his mental powers on Ronnie and sent the deputy rocketing completely around the bend. She felt a wave of anger toward Marshall for manipulating Ronnie, but now wasn't the time to deal with it. "He's down, Ronnie, and he's not going to get up anytime soon. He's not a threat right now. But Lenora is. We have to stop her."

She glanced at the Reliquary where Marshall's daughter still stood, watching the chaos taking place around her and grinning with delight. Terry was walking toward her with a determined stride, and Joanne saw he held a small blade gripped tight in his hand. A scalpel, she realized. The hooded figured who'd attacked her last night had wielded a small blade too. Just like Terry's.

Oh, shit. No . . .

· · · · ·

Lenora's eyes focused on Terry as he approached, but he could see nothing in that gaze of the woman he'd screwed so many times.

"To tell you the truth, I'm glad you're here," Lenora said in a too-masculine voice. "I've got something to show you."

Terry smiled grimly as he raised his scalpel. "You better show me fast. Once you start bleeding, it'll only take you a few moments to lose consciousness."

"The Old One's dreams are starting to leak out," she said. "It won't be long until they flood the county. But here's a sneak peek of coming attractions."

Old One? Dreams? What the hell was the crazy bitch ranting about?

A dark cast came over Lenora's eyes and a deluge of obscene images assaulted Terry's mind. Distorted, alien nightmares beyond human comprehension invaded his brain, tearing into the fabric of his essence and shredding his soul into bloody gobbets.

Lenora's glossy black eyes glistened with satisfaction as Terry screamed the scream of the damned.

· · · · ·

Jesus Christ, this bitch was a wildcat! Dale would've rather fought the Black Beast than Debbie Coulter. His face was bleeding from numerous scratches, and his balls ached from where she'd kneed him. Dale wasn't a gentleman, not when it came to protecting his life—not to mention his balls—but he'd been too busy holding onto Debbie's wrists in order to keep her harpy claws away from his eyes to lay a good right cross on her and put her down. He'd tried kneeing her in the gut, but she twisted and thrashed like a dervish, turning his blows aside. He'd never head-butted anyone before, but he'd seen the maneuver in the movies numerous times. He'd always figured that in real life a person would crack their own skull attempting the attack, but he'd run out of options and was just about to try it when Debbie glanced over her shoulder and saw Terry Birch—where had he come from?—standing in front of Lenora.

Terry started shrieking and slicing the air with his scalpel, as if he were trying to fight enemies only he could see. The slashes came awfully close to Lenora, though she seemed unconcerned. She stood still, smiling and watching Terry's histrionics with eyes that, from this distance, seemed for some reason to be completely black.

"Carl!" Debbie shouted. "I'm coming, honey!" With a savage lunge, she pulled free from Dale's grip and began running toward Terry. Dale stumbled and nearly fell, but he managed to remain on his feet. He saw Joanne talking to Ronnie, Marshall Cross lying on the floor next to them, his shirt stained with blood from where Ronnie had shot him. Marshall wasn't moving, and Dale feared the man was dead.

Dale was trying to decide on his next move when Debbie grabbed hold of Terry's shoulder. She shouted, "Don't you hurt my baby, you sonofabitch!" and spun him around to face her.

Terry's scalpel whipped through the air and Debbie let out a gurgling gasp as her blood sprayed forth.

"Oh shit," Dale whispered.

. . . . .

Terry heard Lenora cry out in anguish, and the horrible images raping his mind vanished. His vision cleared in time for him to see Debbie Coulter slump to the ground, blood pumping from the gash in her throat. He had no memory of cutting her, but the blood dripping from the tip of his scalpel—not to mention the blood splashed on his face and clothes—told him that he had.

Good. That was one last bitch he had to worry about. He turned around, intending to give Lenora a second crimson smile to match Debbie's, but a pair of powerful hands clasped tight around his throat, choking off his air. Lenora's eyes were black and ebon tears oozed from the corners, her face contorted into a mask of rage and grief. He still had hold of his scalpel, but she was pressed too close to his body for him to reach her throat. But that didn't mean he couldn't strike elsewhere.

He heard a roaring in his ears and his vision grayed as oxygen deprivation began to take its toll on his brain. But if he could stay conscious long enough to bury the scalpel in the bitch's stomach. . . .

A shadow passed across Lenora's face, and her countenance blurred, shifted, and reformed into a monstrous apparition that was equal parts reptile and insect. She laughed, the sound like a hive full of angry hornets.

"It has begun," she rasped.

• • • • •

Still holding onto Ronnie's wrist to keep him from killing Marshall, Joanne watched Debbie fall to the cave floor, and though her first impulse was to run to the woman's side and try to save her life, Joanne knew there was nothing anyone could do. And if she'd needed any further proof that Terry was the person responsible for the deaths of Ray Porter and Tyrone, she had it now. She had no idea what his motive might be, nor did she understand what connection he had to Lenora and Carl Coulter. But none of that mattered right now—just like her shock, grief, and feelings of deep betrayal at learning the truth about Terry didn't matter. She had a duty to perform.

"Dale, get over here and put pressure on Marshall's wound!" she shouted. As the reporter rushed over to help, she turned to Ronnie. "Give me your gun."

The deputy looked at her and frowned.

"That's an order," she added. Her tone was calm, stern, and professional, and she could see that it was getting through to her second-in-command. But then something happened. A shadow moved through the cave and the lights flickered. Lenora changed from an attractive blonde woman to something out of nightmare, a bestial, demonic thing, and Joanne didn't need her Feelings to know that the Reliquary was beginning to fail.

Lenora lashed out with a clawed hand, ebon talons slicing deep furrows into Terry's cheek. He cried out and fell to his knees next to Debbie's body, blood dripping from his wounds, pattering onto the stone floor, mixing with hers.

Ronnie shrieked in mad terror at the sight of Lenora's hellish transformation. He pulled free of Joanne's grip, aimed his 9 mm at Lenora, and fired. The demon-thing jerked as a bullet struck her high on the shoulder close to her neck, but her only reaction was to turn and glare at Ronnie with glittering obsidian eyes.

"No," he whispered. "I won't do it. . . ."

But Ronnie jammed the muzzle of his weapon beneath his chin, and before Joanne could stop him, he squeezed the trigger. She saw a last look of apology in his eyes, and then all she saw was blood. She turned her head aside as spatter struck her face, hot and wet, and she heard Ronnie's body hit the cave floor. She told herself not to look at him, not even to think of him. There would be time to mourn him later—after she sent that demonic bitch to hell and made sure she stayed there.

TIM WAGGONER

She knelt next to Ronnie's body, not gazing upon the bloody ruin that had been his face, and grabbed his gun. Blood coated the weapon, and she grimaced as she pried it out of his hand. She rose to her feet in a single smooth motion, leveled the weapon at Lenora and pulled the trigger. That is, she *wanted* to pull the trigger. But her finger refused to obey her command.

"If I can make your deputy blow his brains out," Lenora said in a thick, inhuman voice, "I can certainly keep you from shooting me."

Joanne gritted her teeth as she concentrated all her will on firing the pistol. Her hand shook and her muscles began to ache from the effort, but she could not make the trigger budge. She wished Ronnie had managed to hit Lenora in a vital area with the single shot he'd gotten off. Blood black and thick as tree sap ran from Lenora's wound, but the girl—or whatever she was now—didn't seem to notice, let alone care. The wound certainly didn't seem to be slowing her down any.

Dale crouched next to Marshall. The reporter had taken off his suit jacket, wadded it up, and pressed it against Marshall's chest to slow the bleeding. Joanne looked down at him, hoping to see him looking back at her with a cunning gleam in his eye that indicated he'd come up with a plan to save the county, and in the process, their asses. But he looked lost and filled with despair. She knew just how he felt.

Lenora turned back to the Reliquary and plucked two more icons from their places. She turned back around and held out the statuettes for them to see, as if she were a magician about to perform her grand finale.

"These two should do it," she said. "I drop these, and all hell breaks loose." She grinned, revealing a mouthful of needle-sharp teeth. "Literally."

Joanne could feel power surging all around them in the cave, swirling like a vortex of wind on the verge of becoming a tornado. One last little push was all it needed. . . .

Her Feelings were screaming at her to do something, anything, but she'd run out of ideas.

Marshall opened his eyes. "Terry," he gasped. "He's the key. He killed . . ."

Marshall's eyes rolled back and his head lolled to the side. Joanne didn't know if he was dead or just unconscious, but it didn't matter right now. He'd struggled to deliver a message to them, and they had only seconds to figure out what it meant.

She looked at Terry. He'd dropped his scalpel when Lenora had raked his face, and he was now crawling on the floor, searching for it, his pants legs soaked with blood—some his, most Debbie's. Had Marshall been trying to tell them that only Terry could kill Lenora now? Joanne didn't see how. The woman had become too powerful to be taken out by a simple blade.

She looked to Dale, and this she saw a flicker of understanding in his gaze.

"What do you really want, Carl?" Dale asked.

The demon-thing's glossy-black eyes focused on Dale. Its upper lip curled in a snarl but otherwise it didn't reply. Dale did have its attention, however, and he kept talking.

"Do you want to destroy the Reliquary and unleash the Old One's madness—or get revenge on the person who killed your mother?" Dale pointed to Debbie's body. "And what about you, Lenora? Terry was your lover, and he tried to kill you a few moments ago."

Lover? Joanne supposed she'd already guessed as much, though until now she hadn't wanted to admit it to herself.

Terry, still on his hands and knees, turned to glare at Dale.

TIM WAGGONER

314

"Shut the hell up, old man! Once I slice open Lenora's throat, I'll do you." His gaze flicked toward Joanne, and he grinned. "You too, lover."

Lenora looked at Terry for a moment, the expression on her demonic features indecipherable.

Dale continued. "Carl, Lenora . . . the Crosses don't need your help to destroy themselves. They're committing slow suicide with their endless scheming against one another and their abuse of power. The two of you, along with this whole bloody mess, are proof of that. By destroying the Reliquary, you'll just be putting the Crosses out of their misery. It'll be a mercy killing—and is mercy what you truly feel for your family?"

The woman looked at Dale, and one corner of her mouth lifted in a half-smile, half-sneer. She nodded toward Joanne, and she felt her trigger finger become hers to command once more.

Terry cried out in triumph as he found his scalpel. He grabbed hold of it, stood, and managed to take two steps toward Lenora before Joanne fired, emptying the remaining round in Ronnie's gun into Terry's body. Lenora watched impassively as Terry bucked and jerked like a spastic puppet on quivering strings before finally going limp and collapsing to the ground.

When the last echo of the final gunshot had died away, Dale looked at Lenora.

"You have what you wanted most. Now put those two icons back and leave this place in peace."

Lenora continued gazing upon Terry's prone form for a time, and Joanne knew two separate souls were looking out through those eyes. Then the air around her rippled and she became a young human woman once more, the black blood of her gunshot wound now a normal red. Joanne saw that the injury had bled a great deal more than she'd realized, and it looked like Ronnie's shot had nicked an artery. Lenora was pale, and her body trembled weakly as she turned back to the Reliquary and returned the icons to their proper places. And then with a soft sigh, she fell to the ground.

Joanne ran to Lenora's side and took her pulse. Her heartbeat was weak and fading fast. There was no way they'd be able to get medical help for her in time.

"Joanne?" Dale called gently.

She turned to look and saw that Marshall's eyes were open again. He held out an icon toward her, the one that he'd taken to the morgue to harvest Tyrone's spirit. She understood what he wanted her to do

She walked over to get the icon.

CHAPTER TWENTY-THREE

Two hours later, the survivors were gathered in Sanctity's library. Althea had joined them, and servants had brought everyone refreshments or medical supplies as needed. The doctor Marshall had summoned to care for Debbie had finally arrived and, though his intended patient no longer required his services, he tended to Marshall's wound, then examined Joanne and Dale. Satisfied they'd all survive and that his services were no longer required, he departed, secure in the knowledge that he'd bettered his position in the family.

Joanne and Dale sat on the same couch they'd used during Lenora's questioning. Joanne sipped hot tea from a fine china cup, while Dale drank what he'd assured her was an extremely fine, not to mention expensive, single-malt scotch.

Marshall had taken the same seat he'd used before, and Althea now occupied the leather chair that had once been Lenora's.

"I'll examine the Reliquary more closely after you've gone," Althea said. "But it appears you were successful in preventing its complete collapse."

"But the damned thing was bleeding power like a hemophiliac with a severed artery," Dale said, "and we didn't do anything to patch it up."

"Carl and Lenora were purposely drawing on the Old One's power," Althea said, "leading to a greater spillage than what would have occurred naturally. In addition, their efforts prevented the wound from clotting, I suppose you could say. But don't worry. The Reliquary will be safe enough for the time being, until it has a chance to heal more fully."

Althea then turned to Joanne and smiled. "My dear, you performed splendidly. It's comforting to know that my family's faith in you wasn't misplaced."

"I'm glad you're reassured," Joanne said. "That's all that matters, right? Your power and position are secure, and if a few people had to die to make it happen—including your own grandchild—well, that's just the cost of doing business in Cross County, isn't it?"

Marshall started to protest, but Althea silenced him with an offhand gesture. Though Joanne knew his chest was swathed in bandages beneath the neatly pressed shirt he'd donned, the male head of the Cross family looked as hale and hearty as ever. She wondered if swift recuperative powers were another of the Old One's blessings and decided they probably were.

"I understand how you must feel, Joanne," Althea said, her tone a study in sympathy. "You've not only gone through a trying experience physically, but you've had your sense of identity shaken to its very foundation."

That's putting it mildly, she thought.

"You all knew the truth about what happened to me during my disappearance, and about what I'd become. Why didn't any of you ever say anything?" She turned to Dale. "Why didn't *you?*"

Dale looked down at the dregs of his scotch. "It was part of the deal I made with the Old One. You weren't to know the truth until you were ready. And even then you had to discover it on your own, through the natural—or in this case *un*natural—course of events. Why, I don't know. But I kept my promise, I . . . was afraid of what might happen if I didn't."

Joanne understood that Dale hadn't feared for himself but rather for her. She reached out and squeezed his free hand.

"When Dale told us of his encounter with the Old One, we agreed to guard the secret as long as necessary," Althea said. "My family has always obeyed the Old One's commands."

"Speaking of old," Joanne said, "Dale told me that story of how the Cross family first discovered the Old One. A young girl fell into the mound, just as I did. Only she emerged to become something of a speaker for the Old One—a sort of high priestess, I guess you could say. You wouldn't happen to know what became of her, would you?"

Althea only smiled.

Among all the other abilities the Old One had bestowed upon its chosen people, was increased longevity among them? Joanne wouldn't have been surprised to learn the answer was yes.

Joanne had used the icon Marshall had given her to absorb Lenora's spirit. After they'd returned to Sanctity, Marshall sent a lower-ranking member of the family back with a pair of fresh icons—one to gather Debbie's spirit, one for Ronnie's. Both now resided in an honored place in the Reliquary. Marshall had made arrangements to dispose of the bodies they'd left behind and establish stories to explain their disappearance—arrangements that he seemed a little too accustomed to making. There had been no discussion of harvesting Terry's soul, which was just fine with Joanne.

"What will happen to Lenora's spirit?" she asked. That icon hadn't been placed in the Reliquary. Marshall had taken it with him and still had it tucked away in a pocket of the suit jacket he'd donned after the doctor had finished with him.

"Lenora's *and* Carl's," Dale pointed out. "As I understand it, they've became inextricably linked. Soulmates in the truest sense of the term."

"I'm sorry to say the combined spirits of my grandchildren are too wild for the Reliquary," Althea said. "They'd introduce an unstable element into the mix, quite possibly becoming a corrupting influence on the other spirits. Don't worry. We have a separate place to house such restless ones."

Joanne wasn't certain she liked the sound of that, but then the entire concept of the icons and the Reliquary still struck her as disturbing.

"What of Debbie and Ronnie?" Dale asked. "Neither was exactly well adjusted mentally at the end. Will their addition harm the Reliquary?"

"Unlike my grandchildren, theirs was a condition of the mind, not the spirit," Althea said. "There's no cause for concern. All the pieces of the puzzle have been fitted into their proper places, and all is once again well in our little corner of the world."

"How can you say that?" Joanne demanded. "People have died—your granddaughter among them!" She looked at Marshall. "*Your* daughter!" Her tone softened. "Charlotte's daughter."

Marshall flinched as if she'd just struck him. Joanne supposed in a way she had. He looked down at the floor and refused to meet her gaze.

"We will grieve for Lenora in our own way and in our own time," Althea said, her kind voice replaced by cold steel. "You may be the Guardian, but it is still not your place to question us."

"It's *exactly* her place," Dale said. "Hasn't it ever occurred to you that Joanne's primary function isn't to guard against the Old One's power escaping, but rather to police your family and save them from their own dark temptations?"

Althea looked taken aback, and Joanne knew the matriarch of the Cross clan hadn't considered the possibility before now.

"Think of it," Dale said. "Everything that's happened over the course of the last few days is a direct result of how you Crosses manipulate people for your own ends. Marshall may have truly loved Debbie, but can he say he never used his mental powers to *encourage* her to return his feelings? As a result, Carl Coulter was born, a confused young man who—in true Cross fashion—tried to win acceptance into the family by impressing his father with his cold-blooded savagery. And what are the odds that Lenora didn't use her powers on Terry?"

Neither Marshall nor Althea answered.

"And don't forget poor Ronnie," Joanne said. "Just before he died, he told me that Marshall had made him see and do terrible things. I'm not sure why, but I know that Ronnie didn't have the most stable mind, and your using him like a pawn pushed his mind all the way over the edge into full-blown madness."

Marshall looked up at Joanne, but he was unable to meet her eyes for long, and he averted his gaze once more. "At first I needed someone close to you to keep me apprised on the investigation's progress. But when it appeared Lenora might be a suspect I . . . *encouraged* Ronnie to dispose of any evidence which might incriminate her."

"Which turned out to be completely unnecessary," Joanne said. "The evidence might've shown she'd committed the vandalism at the Caffeine Café, but it was Terry who committed the actual murders. She had nothing to do with them."

"I know that," Marshall said, then in a whisper added, "now."

Joanne stood and Dale followed suit a second later.

"There's no way I could ever bring charges against you for contributing to the deaths of Ronnie, Debbie, and Lenora." Terry too, in a sense. "Not only wouldn't I be able to present any proof to back up the charges, the county—much as it pains me to admit it—needs the Crosses, to maintain the Reliquary if nothing else. But remember this. I know who I am now and what I'm supposed to do. And from now on, I'll be watching you. Closely."

With that, she turned and left the library, Dale at her side.

· · · · ·

Joanne and Dale stood at the bottom of the steps leading up to Sanctity's main entrance. It was late afternoon, and despite everything, it had turned out to be a beautiful day. Sun shining, clouds white and puffy, breeze gentle. It seemed inappropriate at best to Joanne and obscene at worst. So many people dead, and it was like the world didn't care.

"I feel like such an idiot," she said. "How could I have been dating Terry and not know what was going on?" If she had, maybe she could've done something to prevent all the tragedy of the last few days.

"Don't beat yourself up," Dale said. "There are many things we don't and perhaps can never know." He put a hand on her shoulder. "But you know the most important thing of all now."

She nodded. "Who I am."

Dale shook his head. "No. You know you're not who you *thought* you were. As for who you will become . . ." He shrugged. "Only time will tell."

He surprised her then by drawing her close and giving her a fierce hug. When they pulled apart, he smiled at her and she saw tears shimmering in his eyes.

"I'm very proud of you, Joanne Talon. And I'm honored to be your friend."

A single tear ran down the side of his face. She brushed it away, knowing that it wasn't for her but for his lost wife and daughter.

"Not to mention my sidekick," she teased.

He laughed. "Like hell! I'm your designated CJA, and don't you forget it!"

Joanne frowned. "CJA?"

"Cover Joanne's Ass."

Despite everything that had happened, she started to laugh, but she broke off when her cell phone rang. Reluctantly, she answered it.

"Sheriff Talon."

She listened for several seconds, then said, "On my way." She disconnected and slid the phone back into its belt pouch.

"Whatever it is, let someone else handle it," Dale said. "You've earned a rest."

"There's a problem over at Grandfield's Nursery. They were knocking down old greenhouses in preparation for putting up new ones, when they discovered something beneath the concrete foundation of one the buildings—three metal drums filled with blood. Fresh blood."

Dale raised an eyebrow. "Weren't those greenhouses built sometime in the early seventies?"

"Yep."

They looked at each other for a moment, and then Dale let out a long sigh. "I'll follow you."

Lights flashing and siren wailing, Joanne's cruise passed through Sanctity's main gate, followed closely by Dale's Jeep. As they headed toward town, neither saw the trenchcoated figure watching from the side of the road slowly begin to follow on foot.

. . . . .

"Do you think they're right, Mother?" Marshall looked down at the icon in his hand. He could sense the restless spirits of his children trapped inside, and he wished that he had found a way to be a better father to them.

CROSS COUNTY

323

They stood in the hallway outside Althea's quarters, and the woman reached out and gently took the icon from her son.

"We do what we must for the good of the family," she said. "Always."

Marshall nodded and tried to smile. He knew his mother was attempting to comfort him in her own way. He also knew she would sense that her attempt had failed dismally. He turned away and headed for his room, intending to spend some time lying in bed, resting and healing while he stared at the framed maps on his bedrooms walls and contemplated the high price of duty.

■ ■ ■ ■ ■

Althea watched her son head for his room. She did indeed know what he felt, but knowing wasn't the same as understanding. Or caring.

She entered her quarters, not bothering to lock the door behind her. There was no need. No one in the house, from the lowliest servant up to an including her son, would dare to enter her quarters without permission. She moved through rooms filled with furniture and various bits of memorabilia, each one decorated in the style of a different time period in which she lived. Her quarters were the largest in Sanctity, but even so, there weren't enough rooms to represent all the decades of her life. Eventually, she reached the most special chamber in her quarters. She opened the highly polished mahogany door upon which was carved an odd symbol—a triangle bisected by a lightning bolt—and stepped inside.

The light came on automatically as her presence registered, illuminating walls lined with shelves, row upon row. And on these shelves stood icons, hundreds of them. There were a few empty spaces remaining, and she chose one and set her grandchildren down in their new home. Some spirits were well suited for helping keep the Old One slumbering peacefully, but others—the wildest, darkest, ones—they served a very different purpose.

They were her private stock.

She gently brushed her fingers across the surface of the newest addition to her collection.

"I'll leave you two to begin getting acquainted with your new friends. You've a great deal to learn, and not much time to learn it."

With a last smile, she exited the chamber and closed the door behind her. After a bit, the light deactivated itself, and in the darkness, a chorus of soft whispers began.